Sara
Coll
Beva
nove
shor
by fe

regularly on television and radio. In 2014, she was named one of the Saltire Society's 365 Most Influential Scottish Women, past and present.

Sara tweets about her writing life as @sarasheridan and has a Facebook page at sarasheridanwriter.

Praise for the Mirabelle Bevan Mystery series

'Mirabelle has a dogged tenacity to rival Poirot'

Sunday Herald

'Unfailingly stylish, undeniably smart'

Daily Record

'Fresh, exciting and darkly plotted, this sharp historical mystery plunges the reader into a shadowy and forgotten past'

Good Book Guide

'A crime force to be reckoned with'

Good Reads

'Plenty of colour and action, will engage the reader from the first page to the last. Highly recommended'

'Quietly compelling .

Mirabelle Bevan Mysteries

Brighton Belle
London Calling
England Expects
British Bulldog
Operation Goodwood
Russian Roulette

Russian Roulette

A Mirabelle Bevan Mystery

Sara Sheridan

CONSTABLE · LONDON

CONSTABLE

First published in Great Britain in 2017 by Constable

This paperback edition published in 2018 by Constable

Copyright © Sara Sheridan, 2017

1 3 5 7 9 10 8 6 4 2

The moral right of the author has been asserted.

A CIP catalogue record for this book
is available from the British Library.

ISBN: 978-1-47212-237-7

Typeset in Dante by SX Composing DTP, Rayleigh, Essex
Printed and bound in Great Britain by CPI Group (UK) Ltd, Croydon CR0 4YY

Papers used by Constable are from well-managed forests
and other responsible sources.

MIX
Paper from
responsible sources
FSC® C104740

Constable
An imprint of
Little, Brown Book Group
Carmelite House
50 Victoria Embankment
London EC4Y 0DZ

An Hachette UK Company
www.hachette.co.uk

www.littlebrown.co.uk

This book is dedicated to Molly,
my very own mystery

Prologue

True friends stab you in the front

Brighton, 6.45 a.m., Thursday 19 April, 1956

Phil turned over in bed, pulling the sheet around his shoulders. The orange curtains his wife had bought were not lined and early morning sunshine leached into the room. From the garden the sound of birdsong punctuated his thoughts as he stirred and cursed silently. He found it difficult to block out the noise of the dawn chorus. It was worse than an alarm clock, though at least when he and Helen had moved out of their old digs near the front, they had left behind the gulls. Up here it was all blackbirds and doves. Still, there was something difficult to ignore about the noise and now the mornings were getting lighter it had begun to annoy him.

Phil didn't want to open his eyes. It had been a disturbed night. He'd had strange dreams, which he couldn't fully remember. Only half awake, he hovered like a bee over a flower, his consciousness suspended. If he was choosing, he'd go back to sleep, but how likely was that, what with the birdsong and the light? He'd have to get up for work soon anyway. Bluntly, he nudged Helen, hoping she might fetch him a cuppa. Usually she was good that way, but today she didn't move. He couldn't blame her. They were both done in last night when they'd fallen into bed.

Still groggy, he turned over, curling his arm around his wife's sleeping frame. She lay on her side, facing the window.

I

He smiled as he ran his fingers across her skin. She always felt like silk. Sleepily, he planted a hot, early-morning kiss on her shoulder and, feeling suddenly inspired, he continued kissing all the way to her hairline. She smelled of soap, perfume and deep sleep – a familiar combination. He nudged her again and slid his hand downwards, along the curve of her waist until it came to rest on her plump behind. Phil was an arse man. Always had been. The day he'd met Hel, she had been wearing a tight red skirt that framed her bottom perfectly. It had been a joy to behold – love at first sight. He remembered watching her dancing with her mate at the Palais, thinking this was the woman he was going to marry. She'd let him walk her back to her digs and, when he'd pulled her close for the first time, she'd smelled of cotton wool and lavender. He'd wanted to grow old with that smell from the moment he breathed it in.

Feeling frisky now, he snuggled closer, stroking her stomach and nuzzling her neck. Then it came to him that the bed was wet. She was wet. His fingers were sticky.

'Hel,' he tried, nudging her. Then, more urgently, 'Helen.'

He pulled away, opening his eyes and staring at his hands as they came into focus. His fingers were covered in blood.

'Hel.' His voice was panicked.

He recoiled as he pulled back the sheet. She was hurt. A crimson stain spread from her stomach outwards. The blood had seeped into the mattress. Some had even dripped on to the thin carpet. She was deathly pale. Phil scrambled to the floor, tripping over his feet. His chest was heaving. A strange, animal-like sound emanated from his throat. His fingers fluttered as he shook his wife's body, leaving a red handprint on her marble-white shoulder and a smear on the lace-edged strap of her nightdress.

'No.'

The word came out strangled and very loud. Then he backed out of the bedroom and, barefoot, crossed the hallway, banging the front door as he burst outside wearing only striped pyjama bottoms and a white vest. He stumbled down the path, trampling a small line of daffodils that Hel had planted in February. His eyes darted, looking frantically for help. Far off, there was the sound of bottles rattling on a milk cart. Uniformly, all the houses along Mill Lane still had their curtains closed.

'Help,' Phil said, quietly, and then louder. 'Help.'

This was a nightmare, surely. The thoughts came in a jumble and he couldn't order them. 'Help,' he barked again. At first there was no reaction from the early-morning suburb. Across the road a curtain flickered in one window and then another. Old Mrs Ambrose appeared in the doorway opposite, at the same time as Billy Randall walked into the garden next door, pulling a brown woollen dressing gown round his frame and knotting it with a red cord.

'What is it, mate? Are you all right?'

Phil held up his blood-smeared hand as if he was a child. 'I don't know what happened,' he said.

Billy sprang over the low fence that separated the two gardens and, passing his friend, he walked straight into the house. He'd served in Italy. People used to say that he'd seen a thing or two, whatever the ins and outs of the Italian campaign. 'Helen,' he called. 'Mrs Quinn.' He checked the rooms one by one. The small kitchen smelled of dripping. A loaf of white bread had been left on a crumb-strewn board and the door to the larder was askew. Nothing there. He moved on to the living room where a half-drunk bottle of London gin lay open next to two smudged glasses. The wireless had been pulled out from its place against the wall. They'd been drinking and dancing the night before. It looked perfectly normal – not dissimilar to his own house.

Then, crossing the hallway and opening the bedroom door, he started when he came across her body. The room smelled

3

bad – though only faintly. Still, a dry retch rose in Billy's gullet. Then his training kicked in. He checked, hoping for a pulse, though he knew it was too late. Helen Quinn seemed too peaceful for what had happened to her. Her dark hair was curled in a loose bun and her hand was splayed awkwardly, like a child's in sleep. The spill of blood was a shock. She'd been knifed, he reckoned. It must have been violent and it would have taken a while for her to bleed out. When you got hit in the stomach it was agonising. You could last for half an hour before finally slipping away. It was the acid that killed you. Once the stomach was pierced, it leached out and dissolved your organs. It was a horrible way to go. Mystified, he stared at Helen Quinn's corpse as he consciously took in the scene. He knew he'd have to describe it later. Then he turned. The Penroses at number five had a telephone. Their house was closer than the public telephone box, which was four blocks away. He'd rouse them and call the police.

Outside, old Mrs Ambrose had waddled across the road and was attending to Phil Quinn. She cast an accusatory stare at Billy that clearly said, I might have known. She had never given anyone an inch in her life, and she wasn't starting now. It was Mrs Ambrose who had told Billy's wife she thought Hitler had got away. 'I don't trust that one,' she had said, 'not even to die.'

Billy didn't give anything away about what lay inside number fifteen. The old woman, after all, never thought a good thing when she could think a bad one. Still, however it looked, Phil was a nice bloke. Even with his fingers covered in blood, Billy didn't want to believe Phil Quinn had killed his wife. Not Helen who always had a smile for everyone. Not Phil who kicked a football around in the street with the Harrison kids.

'I'll fetch the police. You stay here. Don't disturb things.'

Mrs Ambrose shrugged and her housecoat shifted across her ample frame. She was a busty old woman and her clothes never seemed to fit. At the bottom of the path the latest addition to Billy's household, a tabby cat he'd brought home, sat and watched with its head cocked to one side.

'I don't understand how it happened,' Phil Quinn said again. 'I was asleep.'

Billy wondered momentarily if he was leaving the old woman with a murderer, and if that was wise. But someone had to call in Helen's body. He eyed his friend who, frankly, didn't seem in any state to shoo the moggy at the bottom of his path, let alone hurt anyone.

'I'll come right back,' Billy said sternly.

He headed down the pavement with only a glance behind him. It was too beautiful a morning for something so horrible to have happened. Cherry blossom spilled over the privet hedge at number ten and another cat, a ginger one, with its tail twitching, pawed at the flickering petals. Everything seemed too normal. Billy had encountered death before, but not like this. Nothing so domestic. Passing his own house, he noted the curtains upstairs were still closed. He'd raise his wife later. He didn't like to scare her. Not in her condition.

Chapter 1

The wise are instructed by reason

Superintendent Alan McGregor took the stairs to the office at a lick, and burst into McGuigan & McGuigan Debt Recovery without knocking. Inside, Mirabelle Bevan and Vesta Lewis looked up from the paperwork strewn across their desks. Vesta smiled.

'Good morning.' She got up to put on the kettle.

Without indulging the niceties, McGregor launched himself in Mirabelle's direction. He slammed down a copy of the *Argus*, the early edition. 'They've given it to Robinson,' he said. 'I need to talk to you.'

Mirabelle cast her hazel eyes over the headline, which declared 'Murder in Portslade'. Behind her, Vesta turned on the tap and let the water run.

'I don't want any damn tea,' McGregor snapped. Vesta turned off the tap and, in the same moment, Mirabelle looked up in an icy stare. Poor manners were not acceptable in the Brills Lane office no matter what might have happened to get the superintendent worked up. 'I'm sorry.' He recovered his equilibrium. 'It's been a difficult morning. I walked out of the station and came straight here. You're the only one who can help.'

He proffered the paper. Mirabelle nodded at Vesta to acknowledge the apology. Vesta fiddled with the buttons on her cardigan. Mirabelle shrugged off her friend's inattention and leaned over to read the story – a young housewife stabbed in her sleep. Her husband had been taken into custody. There was a picture of a cosy-looking brick house and another of the couple, titled 'Mr and Mrs Quinn on their wedding day.' In it, Mrs Quinn gazed into the eye of the camera, her white dress framing her tidy figure, her hair coiffed elegantly in a chignon and her lips set in an easy smile. It struck Mirabelle that photographs of murder victims were always strange because they hadn't a clue what was going to happen. With the hindsight of a dead body, it seemed odd that they had simply got on with their lives – taking holidays, attending christenings, or, like Mrs Quinn, clutching her new husband's arm.

'You're the detective superintendent,' she said. 'If you don't want Robinson on the case, can't you ask for it to be assigned to someone else? It seems like you want it, Alan.'

McGregor's eyes burned. 'They won't give it to me. And Robinson has hauled in Phil Quinn for questioning. Straight off on the wrong tack.'

'Well, the husband is the most likely suspect.' Mirabelle lifted the paper as if it underlined her point.

'Quinn didn't do it.'

'How do you know?'

'I know him. And, worse, I know Robinson. The lazy so-and-so won't look beyond the obvious. Someone's framing Phil, don't you see?'

'Why would anyone want to do that?'

'If I knew . . .' McGregor sounded exasperated.

'And how can you be so sure that this friend of yours didn't have a hand in the poor woman's death?' Mirabelle turned the page as she read the rest of the story. 'According to this, he'd have had to have slept through someone stabbing the poor woman in the bed next to him. It doesn't seem likely.'

'Phil Quinn's on the square.'

Mirabelle raised a quizzical eyebrow. She didn't like Masonic terms. Both she and Superintendent McGregor had had a run-in with the Brighton Lodge a couple of years before and she still found the terminology Masons used, suspect. 'How do you know Mr Quinn? Exactly?'

'I've known him for years.'

Mirabelle waited. McGregor hadn't answered her question. Vesta leaned against the sink and slowly crossed her arms. The shocking pink of her nail lacquer stood out against her dark woollen cardigan. This discussion was highly irregular. She was enjoying it tremendously.

'I know him from back home,' McGregor admitted. 'I've known him since I was a kid. In Scotland.'

'And he ended up living in Brighton too?'

'Phil was here when I came down. A friendly face. We were in the same year at school but we lost touch afterwards. He moved to the south coast after the war. He served in the Logistic Corps. He was an army mechanic. Once the fighting was over he went in with a couple of other guys. You know Hove Cars?'

'The taxi company?'

'That's Phil.'

Mirabelle eyed McGregor. They had been involved with each other for, well, she couldn't say exactly how long. The before and after of it seemed to have merged lately and it was impossible to pin down precisely when their affair had started. The superintendent had never mentioned this man.

'If he's such a good friend, how come I've never met him?'

McGregor shrugged. 'We only see each other now and then. You know me. I'm hardly the sociable type. It's like that, isn't it, with old friends? You just pick up where you left off. And it's not as if I'm the only one who knows him, I mean that's what I said when they wouldn't give me the case. Lots of blokes on the force know Phil. My old boss used to say hired cars were the pumping blood of the city. Taxis and coppers go hand in hand. Every man on the force knows Phil Quinn – from beat bobbies up.'

'Are you saying your friend is a police informant?'

McGregor shifted. 'Nothing so formal as that, Mirabelle, but yes, Phil always helps if he can. And Hove Cars don't only run taxis. They've got a couple of Rollers for weddings. The Grand uses them as a chauffeur service. They've pretty much got Brighton tied up. Phil Quinn loved his wife. He was crazy about her. Can you imagine what it must be like, losing her like this and then being banged up, subjected to Robinson's puerile interrogation?'

Mirabelle folded the newspaper smartly. 'Well, I suppose our first stop will be his business partners, if you want to bring me along.'

McGregor shook his head. 'That's the trouble. I can't be seen to be part of this. I'm sorry to ask you. I know it's irregular. Wrong, even. But you're so good at this kind of thing.'

A smile played around Mirabelle's lips as she realised what he was asking. It wasn't that she was gratified in any way by the murder, but still. 'Alan, you've spent years shooing me away from police business. If I recall, once you locked me up to stop me continuing with an investigation.' McGregor tried to interject. He always insisted that had been a mistake. Mirabelle raised a solitary finger. She had the air of a headmistress and wasn't going to be diverted. 'So, just to be clear, are you saying you want me to look into this case? You want me to undercut Robinson's investigation? I mean, that's exactly what you usually object to me doing.'

McGregor quailed. 'I know. I'm sorry. Look, I'll help. I just can't be seen to help. Someone has to have a pair of steady eyes on this and Robinson's eyes, well, they're never steady. And you've got Vesta. I mean, if you would agree to be part of this, Vesta?'

Vesta nodded. 'Sure.'

McGregor checked his watch. 'I have to get back. The chief told me to keep my nose out. He insists I'm too close because of the childhood connection. It's just nonsense. Like I said, everyone knows Phil.' He looked sheepish. 'I lost my rag up at the station. I'm sorry if I came in here at a hundred miles an hour. It's been a horrible morning.'

Mirabelle paused. She wasn't going to crow. 'All right. I just wanted to be clear. Vesta and I will get going straight away. Why don't I pop in later and let you know how we're getting on?'

'I'll keep my eyes open,' McGregor promised. Then he retreated. They listened in silence as his footsteps echoed down the stairs.

'I've never seen him in a state like that,' Vesta said. 'He didn't even take off his hat.'

Mirabelle kept her eyes on the door. McGregor had remained cool under pressure on a number of occasions that she would have thought were far more stressful. Vesta was right – it wasn't like him.

'We better nip up to Hove Cars,' she said, pulling on her spring jacket and pinning her hat in place.

Vesta reached for her coat. Lately she hadn't worn a hat. It messed her hair, which she seemed to dress higher every time Mirabelle took a moment to notice. Today the girl had teased it into some kind of extended bun, which was its tallest incarnation so far. Vesta always looked smart, but Mirabelle couldn't help feel that no woman was properly attired without millinery.

'I'm starving,' Vesta enthused as she did up her buttons. 'Maybe we could pick up lunch on the way back.'

Hove Cars was located in a scruffy set of mews garages that ran behind Hangleton Road. The condition of the garages was in sharp contrast to the gleaming, well-kept vehicles parked outside them, but then, Mirabelle thought, most customers probably never came to the premises. As the women hovered on the cobbles they took in the peeling paint and the smell of engine oil. Clearly on view through a set of open doors, a shiny black Ford was jacked up with a pair of legs sticking out underneath. Mirabelle was put in mind of her investigations into a smuggling ring the year before. The men in question had brought in African diamonds in the sump oil of a racing vehicle. The investigation had not ended well. She didn't like to think about it.

The women paused and Mirabelle wondered if Vesta was thinking the same, but it seemed that the girl was simply unsure how to attract the attention of the fellow underneath the car. Eventually, Vesta cleared her throat. When this did not produce the desired result, Mirabelle leaned over. 'Excuse me,' she said, directing her voice at the man's knees. The legs stirred and then a figure shuffled out, revealing a very young mechanic, most likely fresh out of school. The boy smiled as he dusted himself down – a useless gesture as the oil stains on his overalls could not be brushed away.

'Can I help you, miss?'

'I'm looking for the person in charge.'

'Well, if you mean at the garage, I suppose that would be me, what with there being no one else here this morning. Though if you want a car there are a couple of drivers in the office.'

'Someone left you in charge?'

The boy drew himself up. He skimmed six feet now he was upright. 'Yeah. What about it?'

'Is that because of the trouble?'

The boy sniffed and then nodded.

'I suppose everyone got a terrible fright. A thing like that.'

Once he started, the child seemed eager to talk. 'The police were here when we opened up. Mr Quinn! Who'd have thought? Mr Gleeson went to get a solicitor. I don't know what happened to Mr Fourcade. He didn't even get into his overalls.'

'Are they the owners?'

'Them and Mr Quinn. Mates, like, too.'

'It sounds as if they're close. I mean if Mr Gleeson is engaging a solicitor on behalf of his friend?'

The boy nodded. 'I suppose,' he said.

'What are you doing to this car?'

'Changing the oil.' The boy rubbed his hands together. 'It's the only thing I can do. That and check the tyre pressure. It's an apprenticeship, see. But I've only been here a couple of weeks.'

Mirabelle changed tack. 'Tell me, did you know Mrs Quinn?'

'I saw her,' the boy said eagerly. 'She came down with some sandwiches for her old man last week. She didn't want him going short.'

'How very kind of her.'

'She was a looker. She had one of them fancy sweaters like in the glamour magazines – you know – the ones with shapes on. Do you think they'll bang up Mr Quinn for it?'

'That depends on the evidence. What do you think?'

The boy's eyes burned. 'I ain't no grass.'

'Which would suggest, if you don't mind me saying, that you think that he did do it.'

A flicker of annoyance crossed his young face. 'I'm just the apprentice. What do I know?' He shrugged.

Mirabelle was about to push the boy further when a purring engine sounded and a red Jaguar drew up. A man in a tweed jacket got out and a whiff of aftershave cut through the dense smell of oil that hung around the garage door. He was clearly a more promising prospect, and Mirabelle and Vesta turned towards him as one.

12

'Adrian.' The man nodded as he eyed the women. 'Go and sweep up inside. Can I help you, ladies?'

Mirabelle offered her hand. 'I'm Mirabelle Bevan. And this is my business partner, Vesta Lewis.'

'Tommy Fourcade.' The man's handshake was firm. He was patently a fellow who could handle himself. And he was well dressed – the tweed jacket was immaculately cut.

'We're here in connection with the murder of Helen Quinn,' Mirabelle announced.

Mr Fourcade's tone hardened. 'What's it to you?'

'We're private detectives,' Vesta cut in with rather too much enthusiasm. She was silenced by a cold glare from Mirabelle who considered that kind of comment showing off.

'I see.' Tommy Fourcade's green eyes danced as he decided these women were no kind of threat. 'Lady detectives. Well, well. That's a new one. You should be worrying about little kids lost on the Prom. Don't you get your pretty heads in a state about this. We've got a bigwig lawyer on Phil's case. He'll be out before we know it.'

'You think he's innocent, then?'

'I've known Phil Quinn for over ten years. You can take it from me, he didn't kill his wife.'

'Did you serve together? It was the Logistics Corps, wasn't it?'

Fourcade's jaw tightened. 'You're well informed. Look, Phil loved Helen. He wouldn't have hurt her in a million years.'

'Someone hurt her, Mr Fourcade.'

'Well, whoever did it, they'll pay. Don't worry about that.' His tone hardened again, only barely masking a threat. 'Once we've got Phil out, we'll find the bastard.'

'Do you know who it was?' Mirabelle pressed.

'If I did I'd have told the police and Phil wouldn't be in custody.'

'Did Mr Quinn have enemies?'

'No more than any of us. This business isn't a cakewalk, Miss Bevan. But I've never known another firm to murder a fellow's wife.'

'Someone killed her. Someone had a reason.'

'And you think there's no smoke without fire?'

'I didn't say that.'

Tommy Fourcade bit his lip as he eyed the women up and down. 'Don't worry,' he said, 'if the police don't catch whoever did this to Helen, we'll find them. And, when we find them, we won't hold back.'

Mirabelle let this comment hang. It was the second time he'd made a threat. 'Let's hope they find the murderer soon, then,' she said.

Tommy nodded in the direction of the open garage door through which Adrian could be seen polishing a set of wrenches. 'I've got to get to work. This ain't nothing to do with you,' he said.

A driver walked out of the office, sucking the last smoke from his cigarette before throwing the butt into the gutter. He nodded at Fourcade, got into an Austin and, after pulling on to the road, accelerated in a cloud of exhaust fumes. Vesta lifted her fingers to shield her nose but Mirabelle didn't move as Mr Fourcade removed his jacket and headed for his overalls. He meant what he'd said, she thought. This murder must be especially awful for someone like him – someone who wanted to feel in control. No wonder he wanted them out of there – women asking questions must be difficult, particularly competent women. But, then, perhaps he was the kind of man who always decided when conversations started and finished. Either way, she and Vesta had been dismissed. Vesta was clearly more accepting of the arrangement. She had already turned towards the street and Mirabelle fell into step behind her. As they mounted the pavement, the sun came out. Further along, a grocer's boy polished apples and laid them carefully in a neat pile on display. A whiff of hyacinth snaked towards them from the florist's, mingling with the fresh smell of the fruit. It would be a lovely morning if someone hadn't died.

'He seemed very decisive, didn't he?' Mirabelle pondered.

'He was just being loyal to his mate.'

It occurred to Mirabelle that Phil Quinn seemed to inspire tremendous loyalty in his friends. First McGregor and now Tommy Fourcade.

'Why don't we pop into that café we passed?' Vesta suggested. 'We can chat about it over lunch.'

Chapter 2

*Everyone is made for some
particular work*

Fortified by gammon, white bread, dripping and tea, Mirabelle and Vesta hopped on to the bus for Portslade, asking the conductor to let them know when they reached the nearest stop to Mill Lane. It wasn't far.

'You wanted the stop for that murder, ladies?' the man announced loudly as the bus pulled up. 'Here you go. They'll have a tourist service up here in no time. Non-stop from the front.'

'Well, really,' Vesta tutted, feeling the eyes of the other passengers alighting on her as she and Mirabelle stepped on to the pavement. It wasn't that she cared what other people thought, but it wasn't pleasant that the other passengers were under the impression they were rubbernecking. A lady in a straw hat as good as sneered as the bus pulled away.

'Oh well,' Mirabelle rejoined. 'I expect they think we're thrill seekers.'

Vesta looked dubious. She regarded the beautifully fitted skirt of Mirabelle's peach, glazed-cotton dress and decided that her hem would need to be higher.

As the women turned off the main road, a scatter of small boys in grey shorts kicked a dilapidated football around, making for two bashed-up bins they had set up as goalposts.

'Excuse me,' Mirabelle accosted the nearest. 'Which way is Mill Lane?'

The boy stopped and crossed his arms. 'You here for the murder? They won't let no one in the house.'

'Which way is it?'

'Just up there and left.'

Mill Lane was quiet as the women turned the corner. The houses on either side ran to two storeys. Each had a wooden gate painted either red or black, the glossy colour echoed by the window frames. The gates opened on to small front gardens, some of which were laid out to vegetables. In one, an apple tree was coming into blossom. It seemed too pleasant a place for a murder to have occurred. There was no question, however, in which house Helen Quinn had died. Three-quarters of the way up, on the left-hand side, the front door of number fifteen was open and a police photographer was clearly visible. As Mirabelle and Vesta approached, a plump old woman, wearing a floral housecoat, opened the door of the house opposite and carefully carried a tray of tea things across the street and straight into the scene of the crime. Immediately, she backed out again, shooed by a bobby, who, it would appear, had mistakenly abandoned his post at the front door.

'You can't come in, love.' The officer held up a hand as if he were directing traffic. It struck Mirabelle that the woman reminded her of one of those vans – wide at the axle and thick of tyre, the sort that made deliveries around town. She seemed to steer from the bust.

'I brought some tea, that's all,' the woman insisted. 'I thought you'd be parched. You and the other boys.'

'That's very nice.'

'Mrs Ambrose. Number fourteen.'

'Thank you.' The policeman relieved Mrs Ambrose of her tray. He was a big man with a stony expression. Momentarily, even from quite far off, Mirabelle was distracted by his shoes, which must have been twice the size of her own. She'd bet he always ended up on door duty. It was as if he had been built for the business of obstruction.

'So—' the woman tried to peer past the uniformed giant '—any ideas yet?'

To his credit the policeman humoured her. He might be large but he was even-tempered. 'Who do you think did it?'

The woman sucked her teeth as if not only was this quite some consideration but as if she was speculating for the first time. 'Well, they say each murderer has their own way. I mean a woman will kill very differently from a man,' she postulated. 'I couldn't say without knowing exactly how poor Helen died. I mean, exactly what happened to her.'

The policeman put the tray on the doorstep and turned his attention to pouring the tea. He added milk and three sugar lumps and stirred thoughtfully. The mug looked like a teacup in his hands, and the teaspoon was simply ridiculous, like a child's toy.

'Stabbed,' he pronounced, and then, seeing Mirabelle and Vesta loitering at the gate, he turned his attention to them. 'Don't tell me, you ladies have brought biscuits,' he said flatly. The nicer suburbs were always like this when there was trouble – nosy neighbours pretending to be helpful.

The old woman did not take the intrusion so easily. 'I don't know you.' She rounded on them. 'What are you doing here?'

'We're friends of Superintendent McGregor,' Mirabelle said, as she opened the gate. It was the tactic most likely to elicit cooperation from the constable, no matter what McGregor had said. Sure enough, the policeman stood a little straighter as the women walked up the path.

'Well, I'm glad you're not just here to gawk.' Mrs Ambrose tutted. 'You wouldn't believe what it's been like. When they brought out poor Helen's body, there was a crowd. People came up from the other side of the main road. "Get a picture," I said. And them journalists from the paper. Cheeky beggars. On such a beautiful morning as well.'

The policeman stared at his mug of tea mournfully.

'It seems odd that nobody heard,' Mirabelle said, looking round. 'I mean, if Mrs Quinn was stabbed, you'd think she'd have screamed. It said in the newspaper that she was murdered in the small hours of the morning. Someone must have heard.'

'This neighbourhood isn't what it was. I mean, before the war, but not now.' Mrs Ambrose's eyes sneaked around the officer as she spoke.

The policeman meditatively turned the mug around in his hand before he took another sip. He knew his frame was big enough to fill the doorway and there was no point in trying to stop the old lady when her cause was so patently hopeless. That was the thing about big men, Mirabelle thought, they had a lot of confidence.

'What do you think about the issue of noise, Officer?' Mirabelle asked. 'I mean, Mrs Quinn must have screamed.'

'The detectives will be worrying about that,' the man pronounced. 'Now, Mrs Ambrose, why don't I bring back your tea things later? Civic duty aside, we don't want to hold you up.'

Mrs Ambrose hovered, not wanting to go but realising she had been dismissed. She eyed Mirabelle and Vesta. 'I was first on the scene,' she said. 'I was here before anyone.' The police officer kept his gaze steady. 'Just pop it back when you boys have finished,' Mrs Ambrose continued as she turned. The three figures waited on the doorstep as the old lady walked down the path and closed the gate.

'As for you ladies, I'm sorry but I can't let you in either,' the policeman announced. 'Superintendent McGregor or not.'

He was not the kind of man with whom you argued, so Mirabelle turned her efforts to the business of extracting information.

'Is it an interesting crime scene, Officer?' she enquired.

'There's not much to see now.' The man's expression remained stony. 'And what there was before they took her away, well, I wouldn't describe it as interesting. Mostly we've been looking for the knife.'

'Have you found it?'

'Not yet. We checked the house, but the lads are doing the drains now and seeing if the blighter maybe buried it in the back garden or chucked it into one of the hedges.'

'Mr Quinn, you mean?'

'Yes, miss.'

'So Inspector Robinson thinks Mr Quinn stabbed his wife, let her bleed to death, hid the weapon and then calmly waited for a few hours before raising the alarm?'

The policeman didn't rise to the bait. 'It might not make sense to you or me,' he said, 'but you never know. Most murderers are just normal. Half the time they don't mean to kill anyone – they just lose their rag. And for the ones that are premeditated, the story usually makes sense, you know. But now and then there's an odd case.' The man raised a thick finger to tap the side of his head.

'Did Mr Quinn seem odd?'

The policeman shrugged. 'More groggy. If my wife was dead I expect I might be fully awake. Paying attention. The inspector reckons he drugged the woman. Most likely in her gin the night before.' He leaned in, continuing in a whisper. 'That's how come she didn't struggle. The bottle's gone to the lab to see what the eggheads make of it. You're right about her not calling out, see.'

Vesta's eyes were burning. It was clear that the idea of poisoned gin lent a certain glamour to Mrs Quinn's death. Mirabelle tutted. She disliked this modern vogue for glamourising violence. Cheap paperbacks at the railway station were full of it and in the last few years it seemed there had been a spate of well-dressed gentlemen killers who covered their tracks with war medals and respectability. People wanted to forget what they'd seen during the war, what they knew about death. It was easier, somehow, to cover things up with nice outfits or cocktails. It made crime easier to gawp at it. But the truth was that death, or at least murder, was always the same shoddy business, no matter how you tried to gloss it over.

Mirabelle took Vesta's arm. If the policeman wasn't going to let them in, they might as well try something else. 'Thank you, Officer,' she said.

As they closed the gate behind them, a heavily pregnant woman was making her way up the street. Mirabelle squinted. It seemed the poor woman was unravelling. In one hand she carried a loosely wrapped brown paper parcel and in the other she clutched a crumpled linen handkerchief. The top buttons of her coat gaped, as if she couldn't summon the will to fasten them, and her eyes were pink. Mirabelle glanced back towards the policeman, who had taken Mrs Ambrose's tray into the house and was pouring tea for the rest of the men. Turning back, she caught the woman's eye.

'Oh dear. You knew Mrs Quinn?' she said gently. 'I'm so sorry.'

The woman sniffed. 'I won't talk to the papers,' she said, trying to push past Mirabelle and Vesta and through the gate of number thirteen.

'We don't work for the press,' Mirabelle assured her. 'We work with the police. If you don't mind, Mrs Lewis and I would like a word.'

The woman paused as she held the gate open, her eyes darting. 'You don't have a camera?'

'Nothing like that.'

'I talked to an officer already.'

'It's the detail, you see,' Mirabelle said vaguely. If she was going to get anywhere, she needed people to talk. 'And you live next door.'

'I suppose it'll be all right,' the woman decided. 'I'm Violet Randall,' she said, as she turned up the path and opened the front door. 'It's good they have you. I'd far rather talk to a woman.'

The Randalls' house was full of flowers. Milk bottles with sprigs of blossom peppered the hallway and further in Mirabelle and Vesta could see empty tins arrayed with daffodils and bluebells. The place was spotless, if a little threadbare. A tabby cat lazed in a patch of sunlight by the window.

'I'm sorry for the mess,' said Mrs Randall, as her coat almost fell off her shoulders and on to the chair. 'I'm not terribly domestic.'

'It's lovely here,' Vesta declared with a grin. Mrs Randall looked taken aback as if she couldn't quite believe what Vesta had said. 'You haven't introduced yourselves,' she pointed out, hovering by the door.

'Oh yes, of course.'

They shook hands solemnly. Mirabelle and Vesta gave their names and Mrs Randall said to call her Vi and nodded them towards an old sofa patched with squares of faded houndstooth. Between the tins of flowers on the mantel, Mirabelle just made out last year's Christmas cards. Mrs Randall clearly hadn't read the *Good Housekeeping* guide to the seasons, but the room was bright and the house immediately had the feel of a home. A novel lay open on the chair. Mrs Randall closed it. 'I need to take that back to the library,' she said.

'I'm sure they'll understand if you're late, after what's happened,' Mirabelle reassured her.

Mrs Randall nodded. 'You want to know about it. We all want to know. My husband, Billy, spoke to the policeman. He found Helen's body. The thing is, we didn't see anything. We were asleep. Billy got up first. By the time I came downstairs your colleagues were here and Helen was gone.' She raised the handkerchief to her nose.

'We're just mopping up,' Mirabelle said. 'Sometimes it's the small things. I wondered if you'd heard anything in the night?'

Vi shook her head. 'I sleep like the dead at the moment.' She placed her hand on her baby bump. Then she remembered. 'Oh no,' she said. 'Sorry.' Tears began to well. 'It just makes you tired, that's all. I didn't hear anything.'

'You were close to Mrs Quinn?'

'Helen was a friend. We used to have a cuppa most days. There was no side to her. She and Phil had everything. You should see their place. But she wasn't snooty. I was going to ask her to be godmother to the baby.'

'When are you due?' Vesta leaned in.

'Next month.' Vi sniffed. 'And now I don't know who to get to do it.'

'Mrs Randall, do you know the police have arrested Mr Quinn?'

Vi sat up. She sniffed once more but the crying stopped. 'No,' she said. 'What for?'

'They suspect him of the murder.'

'That's ridiculous. Phil wouldn't hurt Helen in a million years. He adored her.' Vi got to her feet and, with her hands supporting the arch of her back, she began to pace up and down the thin carpet. 'I don't know why anyone would even think that.'

'Well, for a start, he was in the house with his wife's body for a long time – several hours – and didn't seem to notice she was dead. He can't account for that. The police suspect he drugged her, then stabbed her. After that it would appear he waited till morning before he alerted anyone.'

'And they reckon he thought he'd get away with that? I mean, that was his plan?'

'What do you mean?'

'Miss Bevan, I was a nurse in the war. I was in the Voluntary Aid Detachment. If you want to kill someone there are lots of ways to go about it that would give you a better alibi. I mean, if Phil drugged Helen it was premeditated, wasn't it? If you premeditate a murder you generally plan to get away with it. In that respect the theory you're suggesting was a terrible plan. And besides, Helen was stabbed in the stomach. That's painful. It takes a long time to die. Phil would never have been able to watch her suffer.'

'Does Mr Quinn have any enemies that you know of?'

'Apart from the idiot policeman who came up with that cockeyed theory?' Vi's eyes flashed. 'I can't think of anyone. The Quinns were nice people. I'll say that in court.'

'How long have you known them?'

Vi shrugged. 'I know them perfectly well,' she said.

'Not long then?'

'We moved here last autumn. Billy's aunt died and left him the house.'

'And the Quinns?'

'They got married last year. It's almost their anniversary.'

Mirabelle thought of the wedding photograph in the *Argus*. Was that only a year ago? The Quinns really hadn't had much of a chance. She got to her feet. 'Who had you thought of for the godfather?' she enquired.

'Oh, Billy's brother, I expect. In Portsmouth.'

'Not Phil Quinn?'

'You're supposed to spread it around, aren't you? In case . . . well, something like this happens.'

'If you were friendly with Mrs Quinn, was your husband friendly with Phil too?'

'They got on. I mean, Helen and I saw each other every day. The boys only got together now and then in the pub. On a Friday, you know. I can see what you want me to say, but there's nothing in it. Phil Quinn is a good man. He'd lend anyone a hand.'

'Had you noticed anything between Mr Quinn and his wife? I mean, anything unusual? Anything that was different recently?'

'They were trying for a baby. But that's just normal, isn't it?'

Mirabelle noticed Vesta shift in her chair. Vesta had been married to Charlie for two years. They were a happy if, by most standards, unconventional couple. She ignored the girl's awkward movement and continued. 'And you never heard them arguing? Not about anything?'

'Billy and I argue now and then, but, honestly, Helen and Phil weren't like that. They were properly lovey-dovey. They had it easy, I suppose – they were newly-weds. Phil makes a lot of money too. That gives you less to squabble about, doesn't it?'

Mirabelle couldn't comment. She had never married. During the war she and Jack had shared digs but they had been separated for weeks at a time, and even though she and Superintendent McGregor had become close, they didn't share a place of residence, let alone a bank account. Being married seemed completely out of reach, but that wasn't something to think about now.

Mrs Randall continued to rub the small of her back. 'Do you think they'll let Phil go? He couldn't have killed her. I won't believe it.'

'His business partners have secured the services of a solicitor,' Mirabelle said. 'The nub of it is if Mr Quinn didn't kill his wife then who else would want to, let alone have the opportunity?'

'I thought the law was innocent till proven guilty.'

'That's what Inspector Robinson will be looking into. Trying to prove him guilty, I mean.'

'And what are you going to do?'

'We're going to see what we can turn up. Honestly, this doesn't make sense to me either. For the reasons you pointed out for a start.'

'And beyond that?'

'It's a vicious crime. It feels like there's more to it. If Phil Quinn didn't kill her, then I'd like to find something – just a trace – of the person who did.'

Vi sighed, but she seemed to relax a little. 'Well,' she said, 'at least you're on the case . . .'

Mirabelle's eye was caught by a forsythia bush outside the window. She momentarily wondered why Vesta had been so quiet. The girl had hardly asked a single question. Now, she was sitting back in the chair with her eyes on the floor, or, more accurately, Mirabelle realised, with her eyes on Mrs Randall's ankles, which were slightly swollen. Beside the fire there was a knitting basket with a storm of white 3-ply wool attached to a pair of wooden needles – like a flurry of snow piled against a wall. As she raised her eyes from the pregnant woman's ankles, Vesta noticed the knitting and seemed momentarily stumped. Whatever the girl was pondering, it was not Helen Quinn's murder.

'Thank you, Mrs Randall. We mustn't take up any more of your time,' Mirabelle said, getting to her feet. 'Come along, Vesta, let's get going.'

Chapter 3

A cat in gloves catches no mice

The women proceeded down the road. Around the corner, the footballing boys had disappeared and the rubbish bins they had used as goalposts were abandoned, knocked over on the pavement. Vesta bent to pick them up and replace the lids. It was the deciding factor. Mirabelle folded her arms.

'How long have you known, Vesta?' she asked, as the girl pushed the bins back into place.

Vesta blushed. 'What do you mean?'

Mirabelle eyed her and said nothing. Vesta's forehead creased with both guilt and worry. 'Does it show?' she asked. The words came out garbled.

'You refused pudding at lunchtime. You can't bear the smell of exhaust fumes. You were transfixed by Mrs Randall. And her knitting. And you're clearing up after children in the street. Of course it shows.'

'I meant my stomach.'

Mirabelle shook her head. 'I made an educated guess based on your behaviour. That's far more reliable. Have you told Charlie?'

Vesta's fingers twitched. 'They say you should wait three months. You know, just to be sure. Before you tell anybody.'

'I don't expect they mean your husband to be included in that embargo.' The girl didn't respond. 'Congratulations, silly. Aren't you excited?'

27

'Yes.' Vesta's reply was knee-jerk, her tone, more tellingly, was uncertain. 'Of course I am.'

Mirabelle smiled. 'We have to celebrate.'

'I could murder a gin and bitter lemon,' the girl admitted. 'I don't know why, but I could really murder one.'

They continued back to the main road in silence. Mirabelle tried to imagine what it must be like, knowing there was a baby growing inside you. Those days were long gone for her. No woman had her first baby at forty-three and, besides, Superintendent McGregor was always careful. Vesta clutched her bag with an unaccustomed tenacity as they headed down the main road. 'I don't know,' she said out of the blue. 'Maybe everyone can tell.'

'Let's chat about it when we sit down,' Mirabelle said, her tone soothing.

As they passed the turn-off for Hove Cars, she came to a halt outside the off-licence next to the florist's with the hyacinths outside. 'Do you mind if we just check in here?' she asked.

'Of course.' Vesta nodded as she pushed open the door.

A bell sounded as the women walked into the gloomy interior. It was so dark inside the shop it felt like being swallowed. Mirabelle shuddered as her eyes adjusted. Vesta rubbed her arm as if she was trying to keep warm. Inside, an elderly man stood in front of the long mahogany counter. He wore a suit made of material so thick that the creases at his elbows looked like folded cardboard.

'Rabbit again,' he said mournfully. 'Why she can't get duck, I'll never know. I ask for duck but she doesn't listen. A nice juicy breast.'

Halfway up a ladder that reached from the floor to the top of the fitted shelves, a far younger man in a brown apron perused the stacked bottles. He was impressively steady on his feet.

'Well, you've had the Pinot Noir, Major. I mean any light red burgundy would work well . . .'

'I'm longing for a proper, robust Bordeaux. That's the thing.'

The man dismounted the ladder and pushed it past a pile of beer crates, mounting it again to reach a different set of bottles.

'There's this Paulliac,' he said helpfully, lifting a bottle off the shelf. 'It's very good.'

'With rabbit though,' the major tutted. 'I've a mind to go to the butcher's myself. I think it was the war that did it. She'll never get used to real meat again. It's all scraps, you see.'

As if he had only just realised the women had come in, the old man turned towards them. His eyebrows seemed oddly bright in the darkness. He tipped his hat solemnly. 'Good morning, ladies. Goodness, my dear—' he inspected Vesta as if she was a curiosity '—where on earth did you spring from?'

'Bermondsey,' Vesta replied.

Mirabelle heard herself sigh. Then she berated herself inwardly. There was no point in meeting rudeness with rudeness, but still. It was turning out to be a trying morning.

'And you ladies are wine lovers?' the old fellow continued. 'Capital. It's champagne, your tipple, I'd hazard. At your age, I drank champagne most of the time.' The man on the ladder shifted and this drew the major's attention back to the business in hand. 'Give me the Pinot Noir then, Peter,' he said. 'I'll try for the duck again tomorrow. And I need another bottle of that Armagnac. I'm almost out.'

Peter climbed down, carefully placing the bottles on the counter as the old man turned his attention back to Vesta. 'I was stationed in Southern Rhodesia in the thirties. I lived outside Salisbury. Do you know it?'

'Shall I put that on your account, Major Farley?' Peter enquired.

'Yes, yes.' The old man hovered. Vesta smiled indulgently.

'Will you manage all right?' Peter hurried him towards the door. 'We must get on, you see.'

The major tipped his hat. 'Yes indeed. Well then, good day.'

The three of them waited until the bell had chimed and the door closed. A strange kind of calm fell over the shop. Peter looked ruefully at the women. He faced a quandary. The customer had been rude but he was a good customer and besides it was terrible manners to apologise for someone else's bad manners.

'Can I help you?' he asked after he had stopped trying to work out what he ought to say.

'I hope so.' Mirabelle smiled. 'I've called to enquire about Mr Quinn's account.'

'Mr Quinn?'

'From the garage over the road.'

'I'm afraid Mr Quinn doesn't run an account, madam.'

'Not to worry. It was only a thought.'

The women turned to go but Peter cut in. 'Mr Quinn pays cash. All the gentlemen from Hove Cars pay cash.'

Mirabelle caught Vesta's eye. She let a smile spread across her face. 'Well, in that case, I don't suppose you recall Mr Quinn buying a bottle of gin recently?'

The man leaned on the counter, conspiratorially. 'Mr Quinn usually buys gin. That's his tipple.'

'When did you last see him?'

'Why?'

'You haven't heard?'

'Heard what?'

'I'm afraid Mrs Quinn was killed last night. The police suspect she was drugged. There was a bottle of gin, you see . . .'

The man straightened up. 'Well, that's very underhand, I must say. Walking in here asking loaded questions. Casting aspersions on our gin.'

'I'm sorry. I ought to have explained. The police are testing the gin. They don't know for sure yet.'

'Yes. Well.'

'The thing is, I wondered how often Mr Quinn bought a bottle and if he had a favourite brand.'

'What gives you the right . . .'

'We're friends of Mr Quinn. Or that is to say, friends of friends. I might be the first to ask but I imagine the police will get here eventually. I'm simply trying to understand exactly what might have happened.'

'We don't sell poisoned gin, madam. Not a bottle.'

'I don't suppose you'd last long in business if you did. Please. It would be very helpful just to know what kind of gin Mr Quinn favoured and how often he bought it.'

The man drew in a long breath, as he considered the matter. These women, after all, had been most understanding of the major. 'Well,' he said finally, 'I don't see what difference it makes. Mr Quinn buys London gin. Burleigh usually, though it depends what we have. Supplies are not consistent. I suppose he might pick up a bottle most weeks.'

'When did you last see him?'

'End of last week. It was raining. Must've been Friday.'

'Did he buy anything else?'

'Not on Friday.'

'But generally?'

'Fancy American beer. He likes that. In bottles, you know.' Peter tipped his head towards a pile of crates. 'Quite often, he'd buy a couple of crates and send them home in a car. At Christmas, he picked up brandy and port as well. And whisky – single malt – for presents, he said.'

'Thank you.'

'I'm sorry to hear about Mrs Quinn,' Peter said. 'She was a nice woman.'

'You know Mrs Quinn?'

31

'Oh yes. She's a lovely lady. The major would approve of her, all right. She came in regularly for champagne.'

'Champagne?'

'She had good taste. She always took Dom Perignon. She said she liked the size of the bubbles.'

'So the Quinns weren't celebrating with the gin?'

'I shouldn't think so. Like I said, they went through gin regular.'

Mirabelle continued. 'When did you last see Mrs Quinn?'

'Last month. A birthday, I think.'

'And her wedding anniversary would have been coming up.'

'Oh that's very sad. Well.' Peter folded his arms and stood up straight to indicate the interview was over. 'Thanks for telling me about the police. I mean, be prepared, isn't that right?'

It struck Mirabelle that today the men she was coming across seemed to feel they were in charge.

On the street, Vesta took her arm and they turned towards town. The sun had come out and a refreshing breeze whipped up the hill. Vesta squinted into the bright light.

'If Phil Quinn was there last week, that means there was plenty of opportunity for someone to tamper with the bottle,' she observed. 'A whole week almost. Mrs Quinn sounds stylish, doesn't she? Nice to everyone and with a taste for champagne. Dom Perignon is good, is it?'

Mirabelle nodded. She couldn't help thinking about Mill Lane. It was hardly a busy place. A stranger would be noticed. She bet not much got past Mrs Ambrose. Whoever had tampered with the gin was either local or had been lucky not to be seen. 'Come on,' she said, 'let's find you that gin and bitter. I might have one myself, what with your good news.'

* * *

More of the pubs closer to town served women because of the tourists, and Mirabelle guided Vesta through the heavily carved doors of one that looked respectable enough. She nudged the girl towards an empty table by the frosted glass window and ordered two gins with bitter lemon. The barman took a deep draw of his cigarette as if he was considering whether to bother serving them. Then he stubbed out his fag, pushed aside the newspaper he'd been reading and set to mixing the drinks, which arrived in two rather short glasses, a single bottle of bitter lemon shared between them.

As Mirabelle took her seat, Vesta sniffed. 'It smells good. I can't tell you. All I want is lemon. Even Vim. At the weekend, I was scrubbing the kitchen floor and I could have practically licked it.'

'Charlie's going to notice,' Mirabelle said. 'Especially if you start with that kind of thing.'

Vesta looked uncharacteristically shy. 'I can't quite believe it,' she said.

'Have you been to the doctor?'

Vesta nodded. 'He says it'll be a Christmas baby.' She looked as if she might burst into tears. 'I suppose it saves me getting Charlie a present,' she said gamely.

'If you want to leave, you know, Vesta. Work, I mean . . . Or if you need time off?'

Vesta had always said she would never quit the small office on Brills Lane. Now, she hesitated. 'I don't know what it will be like. I mean, it gets a grip of you. It's got a grip already.'

Mirabelle tried not to show that the idea of Vesta leaving work upset her. The girl was entitled to change her mind about what she wanted. Motherhood was a woman's greatest privilege. Before the wedding, Mirabelle had worried that marriage might make Vesta rethink what she wanted. Many women would have quit work to keep house, but the girl somehow managed to hold down her job and look after the place she and Charlie had bought. The upshot was that the Lewises subsisted on fish and chips and meals in a variety of pubs that hosted jazz nights, quite apart from whatever Charlie brought home from his job in the kitchens at the Grand. They managed, though Vesta was certainly no match for her mother, whose fried chicken was legendary. On the upside, her lack of interest in domestic duties left her plenty of time for cross-referencing the ledgers that remained the basis of all McGuigan & McGuigan's invoicing and interest calculations. Still, Mirabelle would have to face that a baby might change things that Vesta's wedding vows had not. She imagined how the office might feel with Vesta's desk empty, or, she considered suddenly, even filled by someone else. Someone new.

'Let's see how you feel,' she managed as she sipped her drink. 'There's masses of time.'

The barman lit another cigarette. He stood under a large mahogany clock and tried to look as if he wasn't listening. Slowly, he turned over the page of his paper.

'The thing is,' Vesta admitted, 'it's one thing putting up with people saying things when it's only me. I can take it. But I'm not sure how I'd feel if they were saying things to my child. Last night I sat at the window and I thought about our neighbours and their kids. They've come round to accepting Charlie and me. But we're always going to be different. People can't help it.'

'I'm sorry,' Mirabelle said. There was no point in pretending that Vesta wasn't right.

'It's no different in America,' the girl continued. 'From what Charlie says. In some places, it's worse.' Vesta took a sip. 'They have different entrances at the cinema.'

'That's terrible.'

Vesta shrugged. Her mind dotted between her worries, lighting on bits and pieces of evidence. Her elder brother had

34

gone back to Jamaica a couple of years ago. He always said he couldn't stand the British weather but Vesta wondered if his decision had been predicated on the fact that their mother was a force of nature. Mrs Churchill expected her children to fall into line. Any dissent caused ructions. Vesta was prepared for the battle – her marriage to Charlie had caused a family fight that was only smoothed over months afterwards. But now it occurred to her, what if Frank hadn't left London because of the cold or their overbearing mother? What if he'd left because of the stares and the comments? The everyday humiliations of not being served in shops or constantly being asked where you came from.

'I think you should tell Charlie,' Mirabelle said. 'I can't imagine you keeping quiet about such good news for three whole months. He's the father after all. It's something you need to talk about.'

Vesta nodded. 'You're right,' she said. 'Maybe I'll tell him this weekend.'

'Do it tonight,' Mirabelle encouraged her. 'I'll get on with this. Don't worry.'

Chapter 4

Doubt grows with knowledge

The light was just beginning to fade from the sky as Mirabelle approached the side entrance of Bartholomew Square police station where Phil Quinn was still being held despite the best efforts of the solicitor his friends had engaged. Superintendent McGregor had arranged a cloak-and-dagger rendezvous. The desk sergeant owed him one and Mirabelle wanted to meet Phil Quinn. Arrangements had been set for the evening – after Robinson and his team had left and McGregor was safely out of the way.

Mirabelle hovered in the doorway. It was odd how the noises on the street changed at dusk – the heavy swing of a pub door that you'd never notice at midday was somehow impossible to ignore after seven o'clock. Especially at this time of year. It was still too early for the mass of tourists that populated Brighton all summer. There weren't any buskers yet – no one-man band on the corner at the Kingsway or the fellow who went round the pubs playing his harmonica. No hurdy-gurdy on the corner at the front. Though the days were mild, the evenings in springtime could be bitter. Mirabelle's jacket was not thick enough. It had been sunny that morning and she had been optimistic. Luckily, she didn't have to wait. Sergeant Belton, a grey kind of fellow, recently transferred from Brighton's other police station at Wellington Road, promptly opened the door and let her through. Inside, he turned, waiting for her to say something.

The passage smelled of bleach. It had been a while since Mirabelle had visited the cells at Bartholomew Square. She had been incarcerated here for a few hours several years ago. For that matter, she'd been holed up in Wellington Road, under Belton's care too. McGregor referred to both these incidents as mix-ups, but Mirabelle had her suspicions.

'Good evening,' she said. 'Superintendent McGregor told you I was coming.'

'This way.' Belton swung a brace of keys on his bent finger. 'I've told the lads to take a break. There's biscuits in the office. We won't see anyone.'

'Busy day?' Mirabelle enquired.

Belton's grey eyes didn't flicker. 'Our busy time is the summer. Lost children. Pickpockets. Misdemeanours. The murders are more regular. One at a time. But you know that, Miss Bevan.'

He'd never liked her. Mirabelle had become inured to the catty comments of McGregor's colleagues. When the superintendent got the ins and outs of a case wrong he took it on the chin, but most policemen didn't like being shown up, especially by a woman. The ironic thing, it struck her, was that being right didn't always help. The victim was still dead. The damage could never be made up in any meaningful way. The most you could hope for was that someone would be punished, and that that person was the one who had perpetrated the crime.

Belton stopped at a closed door. 'Are you sure you want to see him?'

'Of course.'

The line of male cells felt oppressive. They were darker and smaller than the female ones. The sergeant slid back the cover on the viewing square and peered inside. 'You've got a visitor,' he said. 'A friend of your wife.'

Belton couldn't help but make a dig. Women weren't

supposed to count, and, when they did, it made him uncomfortable. Smirking now, he picked out a key and opened the door. A slow creak filled the hallway. Inside, against the painted bricks, Phil Quinn was sitting on the edge of his bed. Looking surprisingly dapper, he wore a pair of trousers with a crease down the front and a shirt that was highly starched, as if he was about to set out for a night on the town. Beside him there was a tray – sausage and mash and a mug of tea. Long cold, a ring of grease had congealed around the rim of the plate. As he looked up, he turned his head away, which made it difficult for Mirabelle to get the measure of him. However, it was immediately evident that, though his clothes were pristine, his spirit was in tatters. His eyes, where she caught a glance, were bloodshot and his nose was swollen. He had picked the skin on his fingers till it was dotted with dried blood. Mirabelle felt suddenly as if she'd intruded: as if she was only adding to his humiliation, never mind Belton.

'Thank you, Sergeant,' she said.

Belton stepped back as she moved forwards, as if the two of them were conjoined in this small conspiracy, like figures on a clock tower. Mirabelle listened as his footsteps retreated down the corridor.

'How do you know Helen?' Quinn's Scottish accent was stronger than McGregor's – his vowels bent out of shape. It made him sound aggressive, but perhaps that didn't mean anything – it was only the way he spoke.

Mirabelle suppressed the feeling of pity that washed over her. Other people's grief only reminded her of her own despair when Jack had died all those years ago. The poor man, she thought. He was still talking about his wife in the present tense. 'I'm sorry. It's Sergeant Belton's idea of a joke. Alan McGregor sent me.'

A dismissive noise escaped Quinn's lips. 'Can't make it himself?'

'He isn't allowed. He wanted to take your case but because of your long-standing connection . . . you were at school together, weren't you?'

'Primary. Alan went to the grammar after the eleven-plus. I was the thick one. Can't you tell?'

'Well, he's asked me to look into things. Inspector Robinson . . .'

'That idiot!' Quinn burst out. 'I said to him, every minute you spend asking me stupid questions is a minute less you're finding out who killed my wife.'

'Who do you think did it, Mr Quinn?'

The man's eyes burned with helpless fury. 'I have no idea. Helen was wonderful. Everyone loved her. Don't you think I've been going over and over it? She must have been in agony and I was just lying there. Jesus.'

'The police believe the gin you were drinking was drugged. I wondered if you know who might have had access to do that?'

'Access?'

'To the gin? And to the right kind of drugs, whatever they were?'

'They don't even know that then? Great. I felt groggy this morning. I thought it was a hangover and the shock. I don't know who could have done what you're talking about – drugging a bottle of gin. Stabbing my wife in the stomach. What kind of monster . . . ? It doesn't bear thinking about.'

Mirabelle reined him in. She needed information and, to get it, he would have to focus. 'When did you last drink from that bottle?'

'The night before.'

'So it must have been tampered with some time on Wednesday? Can you think of who might have visited your house on Wednesday? Was your wife in all day?'

'I don't know. I was at work. We're like everyone else – we

39

leave our door open. Helen's friendly with the neighbours.
The women, anyway. They come in and out.'

'Do you suspect your neighbours?'

'Of course not. I don't know who to suspect. You'd have to
be some kind of phantom. Helen never hurt a soul. It's just
evil.'

'Evil?'

'What would you call it?'

'Is your door usually left unlocked at night?'

'Yes. God help me.'

'Did the gin taste strange, Mr Quinn?'

He shook his head. 'We were drunk already. The both of
us. I got home around six. We had beer with dinner and then
we were dancing.' He stifled a sob. 'Helen loved to dance.
And to sing along. She was just a kid – a sweet kid.'

'What time did you go to bed?'

'Ten, I think. Maybe earlier. We were exhausted. Robinson
said she died between one and two in the morning. But I was
right next to her. We went to sleep as usual.' Quinn stared at
his hand, turning over the palm. 'I was there,' he repeated.

'The way she died . . .' It was difficult for Mirabelle to find
the words. 'I mean, you're right. The stabbing was vicious –
evil, you called it . . . Have you any idea why someone might
have killed her like that? I mean, that way in particular?'

'Jesus, no.'

'Mr Quinn, was your wife pregnant?'

Quinn heaved a sob and his voice broke as he answered.
'No. I mean, she didn't say. God, you can't think that.'

'There's no indication. I'm sorry. I only wondered. Why
stab her in the stomach?'

'I don't know. Why stab her at all? In the heart? At the
throat? What difference does it make?'

'I'm sorry.' Mirabelle didn't explain, but how Phil Quinn's
wife died did make a difference. Of course it did. 'And you

can't think of anyone who would have wanted to see her dead?'

'Of course not.'

'Can you think of anyone who would want to see you suffer, Mr Quinn?'

'By murdering Helen? Look, I've told them upstairs. There have been people who have been unpleasant. At work, I mean. We have the odd complaint. A car arriving late or going to the wrong address. It's my job to negotiate contracts for the garage. Fuel. Insurance. That kind of thing. I cut a good deal. You get the odd guy being chippy about being caught over-charging. But nothing has ever turned nasty.'

'And there's nothing else?'

'You think I'd forget a situation horrible enough to cause someone to drug me and my wife and then stab her to death? I didn't do it and I don't know who did. I certainly don't know why. Some use I am. I've been sitting here going over what happened and none of it makes sense. We're just ordinary people, Helen and I. All I can come up with is, maybe there isn't a reason. Maybe the person who killed Helen is just mad.'

Mirabelle paused. Murder could be random. Just not usually. But now a picture was emerging and it raised a question she hadn't yet considered. 'Do you think, Mr Quinn, it's odd they killed Helen and they didn't kill you?'

'I wish they had.'

Mirabelle didn't doubt it, but it was important he answered the question properly. 'Please. It might be key. They went to the trouble to drug both of you, you see. Doesn't it seem odd they only killed her?'

'They'd have had to drug both of us. I mean, we'd have fought. I'd have fought. I'd have killed the bastard who was trying to kill Helen. And she was no shrinking violet. Helen would have tried to kill any bastard who was trying to kill me.'

Mirabelle sighed. Maybe this was the best someone could come up with to torture Phil Quinn. If it was, it was working. He looked terrible. He clearly hadn't eaten and he wouldn't sleep either. The poor guy didn't know a thing.

'My solicitor had these clothes sent in,' he said, as he picked at his pristine shirt. 'He said it's important I look respectable.'

'Leave it to me. I'll do my best,' Mirabelle said and banged on the door to summon Belton.

At length, the sergeant appeared and opened up with a flourish as if the cell was the entrance to the Ritz.

'Goodbye,' Mirabelle said, trying to sound reassuring. 'I'll do my best to get to the bottom of it.'

Phil Quinn didn't reply. The sound of the cell being locked sent an odd reverberation down the corridor as if the door might never open again. Belton turned to lead Mirabelle out. At the entrance, he motioned her to wait as the clatter of footsteps in the office above suddenly became louder. As the noise tailed off, he pulled back the snib and pushed the door wide.

'Case solved then?'

Mirabelle shook her head. It wasn't going to be that easy. Belton's grey eyes almost warmed for a moment. He seemed eager. 'The boys are saying he'll swing. This kind of crime, he's bound to.'

'I hope not, Sergeant. I don't think he did it.'

'Well,' Belton said simply, his tone making it clear what he meant was 'This man is guilty. No question of it.' The sergeant had started on the force when he left school. He always thought people were guilty. In fairness, most of the people he came across were. Mirabelle stepped over the threshold on to the square and the sergeant nodded. 'Goodbye then.'

Mirabelle shuddered as the door closed. From somewhere far off the wind carried the sound of church bells across the cobbles. Pulling her jacket around her, she hardened herself to the chill and turned in the opposite direction from her flat at the Lawns, away from the sea. She had one more call to make this evening and it was inland. The smell of stale beer and cigarettes leaked out of the pubs as she passed and now and then there was the sound of someone singing and the plink plonk of a piano. As she got on to a bus on Queen's Road, she was glad to be out of the chill. Behind her, a man lit a cigarette and offered her one from the packet.

'Cold night,' he commented.

Mirabelle declined, turning towards the window. She wanted to think. In fact, as the city flew past the glass, she couldn't stop thinking. Helen Quinn's death was like a knot she was determined to unpick.

After getting off at Hangleton Road, she crossed the street and cut down the mews, where three black Austins were parked outside Hove Cars. The garage doors, where the apprentice had been plying his trade, were closed for the night, but a light was still on in the office. Inside, illuminated in the darkness, a young man sat at a desk, taking incoming calls. The ashtray in front of him was piled high with butts and beside him there was a radio control set. Hove Cars had all the latest gadgets. Opposite the desk, a line of drivers sat on a long bench, reading newspapers. Mirabelle ducked out of sight behind a drum of rainwater as a car turned into the mews. A man got out and proceeded into the office. As he entered, she could make out the murmur of greetings. She sneaked closer to the closed window.

'All right, John?'

'Quiet tonight.'

'Still early.'

Mirabelle checked her watch. It was just after nine. As if on cue with the men's comments, the telephone rang and the young man picked it up. 'Hove Cars.' He listened, scribbling down the details. 'Five minutes,' he said as he hung

43

up. 'Willie, go and pick up at Tongdean, would you, and take the girl down to the Grand?' This must be a regular booking and in response there was a murmur among the men, a ripple that felt like some kind of joke. The fellow nearest the desk got to his feet and lumbered outside. 'Keep your hands off the ladies, Willie! Those ones charge, you know,' one of the others shouted. The jollity was silenced as the phone sounded again and another driver was dispatched to pick up a girl called Ruby at an address on First Avenue. Mirabelle thought of the times she had ordered a car. She'd never once given her Christian name to a dispatcher. It wouldn't have seemed right. A minute later and another car was called to one of the dance halls. Inside, as the driver departed, the young man got to his feet. He picked a bottle of beer out of the cupboard and, as he did so, Mirabelle realised that the poor fellow had a wooden leg. He was too young to have been injured in service, but perhaps the Blitz had done for him. Your instinct was always to feel sorry for the people who had been hurt, but the truth was they were lucky to get away with their lives. Once, Mirabelle had helped to dig out a woman whose kitchen had collapsed. When they got through the rubble, the old lady was clutching a small terrier. 'Here,' she'd said. 'Take Sammy first.' It had felt like a miracle, the two of them alive under all the debris. The dispatcher was young – he must have been a child when it happened.

Mirabelle shivered. The later it got, the colder the air became and she'd seen enough to tell what was going on. Stepping on to the cobbles, she rapped on the office door. One of the men got to his feet and opened it.

'Yes, miss. A car, is it?'

'To the Arundel guest house.'

'Yes, miss.'

'It's not the Grand,' she added with a smile, just to check the reaction.

The man behind the desk had the grace to look uncomfortable. He fiddled with the radio control set and didn't meet Mirabelle's eye. Outside, the driver held the car door and she slipped into the back seat. The cold leather creaked. 'I didn't want to walk into town,' Mirabelle admitted. 'Not with that terrible murder.'

'Cold night, anyway, miss,' the man replied as he switched on the engine. 'Poor Mrs Quinn.'

'Did you know the woman?'

'Mr Quinn owns the garage.'

'I didn't realise. I'm sorry,' Mirabelle lied. 'You must all be terribly upset. I can't imagine who'd want to do such a terrible thing.'

'There are bad people out there.' The driver switched on the wireless. The young man's voice sounded. 'Calling all cars. Pick up at the Grand for Eleanor.'

'Is that a regular booking?' Mirabelle enquired.

'We do a lot of work for the Grand, miss.'

Mirabelle felt her lips purse. Hove Cars clearly picked up and dropped off at the hotel, that was no secret, but then what she was hearing wasn't a booking on account of the Grand. It was for quite a different kind of hospitality – a series of young ladies who used their first names. Tomorrow she'd need to look into it. In the meantime, Superintendent McGregor had promised her dinner or at least he'd promised that his housekeeper, Miss Brownlee, would make her dinner.

The driver cruised smoothly into town. On the other side of the pier, he turned down a Georgian terrace and pulled up at the door of the Arundel guest house. Mirabelle smiled. It wasn't like coming home but it was close. The man got out to open the door and she paid him on the pavement, making sure to tip.

'I'll wait to see you safely inside, miss,' he said. 'Like you said, you can't be too careful.'

McGregor had bought the Arundel a couple of years ago and, ever since, Miss Brownlee (who was already resident) had done a sterling job of turning out the superintendent tidily and keeping him well fed. An easy understanding had grown between the two women in Superintendent McGregor's life. Last year, they had exchanged Christmas cards and Mirabelle had bought Miss Brownlee a red silk scarf from Harrods, which she thought would suit the old lady far better than the succession of gaudy rayon squares she habitually chose to wear. 'What a nice box,' Miss Brownlee had said and Mirabelle hadn't minded.

Now, Mirabelle slipped the key from her handbag and silently entered the front door. From the sitting room at the rear there was the steady hum of post-dinner conversation and the clanking of coffee cups. The Arundel was generally fully booked, which was in part due to Miss Brownlee's skills in the kitchen and, increasingly, McGregor's reluctance to take out his profits. Instead, he instructed Miss Brownlee to invest in new fittings. Last year, she had bought fresh mattresses and a refrigerator, which she found herself unable to refrain from mentioning at every opportunity.

Mirabelle crept up the stairs. There was a standing arrangement that the sitting room and its awkward questions were to be avoided. At the top, she knocked and didn't wait for McGregor to call her in. The superintendent had chosen what had once been the house's drawing room as his quarters and Mirabelle opened the door on to the familiar sight of two long windows, shrouded in thick, blue velvet curtains. The room was laid out beautifully with a four-poster bed at one end. At the other, McGregor sat in an easy chair by the fire. The late edition lay open in front of him with the earlier editions piled to one side. Jostling the newspaper, he got to his feet and indicated the drinks tray. Mirabelle nodded. He poured a gin and tonic and she wondered, fleetingly, if this was how Helen

Quinn's last night started – with a deadly measure poured by the man she cared about?

'Miss Brownlee left you some pie,' McGregor said.

Dinner at the Arundel was served at seven o'clock sharp with no exceptions. If they came in at this time of night, regular guests did not benefit from Miss Brownlee's trays. Mirabelle peered at her supper. The wooden tray was laid with a thick linen napkin, highly polished silverware, a slice of pork pie with pickles and a generous portion of pudding on blue and white china.

'Is that cheesecake?' Mirabelle squinted hopefully.

'Lemon cheesecake. She bought an American cookery book from a shop on Duke Street and then, of course, once she'd baked it, she could chill it. She left exacting instructions about the temperature it's to be served at. I expect by now it's too warm.'

Mirabelle couldn't help but smile. Miss Brownlee had a natural aptitude with food. She could tell what you fancied before you knew it yourself. No matter its temperature, the cheesecake was sure to be delicious.

'What a treat. I wonder if she'd give me a slice for Vesta?'

'I thought Vesta would be fully supplied with cake.'

Mirabelle shrugged. He might be a chef but Charlie didn't know yet about his wife's yen for lemons. Mirabelle fell into the chair opposite the superintendent, sipped her gin and drew the tray on to her lap as the fire crackled. The smell of woodsmoke pervaded the room.

'Well?' McGregor was impatient. 'Did you see Phil?'

'He's in shock, I think. His language was a bit ripe.'

Mirabelle regarded the pie. The pastry crumbled in her mouth. She was hungry, she realised as it melted on her tongue.

'Any ideas yet?'

'Not really. They kept their door unlocked, day and night. The neighbours all had access, along with anyone else who

47

wanted it. Apart from that, all I've established is that the bottle of gin they were drinking may have been poisoned – that's certainly Robinson's theory. If it was, that happened some time between Wednesday night and Thursday evening, with the intention of disabling Mr and Mrs Quinn and killing Mrs Quinn, certainly.'

'What do you mean?'

'Well, why didn't they kill him, Alan? I mean, going to all that trouble and only killing her? It doesn't make sense.'

McGregor's eyebrows raised. 'It seemed to me it was a punishment. Or a blackmail attempt. Something that went wrong.'

'Maybe. But Quinn appears to have no idea about it. He's very convincing.' Mirabelle speared a piece of pickled cauliflower. Miss Brownlee really was a marvel. She took another bite of pie and once she'd swallowed it, posited, 'If it was a punishment, that begs the question, a punishment for what? The same goes for blackmail. So, what was Quinn up to at Hove Cars? I mean the most likely thing is that it's something to do with his business.'

'Like I said – taxis are the lifeblood of the city. But beyond a little cash on the side, I don't see Phil getting up to much – honestly, Mirabelle. He's never been like that. Some blokes came back from the war with a chip on their shoulder. A propensity for trouble. A need to take risks. Phil came back with a desire to settle down. He's a family man. That's what he came from. What his father was like.'

'Well, someone has taken offence. Maybe someone about whom he turned in information?'

McGregor shook his head. 'We haven't used the lads up there for any landmark cases. It's only detail. Small clues that build up. Phil hasn't put anyone in prison – not directly.'

'What kind of information do you usually get from him?'

'Surveillance. Taxi drivers waiting for a fare and see people come and go. Details of who they pick up and drop off.

Other cars parked nearby. That kind of thing. It's more about helping to build a case than clinching one. Basically, they help us place everybody.'

'So it's doubtful someone could be harbouring a grudge? A serious one?'

McGregor shook his head. 'I don't see it,' he said.

'What occurred to me is that perhaps we need to look around the taxi company, rather than directly at it. That's the thing. Maybe it's a customer. Maybe it's someone who could be given away but hasn't been grassed up yet. Someone who thinks they're defending themselves.'

'Police work often starts out half gossip.' McGregor nodded. 'But murder is a pretty aggressive act for someone on the defensive. What's on your mind?'

Mirabelle didn't want to tell him that she'd spent the last quarter of an hour hidden behind a water butt, eavesdropping, but she had to admit what she'd come up with. It was her only lead. 'Well, who else is the lifeblood of the city? What other profession makes up the most common police informants and, for that matter, the most common criminals? If the taxi owners don't know what's going on, who else is there?'

McGregor sipped his whisky. He watched as Mirabelle cleared her plate. He didn't like to say the word she was looking for but Mirabelle obviously wasn't going to help him.

'Prostitutes,' he managed.

'Yes. Most customers at Hove Cars might be above board. But what if they're running prostitutes round town? Or more than that – what if they hook up punters? How well are you connected to Brighton's brothels, Superintendent? Do you know who makes their transport arrangements? There's something going on and it's the only thing I can think of that might furnish a way in.'

McGregor stiffened. 'I can't let you go sniffing around whorehouses, Mirabelle.'

Mirabelle pushed away the tray and took a long drink of gin. It was too late for that. Her interest had been aroused. Besides, the seamy world of prostitution had borne evidence before. Still, she didn't say so. Instead, she glanced momentarily at the four-poster bed. She stayed here more often than he stayed at her place. She told herself it was because of Miss Brownlee's breakfasts and that it was more convenient and, for that matter, more discreet. None of these things was entirely true or, at least, they weren't the real reason. The thing was McGregor's long-windowed suite didn't hold memories of anyone else. There was nothing to be reminded of at the Arundel and that was what she liked about it most.

McGregor met her gaze. 'You'll figure it out. I know you will,' he said, as he got up and tipped her chin with his finger. She smiled as he leaned in and kissed her. Lately, she'd found herself greedy for him. For this. He swept an arm around her waist and scooped her out of the chair.

'Come on, darling,' he said. 'Let's go to bed.'

Chapter 5

Imagination decides everything

Vesta sat at her desk, her frame masked by a copy of *Tatler* magazine, which promised news of spring fashion. She had first come across the publication at Goodwood House the year before. Always a fan of the *Picture Post*, her consumption of magazines had risen of late. The last couple of weeks she found it difficult to sleep, waking hungry at seven, making a tottering pile of buttered toast, which she consumed while flicking through the glossy pages, before sneaking guiltily out of the house before Charlie got up. She was glad to have the office to come to.

'Some women get morning sickness,' Vesta pondered as Mirabelle came through the door. 'But I'm fine so far. I just fancy what I fancy, if you know what I mean.' Being pregnant was beginning to feel like something she could share, with Mirabelle at least.

'Did you tell Charlie?' Mirabelle checked, as she hung up her coat.

Vesta shook her head. 'I couldn't,' she admitted, as she poured Mirabelle a cup of tea from the pot on the side, like clockwork.

Mirabelle sipped. It seemed churlish to refuse the cup but Miss Brownlee's breakfast had been more than adequate and more tea was the last thing she felt like. Vesta's magazine lay open on the desk, but she tried not to look at it. *Tatler* made Mirabelle uncomfortable. It was a compendium of the life she'd lost – parties in London, receptions at court and castles in the countryside.

'Look,' Vesta insisted. 'Isn't it glamorous? A spring ball.' She turned to the social column. 'Countess Marianna Iritsin, recently arrived in London from Monte Carlo,' she read. 'Look at that dress. It must be a Schiaparelli.'

Mirabelle peered across the page. The woman was perhaps her own age and beautifully turned out. Still, Mirabelle squinted, she looked as if her smile had been plastered on. But then after Monte Carlo, fog-bound, low-key London must come as something of a shock.

'I wonder what she was doing there,' Vesta pondered.

Mirabelle shrugged. She could hazard a guess. Upheavals in Russia over the last forty years had resulted in a swathe of émigrés across Europe – some had got out with money and some were living in penury. Judging by the dress, the countess fell into the former category. Avoiding looking at any more pictures, she turned her attention back to the case.

'Vesta,' she said, 'we need to find some . . .'

'Biscuits?' Vesta offered.

'No. We need to find some ladies of the night.'

The girl snapped the magazine shut and hooted. She raised her hand and pointed at the clock. 'At nine in the morning?'

Mirabelle laid down her teacup. 'Well, even if it's not till later . . .'

'Wherever do you think we're going to find Nancies? I mean in Brighton?' Vesta continued.

That was a fair point. Mirabelle had never enlisted the help of Brighton's prostitutes before. In London it was easier. Girls famously hung around King's Cross and had done for a century or more. And then you could spot women in Soho. You could tell by the way they flirted as much as anything else. There was something about someone who was selling herself. Something that was always slightly out of place, or perhaps trying too hard to look as if she was in place. The kind of woman who sipped her drink but wasn't thirsty. Mirabelle checked herself. She might notice things but she didn't like to judge. During the war, some of the bravest women had sold themselves, if not for money then for information or even just the freedom to get away. Sometimes for all these things and a dash of pleasure. 'Why shouldn't I get what I want?' Mirabelle recalled one saying at her debriefing. Well, why not? And there was no question that, now and then, these women had provided helpful information. When one of Vesta's old friends had been arrested by Scotland Yard, Mirabelle had found out more about him from the prostitutes he'd visited than she had from his family.

Still, that had been in the capital. In Brighton it would be more difficult. During the summer there was a steady stream of call girls who arrived from out of town and hung around the bars and hotels on the front. One year, when Mirabelle first started working at McGuigan & McGuigan, she had helped one of them to get away. It was too early in the season for those women to have hit the promenade in any numbers. There weren't enough tourists to make it worth their while. Besides, Mirabelle thought, she wanted to find regular users of Hove Cars, which meant her target was some kind of call-out service – yes, that's what she was looking for. Something regular, based in Brighton all year round. 'Come along,' she said, reaching for her coat, 'I have an idea.'

Mirabelle had never introduced Vesta to her friend, Fred, who undertook a healthy trade in contraband from a cottage on one of the laneways near the office. As they set off up East Street, it struck her that she wasn't sure why she had neglected to do so. Over the last few years, she had bought several presents for Vesta from Fred's extensive stock. Still, now she felt uncomfortable as she led the girl up the hill, through the maze of little streets and on to the run-down, muddy lane that ran to Fred's door. The ground was potholed. Hardly anyone came down here – the entranceway was so slim it was easy to miss. Sometimes at night men were dragged down the lane and beaten up. Once, when Mirabelle had arrived, there had been a disconcerting smear of blood along the brick wall that ran down one side. Now there was only a filthy tramp asleep, a thick slick of moss above his head. As the women passed, they caught a whiff of stale alcohol and urine. Mirabelle couldn't help think this wasn't the sort of place she ought to bring a pregnant woman. She found herself considering what Vesta had said the day before – about poor treatment being all right for yourself, but expecting a child to bear the same thing being more difficult. She'd become so fond of Vesta that the prospect of her facing day-to-day difficulties offended her. Perhaps, she thought, she should find the girl something else to do.

Vesta beamed. 'What's down here?' she asked.

Mirabelle stopped in front of the cottage door and tenta-tively knocked on the peeling paintwork. To her right, part of the gutter had come away from the slated roof and bowed over the window, which was spattered with dried mud. At least it wasn't raining today. Every time Mirabelle came here the place was in a worse state. There was the sound of a lock being pulled back, then the door juddered as it opened and Fred peered out.

'Ah. Miss Bevan.'

It was immediately apparent that Fred was ill. Mirabelle had never seen him under the weather. During the war, he'd survived bombing raids as well as prolonged and difficult journeys by sea. He'd been starved in a holding camp from which he'd escaped. On another mission, he'd had to fight his way out of a tricky situation in Spain – a country that remained neutral for the duration of the conflict and, as such, was a hotbed of spies and a natural, if dangerous, route for those who wanted to escape. Despite all that, on none of the occasions Fred had arrived to be debriefed in London had he ever looked as bad as he did today. His shirt was open at the neck and a thin towel was draped around his shoulders. His nose was blocked and his eyes watery. He sneezed and, when he did so, he looked suddenly old.

'Oh hell,' he said, wheezing. 'Maybe you'd best not come in, Miss Bevan. I don't want to give you this.'

'What happened?'

'I got hung out to dry, to tell the truth. I ended up on the Downs by myself. The so-and-sos I was doing a deal with took me out but didn't bring me back. I had to walk all the way in the pitch dark. Got soaked to the skin. I'm getting too old for this game. Who's your friend?'

Vesta put out her hand and Fred shook it. 'Vesta Lewis,' she said.

'Very pleased to meet you,' Fred managed and then coughed because it had taken some effort. Mirabelle noticed his five o'clock shadow was completely white and his neck seemed thin and loose. Old men went ragged at the edges – it was always sudden and strange when it happened – as if the strong men they had been shrunk in the wash of life and they emerged misshapen and devoid of colour in the process. 'What can I do for you, Miss Bevan?' he asked, as he recovered his breath.

Mirabelle looked over her shoulder. There was nobody around, or at least nobody conscious, but still. She tipped her head to indicate that she would like to go inside.

'If you're sure you want to enter the house of suffering,' Fred said cheerily.

On the other side of the peeling front door, the dilapidation continued. Two rough wooden cages, each containing a cockerel, were placed at either end of the counter. The birds made clucking noises that sounded threatening and, here and there, a quivering, feathered limb stuck through the

55

bars. Mirabelle didn't like to think what Fred was up to. That kind of thing had been banned for a long time, but then, the forbidden was his stock in trade. Behind the cages, tea chests were stacked tidily against the wall and in front of the counter Fred had pulled out a grubby old armchair. There was a small pot of Vicks perched perilously on one arm and a yellowing cotton handkerchief crumpled on the other. On the floor, a dusty kettle was plugged into the wall, the spout emanating a thin wisp of steam.

'For my chest,' he said.

Mirabelle couldn't help but think that this was not the best accommodation for a man with a chest complaint. The cottage was damp and it felt colder inside than out.

'Maybe you should go home,' she said.

'And give it to the missus? It wouldn't be fair. Besides, maybe she wouldn't love me any more if I wasn't my usual, handsome self.'

'Perhaps she'd want to look after you,' Mirabelle rejoined.

'You don't know my missus.' Fred grinned gamely and a sparkle lit his eyes. Mirabelle felt relieved to see him look more like the man she knew. 'So, how can I help you ladies? I've got spices somewhere.' He nodded at Vesta. 'If you like that kind of thing.'

'Oh. I don't really cook . . .'

'Vesta's husband is the chef.'

'Well, maybe he'd like some pimento. And there's olive oil. The Italians like all that. I wasn't sure when I first got it in but it's selling like hot cakes.'

'I'll ask my husband. Thank you.'

'The thing is, Fred,' Mirabelle cut in, 'Vesta and I are looking for a particular kind of service. The sort of service some gentlemen require. Somewhere in Brighton that does callouts – to the Grand, certainly, and to private houses.'

It momentarily sounded as if Fred had contracted whooping

cough and it took him a minute to regain his equilibrium. Between laughing and struggling for breath, tears dotted his cheeks. 'Oh, I never know what to expect from you, Miss Bevan. I suppose I should just be grateful you don't want another gun because that day you had me worried.'

Vesta eyed Mirabelle. It seemed pushy of her to ask, but now and then when things came up, she found herself mesmerised by the things Mirabelle got up to when they weren't together. The things she knew about were tantalising enough. Mirabelle ignored Fred's comment.

'It's the death of that woman, you see. Up in Portslade. Did you read about it? Helen Quinn?'

'You don't want to get involved in that sort of thing.'

'We were asked to look into it by the superintendent,' Mirabelle said blithely.

'And you think this woman was on the game?'

'Goodness, no. There's no evidence of that. The thing is, her husband runs a taxi firm. Hove Cars. And our first line of inquiry is that the murder is some kind of revenge killing. The firm cooperates regularly with the police, that is to say the drivers provide information from time to time. It struck me that Mrs Quinn's death might be something to do with his business more generally, and then it struck me . . .'

'That if the murderer was taking revenge for being grassed up or there was something dodgy going on in the company, that hookers might be a way to find out about it?'

'They're mobile. I don't mean like cars. I mean with people. Most people only have contact with a small circle. But prostitutes . . . well, people talk to women like that. And they're savvy. I listened in at the hired car office, Fred, and it seems several of the firm's calls in the evenings are ferrying around women. You know. Women on their own.'

'You ain't lost any of your smarts, Miss Bevan. I'll never forget that time you got me out of—'

'Please,' Mirabelle cut in, casting her eyes towards Vesta, who had settled on a carver chair with her legs elegantly crossed. 'You signed the Official Secrets Act. Remember?'

Fred considered this. 'We're among friends,' he said in his defence. 'Look, I don't know about individual girls. Being a married man. Them days are over. But, now I think on it, there's a bloke who runs the kind of racket you're talking about. Girls, I mean. He isn't pleasant. Well, you wouldn't expect that, would you? He's got a place in Hove – a nice old house. Davidson's his name. Ernie Davidson. He has a few girls regular like. And he runs a poker game. It's an upmarket operation – not Mayfair or anything but still. Don't be fooled. He's a tough customer. He bought a lot of port off me. And whisky too, back when you couldn't get it easily. He drives a hard bargain. I don't know if he uses Hove Cars. In London, in the old days, those guys had their own drivers to ferry the girls about. Bodyguards, really. But he'd be a good place to start. I bet he keeps his finger on the pulse and you're right, of course – brasses hear everything. Maybe the superintendent isn't half as daft as he seems, putting you two on the case. I don't suppose you'd get a police officer in that house, but two nice-looking women . . .'

'What's the address?' Mirabelle asked, deciding not to divulge that the superintendent had specifically warned her off this kind of inquiry.

'Tongdean Avenue, up near the golf course. I've delivered there. Nice houses on that side of town.'

Mirabelle nodded. The name was familiar from the night before. The first call-out she'd heard was to Tongdean.

Fred scrambled behind the counter. 'I'll write it down,' he said. 'Here, if you want, you could get a taxi. There's a telephone box outside the pub. I've got a number for Hove Cars and all.'

'Very funny.' Mirabelle removed the slip of paper and popped it into her purse as Fred heaved and hooted. Vesta slipped off the chair. 'Please, look after yourself,' Mirabelle said, as she ushered the girl outside. The tramp, she noticed, had shifted slightly, which meant the poor man was alive, at least.

'You don't have to worry about me, Miss Bevan,' Fred called after the women cheerily. 'I'll be fine. Always am.'

Chapter 6

I cannot but give way to music and women

Tongdean Avenue was part of a stretch of comfortable suburban streets two miles inland. Developed before the war, the plots were evenly spaced, each containing a single detached property, some of which had been designed in the Tudor style with oak half-timbers between plaques of wattle and daub, and others which were more modern. These last looked like white ocean-going liners, so smooth and white that Mirabelle wondered if the occupants ever woke with tousled hair and crushed night clothes. Between the houses, the gardens were vivid green, each building surrounded by its own grounds and now, some years on from the initial development, the trees were coming into their own and at this time of year there was a profusion of blossom.

Vesta had not been pleased that Mirabelle did not want her company on the expedition. 'Think of your condition,' Mirabelle had said when they got back to the office. 'I can't bring you to a brothel.' Fred's hovel had felt bad enough.

'Why not?' Vesta objected. 'The houses are lovely at Tongdean. It doesn't look dangerous.'

'Those kinds of places seldom do,' Mirabelle replied drily. That wasn't entirely true. Downmarket, dens of iniquity looked exactly what they were, but upmarket, things were gilded and dressed so that even if matters weren't entirely hidden, they might easily be glossed over. But what might happen beneath that gloss was uncertain and Mirabelle didn't want to take the risk. 'It was the telephone that revolutionised how the business worked,' she observed, slipping the pencil in her hand through her slim fingers and bouncing it off her notepad as she distracted the girl.

'What telephone?' Vesta asked, taking the bait.

'The telephone. I mean, before that women had to go out to make their arrangements. Or a man had to call to a specific place. Or send a note. Can you imagine – a telegram. But once it was possible to telephone . . .'

A smile played on Vesta's lips. 'Oh, I see,' she said. 'So somewhere more out of the way, all you'd need is a telephone and you'd be in business.'

'Well, a telephone and a way to get about. That's the point, isn't it? Hove Cars.'

In the end, Vesta agreed to mind the office as long as she could look into the nature of the sedative used to drug the Quinns. She had a friend on the nursing staff at the Royal. Mirabelle thought it would be good for the girl to speak to someone medical. Perhaps it would help her find a way to tell Charlie.

'There might be a clue in the poison, I suppose. I'll telephone to Marlene,' Vesta said, sounding resigned as she eyed the handset on her desk with a new understanding.

Mirabelle left her to it, and half an hour later, as she stepped off the bus on Dyke Road, she could hear children splashing and screeching, out of sight in one of the back gardens. Someone must have a swimming pool, she thought. How nice. It didn't feel like a working day up here – the place was overwhelmingly domestic. As she turned on to Tongdean Avenue there was a burst of butter-yellow blossom on all sides. Mirabelle eyed the laburnum petals that spilled on to the grass and dripped over the hedges. They made quite a show. Although laburnum was poisonous, its deadly pods wouldn't have the effect of knocking out Mrs Quinn, Mirabelle thought.

Laburnum, in even a small quantity, would kill a person outright. She'd seen what the poison could do first hand only a couple of years ago and it always surprised her that the tree was so commonplace. She wouldn't choose to plant it in a garden, but perhaps whoever developed Tongdean Avenue had a fondness for yellow.

Mirabelle unfolded the piece of paper Fred had given her. Looking up, she realised that she had stopped outside the right house, a brick-built, five-bedroom on a corner plot. In the front garden some sorry-looking ice-blue irises were poking through the damp earth. The lead-paned windows were shielded by net curtains and the front gate was closed. A privet hedge ran along the low boundary wall. Mirabelle noticed the door furniture was dull. The house looked expressionless, as if it wasn't paying attention to the outside world.

She took a turn around the perimeter wall. At the rear, more net curtains obscured the windows and there was a long stretch of lawn, a willow tree and a couple of beds of rosebushes. Directly outside the back door a pile of garden furniture lay bundled in tarpaulin. The side gate led to a long garage. It did not have the air of a place where the doors might be routinely left unlocked or where visitors were welcome.

Mirabelle took up a position just past the corner where she calculated she would least likely be noticed from inside. She waited for about half an hour during which time a delivery van deposited two cardboard boxes of groceries at a house across the street. Surveillance always took time. Mirabelle had read the manuals. She'd even helped to compile one or two. Since she came to Brighton she'd had occasion to put her knowledge to good use. Now, she rested against the brick wall, biding her time. At length, a smart-looking car driven by a uniformed chauffeur pulled up – the most interesting thing to happen so far. The man switched off the engine and picked up a newspaper. Within less than a minute, the front door of the house clicked open and a pretty blonde girl, wearing a brown coat and matching hat, marched down the driveway, her heels crunching the stones. Her jewellery was a little showy for the afternoon but apart from that you'd never guess. She spotted Mirabelle and halted at the gate with one eye on the car. The chauffeur bundled his newspaper on to the seat and jumped out on to the pavement to hold open the door, but the girl put up a gloved hand and turned in Mirabelle's direction, her heels clicking as she approached.

'Look, whoever he is, he isn't here.' She sounded exasperated. 'Your husband, I mean. You're wasting your time. And even if he was here, it's hardly our fault.'

Mirabelle faltered. 'But I'm not married,' she found herself saying. The girl raised her eyes as if this fact simply annoyed her more. 'Save me!' she exclaimed. Then she turned on her heel and hopped into the back seat of the car. The chauffeur raised his eyes apologetically. He started the engine and pulled away. Mirabelle checked her watch. It was after three – about the time these girls would start work, she supposed. It was odd to think that all over Brighton men were planning a stolen afternoon before they went home to their wives. She was glad she had left Vesta in the office.

Further down the street, a postman was making his rounds, slamming the gates behind him. Mirabelle glanced at the house. In the old days, the department had surveilled premises for weeks before taking action, but here, she'd freeze before nightfall, and, besides, there was a limit to the amount of time a woman could hang around on a suburban street without anyone asking why. As the postman neared, she accosted him.

'Good afternoon. Anything for Mr Davidson?'

The man searched his bag. 'You staying for a while then, love?'

Mirabelle wasn't sure how to reply. 'Yes,' was what came out of her mouth. 'I'm his sister.'

The man drew three brown envelopes from the pile, pulling aside the taut string that held the mail in place. 'He's got a big family, Mr Davidson.'

'What do you mean?'

'He's always got people staying.'

'Yes.' Mirabelle smiled weakly. She reached out and relieved the postman of the letters. 'I'll take these,' she said. 'Thank you.'

The bell must have sounded deep inside the house because, as she pressed it, Mirabelle couldn't hear a thing. She eyed the knocker, wondering if it might be necessary to use that instead. At least then you knew you had made a sound that might call someone to action. Before she could, though, the door creaked open on to an old woman wearing a wig set in a strange-looking permanent wave. Its colour seemed dark against her raddled skin and her hands were thick-fingered with calluses. By contrast, she was wearing a housecoat that looked as if it might have belonged to Snow White – all starched white cotton with small red bows and zigzagged edging in French navy.

'He's not here, love,' she said wearily. 'Your husband or whatnot.'

'Oh, I'm not looking for anyone like that. I wondered if Mr Davidson might be at home? I live down the road and his mail was delivered to my house.' Mirabelle did not proffer the envelopes.

The woman eyed her up and down. 'I'll take them, miss,' she said, holding out a large, red hand.

'The thing is, I took it as an opportunity to introduce myself. It's important to know your neighbours, don't you see?'

The woman hesitated. Her eyes were rheumy and her skin was so thick it looked as if she had been smeared with pink concrete. As a consequence it was difficult to read her expression. 'Hold on,' she said and closed the door.

'Well, I don't expect she was trained in Paris,' Mirabelle mumbled under her breath. She weighed Davidson's mail in her hand. It was all brown envelopes, only bills, but they should furnish a way in.

The door remained closed for what felt like too long before the maid reappeared. 'He'll see you,' she announced and held it open for Mirabelle to enter.

Inside, the hallway was decorated in muted tones of dun brown and green. A collection of Victorian brass bells covered every available surface from the window ledges to the little shelves above the radiators. The house so totally lacked expression from the outside that this bright decoration appeared outlandish, but there was little time to take it in. The woman, having closed the front door behind her, set off quickly down the hallway without offering to take Mirabelle's jacket. Mirabelle followed her into a large public room, which opened on to the garden. The windows, though covered in the long net curtains she'd seen from the street, let in a good deal of light compared to the hallway and the place was nicely decorated. A thick, pale carpet was fitted wall-to-wall with a red and blue Turkish rug placed at a jaunty angle on top. Beyond that, the place was crammed with oak furniture – two sideboards, an array of chairs and two desks, behind one of which sat a man wearing a slick, dark suit and a thin tie. Clean shaven, puffing an ebony pipe and wearing wire-framed spectacles, he looked more like an accountant than a pimp. He was at least fifty years of age. It was difficult to reconcile Fred's warning about the hard-negotiating, dangerous owner of the house with the man sitting in front of her.

'Mr Davidson?' Mirabelle held out her hand.

The man got to his feet and firmly shook it, motioning Mirabelle towards a scatter of chairs. 'Please,' he said.

'Your mail was inadvertently delivered to my house. I'm

a neighbour.' Mirabelle waved vaguely in the direction from which she had come.

Mr Davidson glanced at the envelopes. 'And you might be?'

Mirabelle didn't falter. She wasn't going to give him her real name. 'My name is Belle,' she said. No one called her that these days but the monicker was familiar – the best kind of cover. Jack had called her Belle for years. And in these circles surnames were superfluous – for women, anyway. 'You've been on Tongdean Avenue for longer than I have, Mr Davidson.'

'Which number have you moved into?' he enquired.

'Are you friendly with many of the neighbours?'

'Not especially.'

Mirabelle didn't bat an eyelid. 'Number twenty-seven,' she replied.

Mr Davidson got up and pulled open an oak drinks cabinet, revealing an array of bottles. 'Might I get you something?' he asked, as he poured himself a brandy.

'Thank you. No.'

'It is a little early.'

'Oh no. I like a drink. But I have shopping to do. I found a decent off-licence on the way into town on Hangleton Road as a matter of fact. I need to pick up some bits and pieces.'

'I know the shop you mean.' Davidson sipped. 'Well, Belle, what can I do for you?'

'Oh, nothing at all.'

'You just came to look then? Out of curiosity?'

'Just to be neighbourly. When the mail arrived on my doormat, I thought I might as well bring it over. I was going out anyway, as I said.'

His stare was unforgiving. 'It's very brave of you. Most of the neighbours avoid this house.'

'Really? Why?'

He didn't reply. Instead, he filled his pipe and spent a

moment or two lighting it. The smell of burning shag wafted over the desk. 'I can't say it's not a nice place,' he posited, taking off his spectacles and laying them on the leather blotter. Without them his face changed. He looked markedly less professorial. His gaze was direct and unforgiving as if he was weighing her up. Mirabelle's skin prickled and her heart rate increased, but she decided to push him. It was the only way.

'Yes. Though did you read about the murder the other night? It happened not two miles away. It quite shook me. I mean, one feels vulnerable. I'm a woman on her own, you see.'

'I understood the woman who died was married. Sometimes that's the more dangerous option.' Davidson eyed his brandy. 'Look, there's no point pussyfooting about. It occurs to me that you've popped in on business. That's the truth isn't it, Belle?'

'What kind of business are you in, Mr Davidson?'

'Entertainment,' he said flatly. 'My clients are performers. I expect you know that.'

'On the contrary, I had no idea. I would have imagined that you might live in London. What with Shaftesbury Avenue and the theatres.' She kept her tone light.

'I lived in London for a while.'

'How long have you been here?'

'Three years. Maybe four.'

'Brighton is friendly, isn't it? And easier to get about. All the London shops deliver – you'd hardly realise you had left town in some regards. Though, as I say, this murder has unnerved me.'

Mr Davidson curled his fingers around the brandy glass and swirled the liquid up the sides. He did not speak.

'I like the bells. In the hallway,' Mirabelle said eventually. During the war, some interrogators used silence to put on pressure. But it struck her that Davidson was not one to crack that way. It was better to put him at his ease and not let the gaps in the conversation become oppressive. The more she could get him to talk, the more chance there was he'd say something useful. This, after all, was a fishing exercise.

'The bells belonged to my mother,' he said. 'She was a collector of sorts. I don't know what it was that so attracted her but she loved them. She was drawn to junk shops – she liked it down here on the coast – all the little shops. She couldn't pass one by. Actually, some of her collection is quite interesting. There's one of a lady in a Victorian dress and the ringer inside is shaped like her legs. I suppose that was quite saucy in its day.'

'It's a lot of polishing.'

'I think my mother found that therapeutic, to tell the truth.'

'Was she in your business?'

'My mother was a cleaning lady.' Davidson's tone was combative. 'I was brought up round the Portland Road. Notting Hill. And proud of it. I don't really belong on Tongdean Avenue, if that's what you're trying to figure out.'

'Not at all. Good for you. Your mother must have been proud.'

'What is it you want, Belle? Why are you here?'

'Why do you think I'm here?'

'I think you're curious. I think you're a little bit saucy. I think you've heard what goes on in this house and you're wondering if you might belong here. I don't think you're a woman who is on the way to Hannington's or off to buy a case of wine. I think you're someone who is looking for a job.'

'A job?'

'You know what I mean.'

'And if I was?'

'I'd say you're well turned out and you've got nerve coming in here like you have. I'd say there's a certain kind of man who might be happy to see you. The kind of man who wants a decent conversation over dinner before moving on to other

68

things. An older gent who feels foolish being seen with a woman half his age.'

Mirabelle's cheeks burned and she cursed herself for being naive. It felt as if she'd waded in further than she'd intended.

'My girls are paid well,' Davidson said. 'In return they do a good job. A professional job. I don't take on anyone lightly.' His eyes lighted on her ankles and travelled upwards – a naked glance. Mirabelle was surprised how disconcerted she felt. She let him stare though. 'Well?' Davidson said when he'd done.

'I suppose I'm here because I don't know if I can. I don't know if it's right for me.'

He sounded satisfied, as if he'd sniffed her out. 'That's fair enough. Why don't you spend the day, Belle? Get the feel . . . ' He got up, poured a shot of spirits and put the glass down in front of her. 'Let's not pretend, shall we? There's only one way to find out if you're that kind of woman.'

He was openly predatory now, but Mirabelle was suddenly sure she could handle this. She just wasn't sure how. When the door opened and a young woman walked in, she felt a mild wave of relief.

'Oh. Sorry.'

'Not at all.' Davidson motioned the girl towards Mirabelle. 'This is Jinty. Jinty, this is Belle.'

Mirabelle nodded hello. The girl was nicely dressed in a lemon-yellow dress and heels. She was wearing too much lipstick for a weekday afternoon. That was where these women fell down, Mirabelle thought. They were slightly too obvious; not, she supposed, that the men minded.

'How do you do.' Jinty smiled.

That, Mirabelle thought, was more like it. The conversation had become rather intense, and none of it about Helen Quinn. Yes, she needed to get back to that. 'I was just saying the recent murder over at Hangleton has quite shaken me. Did you read

69

about it? Everyone knows that in London that kind of thing goes on, but down here, well, I think of Brighton being safer, somehow. Like the country.'

'The country?' The girl flicked open the silver cigarette box on Davidson's desk and deftly fitted a gasper into a short, jet cigarette holder. She waited for Davidson to pick up his gold lighter and elegantly leaned into the flame to get the smoke going. 'Gosh. I don't think of Brighton like that at all. The dancing down here is wonderful. A crowd of us went to the Palais last week and we all remarked that we could have been anywhere. Tottenham Court Road. The Mecca or somewhere. The music was top-notch. And then there's the Variety. Brighton gets its fair share of big acts. I don't think of it as being like the country at all.'

'Perhaps I just lead a quieter life,' Mirabelle managed wistfully. 'And it's such a nasty business. The murder, I mean.'

'Well, they got the fellow.'

'They arrested the woman's husband. Yes.'

Jinty shrugged as if that settled the matter. The doorbell sounded and Davidson got to his feet. 'That will be your car.'

'I take special clients in the afternoon,' Jinty explained. Her voice was comforting, as if she was purring. 'There's a party in a suite in one of the big hotels down the coast.' She met Davidson's eye, to check what she was saying was all right. He didn't stop her. Quite the reverse.

'Maybe you should go along, Belle. You said you wanted to see. Well, now's your chance. Lights, camera, action.'

Mirabelle considered. The truth was if she stayed here Davidson would only become more insistent and she wasn't going to sleep with him. Besides, Jinty was promisingly chatty. This whole thing had turned out rather differently to what she had been expecting, but she felt intrigued, if she was honest. 'All right,' she said. 'If you think I'm presentable enough.'

'Your dress is fine.' Jinty sounded businesslike, as if she was taking stock of a soldier on parade or an item on display in a department store. 'I tell you what, I'll let you use my make-up in the car.'

'You won't panic?' Davidson's gaze was steady upon Mirabelle as she got to her feet.

'I don't panic,' she assured him. 'Well, I never have.'

'Jinty will keep you right, but if someone makes you an offer, you owe me a cut. I don't give freebies and neither should you. I insist on that from the start.'

Chapter 7

Undercover: to disguise identity to avoid detection

The car was a private hire rather than the lush chauffeur-driven model that had taken the blonde girl wherever she had been going earlier. Jinty shoved along the back seat and Mirabelle climbed in behind her. The girl had brought a smart clutch bag and a small leather suitcase.

'Toys and treats,' she said with a smile. 'I'll stay over.'

'Where are we going?'

'Eastbourne. The Grand.' Jinty raised her eyes. 'The Grand in Brighton is the easy job, but sometimes we have to go further afield. Today it's a conference so that makes it worthwhile. We'll get a day or two out of it, I expect.'

'Don't people notice?'

Jinty laughed and shook her head. 'And what if they do?' she said lightly. Her hair smelled of shampoo. The driver started the engine and Mirabelle glanced back at the house. Davidson was standing in the doorway. He raised a hand to wave them off.

'And he looks after you?' she checked.

'The best,' Jinty confirmed. 'Really. He's good at finding new business, too. If you're thinking of joining an operation, this is a good one. Take it from me. How old are you?'

'I'm more than forty.'

Jinty cast a look that said Mirabelle looked good for forty. She settled into her seat. 'So what made you decide to try this?'

'I don't know.'

'But you did it before? I mean when you were . . .'

'Younger? No. Never.'

'That's unusual. Is it the money? Or are you just bored?' Mirabelle must have looked dubious because Jinty's tone became insistent. 'It's more fun than you'd think, you know. Take today: there'll be a party. Being paid takes the anxiety out of things, I always think.'

'What do you mean?'

'The men know, almost always, that they can . . . you know . . . if they want to. So they aren't nervous or in a rush. And we only go to nice places, working for Ernie. It's that kind of shop.'

'I keep thinking of that woman. The one who was murdered.'

'Helen Quinn? What are you thinking about her for?'

'You know her name?'

'I knew her husband. Phil. He was a customer before he got married. I haven't seen him since he met her, though. It must be more than a year now.'

'But if you know him . . . you don't seem perturbed that he's been arrested, Jinty. Do you think he did it?'

'Well, I don't know.'

'Was he ever violent?'

'No. Phil was a pussycat. He used to bring presents – boxes of sweets.'

'Do you know anything about his company?' Mirabelle kept her voice too low for the driver to hear. By now the car had turned on to the main road and the noise of the engine had increased.

'Hove Cars? They're good guys,' the girl said.

'What do you mean?'

'They'll help out if there's trouble. It's never happened to me, but one of my friends had a customer who got out of hand.'

73

'You mean pushy?'

'I mean rape. People think women like us can't be raped but there are some sick bastards out there.'

Jinty lit another cigarette. Her eyes were hard now.

'Why do you do it?' Mirabelle knew she sounded naive.

Jinty shrugged. 'I make a mint,' she said. 'And if you're clear from the start, it hardly ever happens.'

'And the drivers at Hove Cars help?'

'If you can get away. If it isn't a busy night they wait. My friend, the one who had the creep on her hands, she ran out to the car and the driver protected her. Ernie took it from there, of course, but they're good guys.'

'But there was no suggestion that Phil Quinn ever did anything like that?'

'Tough stuff? No.'

'So do you think Helen Quinn's death had something to do with her husband's business? Could it be someone taking revenge?'

Jinty shrugged again. This tactic wasn't working. 'How would I know?' she said.

'But you don't think it's likely Phil Quinn killed her?' Mirabelle pushed.

'Look, it's not my business. You can't tell what people are going to do. Men especially.'

It occurred to Mirabelle that the girl just didn't care about Phil Quinn one way or another. Perhaps that was how you had to be in her position – you couldn't really care about anybody.

'Why are you interested anyway?'

Mirabelle shook her head only slightly. 'Quinn is a friend of a friend. They shouldn't have charged him. I don't like the thought of someone else getting away with murder. Poor woman.'

Satisfied with this explanation, though, Mirabelle noted, not showing any sympathy or even interest, Jinty settled back to look out of the window. Mirabelle wondered if Mrs Quinn knew about her husband's sexual habits before she agreed to marry him. Did she know he visited prostitutes? But then, did any woman know what her man got up to? People had a right to privacy, though that courtesy extended more to men than to women.

Jinty changed the subject by lazily flipping open the lid of the suitcase, to reveal a lace-edged, ivory boudoir set. She scrabbled underneath and brought out a tortoiseshell box. 'Here,' she said, 'try some lipstick. There's powder too.'

Dubiously, Mirabelle clicked open the lid and picked a pillar-box red for her lips. She raised a leather-cased mirror to her face. It felt like putting on warpaint.

'That's better.' Jinty smiled, as if things were settled. She put the box back in place and slammed the suitcase shut. 'When we get there, you have to chat, you know. See how you get on. I don't think there'll be any trouble, but if anything happens, come and find me, all right?'

At Eastbourne, the car slowed as it drew up behind the hotel. The women got out at the entrance to an underground garage. Arrangements had clearly been made. An attendant got to his feet and slickly directed them towards a lift without asking why they were there. Perhaps, Mirabelle considered, that was the virtue of the red lipstick. 'Fourth floor,' he said, pressing the button once they were inside and drawing his hand back quickly so the closing door didn't catch his fingers. It struck her that the ease with which these things were managed was extraordinary. To say nothing of the ease with which she had taken to it. Jack had teased her about her abilities – a cool head, but not really with the right stuff for work in the field, he'd said. Well, this was the field. The lift rang some kind of bell as it halted and the door opened on to a carpeted hallway where the sound of music drew them to the right door.

Mirabelle laid a hand on the girl's arm. 'Are you sure I look all right?' she checked. She couldn't remember the last time she had even considered such a thing, but there it was.

'Oh yes.' Jinty grinned, squeezing her hand. 'Don't worry.'

Inside, it was packed. Men in suits crammed in, the low hum of their conversation providing a base note to the music and the staccato of female laughter. Several waiters served champagne and short glasses of whisky on silver trays. Jinty raised a hand to wave at two girls who were sitting on a low sofa surrounded, it seemed, by several older fellows in dark suits. 'Sandra! Emily,' she squealed and pushed her way through, elegantly picking up a flute of champagne as she passed a waiter. Mirabelle followed.

'This is Belle,' Jinty pronounced. 'She's new.'

Mirabelle smiled. The men, she noticed, behaved quite normally. This wasn't some pagan hellhole or even the kind of orgy she'd heard went on in Whitehall when it was necessary to let off steam. Midday marriages, she'd once heard the parties called by an elderly civil servant who had seen it all. 'From the Greek,' he had explained.

The chap sitting beside Sandra got to his feet and gestured Mirabelle to take his place. A waiter offered her a drink. It was less Bohemian than she expected. A hundred Friday afternoon parties all over the country would feel the same. Out of the corner of her eye, she noticed a girl kissing a man in a suit in a corner. He had her wedged up against the wall with such force, Mirabelle wondered if they might sink into the bricks and pass straight through into the bedroom that was no doubt next door.

'Are you from Eastbourne, Belle?' the man enquired, drawing her attention back to the niceties.

'Brighton,' Mirabelle replied.

'Really,' he said, as if this information fascinated him.

'Though originally, I'm from London,' she continued.

He held up his drink and she clicked her glass. So this was how it happened. Ice-cold champagne. Men with money. Sofas upholstered in thick yellow velvet. And all around, music and chatter. Floors and floors of bedrooms, so very nearby.

'How much do you get?' Mirabelle whispered into Jinty's ear. She really should have thought of this in the car, but the details hadn't occurred to her.

Jinty smiled flirtatiously in the direction of her audience, but her tone was serious as she replied, talking behind her palm. 'Twenty a night. Upfront. Davidson will take a fiver. If you're not living in, that is. If they tip, you get to keep it. It's good isn't it?'

Mirabelle turned and smiled at the man, who started to talk about a rugby match in Barnes. Jinty was right – twenty pounds seemed quite a good amount of money but then these girls were upmarket – the girls who loitered behind Brighton Pavilion, like the women in doorways at King's Cross, wouldn't get anything like that kind of money. The champagne made her feel as if she was floating. She wondered momentarily if she might be anyone. If she might be capable of anything. The man touched her leg as he demonstrated the success of a particular try – the details of a game she wasn't really following. It was a moment of forced intimacy and only then did Mirabelle realise she didn't want him. All this was bewitching, but it wasn't personal. It wasn't McGregor. How strange, she thought. The superintendent had seemed for a long time like a man who was filling in for Jack. But now, when it came to it, it was him she wanted. She shifted along the sofa and tried to focus on the conversation.

As the afternoon wore on, more girls arrived and there was dancing. Mirabelle joined in. The man who had been talking about rugby had long since jumped ship with a sullen redhead who seemed to have some knowledge of the league match he'd been describing. The couple who had stood kissing in the corner had disappeared. Now, across a coffee table, Jinty was playing a game that involved flipping a sixpence in the time it took to knock back a shot of liqueur. As if from nowhere, a young man with dark eyes caught Mirabelle's hand and twirled her around. She laughed.

'Will you come to bed with me?' he asked, slipping his arm around her waist.

'No,' she said simply. 'Sorry.'

'You're booked?'

'Yes.'

'Shame.'

'I'm far too old for you.'

He kissed her neck and she felt a tingle at the base of her spine as his lips brushed her skin. His cheek was rough – a five o'clock shadow. She pushed him away and he stumbled good-naturedly towards a bottle of whisky perched on a side table. He'd be a handful later for one of the other girls, perhaps when they returned from another assignation. Mirabelle popped her handbag under her arm, took a cigarette from a seemingly abandoned packet that was balanced on the arm of a chair, and waved at Jinty. She was surprised by how liberated she felt.

Jinty smiled. 'We meet at the Grand for drinks on Sunday evenings,' she said, mouthing the words. 'I mean, the Grand at home. Half past eight.' Sunday nights were quiet in hotels. Maybe it was the best way to pick up a little business or maybe it was simply a good night to take off. 'Are you sure you don't want to stay?'

Mirabelle nodded. 'Goodbye,' she said and, picking her way across the room, she slipped out of the suite door.

In the hallway, the carpet was so thick it was like walking on marshmallow. She got into the lift and pressed the button to go up, exiting on to a hallway almost identical to the one she had left. Through a swing door, she found what she was looking for – an exit that opened on to a fire escape and out to the fresh air. Up here the view was beautiful. The slate roofs of Georgian Eastbourne stretched on either side, the sea an open vista beyond them and the breeze bracing off the front. Mirabelle pulled a box of matches from her pocket and lit the cigarette, then took a deep draw. It was good to know she could still surprise herself. She wondered if she'd stood out particularly among the rabble. It didn't feel as if she had and there was something good about having got away with her deception. She checked the time. If she hurried she'd get back to Brighton just as it got dark, but now she wanted to enjoy this feeling of independence for a few more moments. Strangely, she hadn't felt like this since Jack. Not since he'd first kissed her and she'd realised she didn't care about him being married.

She leaned against the closed door and thought of what all the people at the party would soon be doing on the floors beneath – crumpled sheets and room service – and, on the ground floor, the pretence of the conference all these men had come to attend. No one had even said what it was a conference about. She laughed as she realised. Still, even if this whole thing wasn't for her, it could have been. It seemed strange. The ins and outs of where you ended up. You could be perfectly respectable and still get drawn in. That, in itself, was something to think about. How much did Phil Quinn know about this world? she wondered. How much did he know about his drivers acting as bodyguards for Davidson's girls? He must have been aware of it. The other night the controller at Hangleton had sent out three cars in less than half an hour to ferry girls to and from jobs. Had Quinn become embroiled? Had his wife found out about his premarital habits at Tongdean Avenue?

She stubbed out her cigarette and flicked it into the gutter, noticing the red lipstick on the heel. She wasn't used to smelling of smoke. When she got home she'd change her clothes, she thought, as she pulled herself together. This had all been very interesting. It was Alan McGregor she wanted, she remembered. That more than anything. And, for that reason among others, she had to get back to Brighton. There was, after all, a murder to solve.

Chapter 8

Mysteries are not necessarily miracles

Vesta met Marlene outside the nurses' quarters at the end of the afternoon. She'd first been introduced by a friend at a jazz club in London a couple of years before. Marlene was a student nurse then, on a weekend's leave, and she had drunk so much that Vesta had organised a cab to take her home. The second time they'd met, Marlene hadn't remembered anything about the first evening until Vesta had suddenly turned, and then seeing her in profile had brought it back.

'Oh yes,' she had said as if she was transfixed, pointing at Vesta as she worked it out. 'I remember. You were the angel. The one who got me back safely.'

'The angel?'

'The black angel,' she giggled. 'I thought my time had come.'

Vesta took this in good humour and, in another dark cellar on another weekend, with Charlie and his friends playing in the background, the women had bonded over bathtub gin and stories of Marlene's training, which took place at a hospital in East Grinstead. Over the course of this conversation, Vesta had been heartily glad she had chosen secretarial college rather than a medical career. Being a nurse sounded grim, though Marlene seemed satisfied. 'I like feeling I can help,' she admitted, her eyes wide and earnest. Vesta liked that feeling too – whether it was with insurance quotes or balancing the ledgers or, like today, trying to unravel a violent murder. Still, actually saving someone's life must be different, she'd thought as she'd listened to Marlene that second night. On that occasion, it was Marlene who hailed a cab and sent Vesta home. Charlie ended up jamming with a recently arrived American saxophonist who couldn't get over the time difference. Marlene said it was medically impossible – there was no reason he hadn't been able to make the change between time zones.

'He's a chancer,' she said. 'He had ten days on that boat. He probably thinks it makes him more glamorous to keep his wristwatch on New York time. Shall we see if we can find you a ride home, then?'

'You're the angel. A proper one.' Vesta poked her friend's arm as they climbed the stairs into the chill London night, the air dense with smog and lamplight. The street was deserted and, till a cab came their way, the girls danced on the pavement to the fading beat of the packed basement. There was something childlike about Marlene and dancing with her reminded Vesta of playing on bombsites when she was younger – of days when a couple of bricks could make a shop counter.

Today, as Vesta approached, Marlene looked angelic – curled blonde hair and sparkling blue eyes, set off by a royal-blue felt cap and a lick of pale-pink lipstick. Her cheeks were glowing in the spring breeze.

'Come on,' she said urgently, as she grabbed Vesta's arm and hauled her away from the tall, brick nurses' quarters.

'What's the rush?'

'Sister,' Marlene hissed, as if no further explanation was required.

Although in civvies, Marlene wore a blue woollen nurse's cape, which she pulled around her frame. Her hair was pinned in a complicated series of twists that looked as if they must have taken hours.

'Well, if Sister's in there, why did you want to meet right outside the place?' Vesta objected, staring over her shoulder.

Marlene shrugged as if Sister and all that went with her was inevitable. 'She's a harridan. She made one girl scrub the lavvies twice. You can't get anything by her.'

'It seems a lot of bother.'

'Oh, I'm not saying Sister is wrong.' Marlene sounded surprised. 'Anyway, Brighton is much better than being at the Queen Vic. The patients were nice down there but it was difficult. Burns,' she explained. 'I much prefer working on the baby ward.'

'Baby ward?' Vesta repeated. She hadn't known.

It was blowy and the wind followed the women down Elm Grove. There was a pub on the corner and Marlene pulled Vesta into the snug. A fire had been set and the place was ready for the evening ahead.

'No nurses,' the barman said, hardly bothering to look up.

Marlene took off her cape. 'Do I look like a nurse?'

The man scratched his head and his mouth widened into an easy grin, which revealed that several of his front teeth were missing. 'You do, miss. And we ain't allowed to serve nurses.'

'Oh, go on.' Marlene nudged him over the bar. 'It's quiet and we're desperate. I haven't seen my chum in ages. Be a pal.'

Vesta drew a large white fiver from her purse to demonstrate it would be worth his while. 'Two double gins and bitter lemon,' she said, laying down the note. 'And whatever you're having.'

The barman shifted his head, tipping his chin at a pair of oak chairs next to the fire. 'If I get into trouble . . .'

'A big man like you? You can't be afraid of Sister,' Marlene teased him. 'Go on. And take sixpence tip.'

It seemed settled. Marlene fell to her knees in front of the grate and lit the kindling with a match. She blew gently to get it started and sat back on her heels. 'That's better,' she said.

'Why aren't you allowed in here anyway?'

'Oh, they don't want us picking up doctors. It's ridiculous. There's no doctors at this time of day.'

Vesta drew out a chair and sat down. Marlene's world was increasingly mysterious. 'So. What's it like?' she said. 'I mean, on the baby ward.'

'Oh, it's lovely. Who doesn't like babies?' Marlene settled into a tapestry-lined bench opposite. Her eyes softened. She had the knack of making anywhere she landed feel like home. Vesta was not to be distracted.

'I mean what's it like for the mothers?'

'They're happy after.' Marlene smiled. 'It's much more cheerful than the other place. Hardly any women die these days and the babies are sweet. The Royal is a good hospital. On nights, I see to the feeds, to let the mothers rest. They just stare at you, little things.'

Vesta felt slightly sick as the barman set down the drinks and a pile of change on the bartop. 'I ain't serving tables,' he said.

Marlene got up and brought everything over. It seemed there was nothing she couldn't just deal with. 'Where did you get a fiver?' she said.

'I always keep one in my purse.' Vesta sounded nonchalant, as if it wasn't a fortune. She'd seen the effect a banknote could have – Mirabelle used them all the time. 'My boss does it. Money can be handy, all right.'

'Any more murders? Any cases solved?'

Vesta's expression was serious. 'Last autumn was the last one. The death looked like a suicide, but it wasn't. He was my boss's upstairs neighbour.'

Marlene's eyes sparkled. 'Gosh,' she said. 'I suppose when you work in debt collection . . .'

'You'd think that, but most of it isn't that way. I mean, it's sad, really. People get out of their depth. They owe rent and they just let it slide. Mostly it's all ledgers. It's only now and then . . .'

'Cheers.' Marlene brought the glass to her lips and sipped delicately.

Vesta sniffed. She didn't feel like the drink now, but she picked it up to make a gesture and, as the rim neared her lips, she caught a whiff of what smelled like acid. It was as if she didn't really know herself – she had become so terribly changeable. She put down the glass.

'How's Charlie?' Marlene asked cheerily.

'Oh, same old.'

'Is he working today?'

'Yes. And, actually, I'm working too. There is a new murder. A woman. And I wanted to ask you something.'

'Really?' Marlene sounded thrilled. 'Perhaps we should have got some peanuts. If you're on expenses.'

Vesta ignored this. Who in their right mind would want peanuts? The thought made her squirm – she couldn't bear the grease. 'I wondered about poisons,' she said. 'Something that would knock you out.'

'An anaesthetic?'

'Maybe. Or more of a tranquilliser. Slipped into a drink.'

'Ah.'

'I mean, if you popped in something and it took a while before it knocked you out. You'd make it to bed, say. But, when the drug kicked in, it would take you out of it so completely that someone could stab you and you wouldn't struggle.'

'Stab you?'

'In the stomach. And you wouldn't feel a thing. You wouldn't wake up.'

Marlene eyed her glass as she considered carefully. 'Well, I can get you something if you want. My friend, Harry, works in the pharmacy. He'll probably want to be paid and I don't know if you could trust him. I mean, if he saw something in the newspaper and made a connection . . .'

'Jeez.' Vesta sounded exasperated. 'I don't want to kill any-one. It's a scenario, Marlene. For this case. I'm trying to figure out how they did it. The poor woman is already dead. That's what happened to her.'

Marlene didn't reply at first. She sipped her gin. 'All right,' she rallied. 'Well, is there alcohol involved in this scenario of yours?'

'Gin.'

'Well, that speeds things up. Alcohol makes most drugs work more quickly or more effectively – too effectively sometimes. It gets things to the bloodstream more quickly. Like when you take an aspirin with a cup of tea.'

'Aspirin?'

'You know. If you have a headache.'

'Well, this drug would need to work quite slowly, I suppose. It must have made the person who'd taken it tired. It certainly sent them to bed before they passed out.'

Marlene nodded. 'Righto,' she said, considering the impli-cations. 'Low dosage, I guess. And if you were drinking gin and it made you woozy, you'd just think you were tipsy. Leave it with me. I'll see what Harry says.'

Marlene had almost finished her drink, but Vesta had only managed a sip. The smell of lemon had entirely lost its allure. Suddenly, she found herself thinking about potato. Soft, fluffy potato. Mounds of it.

'Are you all right?'

Vesta nodded. She hesitated. She hadn't told anyone yet. No one but Mirabelle and she had guessed. 'The thing is,' she said, biting her lip, 'that I might be coming to see you soon. In a professional capacity, I mean.'

Marlene looked blank. 'I'll ask him as soon as I can, don't worry.'

'Not that.' She laid her hand on her stomach. It seemed an outrageous action and she blushed. Marlene's eyes widened.

86

'Oh, Vesta, that's wonderful.' She flung her arms around her friend. 'You must be thrilled.'

Vesta was clearly not thrilled. 'I'm more curious,' she said. 'And a little scared, if I'm honest.'

'What on earth are you scared of?'

Vesta found she couldn't say.

'And Charlie – he'll be a great dad. He's so patient!' Marlene sounded as excited as Vesta knew she ought to feel. Her eyes filled with tears.

'Do you think so?' She sniffed. 'Do you think he'll be all right?'

Marlene regarded her friend. Charlie would be the perfect father. He knew right from wrong, but he'd teach his children that gently. More than that, he'd teach the kid to cook – that had to be a bonus. Vesta looked tortured. 'You haven't told him yet, have you?' Marlene understood suddenly.

Vesta shook her head.

'Why not?'

'I don't know. It just seems overwhelming. Having a baby. Being a mother. I don't know if it's for me.'

'Well, it's a bit late for that,' Marlene said. 'Oh, Vesta, it will be marvellous. There's no need to be afraid. Not of the birth. Not of anything. I'll show you.' The girl sprang to her feet and pulled the nurse's cape around her shoulders with one hand while hauling Vesta to her feet. 'Are you having that?' Marlene asked, gesturing towards Vesta's scarcely touched glass. Vesta shook her head and Marlene smiled, lifted the drink and drained it. 'To the baby,' she said.

As they marched back into the stiff breeze and made their way towards the hospital entrance, it came into Vesta's mind that the Royal had been built as a workhouse. She wondered if it was haunted and how many paupers had brought their babies there, poor things. How many had died. She told herself off for being melodramatic, but she couldn't help it.

Marlene was oblivious. 'It's good it's the afternoon. There's visiting,' she prattled.

Through the heavy double doors all trace of the workhouse was gone. The light through the long windows was opaque and there were notices on the walls about hygiene and keeping quiet. A man with a bunch of flowers overtook them, bursting through the doors and pushing past an old lady who was manoeuvring a tea trolley across the green linoleum.

'New father,' Marlene explained. 'I bet you. Charlie will be the same.'

'How long does it take?' Vesta asked. 'You know.'

In the warmth, Marlene slowed her pace to leisurely. She slipped her arm comfortingly through Vesta's. 'You haven't a clue then? It varies. I mean, different women are different. A couple of hours maybe, if you're lucky. Worst ways, a whole day and night. Maybe more. There's no point in lying.'

'And it's painful?'

'Always. Though you get a baby at the end of it – as a consolation prize. And there's gas and air, which takes the edge off. We'll look after you, Vesta. I'll look after you. I promise.'

'Do many women die?'

Marlene turned to face her friend. 'You shouldn't think like that. And the answer is no. Things have improved a lot and the midwives are marvellous. One or two people don't make it, but most women are fine. Especially young healthy women like you.'

They turned on to the stairwell. 'I think they put the maternity unit up here because of the view,' Marlene said, with a smile. 'There's quite a bit of sitting around in bed, you see. And we do classes. Bathing baby. That kind of thing.'

Along a corridor, they passed a ward full of cots. The long wall was glazed as a viewing gallery, which afforded a panorama of tiny faces. Inside, three nurses in pristine uniforms fussed between the cots. At the window, an older woman, a grandmother it had to be assumed, stared at a child in a pink cardigan. She put a gloved hand up to the glass and just grinned. Inside, a different baby was picked up and taken out by a grey-haired nurse. Vesta's expression asked the question.

'She's taking it to the mother, you dodo.' Marlene rolled her eyes. 'Didn't you have babies in your house? I mean, when you were growing up? Don't you know anything?'

Vesta thought. There had been her younger brother, but she'd hardly noticed him. Along the street, many of the women had had babies, but Vesta hadn't shown an interest. She'd never got involved. 'The thing is, with the Blitz, most kids were sent away,' she said vaguely.

'We went to Devon. It was fun. My brother had to help but I was too small. Where did you go?' Marlene asked.

'We didn't go anywhere. We were black. I mean, people don't want black kids. Mum thought it was best just to keep us. You know, in Bermondsey.'

'Gosh. Were you bombed?'

'The other side of Peek Freans' was bombed. But we were fine.'

'So there weren't many babies then?'

'No.' Vesta knew that wasn't entirely true. The thing was, she had always kept her distance from the business of motherhood. She knew perfectly well that having babies kept women at home. More than that, it kept them in Bermondsey and, from quite a young age, despite loving her parents, Vesta had wanted to leave. That was what she was afraid of now, she realised. That was the thing that was holding her back from telling Charlie. She was scared that she'd love the baby so much she'd end up stuck in the house. She was afraid that she wouldn't matter any more. That she'd get fat and old, scrubbing the floors and washing nappies. Like all the other women. Like her mother. She felt tears well up. Her mother, after all, was an inspiration – wonderful, joyful Mrs Churchill. Everyone loved Ella. She'd worked all her life to look after her family and she'd loved every minute of it. But Vesta did not want to end up that way.

'I just can't see how to do it,' she sobbed. 'That's the thing.'

Marlene withdrew a cotton handkerchief from her pocket. 'Now, now,' she said. 'Nature does it, Vesta. Really.'

Vesta blew her nose. Nobody seemed to understand. 'Come on,' she said. 'Let's go down.'

Their shoes echoed on the stairs and, at the bottom, she handed Marlene back the handkerchief. 'You can leave the tranquilliser thing to me.' Marlene smiled. 'I'll ring on the telephone. There's a payphone in the nurses' home, though I might have to pick my moment. Quite often they listen in case girls are planning to sneak out.'

Vesta gave her a hug. 'Thanks,' she said.

As they came out of the double doors, an ambulance had pulled up and a man was being taken out on a stretcher. Vesta halted, as her attention returned to the larger world. That was the other thing – the way this child, growing in her belly, seemed to drink all of her attention so she had nothing left for herself, or Charlie or any of the things in which she'd normally take an interest. It was controlling her appetite. Her taste. Her inclination to sleep. Now, coming on to the pavement, she blinked as she recognised the recumbent figure being unloaded. Yes, it was him, she thought, pushing her way towards an orderly who was hauling the stretcher on to a trolley.

'Fred,' Vesta called. The man on the stretcher looked up with some effort and wheezed as she approached. He was clearly unable to form a sentence. His chest heaved and he tried to lift his head but it seemed terribly heavy. He looked thinner than when Vesta had seen him only a few hours before and his skin was an alarming colour of grey. 'What happened?' she asked.

'He fell over in the street,' the orderly said. 'It looks like bronchitis. Are you a relation?'

Vesta just stared at him. 'No,' she said flatly. Fred might have looked grey but he was nowhere near black.

'Out of the way, please, miss.'

She ignored him. Instead, she clasped Fred's hand over the thin blanket. 'Can I get anyone for you, Fred? Your wife, maybe?'

Fred shook his head. His breath rattled and the words came out half formed. She leaned in. 'Tell Mirabelle,' he managed. 'My son. Behind the picture. She'll get it.' He fell back on to the canvas, exhausted.

The orderly tutted. 'Now, now. That's enough. We need to get you on to the ward.'

Vesta felt helpless as the trolley was wheeled away. 'Which ward do you think they'll put him on?'

'Twelve,' said Marlene, sounding businesslike. 'They can do a lot for bronchitis, but then . . . if it turns out TB . . . It's on the other side of the building.'

Vesta felt her heart sink. 'Mirabelle is out on a job,' she said. 'I can probably get hold of her later.'

'I'll drop in on the old guy, if you like. Was his name Fred, did you say?'

Vesta nodded. 'He's a friend of my boss. He has this place, where he sells things.'

'A shop, you mean?'

'Not exactly.' Vesta felt ashamed. All these shady dealings and shady people. Usually, she found investigations glamorous, but today, somehow, it didn't feel that way. The hospital was a place of life and death and no glamour about it. 'I'll come back to visit him over the weekend,' she promised, clasping Marlene's hand. As she turned away, she realised she wouldn't mind seeing the baby room again. She hadn't realised that newborns were so tiny. The image of a little dot in a blue cardigan over the nurse's shoulder remained with her as she headed down the street.

Chapter 9

We make war that we may live in peace

That evening, the sunset was particularly beautiful. Returning from Eastbourne in time to strip off her fitted skirt and wash away the make-up Jinty had encouraged her to apply, Mirabelle put on a pair of dark trousers and flat shoes and tied her hair back in a simple ponytail. As she left her flat on the Lawns, the sky was streaked with colour. The black outline of the pier was visible from far off, its lights the brightest stars of early evening. Slowly, a broad shadow crept across the city as darkness fell, the streetlights casting a dim, buttery glow over the paving stones as she walked away from the front. The air smelled of the sea tonight. Waiting to catch the bus, she wondered vaguely how Vesta had got on with the poison.

It was Friday so the top deck was full of young people heading into town, chattering loudly. In the main, they were late for the dance halls, but perhaps it was fashionable not to arrive on time. Either way, Jinty had been right – Brighton's nightlife was particularly lively when you were in the thick of it. The girls wore wide cotton skirts over bright, sugar-starched petticoats – a riot of colours and patterns. The boys wore dark suits, slim cut on the leg, the material emitting a glimmer in the bus's harsh light. Between the sexes, the banter was alive, as the crowd puffed away, sharing cigarettes and offering lights. Mirabelle wondered if she ought to have sat on the lower deck. She'd never be part of that, never had been. Still, she found herself feeling underdressed.

The revellers quit the bus at the city centre, getting off in a cloud of perfume and brilliantine, which lingered with the remains of the tobacco smoke as the driver turned northwards. This time, at least, Mirabelle knew which stop to get off at without having to ask and, as she stepped on to the pavement, the air felt warmer this far inland. Walking towards Mill Lane, the houses looked cosy. The windows glowed with lamplight and, occasionally, from an open casement, there was the sound of laughter or the crackling of voices on the wireless. Just off the main road an old man was digging his front garden. He had balanced an oil lamp on a wheelbarrow. It looked as if he was planting seeds. Mirabelle deliberately didn't catch his eye.

Mill Lane looked no different from any of the other streets off the main road. At number fourteen, the windows of Mrs Ambrose's house were dimmed by drawn curtains, but, across the street, the Randalls hadn't closed theirs and Mirabelle caught a glimpse of Vi and Billy deep in conversation. Vi was grasping her husband's hand, her face lit by the lamplight. From behind, Billy Randall was nodding. Mirabelle smiled – young love was such a blessing, the unalloyed happiness of the first time you felt that connection. Stifling the ripple of remembrance that shifted in her gut, she opened the Quinns' gate carefully and slipped through the gap before it could squeak. Then she drew out her set of SOE lock picks and quickly opened the front door. After slipping inside, she took out her torch. She had come prepared. She switched on the beam, keeping the light low to the floor.

The house felt abandoned already. The police hadn't tidied before they left. The pillows from the sofa were stacked beside its frame and there was an eerie smattering of finger-print dust over the mantel and on the wireless set. This was where they had danced, she thought, and that was the table where the gin bottle must have lain. Mrs Quinn's house was the mirror image of Vi Randall's, though it appeared immediately more luxurious. There were several modern pieces of furniture and a selection of well-made throws and rugs. On the wall, there was a set of paintings, framed in painted wood. Still, even in the torchlight, it lacked character somehow. There were no newspapers. No books. No flowers. On the mantelpiece there were a few photographs – one of the Quinns' wedding and a few others of people Mirabelle assumed were relations – the kind of photographs people had had taken before they went to war. Keepsakes, not memories, taken in photographic studios.

She crossed the hallway, noticing the carpet was new and of high quality. Inside, despite everything, the bedroom smelled faintly of lavender. The door of the wardrobe had been left open, revealing a rack of what looked like well-kept clothes and a row of smart, high-heeled shoes. Several colourful sweaters were folded tidily in a pile. Helen Quinn had certainly kept up with the latest trends. Beside them were Phil Quinn's shirts – a starched stack of white. On the other side of the room, the bed had been stripped and the mattress was stained badly where the woman must have died. Beyond that, there were dark marks on the carpet and a smear along the wall, which, Mirabelle thought, must have been made when they removed the body.

Re-enacting the scene, Mirabelle paced out what the murderer had done. Presumably, they entered the room by the door. The Quinns had been asleep. Helen had lain on the far side of the bed so the killer would have had to go round the base. Mirabelle cast the beam across the wall and, sure enough, there was a clear void in the spatter of blood. That's where they must have stood. Gingerly, Mirabelle placed herself in the spot and drew back her arm. This was how they had stabbed the poor woman. There were two tiers of tiny blood marks on the wall – yes, that meant Helen Quinn had been stabbed twice at least. And then, how long had it taken her to die? It occurred to Mirabelle that even if Mr and Mrs Quinn had been drugged, surely the bed would have shifted with the force of the attack. The direct nature of the crime suddenly became apparent. This was an impossible thing to do to someone you didn't know. Someone you didn't hate. If the murderer was going to drug the Quinns, why didn't they just poison them? It would have been easier.

Mirabelle leaned against the window frame and thought for a moment. The stabbing seemed suddenly a very public way to kill someone, underlining that this was not only a murder but a message too. If Phil Quinn was the recipient of that message he seemed not only unafraid but also unaware. What it clearly said was, *I can come for you whenever I want. I can do anything.* But Quinn had had Helen taken from him – the thing he valued most. What more could the murderer threaten?

Considering this, Mirabelle reached for the bedside table on Mrs Quinn's side. The drawer contained a pack of cards, a box of Kirby grips and some safety pins. On Mr Quinn's side, there was a man's hairbrush and a bottle of expensive aftershave and below that two drawers full of pressed handkerchiefs interleaved with tissue paper and lavender. On the dressing table, a box containing lipstick, a showy compact filled with pressed powder and a flashy marble and gilt talcum holder with a pale, pink-ribboned puff. She was about to investigate the toilet arrangements when she started at the sound of the front door opening.

A man's voice cut into the darkness. 'Who's in here?' he called angrily. 'Show yourself.'

Mirabelle snapped off her torch, called back to real life, and, hardly thinking, she slipped open the bedroom window with the intention of escaping across the back lawn. The sill was on the high side, she realised, as she scrambled up it, dropping the torch and losing her footing. She fumbled, trying to keep away from the bloodstains, desperate not to smear the spatter. Her hands fumbled as she pulled herself up. In a momentary lapse of judgement, she reached down to pick up the torch. Sure enough, the bedroom door slammed open and the man hurtled towards her.

'Oi!' he called, as he crossed the room, a large, indistinct black shadow. He grappled Mirabelle, pulling her back over the sill and pushing her against the wall. Then he grabbed her arm, pinning her against his body and using his weight to force her towards the door.

'Get off!' she shouted, squirming and outraged. 'What are you doing?'

He was a big fellow. She tried to kick him, but he had her pinned too close to his body to give her any purchase.

'Get off me!' she tried again. She wondered if she might manage to stab him off with her elbows, but he seemed to have her rather professionally held in place. At the bedroom door, he squirmed to free one hand and switched on the light. Mirabelle pulled away.

'Go to hell!' she snapped. How dare he? Then she looked. The dark shape materialised into a beat bobby in uniform – a middle-aged, thick-set man with a wide face. He was breathing hard – he might have given her a fright but he'd given himself one too. Breaking into a dark house and grappling an intruder into submission was not for the faint-hearted. As the rush of her pulse slowed, she realised that his uniform smelled of mothballs. She rubbed her arm. It felt as if there was a bruise forming.

'You scared the life out of me,' she said, as they both took stock of the situation. It was clear he expected kids breaking in, if not the murderer returning to the scene. Certainly not this perfectly respectable, slight lady.

'Well. What have you got to say for yourself?' he demanded.

'I'm sorry. I wanted to see where it had happened.'

'This is the site of a murder, madam, not a tourist attraction. I can book you for breaking and entering.'

'I'm a friend . . .' Mirabelle's voice trailed.

'A friend? Of the deceased?'

'Of the accused, I suppose.'

The policeman's face betrayed satisfaction at this admission. The ghost of a smile passed across his lips. People jumped to such conclusions.

'I'm not Philip Quinn's mistress, Officer. Nothing like that. What I mean to say is, I'm a friend of Superintendent McGregor. That's what I'm doing here.'

Light dawned. 'You're McGuigan & McGuigan, aren't you? The debt collector. I've heard of you. Meriel Benton, isn't it?'

'Mirabelle Bevan. I expect you've heard I'm a meddler then?' She tried to crack a smile. The policeman didn't reply, but Mirabelle knew what they said. 'Phil Quinn is a childhood friend of the superintendent,' she continued.

'Yeah. I heard.'

'I wanted to look into this for him. He suggested it, actually.'

'This house is private property, miss. It's a crime scene. You can't just break in, no matter who your friends are or what the super said.'

Mirabelle made no attempt to defend her actions. Instead, she directed herself to the matter of information. That, after all, was the important thing.

'Is Mill Lane on your usual beat? Were you on duty that night, Officer? The night Helen Quinn died?'

The man seemed eager to talk. 'I didn't see a thing,' he admitted. 'I wish I had. I must have passed right by when it was going on. It's a strange feeling. I wasn't going to let that happen again, was I?'

'You mean, seeing me in here?'

The policeman nodded. 'A murder in Portslade, who'd credit it? I don't want to see another.'

'You're right. It seems too nice. Suburban. Quiet. Who do you think did it?'

'Inspector Robinson reckons he's got the man. The husband,' the policeman said flatly.

'I didn't ask what Inspector Robinson thought. You were here.'

'He's charged the fella.'

Mirabelle blanched. She didn't know Quinn's case had progressed quite so far. This was an important development. It meant Robinson probably wasn't even investigating other options any more.

'The accused's on remand,' the policeman said. 'Awaiting trial.'

'Do you think he did it?'

'It seems most likely. The husband.'

'Did you know Phil Quinn? I mean, this is your beat.'

'I know him by sight – going in and out of the house. That's all. "Evening, sir," and that. You never can tell, can you?'

Mirabelle sighed. She knew he was right – Jinty had said the same. And yet, Robinson obviously hadn't made much of an effort to investigate anyone or anything else. She stared at the mattress on the other side of the room. 'What occurs to me, now I'm here, is that it was a big thing to say. I mean, killing her like that. It made a statement. When you look in detail at what he had to do.'

'Yeah. Some of the lads have been reckoning the same. I mean, there was talk that it was to punish Quinn for a misdemeanour. Gangland and that. He ain't got a record though. Doesn't seem the type. But, as you say, you never know. I reckon, he killed her and it was Quinn who was sending the message. Saying something to the world. Or even to her.'

'The dead woman?'

'I've known that. A man who wants to dominate his wife.

99

A fellow minded to get away with doing anything he wants. "I'll show you."'

Mirabelle thought of Phil Quinn sitting in his cell, red-eyed and unable to eat, wearing his ridiculously smart clothes. He didn't seem like someone who wanted to dominate anybody. He must be devastated now he'd been charged. She was about to say something to that effect when there was a smart knock at the front door.

'You stay here,' the constable ordered. Through the hallway, as the officer opened up, Mirabelle saw a man on the doorstep. Behind him, Vi hovered further up the path.

'Billy.' The policeman nodded. 'Evening, Violet.'

'What's going on, Arthur? We saw a light,' Billy Randall said. 'Is everything all right?'

Vi noticed Mirabelle and gave a little nod. 'Hello, Miss Bevan.' She stepped forward. 'Have there been any developments?'

The constable gave himself up to this little gaggle of interested parties and stepped back to let them converse.

'This is my husband,' Vi introduced Billy. 'This is Miss Bevan, Billy, the lady I told you about.'

'I visited Philip Quinn yesterday,' Mirabelle said. 'He is terribly shaken, but he's surviving. He's been charged now. The constable just told me.'

Billy Randall shook his head. 'That's not right,' he said. 'Phil wouldn't have laid a hand on Helen. I told your lot that. You've got it all wrong.'

'I think it's difficult for the police because there's no evidence of an alternative assassin,' Mirabelle cut in. 'There's no apparent motive for someone else to have done it. That's what I'm doing here. I came to see if I could figure out who might have got in that night. Who might have drugged the Quinns' gin bottle, for a start.'

'I was here in the afternoon,' Vi said eagerly. 'Does that help?'

The policeman fumbled with the flap on his pocket to get out his notebook. He let out a low sigh. 'Close the door behind you,' he said, pulling out a pencil.

The four of them clustered uncomfortably in the hallway around the open bedroom door. 'I told the police,' Vi explained. 'But they didn't seem to think it was important. They just kept asking Billy about what he'd seen. He found the body, after all. And then, Miss Bevan, I had a chat with you. But, I suppose I was so shocked that they'd taken Phil into custody that we didn't talk about the afternoon before the murder.'

'No,' Mirabelle said. 'We didn't.'

The policeman's eyes did not betray any emotion about the fact that Mirabelle had interviewed this witness. 'We might as well make sure then, hadn't we?' he said. 'In case we turn something up. So, what time did you pop in, Mrs Randall?'

'About four o'clock,' Vi replied promptly.

'And Mrs Quinn seemed fine?'

'Yes. Absolutely normal. We often had a natter in the afternoon.'

'Did you notice the gin bottle?' Mirabelle cut in.

Vi smiled. 'I certainly did! We had a tot.'

Billy Randall regarded his wife. 'Drinking in the afternoon, Vi?' he tutted. The policeman took a note.

Vi shrugged. Her cardigan shifted over her slim shoulders. 'Well,' she said, 'it was only a little treat. We had a cup of tea and then Helen said why didn't we have a gin and a round of cards. We played rummy.'

'Mrs Quinn liked cards, then?' Mirabelle checked.

'Oh yes. She could deal all fancy. You know. Pivot cuts.'

Billy Randall's expression changed. Mirabelle thought he looked mildly impressed with his wife's knowledge. He clearly had no idea what she got up to during the day. 'You didn't tell me you girls played cards and drank gin,' he said.

Vi's eyes shone. 'Well, it's not all peeling potatoes and cleaning the kitchen floor, you know. You've got to live a little.' She rested her hand on her baby bump.

'But gin in the afternoon, Vi. What did you two talk about?'

'Oh stop it, Billy. It was just a bit of fun. All the girls like a drink and a natter.'

'What time did you leave, Mrs Randall?' the officer cut in.

'Half past five. Billy gets home after six and I wanted to get the fire lit and lay the table. It still gets cold in the evenings.'

'Do you know what time Mr Quinn usually got back?' Mirabelle cut in.

'It varied. I mean, he wasn't nine to five. But Helen knew he'd be home for dinner. She'd got liver in.'

Both Billy Randall and the constable nodded, Mirabelle noted, as if this was a sign of Mrs Quinn doing her duty. She tried to imagine herself preparing dinner for a husband. She scarcely bothered for herself at the end of the day, never mind anyone else.

'So Mrs Quinn probably spent some time in the kitchen after you'd left.' Mirabelle stared up the hallway at the open kitchen door. 'And we can assume she left the bottle in the sitting room.'

'Helen wasn't much of a cook. She wouldn't have spent hours in there or anything.'

'But it must have happened when he got home,' the constable concluded. 'Or, at least, the bottle must have been drugged at some point after you left, Mrs Randall. But Inspector Robinson must know. I take it you suffered no ill effects?'

'Not a bit.'

'Why would Phil want to drug his own drink?' Billy Randall cut in. He looked bereft as he scrabbled for something to get his friend off the hook. 'I mean, if you think he did it, well, he wasn't compos mentis that morning. Why would he drug himself too?'

It was an odd question. The constable didn't reply and Mirabelle didn't explain. It would have been the best way for Quinn to give himself some kind of alibi. Not the best alibi he could have hoped for, but still. Instead of spelling this out, she nodded towards the rear of the house. 'Could I have a look outside?'

The constable dropped his hands to his side as if this was a terrible imposition. 'I suppose so,' he said wearily. 'The boys have finished and you've seen the rest of the place.'

Mirabelle crossed to the window and picked up her torch from the carpet. Then she cut up the hallway and through the kitchen. She slid the bolt on the back door. 'They didn't usually lock it, did they?'

'I suppose the police secured the place before they left.' Vi followed her. The garden was pitch black. The light from the houses illuminated a snatch of ground a few feet into the grass. The moon tonight was slim and the sky cloudy. Mirabelle snapped on her torch and directed the beam into the blackness.

'So the gardens back on to each other? They're contained, I mean?'

'Yes. Mill Lane on this side and Deacons Drive over there.'

'But there are vacant lots, aren't there? Someone might have slipped through and climbed the fence.' She walked up the short path, which cut through a vegetable patch. Beyond that, there was a stretch of lawn. The grass sloped upwards as she stepped on to it. A few doors down, a dog barked.

Vi pointed ahead. 'There's a gap between the houses there, if that's what you're looking for.'

Mirabelle didn't say that she wasn't sure what she was looking for. As the constable pointed out, the police had been all over the garden. She walked upwards. The cool evening air smelled green. Turning, it occurred to her that from here, with the light on, you could see through the kitchen window and into the bedroom too. Had the killer loitered, she wondered, biding their time until they could slip safely through the back door or even through the window on to Helen Quinn's side of the bed? It was an excellent vantage point and, once it was dark, no one in the houses would be able to see who was out here. Then it struck her, with the camber of the lawn, it would be easy to keep an eye not only on the Quinns, but also on the neighbouring houses. With the lights on, you could see what everyone was up to, right around the block. You could wait till everyone was in bed. Robinson's men had been here in the daytime, but it was the darkness that lent the true meaning to this little part of the puzzle. Carefully, Mirabelle crouched down – the grass was young and damp. There were a couple of bushes to provide cover. There was no sign of where someone might have rested, but they had been here all right. She could feel them.

Below her, Billy Randall and the constable hovered at the back entrance to the house, but Vi had stopped further in, next to the vegetable patch. Mirabelle watched as she turned and caught sight of the stain on the mattress through the window. She hadn't seen it before. Slowly, Vi raised her hand to cover her mouth. Billy stepped forward to steady his wife and she folded into his arms. A wailing sound snaked up the garden as Vi took in the grisly evidence. Mirabelle wondered if the years had hardened her. The truth was she felt curiosity more than anything. Phil Quinn hadn't killed his wife, she was convinced of that, no matter what Robinson had charged him with. There were too many small details that predicated against it – a man might kill the woman he loved, but most would do so in anger, on the spur of the moment, and if he did premeditate a killing, well, only a fool would do it this way. Vi had been right about that from the beginning. She walked back down the path. Billy Randall glared as if it was her fault his wife was howling on his shoulder. Vi gradually unfolded, heaving for breath.

'You better find out who did it,' she said. 'You better get Phil off.'

'I'll try,' Mirabelle promised.

The policeman shuffled on the back doorstep, awkwardly aware that Mrs Randall hadn't addressed her comment to him. 'Come along.' He cleared his throat. 'We'd best get all of you home.'

Chapter 10

*An early morning walk is a
blessing for the whole day*

Mirabelle woke to the chime of her doorbell. The bell used to make a muffled sound that was easy to ignore, but the year before Vesta had refurbished Mirabelle's flat after a fire and the new bell was more of a buzzer, and impossible to sleep through. Fumbling across the pillows, she reached for her silver-grey silk wrap in the half-light and stumbled barefoot through the drawing room and into the hall. As she passed the clock, she realised it was scarcely eight o'clock. Vesta was waiting patiently on the doorstep clutching a brown paper bag in one hand and a small bottle of milk in the other. 'Breakfast,' she said, holding them up. 'The rolls are still warm. I'll make us tea.'

Bemused, Mirabelle stepped back to let her in. Vesta knew her way around Mirabelle's scarcely used kitchen better than Mirabelle knew it herself. The sound of the kettle being put on to boil echoed in the hallway. Mirabelle went to find a pair of slippers. As she pulled back her bedroom curtains, the long window revealed a bank of heavy, grey cloud. A man with a sorry-looking collie was walking along the pebble beach beyond the grass. She scrabbled to find her slippers and emerged into the drawing room where she drew the curtains on to a larger version of the same view.

'Awful day,' she said, as Vesta set down a tray on the dining table that Mirabelle never used and proceeded to pour tea into pristine cups. There was no point in asking about jam. Or honey. If you wanted to eat anything in Mirabelle's house, you'd best bring it with you. Mirabelle settled into a chair and accepted the proffered cup, noticing that, though she hadn't seen it before, the design was rather attractive. 'Did you find out about the poison?' she asked.

'Marlene is looking into it. I came because Fred was admitted to hospital.'

'What?'

'I came round yesterday evening but you weren't here. It was his chest. We probably shouldn't have left him in that damp, old cottage. I was thinking about it all last night. A man like that on his own and poorly.'

Mirabelle didn't say that in the past Fred had managed to get himself out of far worse than a sore throat in a slum down an alleyway. During the war, he'd undergone some of the most arduous missions with which she'd been involved.

'He collapsed in the street,' Vesta continued. 'They brought him in in an ambulance.'

'Have they contacted his wife? Did you offer to help?'

'He didn't want me to fetch her. He asked me to get you, Mirabelle. To tell you something about his son and a painting. It was difficult for him to speak, but he said you'd figure it out. Do you know his son?'

Mirabelle bit thoughtfully into the roll. The butter had melted. Fred didn't have children of his own but he had smuggled a boy out of Spain during the war. A Jewish kid or maybe a gypsy. A dark-haired orphan, anyway. He'd felt responsible for the child and had taken him in. 'I met the boy once,' she said. 'It's a long time ago. Fred adopted him. I don't know where he ended up.'

'Where does his wife live?'

Mirabelle pulled a face to indicate she had no idea. Fred had never been keen to discuss his wife. Mirabelle wasn't the curious type – she didn't dig in the files unless she was looking for something in particular. The only time she'd have had to look up details of Fred's wife's whereabouts would have been if Fred had been killed. Doing it out of nosiness would have felt like a betrayal, as if she had given up on him. The sound of rain spattered the long windows.

'He was heaving for breath. It was terrible,' Vesta said. 'He seemed quite desperate about the picture. I was sure you'd know what he meant.'

'Well, if he asked us to look for a painting, we'd better do it.'

'A painting and his son,' Vesta itemised.

Mirabelle nodded.

'Did you find out anything at Tongdean?' the girl enquired.

Mirabelle wasn't sure how to reply. She didn't want to tell Vesta she'd ended up at a party in a hotel suite, considering whether to sleep with any of the men there for a surprisingly generous sum of money. 'Not really,' she said, still taken aback by how tempting it had been. 'Though, it's what American jazz singers call a cathouse all right. I met one of the kittens. And then last night I went back to the Quinns' house. It had the most astonishing atmosphere, as if no one had lived there for years. There's a vantage point outside. On the night of the murder, whoever killed Mrs Quinn was watching from the rear. The truth is anyone could have got into the house but not anyone could have killed Helen Quinn. I paced it through. It was a horrible crime. I mean, so violent.'

Vesta laid down her teacup. 'You better get dressed.'

Mirabelle chose a dark green day dress and heels. She picked out a gabardine coat, tied a moss-coloured scarf over her hair and picked a silver-handled umbrella from the stand. As the women left the house, she opened it to shelter them. Outside, the street was slick, the grass above the pebble beach was swelled and boggy as they turned towards the main road.

'It isn't a day to be on a bicycle,' Vesta said. That was how she usually got about.

Outside a row of shops, several children in wellington boots splashed along the pavement, completely soaked. One child peered hopelessly into a puddle, holding his fishing net as if at any moment a fish might appear. The traffic was only partially slowed by the weather and, as the cars cut through the puddles, they sprayed the pedestrians. Mirabelle and Vesta took shelter in a shop doorway.

Luckily, the buses were operating as normal and it didn't take long to be picked up. Inside, the windows were steamy and, at the back, the two women shared a cigarette to keep warm. They settled in silence as they bought their tickets from the conductor and Vesta cleaned a patch of window. 'Almost there,' she reported. Mirabelle fiddled with a tassel on her umbrella.

Then, dismounting back on to the pavement, she raised the brolly and Vesta grabbed her arm, sheltering from the rain as they turned towards the sea. The laneway outside Fred's cottage was too slim to accommodate two women side by side or, for that matter, an open umbrella, so, taking their chances, they trotted down it single file, the rain bouncing at angles off the uneven ground. Vesta stamped energetically as she came to a halt. On the step a young man stood with his arms folded, an intermittent waterfall of raindrops channelled along the brim of his hat.

'D'you know where he's gone?' he said. 'He's always here on Saturdays.'

'He's sick,' Mirabelle explained. 'Step aside.'

She made short work of the lock, standing in front of the fellow so that he wouldn't see she was using picks rather than a key. The three of them bundled indoors. Inside, it was drier than the laneway, though drips fell through a gap in the ceiling into a wide tin bucket. The light was even more dim than usual. Glad to see the chickens had gone, Vesta went to the counter and lit a camping lamp. Mirabelle took off the sodden silk scarf and laid it over the back of a chair.

'Who are you?' she asked the man.

'I come every Saturday. It's a regular order.' He wouldn't meet her eye.

'Do you know where Fred keeps it?'

The man nodded.

'Well, go on then. If you give me the money, I'll pass it on.'

Round-shouldered, the fellow disappeared into the room to the rear of the cottage. There was the sound of packing cases being moved and then he returned with bulging pockets and thrust several shillings into Mirabelle's palm, mumbled his goodbye and disappeared out of the door. Vesta laughed.

'I don't want to imagine,' Mirabelle said, putting the coins into her purse.

Vesta cast the light around the room, which seemed especially grubby today. 'We have our mission,' she said. 'A picture and something about his son. We'd better see what we can find.'

They began to root around. Fred certainly had a diverse stock. There were boxes containing bottles of Argentinian orange liquor and a mixed case of Italian perfume packed in straw and sealed with wax. A jute sack turned out to contain Hershey bars that Mirabelle guessed had been stolen from the US army. The Americans still had a base in Yorkshire and, even though rationing was over, there were some things it was difficult to get – American chocolate being one of them. Behind the counter, there were shoeboxes full of insoles, perched on three brand-new refrigerators. Then, in the back room, there were medical supplies. 'This will be what that boy wanted,' Vesta said, lifting a condom between her thumb and first finger and looking delighted. Mirabelle ignored her.

'You said a picture.' She leafed through a stack of paintings propped against the plaster, protected by old blankets. They were traditional oils, framed in gilt. They looked valuable and she wondered momentarily where Fred had got them. One in particular looked disconcertingly familiar. 'Do you think this is what he meant?'

'I don't know.' Vesta checked the rear of the pictures one by one. 'But look, there's a note on the back.'

'Delivery instructions,' Mirabelle said flatly. 'I doubt we'll find anything directly helpful, to be honest – nothing personal for a start. Fred knows what he's doing.'

'I had a vision of a child being trapped,' Vesta said. 'Fred seemed to think it was urgent. Life or death.'

Mirabelle shrugged. She tried the back door. It opened on to a miserable backyard with an old-fashioned privy. The water ran in rivulets off the back wall. She picked her way across the mud and opened the thin wooden door of the outhouse. Always check everywhere – those were the rules. Just keep going.

Inside, the privy did not smell as bad as she expected and it was dry. Beside the pan there was a pile of newspapers torn into strips. Above it, Fred had hung a clipping taken from the *London Illustrated News* Coronation edition, published three years before. It portrayed Her Majesty arrayed in her coronation regalia. Fred had always been patriotic. Mirabelle cocked her head, pausing only momentarily before carefully removing the picture, trying not to tear it.

Removing the cutting revealed a hole in the wood. Behind it was the brick boundary wall. Glancing over her shoulder, she decided not to call Vesta, not just yet. Mirabelle ran her hand over the facings. Sure enough, several of them were loose. Carefully, she drew out one brick. Then another. In less than a minute, she had a space big enough to put her hand inside. As she fumbled, she found three guns – all ex-service pistols. One of them had three notches cut into its handle. She tried not to think what that might mean and moved on, removing half a dozen boxes of bullets, a stack of money wrapped in oilskin and a couple of notarised deeds, which looked as if they were ownership documents for properties in London – a freehold in Notting Hill and a leasehold in Chelsea. Mirabelle stepped back and surveyed the pile as she leaned against the wall.

'Oh God.' The words only barely crossed her lips. 'Fred thinks he's going to die.'

Vesta appeared in the doorway. The rain had worsened and water was beginning to seep over the makeshift threshold, which was only an old piece of wood tacked on to the ground. 'What is it?'

Mirabelle held up the money.

'What's wrong?'

'It's his legacy. That's what he meant. Life or death. He wants us to find his son and give him this.'

'Marlene said they can do wonders for bronchitis.' Vesta didn't sound convinced.

'Poor Fred,' Mirabelle said sadly. She bundled everything into her arms and handed Vesta the boxes of bullets. Back in the cottage, they found a shopping bag to pack them in. Mirabelle checked each item, then wrapped the guns in tea towels and stowed them safely. Vesta watched, impressed by her competence. 'I'm not going to ask,' she promised with a grin.

'I suppose we better go and visit him,' Mirabelle replied.

'The son?'

'No. Fred, of course.'

Mirabelle locked the front door and the women splashed up the lane. On the main street, the pavements were busy with Saturday shoppers and people were heading into restaurants for an early lunch. Mirabelle checked her watch. It was only midday. It seemed like a lot more than forty-eight hours since Helen Quinn's body had been discovered and Superintendent

McGregor had hammered up the office stairs, demanding she look into it.

Ahead of her, a woman in a smart red two-piece was picking her way across the road under a stylish green umbrella. Mirabelle caught herself wondering just how many women were funding themselves by means of the kind of party she'd attended only the afternoon before, in the very way she'd considered. How much of this tawdry trade was hidden in Brighton, just below the surface?

Vesta took control of the umbrella. 'It looks as if it's set,' she said. 'Makes you wish you had wellingtons, doesn't it? Like the kiddies.'

Mirabelle took her arm. The girl would make a good mother, she thought. Though she obviously hadn't yet come to terms with her condition or, for that matter, told Charlie. There'd be a new air about her when she had. Mirabelle had noticed it before – a kind of confidence that came with pregnancy. A very female kind of triumph.

'We'll be lucky to get a cab in this weather,' she said, 'but let's go up North Street and give it a try.'

Chapter 11

There is no instinct like that of the heart

A miasma of overcooked vegetables hung around the main hallway of the hospital. Lunch had been served and, though the plates were now cleared, the odour lingered. Vesta tried not to retch. She felt quite peculiar. She took a couple of deep breaths and watched as two little boys with aggressively combed hair and matching coats marched up the hallway in the direction of the Maternity Ward. Ahead of them, a flustered man, carrying a formal flower display and a large box of Fry's chocolates adorned with a wide red ribbon, urged them to keep up.

'This is where I'll have mine, I suppose,' Vesta managed. 'The baby, I mean. If I don't do it at home.'

'Perhaps I'm mistaken but I think most women prefer hospital these days. It's safer, isn't it?'

'I know.' Vesta cut her off.

The hems of their coats dripped on to the linoleum as the women turned down the corridor and followed the signs for Ward 12. Along the hallway there were seats – old wooden benches – for people to wait. A young man was reading a copy of *The Times* at the entrance to Ward 12. He was wearing a brown gabardine coat and hat. Both were dry so it appeared he had been inside for a while. He peered over the top of his newspaper as the women passed and then returned to the sports pages.

Inside the double doors, the main body of the ward lay

straight ahead. It was airy and bright with more than a dozen beds. Here, the long windows were open despite the rain, and the smell of cooked vegetables had dissipated. Vesta felt her stomach settle, as a tidily turned out nurse directed them to Fred's bed, beside which a woman was already stationed. An angular navy hat was perched on top of her greying, smartly set hair and she was curiously stationary – like a statue set in place covering the frail figure in the bed – as if she was smothering him. She was talking in a low voice. 'Well,' Mirabelle managed to catch the words, 'I'll have to deal with the delphiniums, of course, but now I'll be coming up and down, I can't say when I'll have the time.' Behind this figure, Fred's breathing was strained. 'It's just as well they found me. What were you doing out here in the sticks, Fred? What a place for it to happen.'

Mirabelle coughed and the woman turned. Her mouth pursed as she eyed these newcomers and then, clearly annoyed, let her steely gaze rest on Vesta. 'What is it?' she said. 'What do you want?'

'I'm sorry to bother you, Mrs Fox. We haven't met. I'm Mirabelle Bevan and this is my business partner, Vesta Lewis. We're friends of Fred.' She held out her hand.

Fred's wife's eyes narrowed. She ran a hand around the back of her neck, her fingers dipping in and out of her bun. Then she straightened her blue cardigan as if she was limbering up for a fight. 'Oh,' she said, her jaw so tight with disapproval that Mirabelle thought it might pop. 'He never mentioned you.'

Fred lifted his head and strained to speak, but before he could do so, his wife stepped across the bed as if she was defending a beach in Normandy, spitting her words like well-aimed bullets. 'You can't just come here and upset him like this. He's ill. Really, it ought to be family only. I'm surprised they let you in.'

'Are the rest of the family coming?' Mirabelle enquired smoothly. These were difficult times for everybody. She should try to diffuse them.

'Oh there's no one. Not a soul. Only me.' Mrs Fox sounded satisfied. Mirabelle let the statement lie. She glanced around the woman's frame as Fred raised his hand and reached out vaguely, motioning her closer with weak fingers. Mrs Fox cast a fiery glance, peppered with outrage. 'How did you meet my husband?' she asked loudly, as if poor Fred wasn't there. 'I mean, he can't know anyone down here.' Her voice was thick with suspicion. Brighton was clearly beyond the pale. Mirabelle wondered what Mrs Fox might think of the rest of the county – or even the countryside. Perhaps the whole of England outside London was unacceptable.

'We have a mutual friend, Mrs Fox. Up in town.' Mirabelle tried to smooth things over as she bent towards Fred's pillow. She wanted to catch whatever he was about to say. Mrs Fox let out a sharp exhalation, outraged at this imposition. She looked as if she was about to interpose herself, but, making a supreme effort before she could, Fred managed to raise himself on to his elbows and grasp Mirabelle's wrist. 'Is it all right?' he rasped.

'Mission almost accomplished, Fred. That's what I came to tell you. Don't worry about it.' Mirabelle kept her voice low.

Fred held her gaze. His eyes were watery and they seemed to be pleading. 'Good,' he managed. The word seemed to come from very deep inside him. Then he slumped on to the pillows and closed his eyes, his fingers falling away. Mirabelle nodded as if something had been settled – Fred's son was his and his alone and the goods in the shopping bag were a secret. This woman didn't know anything and wasn't to be informed.

'Well, if you don't mind, as I'm sure you can see, my husband is too ill to have visitors,' Mrs Fox cut in, stroking Fred's arm almost as if she was polishing him. Mirabelle wondered how long Fred had left his wife alone at a time. He'd been married all the years she'd known him, but she didn't blame him for keeping Mrs Fox out of the way.

'Of course. I'm sorry.'

She stepped back. Mrs Fox bent back over the bed, as if the women had been dismissed. As they walked off, she glanced over her shoulder and, seeing her rivals on their way out, resumed whatever she had been saying. 'Well, really,' she started. Mirabelle steeled herself. Walking away felt as if she was abandoning a comrade in arms. But you couldn't trump a wife's right to her husband's final hours. Vesta bit her lip and Mirabelle shoved her gently, moving her on. There was nothing they could do. Once they were out of sight, Mirabelle accosted a young nurse. The girl was preparing medication on a trolley, tipping pills into small cups.

'Excuse me. I'm an old friend of Fred Fox. Over there. Bed seven,' she gestured. 'I wondered if you could tell me, is his prognosis good?'

'I'm sorry,' the girl replied sympathetically. 'I'm not allowed to say. If you aren't family, that is.'

There was no point in arguing. Those were the rules and Mirabelle was well versed in them. Vesta pulled her by the arm. 'Come on.'

Outside in the hallway, the girl couldn't hold in her outrage. 'Family? What does that mean? You're closer to Fred than that horrible, spiteful woman and anyone who knows anything can see it a mile off. Do you think she's going to stand guard over him until he dies, like some kind of banshee . . . it's just downright nasty.'

Mirabelle raised a finger to her lips. She shook her head – only a tiny movement, but it stopped Vesta speaking. The green linoleum stretched ahead, so shiny they could see their vague shadows reflected in it. Two outsiders, waiting. Then

Mirabelle's heels echoed as she stepped up smartly, stopping just in front of the bench. She peered around the newspaper the man sitting there was using to shield his face. He was the right age and he was dark – sallow, people might have called it. When he raised his eyes, they were the striking shade of green that she recalled. He removed his hat as he scrambled to his feet.

'Miss?' he said, as he folded the paper, bundling it on to the wooden seat.

'You're Fred Fox's boy,' Mirabelle said flatly. 'I hardly recognise you, but I suppose you must be. I haven't seen you in, let me see, more than fifteen years – you were only a child, a skinny thing. I don't suppose you remember me.'

The man grinned and held out his hand. In contrast to Mrs Fox's behaviour this felt like an embarrassment of good manners. 'I'm sorry,' he said. 'I suppose I was quite young.'

'Fred brought you to a hotel in London. He had a meeting. You had to wait.'

The young man's green eyes flickered. 'There was a grey sofa – they left me in the corner for ages. Was it you who gave me a ginger drink?'

Mirabelle laughed. 'It wasn't me. But that's right. You had a bottle of pop and a blue straw. Your shorts were the same colour as the sofa.'

'Marcus Fox,' the young man introduced himself.

Mirabelle shook his hand. She couldn't see any trace of the scared, skinny boy except that his eyes hadn't changed, or not much. 'I'm Mirabelle Bevan and this is my business partner, Vesta Lewis.'

'And you came to visit my father? That's very kind.' Marcus's tone became serious. He cast a glance towards the ward as if he was nervous his stepmother might emerge like a wrathful harpy.

'Didn't Fred ever tell her about you? Mrs Fox, I mean? I

thought he was so courageous – I mean, he saved you. He brought you back.'

'I don't know, to tell you the truth. If he told her, the reception probably wasn't good, let's be honest.' The young man didn't sound bitter. If anything, he seemed extremely cheerful, which, after all, was only sensible. Life in England in 1942 was probably better than where he'd come from and a brave, interesting, if unconventional father might, she supposed, make up for having two parents. 'I always felt I'd dodged a bullet.' He smiled. 'I didn't like to ask Dad much about it.'

It struck Mirabelle that all his life Fred had dealt in secrets – secrets of state, secret desires, secret people. He'd kept everything under control and everyone happy. Till now. It must be difficult for this handsome young man to sit, waiting, while only a few yards away a woman who should have been his mother was standing proprietorially over the man who had saved his life all those years ago. But that was how things were around Fred. She wondered if he was addicted to intrigue. She could see how that could happen.

'I'm so sorry.' She turned to Marcus. The boy was solicitous. Mirabelle wondered what was behind the manners. 'How did you hear about Fred's collapse?' she asked.

'He was supposed to turn up last night. We always have a meal on a Friday and Dad didn't show.'

'In London?'

'We were going for a curry. I waited for two hours in a restaurant off Regent Street. Veeraswamy. It's one of his favourites. In the end, the waiters got annoyed because I hadn't ordered. I knew something was wrong. He can be eccentric, my dad, but he's rock solid reliable when it comes to food. He works out of Brighton a lot so I figured that's where he would have been coming from. I caught the next train. It didn't take long to track him down.'

'Have they said anything about his chances?'

'Not good, I'm afraid.'

'I'm so sorry. Your father is a wonderful man. It must be awkward for you with Mrs Fox here.'

Marcus shifted. His eyes lingered on Vesta for a moment then he seemed to rally. 'I explained to the ward sister. I don't expect we're the only family with a secret. Or that doesn't get along, for that matter. "Estranged" they call it. Anyway, Sister was understanding about the whole thing. She has it in hand and Elsie won't know I'm here – not from the nurses, anyway. I suppose she might notice me though. Like you did.' He halted. They all knew that Mrs Fox was not the kind of person to notice anything on the sidelines. Marcus continued. 'She thinks he was down for the racing, though there are no races this week. He was knocking stuff out down here, wasn't he, Miss Bevan? That's why he was spending such a lot of time in Brighton. He was selling stolen goods.'

Mirabelle nodded. 'Yes,' she said. Now Marcus had said it, it sounded worse than it had felt when she had periodically visited Fred in the cottage to pick up bits and pieces.

The young man smiled. 'I'm going to stick around anyway. Poor Dad. I can probably sneak in a visit early doors. I'll take him some brandy. He likes a tot. I'll just keep an eye on him, you know, till he goes.'

This recalled Mirabelle to the reason she was there. She checked over her shoulder. Then she opened the shopping bag. 'Fred asked me to fetch these for you. It's some money and the deeds to a couple of properties. There are also three guns, but, if you don't mind, I'd rather dispose of those.'

'Guns?' Marcus peered over the rim of the bag.

'Service pistols. I think all this is his legacy to you. Unwritten, of course, but he wants you to have it.'

Marcus took the shopper. 'Thank you. Leave the guns to me,' he said. 'A lady like you shouldn't have to do that kind of thing.'

A ghost of a smile crossed Mirabelle's face. The boy was personable, but he clearly didn't recall anything other than the ginger drink from that day in the Charing Cross Hotel more than a decade before. However, she didn't quibble. There was something about Marcus Fox, she realised – something competent. She watched as he secreted the goods around his person with admirable discretion – maybe he'd learned a thing or two from his father apart from good manners.

'Well,' she said, holding out her hand. 'If you need me you'll find me at McGuigan & McGuigan Debt Recovery on Brills Lane. Please keep in touch.'

Marcus scrambled to shake it. 'Of course,' he said. 'I'll let you know when he goes. She'll want to bury him, you see. In her mind it'll only be her at the graveside, the grieving widow, but I'm minded to go to the service. And you could come too, if you like. Once she can't hurt him any more.'

Mirabelle didn't ask what he meant. 'Goodbye,' she said and Fox nodded gravely.

The women walked in silence to the main entrance. Outside, the rain was bouncing off the steps. Vesta stared up the corridor towards the staircase – inside where it was dry. 'Do you mind?' she said. 'We could have a look at the baby ward.'

Mirabelle followed. It was better than walking through puddles and more cheerful than where they'd been. Upstairs, the hallway smelled of talcum powder and hot milk and the atmosphere was businesslike with nurses moving around efficiently behind the glass wall. Vesta peered in. The cots were alive with squirming babies. Mirabelle laughed. 'Look at them. Isn't it heartening? I mean, Vesta, it's normal.'

Vesta focused on the tiny faces and the tiny hands. The tidy, coloured blankets. She stopped when she came to a black face, solitary among the sea of pink. A little boy swaddled tightly in blue. One of the nurses spotted her. She went to the cot and picked up the child, holding him aloft, assuming Vesta was a relation. The boy dribbled and the nurse wiped his chin. Vesta put up a hand in thanks.

'Maybe it'll be all right,' she said, sounding less dubious than she had previously. As they turned to go, a pretty blonde nurse carrying two babies rounded a corner.

'Oh, Vesta,' Marlene said without missing a beat, as if she had expected her friend to be there. 'I meant to ring you. Morphine. That's what's most likely in your gin bottle. But they'd need to be careful with the dosage.' She lowered her voice. 'It's easy to stop breathing, do you see? If you have too much.'

Vesta started to introduce Marlene to Mirabelle when the nurse noticed something over her friend's shoulder. 'Sister,' she hissed in a tone of pure panic, and then, more loudly and in a normal voice, she said, 'It's not up here. You need to go downstairs, madam. Turn left at the bottom. Good afternoon.' Then, with the children gurgling, she sped off in the direction of the ward.

'Morphine,' Vesta said when she'd gone.

Mirabelle nodded. That made sense. It would have made the Quinns woozy, it would make them sleep. The puzzle was who had done it – sneaking into the house and knocking them both out. The puzzle was why. The sound of a crying baby echoed down the hallway.

'Are you feeling better about everything?' Mirabelle asked.

Vesta nodded. Maybe tonight was the night. 'Charlie's home later. He's going to cook dinner,' she said.

Chapter 12

Love is not a fire to be shut up in the soul

That evening Mirabelle had just drawn a bath and drizzled in some lavender oil when the buzzer sounded. She checked the clock. It was only seven. The rain had continued all day and now the light was beginning to fade and the street-lamps were casting their honey glow. Inside, the curtains were half drawn and the flat felt unusually warm. She had spent the afternoon thinking about the case. About Fred and poor Marcus, the boy just sitting there, waiting for his old man to die. Now, she found herself running over tiny details and sorting her laundry as she did so. The bed was piled with clothes as she swept past barefoot and opened the front door. On the doorstep, Superintendent McGregor's hat was dark with rain.

'I finished early,' he said. 'I thought you might like dinner. There's a French place opened in Rottingdean.'

Mirabelle kissed him lightly on the cheek. 'That sounds nice.'

McGregor hung up his coat and hat and strode into the drawing room to pour a drink. 'It smells good in here.' He smiled, the cut glass shimmering.

'I was going to have a bath.' Mirabelle tipped her chin towards the drinks tray, encouraging him to pour her a tot of whisky.

'You still could, if you like. I'll wash your back.'

Mirabelle settled into one of the armchairs by the fire. She liked it when he flirted with her.

'Aren't you going to ask me?'

'May I wash your back?'

'No, silly. About the case.'

'Of course.' He became more serious. 'Actually, I have some news. I managed to get a copy of the post-mortem. Helen Quinn was stabbed with a thin, sharp blade, probably a flick-knife. We're looking for a slasher.'

'Did Phil Quinn own a flick-knife?'

'Phil hates that kind of thing. There's a lot of knife crime at home. When it's around you, you go one of two ways. Have you heard of a Cheshire grin? Or rather, in Scotland, we call it a Glasgow smile?'

Mirabelle shook her head.

'It's a gang punishment. It's becoming more common down here. Knife crime is on the rise in London but we haven't seen much in Brighton. Not yet.' The superintendent paused, finding it strange talking to Mirabelle about this. She looked beautiful in the lamplight. Why had he thought she'd know about the Glasgow smile? She was a lady. Perhaps it was that contradiction – Mirabelle's grace set against her grit – that always reeled him in. He turned his attention back to the case. 'None of the knives in the house – in the kitchen, that is – match the weapon that killed Mrs Quinn. It was a four-inch blade and it would fillet you. Robinson hasn't been able to find it.'

'But he's charged Quinn anyway?'

'The evidence is purely circumstantial. But Robinson doesn't mind that. I managed to speak to Phil before they took him up to Lewes. He hasn't taken it well. I told him we're working on it.'

'And Robinson?'

'I tried. The knife that killed Helen Quinn was a criminal's weapon, but, when I pointed that out, he just snorted. One way or another, it looks like there's a gang involved. It's made me jumpy. I don't understand. There's never been anything like that around Phil.'

'And the drug used to knock them out was morphine?'

'Yes. How did you know?'

'Educated guess.'

'The doc reckons Helen Quinn might have still felt some pain – if it was only that. He said she'd been drugged on top of the stuff in the gin bottle. The morphine knocked her out and then she was injected. They found a mark on her arm. In any case, both drugs are too widely available to be easily traced – any pharmacy or hospital would have them in stock and there have been no recent break-ins or thefts that could be the source. There's nothing like that recorded in Brighton over the last six months – more, actually. There have been a few in London, but it's impossible to link the drugs to a particular robbery. Tell me, what else have you been up to, apart from making educated guesses?'

Mirabelle thought of her introduction to Mr Davidson at Tongdean, her afternoon in Eastbourne, being caught by the beat bobby at Mill Lane, Fred heaving for breath and then she and Vesta in the long hospital corridor handing three illegal guns to Marcus Fox. 'I'll go over it with you when I'm in the bath,' she said. 'Come and talk to me.'

Vesta had chosen peach for the walls. Above the sink, there was a wide mirror in a gilded frame. It reflected the steaming tub, from which lavender scent was wafting through the flat. On the shelf, a line of glass bottles dripped with condensation. The clock on the wall ticked. McGregor settled by the door and watched intently as Mirabelle slipped out of her clothes and stepped into the warm water. He sipped his whisky, his eyes still, as her skin distorted under the surface and the water lapped against the enamel. Once she was comfortable, she offered him a large sponge. He laid his glass on the side and began to wash her, planting kisses on her slick skin. She picked up his drink and took a sip, letting the whisky evaporate on her tongue, the taste smoky in contrast to the lavender on the air. He bit her shoulder.

'We'll never get to dinner if you start that,' she said.

'Damn dinner.' He smiled, as he took back his glass and leaned against the wall so he could look at her. 'You're the most beautiful woman I ever saw.'

Later, they shared fish and chips instead of going to Rottingdean and walked along the front. It was dark and the rain had eased to a fine drizzle, almost like lace. Now and then, they stopped to kiss under the umbrella. The pubs would close soon and the first people to leave were stumbling towards their bus stops or starting the long walk home. A line of taxis waited at the bottom of the road, the drivers smoking.

'Want to dance?' McGregor suggested.

'Where?' Mirabelle didn't fancy the ballrooms around the pier with the girls in bright skirts and their keen young men. It was too raucous. Her dubiety showed. McGregor laughed.

'Don't worry. I know somewhere,' he said, pulling her up Queen's Road as if they were young and in love.

After turning off, he bundled her through a glossy black door and up a steep set of red-carpeted stairs with a banister of thick rope on brass loops. Inside, the windows were blacked out. There was a polished ebony bar in one corner and several tables around which comfortable chairs were arranged, some plush to match the carpet and others upholstered in brown leather. The place glowed red with a hint of neon and the effect was luxurious and forbidden. In the background, music was playing. A love song. Mirabelle liked it immediately. Most of the tables were vacant, but at one a young couple, deep in conversation, were drinking cocktails, while at another, three old men in evening dress smoked cigars and played cards.

'This is lovely. What's it called?' Mirabelle asked.

'I don't know. There's no sign.'

'They'd call it a *boite* in Paris.'

'Let's call it that then. The Boite.'

A maître d' emerged. He sported a moustache and his hair was slicked back so it shone. 'Alan,' he said, shaking McGregor's hand heartily and laying his palm on the superintendent's shoulder to guide him to a table. 'Nice to see you.'

'I thought you might have music tonight. We felt like dancing. You haven't met my girlfriend. Mirabelle Bevan.'

Mirabelle felt a frisson as she shrugged off the strangeness of being described that way. There was hardly ever an introduction, hardly anyone to say it to. All those years ago, Jack had never called her that. Not once.

'How do you do, Miss Bevan?' The man indicated where they should sit.

McGregor perused the bar. 'Have you any champagne? I feel like a celebration.'

'Of course. There's some Argentinian liqueur that came our way this week. I can recommend it – just a whisper of orange in the glass to bring up the taste of the bubbly.'

Mirabelle smiled. That was Fred. Grafting to the last.

'Champagne cocktail?' McGregor offered.

'Yes. Lovely.'

A discreet, Italian-looking waiter appeared with an ice bucket and two crystal flutes while another man removed two tables to make a dance floor. This place ran like clockwork, she realised. It was comforting to know that on a rainy Saturday night there was somewhere so smart up the road.

McGregor held out his hand and Mirabelle got up and folded into his arms as they moved to the rhythm. She laid her head on his shoulder. From far off, she could hear ice chink. It felt a luxury to have the place almost entirely to themselves. When the song finished, McGregor caught Mirabelle's hand

and kissed the tips of her fingers. She laughed. They sat down and sipped their drinks.

Then, as the song changed, Mirabelle noticed a plump woman appear in the doorway. She was wearing thick make-up and her auburn hair was swept into an old-fashioned bun. Handing her coat and umbrella to the waiter, the woman revealed a well-cut, jade taffeta cocktail dress. Mirabelle wondered momentarily if she was a retired madam. She had a seedy but matronly look and then there was that lipstick. The maître d' rushed to kiss her on the cheek. Then, they pushed into the room together, Mirabelle noticed, rather than him leading her to a table. As they came closer, she caught the words: 'I'm bored, Dan, all the way out there on my own. I thought I'd nip into town for a bit of fun.' The maître d' smiled apologetically as if he was trying to shoo the woman along, but McGregor's interest was piqued. He rose to his feet.

'Good evening,' he said.

'Good evening.' The woman stopped. She looked suddenly almost regal.

Put on the spot, the maître d' fumbled before introducing her. 'This is my wife, Superintendent,' he said sheepishly. 'Ruthie.'

'Mrs Gleeson.'

Mrs Gleeson grinned, as if this was more than she was expecting. 'Bring me a brandy on ice,' she said dismissively to the waiter and then moved forward with her gloved hand outstretched. 'Alan McGregor,' Gleeson continued the introductions. 'And Mirabelle Bevan.'

'How do you do.'

Ruth Gleeson stared pointedly at the chair in front of her. 'Do you mind?'

'Not at all,' said McGregor, 'please join us. We're having a lazy Saturday night. Your husband has brought a little bit of Mayfair to Brighton.'

'Ruthie, please,' she replied. 'Well, it's better than those dreadful coffee shops that are opening willy-nilly. We always liked a nightclub, didn't we, dear? During the war, when Dan came home on leave, we were always out on the town. No kids in those days. And hardly any money either.' She gave a little laugh as if she was nostalgic for old times, which Mirabelle suspected she wasn't. Close up, it was apparent that nothing on Mrs Gleeson's person was understated. A thick bracelet of diamonds peeped from under her cuff.

As the waiters fussed, serving drinks, and the Gleesons sat down, Mirabelle whispered in McGregor's ear. 'Isn't Gleeson the name of one of Phil Quinn's partners?'

'Yes. That's him. He sank money into this place last year on top of Hove Cars.'

She eyed the superintendent with a smile as she took in this information. He hadn't simply brought her here for fun then. They were, to all intents and purposes, working. Pulling in her chair, she leaned towards Mrs Gleeson. 'How many children do you have?' she asked.

'Three,' Ruthie replied. 'Can you believe it?'

Gleeson looked mildly uncomfortable. He was a good-looking man and he seemed aware that his wife didn't match him, though maybe it had been different when they first met. Sometimes couples became more like each other, other times they diverged. Mix and match, Vesta called it. The gramophone was set going again, this time with big band music.

'We've done all right.' Gleeson sipped his whisky, before he brought up what was really on his mind. 'It's a bad business about Phil,' he said. 'He's charged and on remand now. Did you know?'

'I heard you engaged a solicitor,' McGregor said.

'Fat lot of good it's done us.'

'Where are you from?' Ruthie asked Mirabelle, turning

towards her as if they were girls sharing a conversation and there was nobody else at the table.

'We just live around the corner,' Mirabelle replied, without specifying that she and Superintendent McGregor resided around different corners even if both of them were close. 'This club is lovely. Did you help set it up?'

'Dan always wanted a place. He knew how to get it right all on his own.'

'I would have thought you wanted a garage, Mr Gleeson? I mean, you're one of the partners at Hove Cars, aren't you? This is another thing entirely.'

Gleeson lit a cigar. A spiral of smoke floated across the table. 'The garage was Phil's idea. It's a corking little business and we've all done well out of it, but—' Dan gestured openly '—I could come here every night and never feel done in. It's a pleasure.'

Ruthie smirked. She sipped her brandy. 'You do come every night,' she said.

'Gosh. It must be tiring,' Mirabelle insisted. 'I mean, Hove Cars during the day and then this.'

McGregor watched her. Really, she was remarkable. Never off the job.

Gleeson shrugged. 'There's less and less for me to do at Hove these days. At the beginning, we only had two cars and we drove them round the clock between the three of us. I'm not kidding. We had a twenty-four-hour service. We used to kip in the office if there weren't any calls. Now, that was tiring. But then business took off and we bought more cars and took on drivers. These days, Phil runs the contracts and the men – until this awful business. Tommy Fourcade sees to the cars – he's the mechanic.'

'What do you do?'

'Accounts. I'm good with figures. But the way I've set it up, the place runs itself. I pay in in the morning – always up to the bank myself. Then there's monthly figures – cash flow – but that's all. Except I've been in the last few days helping out because of what happened.'

Ruthie shook her head. 'Terrible,' she said. 'I never would have thought it.'

'None of us thought it—' her husband's tone had an edge '—cos Phil didn't do it, love.'

Ruthie tinkled the ice in her glass as a form of protest. 'Well, if Phil is innocent, who killed poor Helen then?'

Gleeson deferred to McGregor. 'We don't know yet,' the superintendent said. 'There's a difference of opinion.' He attempted an unaccustomed level of diplomacy. 'My colleague thinks Phil did kill her . . . he's charged him.'

'Exactly,' Mrs Gleeson cut in. 'It's only logical. It's always the husband. You see it time and time again in the papers. What else did she have, little Helen Quinn? She was pretty, but what else did she have but her husband and look what he did to her?'

'Now, Ruthie.' Gleeson stopped his wife. 'Phil and Helen were a cracking couple. They were devoted.'

'She must have done something to set him off.'

Mirabelle's eyes widened. The champagne felt suddenly refreshing as she realised Mrs Gleeson had made a good point even if it was misdirected. She was surprised she hadn't thought of it before. What if Helen Quinn had done something – Helen herself – not Phil. Everyone investigating the poor woman's death had assumed the murder must be something to do with her husband – either that he did it or that it was some kind of blackmail attempt or revenge. But what if Helen Quinn was murdered on her own account? The idea rankled. If it had been a man who'd died, such assumptions never would have been made. Robinson obviously hadn't considered it either, or, if he had, he'd dismissed it straight away.

'I've been so stupid,' she muttered under her breath.

'Sorry, dear?' Mrs Gleeson leaned in. 'What did you say?'

Mirabelle looked up. 'Did you know Mrs Quinn well?' she asked. 'Where did she come from?'

'I don't know. She wasn't really a friend. Helen was much younger and they had no children.' Mrs Gleeson sat back as if she was retiring from battle.

It wouldn't have surprised Mirabelle if the woman had raised her hands in surrender. She cast her eyes towards Dan Gleeson. 'Do you know? Anything about Mrs Quinn?'

'I haven't a clue,' he said, puffing on his cigar. Ruth held out her hand and he dug in his pocket and withdrew a silver cigarette case from which she extracted a smoke. Gleeson fired his lighter so she could kindle it. He seemed to be trying to recall the details of the year or so since Helen Quinn had arrived. It was interesting – clearly neither of the Gleesons thought of the poor woman as anything other than Phil Quinn's wife. 'Phil met her at the Palais,' Gleeson reflected. 'She was down from London. It was one of those whirlwind romances. He snapped her up pretty quickly.'

'Did she work in London?'

'She must have. She wasn't posh or anything. Whatever she did, she gave it up when they got hitched – no need, you see. She was a nice woman. Terrible cook, though. They made a kind of joke of it.'

Mirabelle's eyes darted. She thought of the apprentice at the garage who'd said Mrs Quinn had brought her husband sandwiches. Perhaps that was part of their joke. Maybe breakfast that morning had been inedible.

'What is it, Mirabelle?' McGregor laid a hand on her arm.

'We've been looking at the wrong thing. We've been concentrating on him. Don't you see? We never considered Helen Quinn might have been killed because of something she'd done.'

Mrs Gleeson snorted. 'That scrap of a girl!' she said. 'Ten years younger than Phil? What could she possibly have done?'

Mirabelle thought of the women at the party in the suite in Eastbourne. They all had secrets that ordinary people wouldn't believe. Being a fallen woman wasn't written large on you any more than anything else. It was only a matter of detail that most people wouldn't even notice. Helen Quinn might have had secrets and it seemed, if she did, she was good at keeping them.

'I'd like to know more about her. Did you meet her family at the wedding?'

Mrs Gleeson thought for a moment. 'I don't know that she had any family. Maybe an uncle. Do you remember, Dan? An old fellow. He sat at the side all afternoon and went through a power of stout.'

The waiter poured more cocktails. 'Have you got any of that rock and roll?' McGregor asked.

Mrs Gleeson rolled her eyes. 'That rubbish! What would you want to put that on for? You can't dance properly to rock and roll. Put on "Mambo Italiano".'

The waiter rummaged till he found it and there was a burst of brass. 'Let's mambo,' she said and Mr Gleeson got to his feet. You could see they were a couple now. Dancing knocked years off Mrs Gleeson.

'I want to take you home,' McGregor whispered, as he eased his arm around Mirabelle's waist. A smile played on her lips. It was too late to take this line of inquiry any further tonight but it was a step forward at least. 'All right,' she said, as it occurred to her that they were becoming adept at enjoying themselves. 'Let's go.'

Chapter 13

A clue is guiding information

The Sunday bells were ringing all over the city as they ate breakfast in McGregor's bedroom. No meals could be taken in the Arundel's dining room outside the times allotted for guests for fear that the guests might expect similar privileges. Miss Brownlee had accommodated McGregor, however, with a generous tray of toast and tea and a crumpled copy of a Sunday newspaper. The butter was refrigerated almost solid and was impossible to spread, so Mirabelle spooned a thick layer of marmalade over her toast and bit into it with a satisfied murmur. She was hungry. When she'd eaten, she'd get to the business of finding out more about Helen Quinn. In the meantime, she glanced at McGregor sipping his tea, engrossed in the sports pages before he moved on to the crossword. It felt like a comfortable arrangement, if rather domestic. Maybe I'm getting used to this, she thought.

When the front door sounded neither of them paid much attention. There were a good deal of comings and goings, especially around late morning and early afternoon when people checked out and checked in. As a result, when, in less than a minute, there was a smart knock on the bedroom door, they were taken by surprise. As a fresh-faced constable peered nervously into the room, Mirabelle glanced at the curtains, wondering if she ought to make some effort to conceal herself despite the fact it was clearly too late. The boy must have at least rudimentary observation skills. The force didn't take them otherwise.

'Sorry, sir,' the constable apologised. 'I'm sorry,' he repeated.

'Ellison, isn't it?'

'Yes, sir.'

'Well?'

'There's a body.'

McGregor continued to sip his tea. 'Murder?'

'No, sir. Suspicious circumstances.'

'How suspicious?'

'Suicide, sir. The body was found on the Downs.'

'Apart from the fact the Downs are outside our jurisdiction, I can't see what's suspicious about that.'

'Well, that's the thing, sir. He killed himself elsewhere. Someone must have moved the body. Dumped him. And he'd been staying in Brighton. He was last seen in his hotel on Friday afternoon. Ex-military, it seems. The Chief wanted a senior officer to take charge and Inspector Robinson is . . .'

McGregor cast his eyes to the ceiling. 'Robinson is resting on his laurels over the case I ought to have had.' He drained his cup. 'All right,' he said and got up. 'You were assigned to the Quinn murder, weren't you?' he asked, casually, as he put on his jacket.

Ellison nodded. 'Yes, sir.'

'Know anything about the girl's family? Her past?'

Constable Ellison shook his head. 'I was searching for the knife.'

'Was Inspector Robinson interested in her family?'

'You have to inform the family, sir. If there is one.'

'Yes, Ellison. I know. And did he?'

'No one mentioned it, sir.'

'I see.'

'Then you've no idea where the dead woman came from?'

'No, sir.'

McGregor kissed Mirabelle on the cheek. 'There,' he said. 'I'll see you later.' He squeezed her arm before grabbing his hat and ushering the boy out of the door.

Mirabelle leaned against the window frame and watched as McGregor left the house and slipped into the back seat of the Black Maria that was parked at the top of the street. She savoured the slant of his shoulders beneath his dark coat as Ellison dotted around him. The sky was blue today and she lingered for a moment at the window, watching the wheeling gulls as she finished her toast and wondered about Helen Quinn and whether somewhere she had relations who were unaware of her death. She'd better get to it.

She grabbed her coat and slipped out of the house, closing the gate behind her. Walking westwards, she strode out smartly for Old Steine and from there caught a bus north, getting off at the now familiar stop for Mill Lane. The neighbourhood had scrubbed up for Sunday and the few people she passed were in their best clothes, either on their way to church or coming home again. The men tipped their hats as they passed and the women murmured their good afternoons. Halfway up the street, Mirabelle strode up the garden path at the Randalls' house and knocked on the door. It was as good a place to start as any. Vi Randall had known Helen Quinn better than anyone. The door burst open in seconds to reveal Vi wearing a yellow apron, her extended stomach outlined by the daffodils printed on the surface of the cloth.

'Oh God,' she said, 'they send a female police officer when someone dies.' Her fingers were quivering and her eyes were pink. She'd clearly been crying and she looked as if she hadn't slept. She'd pinned her hair into a roll, but it had slipped into a lopsided mess. The effect would have been comical if she hadn't been so upset.

'I'm not actually a police officer,' Mirabelle admitted. 'Are you all right, Mrs Randall?'

Vi seemed unsteady on her feet and her eyes darted up and down the street as she grabbed Mirabelle's arm. 'Is he dead? You can tell me,' she gasped.

'Is who dead? What are you talking about?'

Vi heaved a sob that came from somewhere deep in the daffodils. 'Billy didn't come home last night. I don't know what's happened to him.' She stepped back, pulling Mirabelle into the bright hallway. Today there was a bunch of hollyhocks in a long bottle that must have once held cordial. 'I don't know what to do,' she said, closing the front door.

'Good gracious,' Mirabelle replied. 'Has he ever not come home before?'

'No.' Vi was insistent. 'Not since we moved to Brighton. When we were first married it used to happen now and then in London. But never down here. It's a clean slate in Brighton. We both promised. He wouldn't. Not with me in this condition. Oh God, something terrible must have happened.'

Distractedly, she set off into the sitting room and Mirabelle followed her, watching as the pregnant woman paced up and down the threadbare carpet with the palm of her hand pressed into the small of her back, just as she had the day Vesta had been there. It didn't seem right to sit down, so Mirabelle hovered behind the patched sofa.

'How long has your husband been missing?'

'Since yesterday. It's half-day at the factory on Saturday. They knock off at lunchtime. I had eggs on toast all ready to go and he was going to fix the cupboard upstairs. It's coming off its hinges. I waited and waited but he didn't come home.'

'Did you call the factory?'

'There's nobody in the office at the weekend. I don't know what to do, Miss Bevan.' Vi sounded hysterical.

Mirabelle kept her voice steady. 'Where does Mr Randall work?'

'CVA. On the other side of the railway. At Portland Road by the cricket ground. It's only half an hour's walk. He's usually back by one on a Saturday.'

'What do they make?'

'Machine tools. He's got a mathematical mind, my Billy. The pay's not bad, just not good enough, not quite. Oh, Miss Bevan. He's never done anything like this before.'

Mirabelle did not point out that Vi had already said her husband had stayed out all night several times when they lived in London. She wondered why this seemingly devoted couple had needed the fresh start to which Mrs Randall had alluded. Vi paced up and down one more time and then turned.

'Oh God,' she said.

'Do you think we should call the police?' Mirabelle suggested. 'I mean, if you're really worried and, well, there are suspicious circumstances.'

'What suspicious circumstances?' Vi sounded hysterical.

'Well,' Mirabelle had started now and she might as well say it, 'the murder next door.'

'But they locked Phil up.' The poor woman was frantic.

'Why don't you sit down?' Mirabelle suggested. 'Can I get you a glass of water? A cup of tea?'

Vi Randall glared at Mirabelle, but she relented and flopped into the armchair by the fire. 'If you aren't here to tell me Billy's been done in, then why did you come?' she asked.

'I came to talk about Helen Quinn,' Mirabelle admitted, her mind racing to figure out what might have happened to Billy. Was there some connection she'd missed?

'Helen? What about her?'

'I wondered, where she came from? If you knew her maiden name?'

'Maiden name? She was Helen Quinn when I met her. I think she was brought up in London. All very respectable.'

'Did she have a job? Before, I mean.'

'I suppose so. She never talked about it.'

'Did she have any family?'

'She never said.'

'I wondered about those pictures on her mantel.'

'That's Phil's lot. Some uncle who went out to Burma and his mum and dad. None of them are Helen's. I miss her.' Vi let out a sob. 'The thing is, once you're married, you're on your own all day and Helen was my pal. She was ever such fun, Miss Bevan. If she were here, she'd know what to do about Billy not coming home. Helen was practical that way. Everyone round the doors is nice, but she was a real mate. It's been a terrible week. Where on earth is he?'

'When your husband stayed out before, Mrs Randall,' Mirabelle tried, shifting slightly because she wasn't sure how Vi might react, 'where was he then?'

'I don't know.' The words came very loud. 'I mean, when you're first married, it can be hard. You just have to get on. He'd go off with his mates, I suppose. Drinking and that.'

'His mates?'

'Yeah. Friends.'

'Do you think that's what he's done now?'

'Brighton's different. I mean, I'm having a baby. When blokes go out in Brighton, they go to the pub down the road and they're home by eleven. I went down last night before closing time but no one had a clue where Billy had got to. You don't want to be the kind of wife who goes looking for her husband, do you? It's embarrassing. But it got so late.'

'And no one had seen him?'

'No.'

Mirabelle was about to suggest again that they call the police and then make a list of places Billy Randall frequented, apart from the local public house. She wasn't sure how Vi might take the idea. The poor girl said she wanted to be practical, but she wasn't behaving that way.

'Well, perhaps it would be best—' Mirabelle started, but she was cut off by the sound of the front door opening. It banged closed and there was a cheery call from the hallway.

'Vi!' Billy Randall took off his hat as he walked into the room. Vi's eyes lit with fury. She sprang out of the chair, launching herself at her husband.

'Where the hell have you been? Where have you been?' she shrieked, hitting him as she asked the question. It was like watching an insect banging repeatedly against a window. 'You promised you'd never do it again. I've been worried out of my mind.' When her open hands had no effect, she balled her fingers into fists and began punching. It took a moment for Billy to catch hold of her wrists. 'Let go,' she shouted. 'Let go.'

'Jesus,' he said. 'That's some welcome. And in front of a guest. Calm down, Vi, would you?'

'Where have you been?'

'What do you mean?' He sounded nonchalant. 'It was a big order, love. There was overtime. I thought we could use the money. You wanted that pram for the nipper. Putting the baby to sleep in a drawer is all right in the house, but what about when you need to go out, eh?' He let go of Vi's wrists and strolled over to the fireplace. 'This'll sort it out,' he said, taking several coins out of his pocket and popping them into a tin next to the old clock. 'Now you can pick whichever pram you fancy. Cash in hand,' he said. 'I'll take more overtime if I can get it too. They say there's a busy spell coming. It's irregular hours, but it could be good for us. Well, what have you ladies been up to? Hit the gin have you?'

'Oh no,' Mirabelle said. 'I only popped over to ask a few questions.'

'Questions?'

'About Helen Quinn.'

'Well, that's enough of that. You can see Vi's upset, Miss Bevan. And in her condition. I'm starving. I thought you might cook me a little something, love. Returning breadwinner and all. I could murder a fry-up.'

'I thought you were dead, Billy. I thought you were done for. When Miss Bevan appeared, I thought she'd come to tell me they'd found your body.'

'Don't make a fuss.'

'A fuss?' Vi was still furious. 'I'll give you a fuss. You can get your own bleeding dinner.' She swept out of the room. Mirabelle shifted uncomfortably. From the hallway there was the sound of a cupboard door being slammed closed, then Vi swept back in. She was wearing a blue summer coat and, Mirabelle noted, quite a nice hat decorated with a silk flower and some pink ribbon. 'I'm going out,' she said, 'see how you like it when you don't know where I am.'

'Vi,' Billy pleaded. 'Don't be silly. You know you'll just go to your mother's.'

This infuriated Vi further. She snorted, turned on her heel and burst out of the room, slamming the front door as she left. Mirabelle cast Billy Randall a sympathetic look, although he had clearly brought it on himself. Calmly, as if accepting his fate, he reached into his pocket and pulled out a pack of cigarettes. 'Makes 'em feisty. Having a baby,' he said as he lit up and then, remembering his manners, offered Mirabelle the box. She declined. Out of the window, she could just make out Vi's hat, bobbing above the privet hedges in the direction of the main road.

'I think she was rather worried, Mr Randall. She'd been up all night.'

Billy shrugged. 'She'll be all right,' he said.

'Where did you meet your wife? She strikes me as a talented sort of person.'

'Talented?'

'She keeps the house beautifully and I think she trimmed that hat she was wearing. And then there's all of this.' Mirabelle gestured around the living room. It was shabby but everything had been carefully looked after. 'She has a nice touch.'

'Oh yes. Vi's good at that. She's a homemaker, see.'

'You met her in London?'

Billy looked momentarily nostalgic. 'Yeah,' he said. 'We were at a party. She could do card tricks.'

'Ah.'

'You'd have to admire her Find the Lady. She has nimble fingers, my wife. She'll be all right once the nipper turns up, you'll see. It'll keep her busy.'

'Couldn't you have called last night? Sent a message?'

Randall took a deep draw. 'I wasn't going to trouble anyone. The neighbours, I mean.' He shrugged. 'We've been short of money, to tell the truth. I thought she'd be pleased. I don't mean to be rude but . . .' He cast his eyes to the door.

'Of course. I'm sorry.' Mirabelle moved to go and Billy followed. She lingered a moment in the hallway. 'You don't happen to know what Mrs Quinn did before she was married, do you? If she had any family?'

Billy shook his head. 'Helen? What she did?' he repeated, as if this was the oddest question anyone had ever posed. 'I haven't a clue. Terrible cook though. I'll tell you that.'

'Yes, I heard.' Mirabelle smiled. 'I'm rather that way myself.'

'She was an orphan,' he said. 'I know that much.'

'I see.'

'One night we were all having a drink and she said meeting Phil had given her a family again. I think she had been, you know, alone. It's a tragedy what happened.' Billy's eyes were hard. 'A rotten bloody tragedy, pardon my French.'

'What'll be a tragedy is if Mr Quinn is convicted for his wife's killing, because, if I'm sure of anything, it's that he didn't do it.'

Billy Randall didn't meet her eye. He opened the door. 'He couldn't have done it. Not all drugged up,' he said. 'They'll let him off. No murder weapon or nothing. No motive either. They'll have to.'

Mirabelle felt her fingers tingle as she walked down the path. People said the oddest things sometimes. They said what was on their mind, without realising. Really, she thought, she ought to try Mrs Ambrose. If anyone on Mill Lane would know about Helen Quinn it was the archetypical nosy neighbour. Yet somehow she found herself walking in the opposite direction as she figured out the way to the cricket ground.

Chapter 14

Vices are only virtues carried to excess

Up on the Downs, Superintendent McGregor hovered beside the body. At first the man looked unharmed, as if he was asleep on the grass. His skin was smooth and his pallor was fresh, brushed with a light suntan that he could not have acquired over the English winter. Then, after a few seconds of observation, it became clear the back of his head had been blown away.

'Wherever he killed himself, there'll be some mess,' McGregor observed.

Ellison nodded sagely and only stopped when one of the other constables at the scene cast him a barbed look.

Ignoring this nascent rivalry, McGregor checked the man's pockets, but there was nothing. The suit was evening wear – well made too. They'd look into that. 'You said he had been staying in a hotel?' He looked up.

'Yes, sir,' Ellison confirmed. 'They called it in. He hadn't slept in his room for two nights running and apparently he'd been drinking heavily. He's Flight Lieutenant George Forgie. Ex-RAF.'

'Who found him?'

'A lady out hacking this morning. There's a stable over the hill. She was a sturdy type – she took it well.'

'Has anyone formally identified him?'

'No, sir. It's only from the description – the one the hotel rang in.'

McGregor hesitated. He hadn't seen active service during the war. He still felt guilty about that and, as a result, he lacked sympathy that many men found it difficult coming home again. There had been quite a bit of this sort of thing in the early days – men who couldn't take peacetime after they'd seen war. The aftermath of the conflict dragged on even now. There were men who had been damaged through torture or starvation in prison camps and those who simply couldn't settle after the adrenalin rush of executing duties of national importance. There were some who found they liked killing and came back to civilian life unable to shake off their murderous impulses. Others, having fought through the war's deadliest battles and held their nerve, fell apart over small domestic tragedies, as if they had no steel left after what they had been through. Still, suicide was extreme.

'We need to find somebody who knew him. Someone who can identify the poor chap.'

'Yes, sir.'

'And we'll need to find the last person who saw him alive.' McGregor judged the timing for himself. Forgie's body was fresh. He hadn't been dead for long. 'Where was he last night – assuming he killed himself at night?'

McGregor stared at the man's bow tie. Then his eyes ran down the body until he came to the shoes, which were devoid of mud. It had been rainy for the last several days. There was no question he hadn't walked up here on to the rolling hills. McGregor took a deep breath. It was a puzzle, but he was sure he'd get to the bottom of it. Military men, after all, tended to range in groups – Forgie's friends and acquaintances would fill in a good deal of the detail when he tracked them down. He was about to issue orders to move the body back to town when he noticed the corner of the man's jacket. Corpses often lay in unwieldy positions, especially when they had been dumped, but the way the jacket had fallen was all wrong.

McGregor ran his fingers over the seam and, sure enough, he felt something concealed inside. He pulled a pen from his pocket and slipped it between the stitches, which came away easily to reveal half a dozen gambling chips – blue and silver, each marked fifty guineas.

'A man for the tables,' he said, as he stared into what was left of Forgie's peaceful face. Nobody would conceal this kind of currency about their person if they weren't a hardened gambler. Items sewn into the seams of a person's clothes were intended for emergencies, but anyone who foresaw a need for gambling chips more than anything else had a very particular take on the essentials of life. Three hundred guineas was very high stakes.

'Oh dear,' he said. This kind of thing made a case more complicated. Gamblers didn't usually kill themselves when they were three hundred guineas up. Quite the reverse. 'Right,' McGregor said, 'let's get the body back to town and try to figure out what this bloke was up to.'

Chapter 15

All evil comes from a single cause:
man's inability to sit still in a room

The gates at CVA were closed. Mirabelle peered at the factory through the wrought-iron bars. She rattled them, but the lock held fast so, instead, she began to walk around the perimeter. From the cricket ground next door she could hear the soft thump and whack of a game under way. Now and then the patter of a crowd clapping floated across the spring air like some kind of natural phenomenon – birds flocking or water flowing downhill in a rush. It was sunny but there was a cold nip in the air – the promise of changeable weather. You could never trust it to hold, especially not in spring. It was game of the cricket club to start a match that would last several hours, but if you waited for the weather in England to be just right, you might wait a long time. Ahead of Mirabelle, two women carrying baskets piled with Tupperware wheeled round the corner giggling, and rushed towards the ground, checking their watches. Sandwiches and scones for half-time, she thought. Cricket was a game that involved tea – a sociable concern. She considered following the caterers. You never could tell where you might pick up information, but then she spotted something undeniably more promising. A side door in the factory wall was slightly ajar. She checked no one was watching and then she pushed it, but the door wouldn't budge any further. Then the smell assailed her. A rank whiff of rotting food and chemicals that came from the other side.

She lifted a handkerchief to cover her mouth and nose, and peered round the edge of the wood where she discovered several old bins stacked on top of each other. Sighing, her eye was drawn upwards to the small space above the door as she realised it was the only way in. Two empty beer crates lay a little further along the wall and she pulled them into place, then stepped up, fearless in high heels, and hauled herself over, coming down on the other side safely with the help of the stinking buckets on which she gingerly balanced as she made her way down.

The factory site was sizeable and, from what she could make out, this side of the building housed the canteen. Through the barred windows, she spotted a bank of tea urns and some large aluminium pots. Checking her heels were not smeared with dirt, she suppressed the urge to gag and moved off smartly into fresher air, to investigate. There must be somebody here, she thought. But the factory's long windows were dark as she rounded the building and the tarmac was deserted apart from two dusty vans parked near the main gates. Opposite them, she peered through a window and could clearly make out the factory floor and behind it a series of small offices. During the war, a place like this would have been blacked out, but these days you could see what it was making. Piles of mechanical parts were lying around. Oilcans were stacked in a row, ready for action when the workforce arrived on Monday morning. There was not a soul here now, though.

As Mirabelle rounded the last corner, a large Alsatian dog came bounding towards her from the other side of the compound. She froze and the animal came to an abrupt halt a couple of feet away, letting out a deep bark. Mirabelle's heart raced, but she held her ground. Somewhere, she'd read that was the thing to do. Hold your ground and show no fear. It seemed to work, or, at least, the dog stopped barking and cocked its head sideways, looking confused.

'Don't worry, miss,' a voice shouted. The dog looked around and barked again, this time at a small boy who was perched high on the brick wall on the other side of the courtyard. 'His name's Napoleon. He's hopeless.' The boy grinned. 'He won't hurt you. Honest.'

Mirabelle felt her ribcage lower. The dog wagged its tail. 'What are you doing up there?' she asked.

'I could ask you the same thing. It isn't trespass if you don't go over. You're the one that's inside, miss.'

The boy had a point.

'I'm hoping to find someone. A caretaker, maybe,' Mirabelle explained.

'Well, you found Napoleon. Not much of a guard but that's all there is. He'd lick you to death, wouldn't he?'

Mirabelle regarded the dog, which was now panting heavily. 'Hello, boy,' she said, trying not to sound nervous. 'Hello there,' she tried again, this time reaching out to pet him. As she sank her fingers into Napoleon's thick fur, the dog's tongue lolled with pleasure. 'You're right,' she said, as he whimpered, 'he's not much use, is he?' As she stood up, the dog fell in at her heel, which made her think of Bill Turpin, the third member of the McGuigan & McGuigan team, who had the knack of taming any animal. Maybe his influence had rubbed off on her.

'Sometimes kids throw stones at the poor fellow. Them dogs is German. But I think he's a good old boy and it isn't his fault, is it? I always bring him a biscuit. I throw it down first of all and he lets me sit here. Once, he tried to jump up but he can't reach me. He knows that now.'

'But what are you doing?' Mirabelle repeated, patting the animal absent-mindedly as she stared upwards. Little boys were often quite strange, in her experience, but the thrill of sitting on top of a brick wall must be limited and it appeared the boy did so regularly.

The child nodded vaguely over Mirabelle's head. 'Best view I could think of,' he said. 'They won't let you in. Not unless you're a member. Very toffee-nosed, they are at the cricket club. My dad says we come from the wrong side of the tracks.'

'You're watching the match?'

'I can see most of it from here. You won't tell them, will you?' The dog woofed forlornly and stared at the child's leg, clearly wishing he could reach it. 'I think he likes a bit of company,' the boy said with a smile. 'It's a mutual arrangement, isn't that what they call it?'

Mirabelle sighed. Napoleon was having a busy day between the interloper on the wall and the woman who had made it over the top of the stinking bins. 'And there's no one about? No one from the factory?'

The boy shook his head. 'Not till tomorrow. Six a.m. the first lot arrive. What are you after them for?'

'I'm trying to find out if there was a late order placed last night. If the factory was open for overtime?'

'Late order? What do you mean?'

'I want to see if work ran on all Saturday afternoon and evening.'

'There was nobody here yesterday. Not after lunch.'

'Are you sure?'

'I watched the juniors,' the boy said smartly.

'So what time did the place close?'

'Lunchtime as usual. Twelve noon on a Saturday, miss.'

'And you're sure there was no one inside? No one at all?'

'My dad works in the stockroom. I'm sure all right.'

'And you were sitting on this wall yesterday afternoon?'

'Yeah.'

'And you didn't see anyone?'

'The union wouldn't have it for one thing,' the boy pointed out.

'How did you get up there?' Mirabelle wondered out loud.

The boy grinned. 'My cousin gives me a lift. He's not interested in cricket.'

'And he'll help you down?'

'I can drop down myself. It's high, but you just dangle and then roll. Like a parachute soldier.'

'SAS?'

The child looked delighted. Mirabelle sighed. It seemed her only way out was back over the stinking bins. I should have looked up earlier, she thought.

The boy was momentarily distracted by something on the far side of the wall. 'That's a six,' he reported. Then he turned his attention back to Mirabelle. 'What did you think they were doing anyway? If the factory was open all night?'

'It's my friend's husband. He got home late and said he was working.'

The boy chortled. 'Got caught, did he?'

'I suppose he's been caught. Yes.'

The question was, caught at what? Napoleon woofed good-naturedly. Mirabelle wondered if the boy might be able to haul her up, but she judged him too small and she didn't want to topple him. 'Thanks,' she said. 'Enjoy the match.' The dog followed her back to the side door and whimpered as she disappeared over the top.

Back on the street, she walked quickly away from the rank air. The sound of the cricket proceeding felt soothing. Really, it occurred to her, the club should be encouraging a boy who was keen enough to spend his weekend perched precariously on twelve feet of bricks just to watch some amateurs whack a ball around. From her point of view, it was just as well he had. The match must have broken for half-time and voices raised in conversation floated in her direction. She walked away from them, back towards the railway. Billy Randall had lied. He had come home with money that he said was from a shift he couldn't possibly have worked. What had he got up to last night? she wondered. Where had the money come from and, more than that, why did he lie to his wife about it? The obvious thought was that he'd been out gambling, but most men would boast if they won, not keep it a secret.

Feeling a cold spit of rain on her skin, she could just make out the sound of groaning in the distance as the club's worthies picked up their tea and headed, no doubt, for shelter. Mirabelle hurried her pace. Walking often helped when she wanted to think things through. It occurred to her that this line of questioning might be a distraction from what she was supposed to be doing. The idea of looking into Helen Quinn and her background was at least as promising, but so often it was the small details that mattered when it came to figuring things out. The lies. The things that didn't fit. She couldn't just ignore the fact that the man who had found the body was behaving strangely.

Heading up Mill Lane, she cast a glance at the Randalls' house. Billy was sitting by the fire, asleep in his chair, exhausted after his night out. There was no sign of Vi. Reverting to her original plan, Mirabelle turned up the path of number fourteen and knocked on Mrs Ambrose's door, which opened rather quickly as if the old woman had spotted Mirabelle coming up the path. 'What are you doing back here?' Mrs Ambrose snapped.

'I came to find out more about Helen Quinn. I'm helping the police with their inquiries.'

Mrs Ambrose cast a low murmur in Mirabelle's direction and it occurred to her that the old woman was wondering why she hadn't been asked to help.

'I wondered if you knew anything else about the murdered woman?' she tried. 'Anything that hasn't been covered yet?'

'What do you mean?'

'Her maiden name? Or what she did before she was married? You know – her job.'

Mrs Ambrose flicked her hand dismissively in the direction of the murder scene. 'Mrs Quinn came here married. I don't know anything about her life before. You should ask Violet Randall. They were thick as thieves, those two. Like children.'

'You struck me as someone who was very observant, Mrs Ambrose. I wondered what you'd seen of Mrs Quinn during the months she lived here? What impression you had?'

'I'm a nosy old woman, you mean?' Mrs Ambrose didn't wait for a denial. 'Helen was no better than she should have been. Just a young woman with a taste for gin. We never had time for that in the old days. I mean, only on special occasions. But the Quinns liked a tipple, both of them. I expect he understood.'

'And they never fought? The Quinns, I mean?'

Mrs Ambrose crossed her arms over her ample chest. 'Everyone fights. You must know that, dearie, by your age.'

'Do you know what they fought about?'

'I'm not an eavesdropper. But she couldn't cook. Not at all. You could smell it burning all the way over here. Her mother can't have taught her anything. Many's the night he gave up and just got fish and chips.'

'Do you know where she came from?'

Mrs Ambrose snorted. 'Clothes like that? London.'

'And did her relations ever visit?'

'Not a one. Nor his neither for that matter. It was just the two of them.'

'I can't help wondering what she did. You know, before she got married?'

Mrs Ambrose shrugged. 'How would I know? She never said. A shop girl, I reckon.'

'What makes you think that?'

'Them clothes.' The woman's tone was insistent. 'You mark my words.'

Mirabelle took her leave. She found the idea of keeping a

house quite mystifying. She ran her flat, of course, but only barely. A marital home was different and it always fell to the woman. Vesta had been nervous about taking it on before she married Charlie, and Mirabelle hadn't understood entirely, but suddenly, here on Mill Lane, she realised how alone some of these women must feel. Girls got married and were flung together, meant to stay in the house whether they were good at domestic duties or not. They were judged on the state of their husband's shirts and their ability to turn out a home-cooked meal. No wonder they ended up hitting the gin.

She wandered around the block on to Dyke Road and cut through the gap between the houses into the Quinns' back garden, where she crouched close to the hedge, knowing she would be difficult to spot. A few gardens along, three little boys threw a clapped-out ball against an old wooden hut. On the back doorstep, a couple sipped mugs of tea and talked animatedly, watching the boys out of the corner of their eyes. Somewhere, someone was playing a piano, practising the same tune over and over – Hayden, Mirabelle thought, though they were mangling it. And, ahead, the Randalls' house was still and next door, inside the Quinns, it looked just as it had the night she'd broken in to recreate the murder. This is where they'd stood, all right, Mirabelle told herself, hunkering down. This was the spot exactly.

Chapter 16

All travel has its advantages

Mirabelle was stirred from her meditative state later that afternoon by Billy Randall entering his kitchen to cut a slice of bread and spread it thickly with butter. Vi had still not returned. He chewed and swallowed as he stood at the sink, filling his belly in a workmanlike fashion. Then he straightened his tie. There was something about the movement that made her realise he was readying himself to go out. Mirabelle got to her feet and sneaked back on to the street down the side of the Quinns' house. Mrs Ambrose's curtains twitched as she loitered by an apple tree covered in blossom so she raised her hand in a cheery greeting – she didn't want to be accused of sneaking around. The curtain fell back into place. Then, sure enough, Billy left the house and began to walk down the road. Mirabelle fell into step behind him, carefully keeping her distance. Tailing someone in the suburbs was tricky. The streets were quiet and strangers stood out. On the plus side, men's hats restricted their field of vision. Mirabelle hung back and watched Billy turn on to the main road. The Sunday service meant that buses were few and far between and he didn't loiter at the stop, instead striding towards town past the shuttered shops. The pavements felt too wide without the outdoor displays at the grocery and the florist. Billy checked his watch. He must be meeting someone.

Further towards town, the sun came out and he opened his coat. A car drove past, the first Mirabelle had seen on the road – two young children peered out of the back window, one with a smear of chocolate on her face. A family outing. Could Billy Randall have committed the murder? Could he? He was the one who'd found her body. He had been there that night – all night. Had he had an affair with Helen Quinn? It hardly seemed the kind of thing you'd get away with on Mill Lane, but people did fall in love. It happened all the time. And he was behaving erratically.

As she kept her distance, Mirabelle was so busy running through the possibilities that Billy Randall's destination took her by surprise as he cut into Brighton Railway Station by the side entrance, crossed the plaza, bought a ticket and headed for the London platform. There were regular trains to the capital, even on a Sunday. Today, there was a gaggle of women who had clearly enjoyed a day out by the seaside, early though it was for tourists. Two of them were holding prizes won at stalls on the pier – a toy bear and a jar of Brighton rock. Periodically, they hooted with laughter, almost like gulls. Billy Randall took a seat on a bench, checking his watch once more. It wasn't an appointment he was heading for, Mirabelle realised, it was a departure time. Billy was going up to town. The Randalls had moved down from London, she recalled. They had come to Vi's hometown to build what she'd called 'a new life'. Perhaps Billy hadn't given up his old one.

There was nothing for it. Mirabelle bought a ticket and, using the tourists as a screen, she stood further up the platform as the train chugged in.

Victoria Railway Station was busy when she stepped off at the other end, carefully keeping Billy in her sights. The smell of frying bacon emanated from the station café. Mirabelle felt her stomach growl but she ignored it. It was almost seven o'clock as Billy Randall passed underneath the huge station clock and she tailed him to the main road. He paused to light a cigarette and then crossed in the direction of Belgravia. It was always easier to blend in somehow in London. There were simply more people. Careful not to be noticed, Mirabelle followed Billy in the direction of Ebury Street where he disappeared through the doorway of a pub. Mirabelle bit her lip. She couldn't go in. If he recognised her she'd have wasted her time. On tiptoes, she peered over the frosted glass of the window, through a clear, thin strip that afforded a view. Randall ordered a half-pint of bitter and sipped it standing at the bar. There were no women inside and Mirabelle couldn't make out a snug. She laid a hand on the cool stucco as she took in the rest of the street. She wouldn't be able to stand here for long. A woman hanging around outside a public house was easily spotted. Vi Randall was right – following your husband into the pub was undignified and that's what people would assume she was doing. There was a small hotel over the road, its dining room overlooking the street, so she turned on her heel and went inside.

The place smelled pleasantly of toast. A solicitous waitress in black and white guided Mirabelle to a table by the window. 'I do so like being able to see people go by,' Mirabelle said lightly.

'On your own, madam?'

This phrase was a judgement and Mirabelle knew it. 'Yes,' she said, ordering a pot of tea and a pork chop. A man sitting at a table near the fireplace smiled weakly in her direction, but Mirabelle ignored him, keeping her eyes on the street. It had been a long time since breakfast and she was hungry. Maybe this was for the best, and, besides, if Billy Randall emerged, she could leave money to cover the bill. The waitress disappeared through a swing door to the clatter of crockery being assembled. Across the road, the pub seemed quiet. A man went in with a dog on a lead and another came out and turned on to Eccleston Street. As the sky darkened, the dim pub lights glowed through the opaque glass. When it was served, Mirabelle poured her tea and ate the pork chop. It was a meal best approached with a sense of purpose. The chop had the texture of felt and the vegetables were overboiled. Still, it was warm and it filled her up. She checked her watch as she finished.

'Pudding?' the waitress offered. 'There's spotted dick.'

Mirabelle considered. Heaven knows what culinary horror the hotel's cook might be able to unleash on raisins, flour and suet. 'There's custard,' the waitress added.

'Thank you. That was quite enough.'

The girl went to fetch the bill and Mirabelle kept her eye on the view. It was after half past seven now, nearer eight, and Belgravia was quiet, the chimney stacks smoking. Most residents would have spent the weekend in the country. Now and then, a car passed – latecomers returning to town in time for dinner. Mirabelle paid, leaving a small tip, and resumed her place outside by the strip of clear glass. Billy Randall had left his spot at the bar. She checked the few seats she could see to the side but he hadn't settled there. She waited. Perhaps he had gone to the lavatory. After five minutes there was still no sign. Mirabelle felt frustrated. This whole case was annoying, somehow – there were too many clues, they seemed to lead nowhere and she could imagine no motive to justify Helen Quinn's murder or Phil Quinn's incarceration. She checked once more on tiptoes, but there was no sign of Billy. Slowly, she took a deep breath and opened the bar door, aware that as she did so, the eyes of everyone inside fell upon her.

'No women,' the barman growled.

'I'm looking for someone. Billy Randall. He came in almost an hour ago. Brown coat? Aged about thirty? He ordered bitter.'

The barman leaned forwards. 'I don't know who you mean, love.'

'He was standing right there.' Mirabelle indicated the place she'd seen Billy leaning against the bar.

'Sorry, love. No women.'

Mirabelle ignored him. She walked towards the exit to the privy. 'Oi!' the barman objected. 'You can't go out there.'

Two men chortled as Mirabelle speeded up. 'She's a harridan all right,' someone said loudly and there was a murmur of agreement. But it didn't stop her. Outside, the privy door lay open and there was no sign of Billy Randall. Behind it, the back gate was closed. Mirabelle turned the handle. It opened on to a mews. She looked both ways. It was getting darker and the laneway was not well lit so it was difficult to make out what lay further along. As far as she could see, it was absolutely still. Mirabelle cursed silently – he must have left this way while she was just sitting there, eating that horrible meal. He could be anywhere by now. Had he seen her? she wondered. She'd been so careful. Burly, in an apron with a cloth tucked at the belt, the barman burst out of the back door. He was furious, ready for some kind of fight, with his sleeves rolled up. 'Look, love, you can't just steam out here. Your fellow's got a right to privacy. He won't appreciate . . .'

'Have you seen him before? Has he been here before?'

The barman shrugged. Even in the half-light his face looked flushed.

'Look,' Mirabelle explained, 'he's not my husband.'

'What then?'

'Police.'

The barman laughed. 'You're a copper? Come on, love.' He eyed her, lingering on her shoes. 'Special Branch is it?' he snorted. 'Set up a ladies' division, have they?'

Mirabelle kept her gaze steady. 'Has he been here before or not?'

The barman relented. You never could tell what women might get up to these days. 'He was in yesterday,' he said. 'I never saw him before that.'

'Same time?'

'More or less. It's none of your business.'

'Did he leave this way yesterday too?' The barman kept his mouth shut so Mirabelle repeated the question. 'Did he leave this way yesterday?'

The man relented once more. 'Yeah. Some fellows just like a bit of intrigue. He paid his tab all right. What do I care?'

Mirabelle considered. Billy was certainly being prudent. It was an old trick to use a bar or café that way. During the war they'd called this kind of place 'a portal'. Agents had navigated their routes entering by one door, leaving by another, building in routine dodges to guard against detection. She cursed herself for not watching closely enough. Now she'd never find out what on earth he was up to. At least, she figured, it was less likely Billy knew she'd followed him if he'd come in the front entrance and out the back one the day before. At least there was that. 'You go in and tell them you saw me off,' she said generously. 'Tell them it was a cheek and you threw me out on my ear.'

'Quite right. You can't come into a public house and disturb everyone.'

There was no point in fighting about it. 'All right,' she said.

The man blustered. 'Really,' he muttered but he went back inside.

The backyard fell silent and Mirabelle closed the gate behind her and stalked along the cobbles just as Billy must have done half an hour or more before. There was no point berating herself. He was long gone. A thousand agents had fallen for this old trick – she'd just be more careful next time. She checked her watch, recalling there was another lead she could follow up. It was Sunday night, after all, and she'd been invited to a party.

Chapter 17

Make the most of your regrets

As she arrived back in Brighton, Mirabelle checked the station clock and set out in the direction of the front. Ten minutes later, the ease with which she wandered into the Grand Hotel felt somehow taboo. She relaxed in the warmth – there was a stiff breeze off the ocean tonight. At the mahogany front desk, a woman wrapped in thick furs, far beyond what might be necessary for the spring weather, complained loudly in a foreign accent. To one side of her swaddled frame, two men hovered uncertainly and, on her other side, it seemed as if she had washed up on to a hilly beach of expensive luggage. 'It is your largest suite?' she berated the man on the desk. 'I only want it if it is the best.'

'Yes, madam,' he assured her.

Mirabelle smiled as she recognised the lady – the Russian countess who had been featured in Vesta's *Tatler*. Today she was wearing Chanel beneath her fox furs, but it wasn't making her happy. The woman turned to her companions, as if the clerk wasn't there. 'I hate staying in a public place. Eating in public. People seeing you go in and out. I wanted the house to be ready,' she whined.

Passing the empty seats and potted palms in the hallway, Mirabelle pitied the fellows who had to deal with this tricky customer. Most people who were featured in *Tatler* were probably difficult to handle, she thought, let alone a white Russian aristocrat who had recently returned from Monte Carlo.

'But, Marianna, it's five star,' she heard one of the men object.

A smile playing on her lips, Mirabelle left them to it. She made for the bar where, ensconced in a booth, Jinty was sipping a smart-looking cocktail with another girl, whose hair was tied up in a ponytail and secured with a diamanté clasp. In the corner opposite them, a thin young man wearing a badly tailored dinner jacket played a piano – the kind of music you might scarcely notice. As she approached, Mirabelle realised there was a cloud of expensive perfume around the girls. The booth smelled both feminine and exotic after the salty evening air. 'Belle.' Jinty smiled. 'I wasn't sure if you'd make it.'

'Sorry I'm late. I wanted to catch up,' Mirabelle said, raising a finger to call the waiter and indicate she'd have another round of whatever the girls were drinking.

'This is Lisa. She's new.' Jinty introduced her friend, whose high cheekbones looked as if they could slice paper. Between the cheekbones and the jaunty ponytail, Mirabelle found herself imagining the execution of some kind of circus trick. 'Belle is considering joining us,' Jinty said. 'You are still considering it, aren't you?'

'I don't know if it's for me,' Mirabelle admitted, sliding into the seat. 'What made you think of it, Lisa? As a career?'

Lisa shrugged. When she spoke her accent was, in contrast to her looks, rather homely. She was from Yorkshire, Mirabelle guessed. 'How else is a girl to make a living?' she said, sounding out of place in the lush surroundings. The truth was, girls like Lisa were generally serving the drinks, but then, that rather made her point.

'Did you work like this before? Up north, I mean?'

'I like to move round,' she said enigmatically.

'Regulars.' Jinty settled into her seat. 'They can be a pain. After a while it's easier to ship out.'

Lisa nodded. 'They get obsessed, some of them.'

'It can happen to anybody,' Jinty cut in.

'Who's your best regular?' Mirabelle asked, going fishing. 'I mean, one you like most?'

'That would be telling. You make me think you fancy the thrill, Belle. You make me think that you are still considering.'

The waiter arrived with the drinks on a chrome tray. The glasses were frosted, their contents cloudy with lemon juice. The women fell silent. Jinty pushed an empty glass away and the waiter lingered, wiping the table unnecessarily. The girl sighed and stared pointedly at him till he walked away.

'Considering? Yes, that's why I asked.' Mirabelle smiled, resuming the conversation seamlessly. She sipped her drink. It was perfect. 'I wonder about the men,' she said. 'That's why I asked. I mean, do you prefer the private clients – the more upmarket ones? Or do you like the regular, local boys? It must be very different in Brighton during the summer. There are so many tourists once the season starts. You must see all sorts.'

'Well, you can't be choosy,' Jinty said. 'But I feel safe with doctors. They're usually adventurous. They have nice hands. Come to that, I like policemen because they know the score.'

'Policemen?' Mirabelle hadn't thought of it. 'You mean bobbies? Brighton bobbies?' The idea of Bill Turpin, as he had been, or Sergeant Belton, for that matter, visiting Ernie Davidson's house in Tongdean – the notion shocked her. It felt too close to home.

'Oh, they can't afford . . . the guys on the beat must make other arrangements. There are plenty of girls who work out of flats off Old Steine.' Jinty wrinkled her nose. 'But some of the detectives. Higher up. Police pay isn't bad, you know. Tommy Robinson drops into Tongdean. He's a dish and, believe you me, they aren't all oil paintings. He took me to London once, out on the town.'

'Inspector Robinson?'

'Do you know him? He's a nice bloke. You'd think more

of them would get married, but it's the job, isn't it? A call girl and a copper – it's a good combination. We've seen it all, between us.'

This was unexpected. Things seemed to be running away with Mirabelle today. The idea of Phil Quinn being one of Jinty's customers was just part of the case, but if Robinson was a customer, well, she couldn't help wondering who else might visit Tongdean Avenue. Her fingertips tingled. She ran one down the cool cocktail glass, following its curve as her heart pounded. She couldn't stop herself asking, though she tried to sound nonchalant. 'I met someone who worked with Inspector Robinson. A Scottish guy. Greying hair and grey eyes. On the tall side.'

'Always wears a blue woollen scarf? Light blue. Unusual.'

Mirabelle's heart jumped. She'd given McGregor that scarf a couple of years ago at Christmas. She'd picked it out at Hanningtons.

'His name's McGregor,' Jinty hooted.

Mirabelle set her jaw, determined not to show the horror that was creeping over her. 'Yes. I think that's him.' She tried to sound unsure, light, as if it didn't matter.

'He's been to the house a few times. He's a bit older but dishy. He pops in for a whisky and a chat with Davidson about whatever he's investigating. I don't know what they talk about – policemen can use us, can't they? Superintendent McGregor, he is, I think.'

'And has he stayed? I mean . . .'

'He's a straight kind of guy. Though sometimes those are the ones, aren't they? With the irregular requests.'

Lisa nodded, as if Jinty had said something profound. Mirabelle felt her chest constrict. Suddenly, she found it difficult to breath.

'So he's a customer?' It occurred to her she must be blushing and there was nothing she could do about it.

'Not one of mine. I don't know what the superintendent gets up to. Ernie can be very discreet. McGregor's probably got some boring Scottish wife at home. Calvinists, aren't they, the Jocks? I'd say he might be married. He has that look. He only ever sees Irene, I think.'

Lisa rolled her eyes.

'Irene?' Mirabelle enquired, deciding the bar was too warm.

'She's the baby of the house. Little Rene,' Jinty continued. 'Eighteen years old and never been kissed. Blonde like a little angel. If I were betting, I'd have reckoned you were more McGregor's type, Belle.' She smiled. 'You'd bring him out of himself. But maybe that's not what he wants.'

Mirabelle shrugged off the comment. Her jaw was tight. She told herself it was important to keep going, though there was a quivering fury alight in her belly. It was an effort to drag her attention back to the case. 'McGregor is a friend of Phil Quinn's,' she said. 'You know, the man accused of murdering his wife.'

'Oh not that again.' Jinty pulled a cigarette out of the pack in front of her. 'Anyone would think you were Phil Quinn's mother. Oh God, you aren't, are you? His mother, I mean?'

Mirabelle shook her head. It interested her that that kind of connection had occurred to Jinty, while the real connection, the one that mattered, had clearly passed her by. 'I'm not quite that old,' she said lightly. 'I don't have any children. I just think it's a mystery.'

'Oh yes. The man who killed his wife.' Lisa leaned in, taking an interest.

Mirabelle nodded. 'He was one of Jinty's customers. Before he got married. Did you know him?'

'Not him. Just her.'

Mirabelle stopped. There it was. At last. A connection to Helen Quinn. And just in time to take her attention away from McGregor's indiscretion. 'You knew her?' she asked.

'Only in passing. I like to swim. She was a swimmer too.'

'In Brighton?'

'Hold your horses. I only got here on Friday. In London. I recognised her in the newspaper – the picture when she died. That's where she went, I thought. To Brighton. To marry a man who killed her.' Lisa's tone implied that any man you married might kill you, that it was only to be expected.

'So you knew Helen Quinn from London?' Mirabelle pushed.

'Yeah. From the pool in Chelsea.'

Mirabelle sipped her cocktail – she needed refreshment. The conversation had been more of a roller coaster than she had anticipated. It looked as if Lisa had operated in a mixed area of town on the fringes of Belgravia. 'Did she live round there, do you know?' Mirabelle enquired.

'I don't think so. She worked in one of the shops along the King's Road. A clothes shop, I think. She always had a bag from there – what was it called? A bloke's name? Anyway, she'd go for a swim after work and I like to swim before.' Lisa had a gleam in her eye. 'I like to be clean.' She spelled it out. 'At the start, anyway.'

'Did you speak to her?'

'Only once or twice. "Nice day", that kind of thing. Very English. "Sorry" in the showers. Then one day she didn't turn up. I didn't think anything of it. I suppose she met the fellow – the one who killed her. Love's young dream.'

'Belle doesn't think he did it.' Jinty's tone was dismissive, as if Mirabelle was a child, ignorant in the ways of the world.

'It doesn't make any sense, that's why,' Mirabelle objected. 'I mean, if Phil Quinn meant to get away with his wife's murder, the way he killed her, well, it was a terrible plan. And besides, he seems to have loved her.'

'Oh those are the ones.' Lisa wagged a finger. 'Those are the worst ones.'

'So you worked in Chelsea?'

'Mostly. Kensington too. I had enough, though. Solicitors. Accountants. Weirdos. Brighton is a fresh start. I'm a history buff. I went to see the Pavilion and the Pier yesterday. Next week I'm going to Mrs Fitzherbert's house.'

'It's a hostel now,' Jinty laughed. 'The most famous whore in Brighton and her house is a hostel. YMCA.'

'Fresh start,' Mirabelle repeated. The Randalls had hoped for that in Brighton too.

'Yes. Fresh,' Lisa confirmed.

'And you don't think London will follow you? It's not so far away.'

Lisa shrugged. 'I'll let Ernie deal with that,' she said without spelling out whatever it was. 'Meantime, who knows? Maybe I'll swim in the sea here, come the summer.'

'I went to a new club the other evening.' Mirabelle decided to share.

'Did a fellow take you?' Jinty leaned in, curious about what Mirabelle got up to between their meetings.

Mirabelle didn't answer. The thought of McGregor laying his arm on her shoulder was uncomfortable now. She tried not to think about what they had done back at his place afterwards. 'It's new, just off Queen's Road. Quite cosmopolitan. If you're ever missing Mayfair, Lisa . . .'

Lisa grinned. 'We'll see how much I miss it. Not so far.'

Jinty regarded Mirabelle with fresh eyes. 'I've never heard of anywhere like that off Queen's Road,' she said, surprised that such a thing could happen – a woman in her forties who knew about a smart new bar that had eluded her.

'You should try it,' Mirabelle enthused. 'I think they have a singer some evenings. We called it the Boite – as in the French – but it doesn't have a name.'

'A bar without a name,' Jinty said. 'I like that. It's Soho, but smarter.'

Later, the girls called a car to take them home. They hovered in the hallway, waiting. Mirabelle felt the front desk seemed rather deserted without the Countess Marianna Iritsin and her luggage. For a slim lady she had filled a very large space. The desk clerk was filling in a ledger in what now seemed like a tremendously peaceful moment, the countess presumably dispatched to the best suite on his books.

'Do you want a lift? The driver won't mind a detour,' Jinty offered, but Mirabelle elected to walk. She didn't want the girls knowing where she lived and, quite apart from that, she needed to clear her head.

'I'm fine,' she said crisply. 'I'll make my own way.'

'Car, ladies?' The doorman came to fetch them.

'Thanks, Bob,' Jinty said, taking Lisa by the arm.

Mirabelle followed the girls outside and watched as the car whisked them away. She felt a kind of fondness for Jinty and her worldly wise. Some women, she knew, would blame these women for their lovers' indiscretions, but she knew better. It was down to the men. She remembered the offers she'd received in the suite down the coast. The possibilities had confirmed that it was McGregor she really wanted. Had he been sneaking off to Tongdean all this time? It didn't bear thinking about.

'Madam?' Bob enquired.

'I'm fine,' Mirabelle assured him.

On the front, instead of turning towards the Lawns she took the long way round. The bars were closing and, as she passed the Boite, she realised that the door to the stair was closed. Perhaps things were even slower on Sunday nights than they had been on Saturday. Everything seemed closed or in the process of closing. People needed a night off, she told herself. Taking the hill briskly, she thought Mrs Ambrose had got Helen Quinn spot on – she was a shop girl from London just as the wise old bird had said. Then she found herself wondering about poor Vi Randall, her husband out for the second night in a row. She hoped this time the poor woman wouldn't be too frantic – after all, by now, she must have returned from her mother's house and, after a sleepless night and in her condition, she would be exhausted. Then, Mirabelle realised, quite suddenly, that she was tired herself. She wondered if she'd manage to get any sleep, with all this battering back and forth inside her brain. Vi and Helen and their men. McGregor in conversation with Ernie Davidson, picking up some little blonde. Someone younger. Someone more compliant. Jinty didn't know, she told herself. She couldn't be sure. She mustn't jump to conclusions. But still, the vision of McGregor removing his tie while the youngest girl in the brothel sat on the edge of her bed, wouldn't go away. Shaking her head, she took a deep breath of sea air and speeded up. At this pace, home was only fifteen minutes off. And tomorrow she knew what she had to do.

Chapter 18

No one ever became wicked suddenly

Davidson welcomed McGregor enthusiastically as the old maid showed him into the study. It was late, but that wasn't unusual – the superintendent popped in at all hours. Tonight, the house at Tongdean was quiet. The girls tended to go out on Sunday evenings. Davidson closed the ledger in which he had been writing and turned to the drinks cabinet.

'I have a couple of nice malts,' he said, pleasantly. 'I expect you could do with one.'

McGregor took a seat. 'Thanks. It's been a long day.'

Davidson poured two generous measures and topped them with a splash of soda.

'It's an investigation.' McGregor took his first sip and let a sigh emanate from his lips.

'I don't expect to see you any other time – though you're welcome, of course. Unless you've come to book me, that is?' Davidson's tone was jocular, but he knew that if he wanted to the superintendent could.

'You know our policy, Ernie,' McGregor reassured him. 'The girls are safer here than they would be on the street. And besides, you're cooperative.'

'How can I cooperate this evening?'

McGregor pulled out the gambling chips he'd found in Flight Lieutenant Forgie's jacket. 'I wondered if there was a new game in town? High stakes?'

Ernie paused.

'You don't run to fifty guinea chips here, do you?'

'A little poker now and then . . .'

'Which is illegal if you're playing house.'

'Just a few friends,' Davidson said vaguely.

McGregor allowed him. There was no point pursuing that. There were larger fish to fry. 'I wondered if one of your friends was an RAF officer. Highly decorated. Quite the war hero. He wintered in Monaco this year. Likes to gamble. Early forties. Small moustache. Name of George Forgie.'

'Georgie Porgie?'

'He's dead,' McGregor said flatly. 'It's not a casual enquiry.'

Ernie Davidson raised his hands in surrender. 'He's not one of mine. And, for the record, fifty guinea stakes is too rich for my blood and, I imagine, for the blood of my friends. My table stops well short of that.'

McGregor sipped again. Davidson denying knowledge didn't mean anything. Criminals always said they didn't know. They had never done it, whatever it was.

'Would you like me to fetch Irene?' Davidson asked.

McGregor smiled. If Davidson was trying to distract him from the inquiry, it meant he was on to something. 'Not tonight. It's not a murder inquiry, Ernie. The poor bloke topped himself. But I do need what you know about him.'

Davidson was visibly relieved. He relented. 'He's a gambler,' he said.

'Evidently.'

'He's a well-known gambler. A good one. I've heard of him is all. High stakes like you said, but with a little—' here he gesticulated '—madness, I suppose. I heard he flew over a hundred missions during the war. No one expected him to survive. It left him with . . . ideas about risk. I heard he'd gamble on anything.'

'Anything?'

'Cards. Backgammon. Horses. But aside from that. Crazy

bets. Drunken bets. I don't know exactly. Who can hold their hand over a flame longest? You know how guys get sometimes.' His laugh did not sound convincing.

'Are you sure Forgie didn't play cards here?'

Ernie shook his head. 'We don't get famous gamblers. We don't get famous anybody. It's all solicitors. Accountants. Local dignitaries. Business people. But not the big time. This house is safe, Superintendent. Steady. That's what you like about it, isn't it? If you want to find the table George Forgie was sitting at, you need to go upmarket.' He pointed upwards, as if indicating some kind of deity. 'I wish I had that business, but I don't.'

'And in Brighton?'

'There's nothing like that. But I'll keep my ear to the ground.'

'If you turn up anything . . .' McGregor finished his drink. His eyes were dry and tired. 'Someone moved his body,' he said. 'Wherever he died, someone didn't want him found there.'

Davidson nodded as if he understood. 'I'll see what I can do,' he said. Though he didn't add that the kind of people who ran the sort of game George Forgie took part in were not the kind of people you shopped to the police.

Chapter 19

Silence is one of the great arts of conversation

Mirabelle had her key in her hand, ready to open the door to McGuigan & McGuigan Debt Recovery at half past eight the next morning, when she realised that Vesta was already inside the office. The sound of someone typing with great efficiency assailed her from halfway up the stairs. As she opened the door, the girl looked up.

'You didn't tell him yet, did you?' Mirabelle sighed.

Vesta's eyes flashed. 'I will,' she said. 'He must think I'm half mad. I keep starting, but I can't get it out.'

Mirabelle removed her jacket.

'What are you doing here this early? Is there something on your mind?' Vesta asked in a bid to change the subject.

'I was going to leave a note on your desk. I'm going to London,' Mirabelle said, deciding to hold back the salient details from the night before about Superintendent McGregor's indiscretion. It wasn't relevant. 'I wondered if you'd mind looking into something while I'm away?'

'Sure.' Vesta had her notepad poised.

'I suspect Billy Randall is lying to his wife. I don't know what he's lying about exactly, but he's up to something.'

'Oh no. And Vi's expecting too. The snake.'

Mirabelle wondered momentarily what Vesta might call McGregor. Then she hauled her attention back to the case. 'I want you to ring Mr Randall's employer and look into his hours. He works at the CVA factory. Near the cricket ground.

You'll have to say you're from an insurance company making life insurance checks or something. See what you can turn up.'

Vesta nodded and wrote 'Prudential Life Insurance' on the first sheet of her spiral-bound pad. People disclosed the most extraordinary amount of information over the telephone if they believed you were filling out a form. The women had remarked on this on several occasions.

'And what will you be doing?'

Mirabelle again restrained herself from replying that she would be wondering about McGregor's sexual integrity. 'I'm going to find out more about Helen Quinn,' she said very definitely. 'So far I haven't managed to discover her maiden name. But yesterday I turned up a lead that she used to work in a clothes shop on the King's Road.'

Vesta nodded slowly. 'So she must have left there about a year ago.'

'It seems that way. I'm curious about where she came from. She's the one who was murdered, after all. We know all about Phil Quinn, but Helen – well.'

'Just gin and cards.'

'And clothes,' Mirabelle said. 'And she's the victim, poor girl. I think she deserves more attention. Vesta, maybe you should write to Charlie. I mean, if it's too difficult to say about the baby . . .'

Vesta's raised her eyes to the ceiling. 'I just feel so ashamed,' she said, trying to control her emotions. Over the weekend she had burst into tears twice, out of the blue.

'Ashamed of what, dear?'

'It's so uncomfortable. If I tell Charlie then I'll have to tell everyone. And they'll all know that we . . . you know.'

Mirabelle leaned forward. She tried not to laugh. 'You're married,' she said. 'It's not as if you're in the position of having an illegitimate baby. Having babies is what married women are supposed to do.'

'Well, it's embarrassing. And my mother will be delighted.' Vesta made this sound ominous. 'Everyone will start expecting things. To be some kind of perfect mother. To stay, you know, at home. I let them down about that when I married Charlie and now this will bring it all up again.'

'Charlie didn't feel you'd let him down. I think you should trust him.'

Vesta let out a heartfelt sigh. 'I can't face it.'

Mirabelle shook her head, but she understood Vesta's fear of bringing things into the open. She had considered visiting the Arundel on her way to the office this morning, but telling McGregor what was on her mind, or worse, having to actually ask him about his visits to Tongdean Avenue didn't bear thinking about. Still, for Vesta it should be different. The baby, after all, was a good thing. 'I wouldn't worry about other people,' she said sagely. 'I don't expect you to stay at home if you don't want to. Actually, I hope you don't. We need you round here.' She got up. 'The thing is, it's going to become apparent. You're better choosing your time than having Charlie notice. He will eventually.'

'You're right.' Vesta fiddled with her pencil. 'I know you're right.'

Mirabelle dusted down her coat. 'Well then,' she said.

It was sunny in London – one of those bright-skied, spring days that lodge in the memory. Mirabelle was glad to be out of town. Briefly distracted by the newspapers on the stand at the station, she ignored the headline in the *Argus* in which McGregor appealed for information about the suicide case. Then she picked up and put down the *Telegraph* in which several society figures said they would miss George Forgie and that World War II could not have been won without him. She noticed Countess Marianna Iritsin had given a sorrowful comment on his abilities and said the world was a poorer place. Her eyes flickered back towards the *Argus* headline. What was it McGregor wanted to know? she wondered. What information was the superintendent fishing for? She realised the very mention of his name left her suspicious and she berated herself for that. There was a job to do that was more important than the way she felt.

At Victoria, she caught the tube to Sloane Square and started searching for vestiges of Helen Quinn at the top of the King's Road. She liked Chelsea – she and Jack had lived here in a run-down flat that he'd rented on one of the backstreets. Not too smart, not too shabby, he'd always said. The two of them had used these shops – Mirabelle had bought light bulbs at the hardware store and had taken advice from the butcher on how to spend her coupons, though the truth was that mostly she and Jack had eaten in the staff canteen.

It occurred to her that she'd discovered a lot about Jack when she had visited Paris a couple of years before. And nothing she had discovered had stopped her loving him. Still, with McGregor these revelations felt different. Jinty's words kept popping into her mind. What does it matter, she scolded herself, if he has or he hasn't. It might well have been before they were attached, after all. But it did matter. It was about what kind of man he was. Only the other day, she'd turned down the opportunity to be unfaithful herself. If McGregor acted differently when the chance came his way, that meant something.

Passing the grocery on the corner, Mirabelle turned her attention back to the case as if she was dragging a naughty puppy away from a bone. In this part of town, the first time she'd investigated anything at McGuigan & McGuigan, she'd broken into a flat on Cadogan Gardens and then a nightclub on one of the mews. It was comfortingly familiar somehow to be back and, it occurred to her, Helen Quinn had known these streets too. That felt like some kind of link. Had they both frequented the same bakery and walked in the same park? Different women at different times, living in the same place. It was something.

Keeping to the left-hand side of the road, she began methodically to check the shops. Several maids were out with their shopping baskets over their arms, dipping in and out of different establishments. The smell of the bakery sallied pleasingly towards her. The scones had been particularly delicious in the old days. Mirabelle wondered if they still made them. Then she spotted the clothes shop. Oh yes, she thought. She had forgotten it was there – just on the arcade. Two dummies placed in the window sported wide cotton skirts for summer and silk blouses held in place by patent leather belts that fastened at the base of the spine. At the front of the display there was a tidily constructed pile of cotton and silk scarves – an array of colour that stretched around the corner. It hadn't looked like this during the war. Mirabelle couldn't see herself wearing any of these clothes. The display might appeal to someone more frivolous.

Abandoning all thought of the scones, she opened the door. Behind the counter, a woman was folding a mauve woollen cardigan. She looked up.

'Good morning, madam. Can I help you?'

Mirabelle smiled. 'I'm looking for someone who used to work here. Her name was Helen.'

The woman's eyes flickered. 'Oh dear,' she said. 'I'm afraid Helen is dead. She died, you see,' she added unnecessarily.

'That's why I've come. I'm looking for information. I'm from Brighton. I work with the police.'

The woman's hands fluttered and a piece of white tissue paper sailed to the floor. As she bent to pick it up, the paper crinkled between her fingers. 'Oh dear,' she repeated. 'The police.'

'I wondered if you might be able to help. We don't know a lot about Mrs Quinn's life before she moved to the coast, not even her maiden name. That's why I've come, you see. To fill in the details. Do you have any idea of the name she used when she worked here?'

'Well, you'd find that on her wedding certificate, I expect.'

'Yes. But I'm looking for more than that. It's been difficult to find people who knew her, you see. So, do you know Helen Quinn's maiden name?

The woman looked serious. 'Lindley,' she trotted out. 'She was Helen Lindley.'

'Thank you. And did she live nearby?'

'Further down, near the river. She used to get the bus.'

'I was told she was an orphan.'

'If you can call a grown woman an orphan. I'm an orphan too then.'

'I mean, did she have any family? I heard there was an uncle who came to her wedding.'

'I never met an uncle, but she only worked here. We weren't bosom buddies. She rented a room from an old bloke. He took an interest, I think. He let her pay her rent late. Maybe it was him who came. They were quite pally.'

'Do you know his name?'

'No. I'm not saying there was anything untoward, either. She was fond of him, that's all.'

'Did Helen have any brothers or sisters?'

'She never said.'

Mirabelle sighed. It felt like wading through mud. Helen Lindley seemed as elusive before she married Phil Quinn as she was afterwards. 'I wondered if you could think of any reason someone would have wanted to hurt Helen? It seems such a senseless crime. It's been difficult to get a handle to.'

'It was the husband, I heard. That's what it said in the paper.'

'Did she talk about him? I mean when she met him?'

'Phil, wasn't it? Yes.' The woman chuckled. 'She wouldn't shut up about him.'

'Did she seem afraid?'

The woman laughed. 'She was thrilled. Prince Charming, he was. Sent a car for her at the station when she went down. And look what goes and happens.'

'We're not sure it was Mr Quinn, that's the thing. As I say, we couldn't find out much about her life before she married. I wondered if you know anything about her that might have spelled trouble? Anything that might have followed her down to Brighton?'

'Trouble? I mean, Helen wasn't a goody-goody, don't get me wrong. She liked a drink. But she was reliable. Just normal, really. They wouldn't have kept her on here if she was trouble.'

Mirabelle bit her lip. All the people involved in this crime seemed too normal. That was the problem. They were all getting on with their lives and then this happened. But violent murders never came out of the blue.

'And boyfriends?' she pushed. 'Did she ever have a connection to a man who might have been part of a gang?'

'Helen?' The woman looked horrified. 'Look, she went dancing. She liked a laugh and she was popular. I mean, there were plenty of young men who wanted to take her out. But she wasn't a gangster's moll, if that's what you're trying to say. I wouldn't even say she was fast. She went down to Brighton cos she preferred it – sleepy by the seaside, she said. She was looking for someone who was just the opposite of what you're suggesting. Well, that didn't work out, did it? But she could have had something more exciting if she'd wanted. Teddy boys, they call them. Rockers? But that wasn't her bag. She might not have been my best pal, but I won't have you saying things about her. Helen was a decent sort.'

'That's the thing. It's just a mystery,' Mirabelle cut in. 'I don't understand.'

'You think you can understand murder? I'm sorry.' The

woman was getting into her stride. 'There's no possible reason for something like that. And it's slander to say so. I'm surprised, you being with the police. You should know better than to cast aspersions on an innocent girl who got killed.'

'We have to ask.'

'Yes, well.' The woman laid her palm on the mauve cardigan as if she needed to steady herself. 'You shouldn't speak ill of the dead.'

The door opened and a cheery boy walked in, struggling with a large brown cardboard box. 'Delivery, Ida,' he announced.

'Pop it down there,' the woman instructed, indicating a space beside the counter.

'Morning, miss.' The boy somehow managed to tip his cap in Mirabelle's direction.

Mirabelle nodded at Ida. 'I'll go,' she announced. 'You said Helen lived near the river?'

'Yes. Luna Street. Like the moon,' Ida said. 'Number nine.'

Mirabelle walked down King's Road past the World's End pub and on towards Cremorne Gardens. When she'd lived in Chelsea with Jack, they'd directed their lives towards the Sloane Square end of the street, hardly ever turning in this direction when they got to the main road. The further she continued, the more dilapidated the buildings became and the more unfamiliar it felt. The brick Victorian and Edwardian apartment blocks sporting geometric facades disappeared, the artists' mews trailed away and gradually Georgian houses, perhaps three storeys high, took their place. The railings that survived wartime requisitioning were rusted and the roofs ramshackle. Paint peeled from the windows and flaked over the sills. Helen Quinn had brushed up well, but where she'd come from was more or less a slum. A musty smell of rotting wood and ineffective plumbing seeped over the pavement.

Looking up, several of the windows were missing and here and there a greying net curtain billowed through the gaps. Mirabelle asked a policeman for directions to Luna Street and he told her where to turn off the main road. As she did so, she noticed a group of three young girls, no more than ten years of age, giggling on the doorstep of the house next door to number nine. One of them clutched a grubby doll, moving it on to her shoulder to rub its back. 'Come on, Isabel,' she said. 'Let's have a burp, shall we?' The other two girls collapsed in giggles against the door frame, only managing to pull themselves together as Mirabelle's elegant outline came into view.

Mirabelle smiled kindly and knocked on the door to number nine. 'It's open, miss,' the girl with the doll said. 'No one locks their doors round here.'

'Thanks.' Mirabelle waited. No one seemed to lock their doors anywhere – that was the trouble. She shifted her weight. The youngster moved her doll to the other shoulder. 'Here,' she said. 'I'll get him.'

She marched round the railings, opened the door and wandered into the thin, dark hallway, which stretched ahead. 'Ed,' she shouted.

'Yeah,' came a low voice.

'It's a lady.'

'Tell her I ain't got no rooms,' the voice instructed.

The little girl looked at Mirabelle and motioned with her hand to relay the information.

'I'm not looking for a room.' Mirabelle was beginning to feel out of her depth.

'She's not looking for a room,' the little girl called.

'Well, what does she want?'

The girl's clear blue eyes turned back.

'Oh for heaven's sake,' Mirabelle said. 'I've come about Helen Lindley,' she called. 'I want to ask you some questions.'

There was the sound of a chair scraping across a wooden floorboard and then a man appeared at the other end of the hall. 'What?' he said. It was more a grunt than a word.

Mirabelle took in his appearance. He was, if anything, shabbier than the house. His greying hair was slicked back, but his shirt, though open at the neck, was pristine. He looked as if he might have been a boxer when he was younger. There was something about the way he held himself. One of his eyes was veiled by a cataract.

'Helen Lindley,' Mirabelle repeated. 'I came to ask some questions.'

In the gloomy hallway, she only just made out a tear leak from the man's bad eye and trickle down his pockmarked cheek. 'Come in,' he said. 'Shoo, Sally.' He motioned the little girl away. Sally turned reluctantly, peering at Mirabelle as she passed, as if her high heels were some kind of wonder. She didn't take her gaze off them till she rejoined the group back on the doorstep. The man took a handkerchief from his pocket and dabbed the tear away.

'Close the door,' he said.

Mirabelle did so, immediately rendering the hallway so dark it took a moment for her vision to adjust. 'I come from Brighton. I'm looking into what happened. It's not official.' She didn't want to alarm the old man by mentioning the police. 'I'm Mirabelle Bevan.'

'I can make you a cuppa.' He turned away before she could answer. 'Come on.'

The back room was some kind of kitchen, although the range was probably a hundred years old and showing signs of rust. A battered brass scuttle sat half empty beside it. 'Ed Hodge.' The man introduced himself, as he filled the kettle. The room contained only one chair – a filthy wing-backed armchair, which was positioned next to the stove. Apart from that it was empty – in a poor state even for a slum.

182

Mirabelle had had to collect money from far nicer addresses.

'Did Helen live here, Mr Hodge?' she asked, as she cast her eyes around. The walls were streaked with smoke from the fire. The ceiling was yellow with decades of tobacco. The windows were grey with soot. Behind Ed Hodge there was a single shelf that contained a packet of tea and some milk, a solitary onion and a tin of Bird's custard.

'Helen lived upstairs. First floor. Nothing fancy,' he said.

'Were you related to her?'

The man smiled, revealing several black teeth, a few yellow ones and some gaps. 'I wish,' he said.

'I wondered if you'd attended her wedding?'

'She wanted someone from her side. Lovely it was. A nice little pub with a room upstairs. She did well, did Helen.'

'And did you keep in touch?'

'No. She had a different life, didn't she? Nice new husband. Nice new house. I understood.'

Mirabelle thought about the Quinns' house on Mill Lane with its new furniture and freshly painted walls. It was a million miles from this. The old man shrugged his shoulders as if he understood what Mirabelle was thinking. 'And why shouldn't she get on in life?'

'She'd had it hard then?'

'She was on her own by the time she came here. Lots of girls would have jumped on the first fella who offered, but not Helen. She had dignity. There were those who thought she liked the bloke she married cos he could give her everything, but she wasn't like that. Don't get me wrong. She enjoyed the house and she already had clothes. She could appreciate a nice set of threads, could Helen. But the thing was, she loved him. Phil, wasn't it?'

'They've charged Phil Quinn with the murder.'

Ed Hodge shook his head. 'That bloke served his country. He was stand up. I don't believe it.'

Mirabelle considered sitting down on the chair but decided against it. 'I don't believe it either,' she said. 'That's why I'm here. I'm trying to figure out what happened. Mr Hodge, was there anything you can think of, anyone unpleasant Helen knew from her time in London? Anything that might have led to what happened?'

'There's men round here who'd gut you.' The old man's tone was businesslike, as he poured water from the kettle into a badly chipped teapot and set it aside to brew. 'Plenty of them. But they wouldn't kill a woman who wasn't their wife. Helen kept herself to herself the whole time she lived here. I was the only one she ever really talked to.'

He looked around for a cup, his face showing a certain amount of confusion. Mirabelle was unsure if he just didn't know where the cup might be or if he had truly not considered who might have murdered his friend. 'What happened sounded bad,' he said, almost under his breath.

'The murder?'

He nodded, rinsing the cup in the sink.

'Did you read about it in the paper?'

Ed Hodge shook his head. 'I can't read. One of the neighbours told me. One of the women popped in to let me know.'

'Did they know Helen then?'

'A little. She went to the laundry down the road. She met some of them there. She was good with clothes. She knew what to do with a stain. I miss her. I know that's stupid. I haven't seen her in a year. But still, knowing she isn't in the world . . .' His voice tailed off and the tear reappeared in the corner of his blind eye. 'Do you know what happened, Miss Bevan?'

Mirabelle didn't want to describe it, but the old man's cloudy gaze was impossible to dodge and she wasn't going to lie. 'I'm sorry. Helen's death was especially violent. She was drugged. She was stabbed. We don't know who did it. Didn't the neighbour tell you the details?'

Ed shook his head. 'Just Brighton they said?'

'Yes. In Brighton. At home. In her sleep.'

Deciding the tea had had its chance to brew, the old man poured some into the cup and held it out. 'Horror show, innit?' he said.

Mirabelle took the cup and sipped. She'd heard somewhere that tea was mildly antiseptic. She hoped so. Despite the old man's efforts, the cup definitely wasn't clean. 'Yes,' she said, 'I suppose it was.'

Outside the window, the three little girls ran past in a jumble of pigtails. This was where Helen had come from and Mirabelle could see how it could feel like home. Still, no wonder Helen Quinn coped with everything life threw her way at Mill Lane. After Luna Street, anything would seem easy. 'She made a friend down there,' Mirabelle said. 'I don't want you to think she was unhappy or that she was alone. She made a friend right next door.'

Ed Hodge nodded. 'That's good,' he said. 'I suppose that's all right.'

Chapter 20

Grit: courage, resolve, strength of character

Vesta shut the office for lunch, but instead of wandering over to the café, she turned along the front. Mirabelle was right, she decided, as she took in the vista. She mustn't prevaricate. Charlie was her husband and she'd have to bite the bullet. Distracted momentarily by the picture-postcard view, she noted the sky was the way you imagined it should be in springtime. The way a child might draw it. Then she turned off Kingsway and up the side of the Grand Hotel. At the service entrance, ahead of her, a truck was belching exhaust smoke. Vesta coughed. She hated feeling so uncommonly sensitive. She shifted to the other side of the door, as the cab opened, and a man jumped down and efficiently pulled out a couple of boxes of vegetables. In contrast to the fumes, the fresh scent from the boxes was a relief – clean cardboard mingled with turned earth and the green that grew from it. Vesta would never have believed she would be able to make out the smell of a cauliflower, but it had been a revelatory few weeks.

'All right, chief?' The delivery man's eyes were focused on something behind her.

Vesta turned. A young commis chef had appeared in the doorway.

'All right,' he confirmed. 'Can I help you, miss?'

'I'd like to see Charlie Lewis,' Vesta said. 'You know, the chef.'

The boy shook his head. 'Lunch service,' he replied. 'They won't let him out till after. Are you his lady friend?'

Vesta nodded. 'I only wanted a quick word.'

From further inside the hotel there was the sound of shouting as if to demonstrate the high-pressure activity going on inside.

'Lunch,' the boy repeated as he took one of the boxes from the delivery man. 'It'll be done by half two.'

Vesta checked her watch. She couldn't leave the office for that long. And now she'd made up her mind to tell Charlie, she wanted to do it. The boy disappeared and the driver followed him. As the door banged shut, Vesta inserted her foot to stop it. She checked to see if anyone might have noticed, but the commis chef and the delivery man hadn't checked behind them and there wasn't a soul nearby. Above, the hotel towered so steeply no one looking out of a window would be able to make her out. Turning like a guilty child, she sneaked a peek through the crack – the passage was empty. Now she had to decide what to do.

Vesta was always careful not to trouble Charlie at work or when he was playing jazz. She never asked him to come home early nor did she enquire where he'd been when he got home late. But this was an emergency. Sticking her courage like a pin in her lapel, she sneaked into the corridor.

It was warm inside and the electric light felt heavy after the brisk spring sunshine, but the air sang with a cocktail of cooking smells, none of which seemed to upset Vesta's stomach. It was a warren down here – laundries and kitchens, pantries and cloakrooms. With a sixth sense she was unaware she possessed, Vesta dodged the delivery man on his way back out, slipping behind a chamber maid's trolley piled with clean hand towels and soap. Secreted no more than two feet out of the way, the man walked right past her. Once he'd gone, she followed the smell of baking like a hound on the hunt and, sure enough, she discovered the pastry kitchen and its Carrara marble worktops. This is where Charlie ought to have been. A tray of choux swans and a piping canvas filled with cream lay on the worktop, but there was no sign of either Vesta's husband or his sous chef. Vesta peered at an elegant swan's neck and, unable to resist, picked it up, dipped it into the cream and let it melt in her mouth. Charlie brought home cakes, pastries and bread almost every day, but they were never quite so fresh. Vesta moaned with pleasure and considered stealing the body of the swan – after all, what use would it be now, without the rest of it? She recalled Charlie's choux swans came with a glacé cherry and, with the swan's body in her hand, began to search for one as a boy in chef's whites returned to the room with an empty plate in his hand. He put it down on the worktop with a decisive click.

'Oi,' he said, 'you can't nick that. Them's for afternoon tea.'

Vesta felt herself blush. Then she grinned – almost as a defence mechanism. 'I'm sorry,' she said. 'I'm looking for Charlie Lewis.'

'Chef's busy.'

Vesta regarded the swan in her hand, unsure what to do with it.

'You might as well have it,' the boy said, reading her body language. 'I bet you didn't even wash your hands.'

'Sorry.' Vesta eyed the swan. Somehow it didn't seem right now to wolf it down. 'Do you know where Charlie's gone?'

'Some woman,' the boy replied. 'In a suite.'

'How long do you think he'll be?' Vesta wondered vaguely how much of her husband's time at the Grand he spent with female guests in suites?

'I dunno. She's a tricky customer. She's complained every meal – that's what the front desk say.'

'What did she want?'

'Well, not our Victoria sponge, that's for sure.' The boy lowered his voice. 'She said the jam was cheap.'

Vesta took a sharp breath. Charlie's jam was as good as the Women's Institute ever produced, if not better. There was nothing cheap about it. 'He won't like that.'

The boy chortled. 'You bet he didn't. Well, go on then.'

Vesta tucked into the swan. 'It's very good,' she said.

'We always make half a dozen extra. Are you his missus then? Vesta, like the matches?'

Vesta nodded. 'Like the goddess,' she corrected him. It was a line she used to use when she was single and frequented the dance halls. It seemed odd to be trotting it out again. These days everyone around Vesta knew her name, and once you were Mrs Lewis you couldn't be quite so flirtatious as when you were Vesta Churchill, the black girl easily picked out of a crowd.

'I've heard all about you.' The boy grinned.

'Really?'

Charlie never mentioned anyone at work.

'Congratulations are in order, I hear,' he said.

Vesta felt herself reel. 'What?'

'Good news. About the nipper.'

'But,' she stuttered. 'Charlie doesn't know about the baby.'

The boy eyed her. 'What are you talking about? Made up he is. Over the moon.'

Vesta climbed on to a high stool. 'But how?' she said.

'Well, if you don't know that . . .' The boy's eyes sparkled. 'I thought you was married.'

Vesta managed a disapproving look. This was exactly the kind of conversation she had been trying to avoid. Luckily, the boy didn't linger on it. He started to separate a tray of eggs into two large bowls. The movement was mesmerising. She was going to ask him a question, but, before she could, Charlie stormed into the kitchen.

'Hi, baby,' he said and cracked what could only be described as an endearing grin. 'You've met Henry.' The sous chef saluted cheerily, between attending to the eggs. 'What are you doing here?'

Vesta slid off her seat. 'I finally plucked up the courage to tell you that you're going to be a father. That's all.'

Charlie leaned in and kissed her. He smelled of toffee and butter. 'You'll be a swell mum. About time, I'd say.'

'How did you know?'

Charlie turned to wash his hands. 'I thought you were sick. You turned down those meringues I brought home. Twice. And then I realised it must be something on your mind because you went out before breakfast three days in a row. I kind of figured it out from there.'

Vesta folded her arms. Was she really that transparent? 'Well, if you've got any meringues left,' she said, 'I'd take one now.'

'You want a coffee with that? The head chef has had a machine installed. He's French.'

Vesta shook her head. She couldn't face coffee. It was one of the inexplicable changes in appetite the pregnancy had provoked.

'Tea,' she said. That was better.

Charlie nodded at Henry and Henry took off.

'I've been terrified of telling you for days,' she admitted.

'Terrified?'

Vesta gave a little shrug and Charlie wrapped his arms around her. He kissed the nape of her neck. 'It's going to be wonderful. We'll make a great family.'

'I don't want to stay at home, Charlie.'

'So don't stay at home.' He shrugged. 'Not a minute more than you want to, baby. We've got money, what with both of us working. We can get a minder. A nanny, you call them, don't you? The way I see it, I'd rather have a nanny than a holiday, any day of the week.'

Vesta smiled. She let Charlie do whatever he wanted, but in return he let her do the same. Most men would be horrified by the arrangement. 'Nannies are for posh people. I wonder if there's someone nearby. One of the neighbours? A mum who'd help out? Someone who'd enjoy it and appreciate a bit of extra cash.'

'I'll bet there is.'

'People might not like it, Charlie. I mean, you know how they were before.'

It hadn't been easy for Vesta and Charlie when they had first moved to the suburbs. They were the first black residents on the block. Actually, the first black residents in over a mile. The local Conservative Association had sent a delegation door to door – not to speak to the Lewises, but to spread the word that voting Labour would only bring more blacks to the district. Things had settled now, but Vesta knew some of the neighbours were still unhappy. There was an old lady who hissed as she passed as if she was an evil spirit. Charlie had baked her a cake, but it hadn't made any difference.

'It doesn't matter what anyone else thinks,' Charlie said. 'It's up to us. You must have figured that out by now.'

Henry returned carrying a small tray on the tips of his fingers. He laid down a teacup with the name of the hotel painted on it and a plate with two meringues. Charlie patted Vesta's bottom and went back to work. Vesta picked up the cup. A smile spread across her face. 'That was better than I thought it was going to be,' she admitted.

'Feel good?' Charlie checked.

Vesta nodded 'What did the woman want? The one with the jam?'

'I think she just takes exception to anything red.' Charlie was assembling swans with impressive precision. 'Russian,' he explained. 'And a countess, no less. Though Lenny on the front desk looked up her title in some book and he couldn't find it. Anyway, we've got to keep her sweet. She's spending a fortune up there.'

The meringue crumbled as Vesta bit into it. 'Intriguing,' she said. The crust melted in her mouth. It felt like a long time since she had eaten with Charlie present. The changes in her appetite had been a guilty secret and she'd done her best to keep out of his way.

'My money is on the fact that she just likes to complain,' Charlie continued. 'I took her up some Hartley's in a silver dish.'

'You never. Instead of your jam?'

'I told her it was our premier boiling, reserved for special guests.'

Henry beamed. Charlie let out a giggle. 'She loved it,' he said. 'That's the thing. Most of them have no idea. She is just the most horrible snob – when I went in she was running down our dining room, at the Grand. Said she couldn't bear to have people watching her eat, as if anyone would even notice.'

Vesta rolled her eyes. She drained the cup. 'I better get back to the office,' she said.

Charlie raised a cheery hand and Henry bowed, sweeping the tea things away before returning to his eggs. 'I'll see you later, honey.' Charlie waved. 'Look after my eldest son.'

Vesta felt herself blush. Peering down the corridor and feeling flustered, she turned in the wrong direction for the back door and made for the service stairs. A waiter carrying a metal tray with a cloche on top eyed her as he overtook and she fell into step behind him. The stairs came out inside the hotel restaurant and she felt her heart rate increase. She hadn't expected to be quite so visible. The waiter took off towards a table. It occurred to Vesta that everyone would look at her, but then she smiled to herself. This was the same ridiculous worry the countess had. Still, she had hoped to emerge into the busy hotel lobby. That's what she felt like – a comfortable chair for a few minutes. The opportunity to watch people while she collected her thoughts. The Grand was like a maze. There must be another set of stairs, she decided, but it was too late now. Two women eating Dover sole put down their cutlery as she stepped on to the dining-room carpet. One whispered to the other. Customers at the Grand were not accustomed to dark-skinned women emerging from the swing doors. 'Madam?' a voice enquired from behind and Vesta almost tripped over her ankles as she turned. 'Can I help you?' a tall maître d' leaned over. He smelled faintly medicinal.

'I'm lost,' Vesta explained. 'I need to get to reception.'

'This way.' It felt humiliating, somehow, to be led out of the restaurant, still, she kept thinking of Charlie's smile and how delighted he'd been. Then, out of the blue, tears welled in her eyes. She knew she was oversensitive at the moment, but still. The maître d' held open the glass door with a flourish and she slipped past the menu board and on to the tiles of the main hallway, holding her chin up, in a vain attempt to hold back the tears. She made for a scatter of comfortable chairs, pulling her handkerchief from her bag as she took a seat. She'd done it. She'd told him. She settled down and waited as if in this first quiet moment there would be a thunderclap. But there was nothing, only tears and a feeling of power. Now Charlie knew and, more than that, he was delighted, Vesta didn't feel afraid any more. She could tell her mother. She'd write this afternoon. The Churchills didn't have a telephone and Vesta wasn't keen to call the Kellys – the nearest handset – and have all the neighbours know at the same time as her mother. Mrs Churchill might take a few moments to adjust. After all, she had never been a grandmother before. Vesta took a deep breath and patted her stomach. Then she spotted them – Marlene and Marcus Fox coming out of the bar. Marlene was attired in a pretty spring dress and a hat fixed in place with a striking feather pin. Marcus laid his hand protectively on her shoulder. Vesta's instinct was to sink back into the chair, out of the way, but, before she could, her friend waved.

'Hello.' Marlene came over, ebullient as ever. 'What are you doing here?'

'I was visiting Charlie,' Vesta admitted. She must have let a smile slip.

'Did you tell him?'

Vesta nodded. Marlene grabbed Vesta's arm. She seemed on a high. 'Oh that's wonderful. Have you met Marcus? This is my friend Vesta,' she said. 'She's having a baby.'

Vesta realised as soon as the words were out that she didn't mind now.

'You're Miss Bevan's business partner.' Marcus tipped his hat. 'Congratulations.'

'I met Marcus on his father's ward. Remember I said I'd keep an eye out?'

'How is Fred doing?'

Marcus shrugged. 'We don't have high hopes.'

'No,' Marlene agreed. 'It's not looking hopeful.'

'Poor Fred.'

'I'll see if I can get the doorman to find us a taxi, shall I?' Marcus wandered up the hall.

'Isn't he gorgeous?' Marlene hardly waited for the tall figure to move out of earshot. 'This is our second date.'

'You're a fast operator!'

'It was him. Keen as mustard. Drinks at the Grand. Not too shabby,' Marlene whispered, as if she was reporting on an endeavour of national importance. 'I can't believe my luck,' she continued. 'Most of the fellows I meet are practically indigent, or, if not, they're terminally ill or new fathers. New fathers are the worst.' She rolled her eyes.

Vesta grinned. 'That's brilliant.'

'He's such good fun. Full of stories. I'm going to let him

take me out for dinner. I'll have to sneak out of the nurses' quarters, but it'll be worth it and I don't care if I get caught, as long as it's not till after.' She sneaked a smile.

'I'm so glad, Marlene.'

'You're a pal. Imagine if Marcus and I get married, I'll have to move to London. Me.'

'Married?'

'Oh, not yet.' Marlene brushed away the suggestion as if she wasn't the one who had made it.

Marcus gestured from the doorway. Marlene preened herself. The feather in her hat was yellow and Vesta couldn't help thinking of a budgerigar. There was something in the way she moved, readying herself before she set off across the tiles, puffing out her chest and fluffing up her feathers. 'Bye,' Vesta called. It felt as if the Grand was the centre of everything today. She smiled, the ting of the lift opening distracting her, as a woman swathed in fur stalked into the hall. Every member of staff in the hallway stiffened. A man rushed forward.

'Countess,' he said, 'Can I help you?'

'I need a taxi,' the woman replied, each word distinct as she spat her request.

Vesta kept thinking about Hartley's jam. This was a piece of luck. A piece of theatre. The countess was beautifully dressed. Like a jigsaw piece falling into place, Vesta realised she was the lady from *Tatler*. She gazed at the woman's elegant stilettos and the large ostrich clutch bag that seemed to sink into her lush fox-fur stole. She might have felt jealous, but then, the poor woman didn't know a thing about preserves. Sometimes people aren't quite what they seem, Vesta thought. Sometimes you might notice a black woman in an armchair and she is in fact a goddess. Sometimes you notice the back of your friend retreating and you'd never guess how many lives she'd saved. Sometimes you start the day too nervous to even face toast and by the afternoon you've had cake for lunch.

'Where shall I instruct the cab?' the man enquired, as the countess passed.

'What business is it of yours?'

'It's customary. To tell the driver.'

The countess glared. 'I should have brought my own car,' she said. 'It saves backstairs gossip.'

Vesta got to her feet. She checked the buttons on her jacket were fastened and fell into step. 'Really—' the countess sounded as if she was despairing '—this whole trip has been a trial. It is so small here. So quiet. I'm not sure about Brighton.'

'We can organise tickets for the Variety if you'd like.'

A smile played on Vesta's lips. The countess did not honour the man's suggestion with a reply. Outside, she slipped into the back seat of the car with a sour expression on her face, as if the vehicle was inadequate in every way. Vesta wondered why the hotel hadn't organised one of Hove Cars' Rolls-Royces, but perhaps there hadn't been time. From the ting of the lift to the countess's departure had been perhaps ninety seconds. What a very unpleasant woman, Vesta thought, and in *Tatler* too, as she turned towards town and the car pulled away.

Chapter 21

Experience is the name we give our mistakes

Mirabelle walked for miles in London. It was a bright, clear, spring afternoon and she passed several wartime haunts, but she was so busy going over the details of Helen Quinn's murder that she scarcely noticed. The information she had picked up at Luna Street and on the King's Road had taken her nowhere new, although it had left her with a more detailed picture of Helen Quinn and what she had achieved. Turning back towards town, Mirabelle realised she was mirroring Helen's journey from poverty to affluence as the slum housing fell away and smart shops with their canopies took over. Children no longer played in the street and dogs were kept on the leash. At Cadogan Gardens, a Harrods van passed and the flash of green prompted her to make for the park. As she swept through the wrought-iron gates, the spring flowers were in bud and a scatter of blossom flecked the grass. She didn't miss London like she used to. In fact, if anything, she found when she was in town she missed the sea. Had Helen Quinn made the same transition from the excitement of the capital to the freedom of the open view along Brighton's pebble beach? Did she know her husband had visited the house at Tongdean? And, if so, did she care?

Through the wrought-iron gate on the other side of the wide lawns, Mirabelle turned back on to the pavement and realised that the Quinns were well matched. They inspired the same loyalty in people. She wondered how Inspector

Robinson could discount that just because it made his life easier. Poor Phil Quinn. She hoped he was managing on remand.

Back in the hurly-burly, she tried to stop her mind wandering to Alan McGregor. As she reached Regent Street, she found she couldn't help herself. She'd spent time with McGregor in this part of town. The memory of the shared lunches and drinks at the bar felt tainted by Jinty's revelation. McGregor was a police officer, of course, but she hadn't fully realised the roughness of the world he inhabited. The sleazy places he'd been and what he might have got up to. The superintendent always seemed straightforward – this was a new side to him. She felt angry and that scared her. Her fury in the past had always been reserved for real enemies. For murderers. For enemies of the state. Now she wondered if this painful edge that folded in her gut was only hurt feelings? She couldn't bear to think about it – not for long.

As she passed the turn-off for Swallow Street, she looked up at the Indian restaurant where Marcus Fox was meant to meet his father the Friday before. She'd gone for dinner there once and Sir Winston Churchill had been installed, eating curry and chapattis, with two chaps from the Foreign Office. She hadn't meant to overhear, but they had been discussing watercolours, as if painting was more important than politics. She must focus, she decided. She must put this nonsense with McGregor out of her mind. She hadn't thought about Fred all day. She hadn't even known he was partial to spicy food. How little we know people, she berated herself. How little we notice. Rounding the corner, Mirabelle turned into St James's, passing an elderly gentleman in full military regalia, who was making his way slowly but surely towards the tobacconist's on Duke Street.

When she reached Victoria, she made for a telephone box and got through to the office.

'Oh hello.' Vesta sounded light-hearted as she answered. Mirabelle smiled. The sound of the girl's voice lifted her spirits immediately.

'It's good to speak to you,' Mirabelle said. 'How's your day been?'

'Good. You'll never guess what,' Vesta reported proudly. 'Billy Randall is no longer employed at CVA. The lady said he just walked out. He didn't even give proper notice and he's supposed to. She said he was not a promising candidate for life insurance. Too unreliable.'

'Did she say why he left?'

'No. But she said when.' Vesta's tone became even more triumphant. 'It was the twentieth. The day after Helen Quinn's murder.'

Mirabelle leaned against the cool glass panes. On the other side of the station, she could see a porter waving a red flag and a train pulling away from the platform in a cloud of steam. Her legs felt tired and she wanted to sit down. She had walked for hours.

'Are you still there?' Vesta checked.

'I'm thinking.'

'Do you reckon he could be the murderer, Mirabelle? Billy Randall, I mean. He reported the crime. He could have sneaked over in the night and done it, and, as for drugging the bottle of gin, well, he was only next door. Perhaps it's no wonder nobody spotted anything unusual.' Vesta waited, but Mirabelle did not reply so the girl continued playing out the scenario. 'Then maybe he was overtaken by guilt afterwards and quit his job . . .' she gushed. 'As if he was having some kind of breakdown.'

'He didn't seem overtaken by guilt when I saw him at the Quinns' house the other evening,' Mirabelle cut in. 'He chatted to the beat bobby for quite some time. He was adamant about Phil Quinn's innocence, which I wouldn't expect if he were the murderer. If he did it, you'd think he'd be delighted the police had fingered Helen's husband.'

'What do you think he's up to then?'

'I don't know. The Randalls and the Quinns seem so terribly nice despite everything that's happened. I spoke to Helen Quinn's old landlord today – he was genuinely fond of her. I think she was a really nice girl.'

'Well, it's the first time something interesting has happened. Something suspicious, I mean. Billy Randall going off like that and not telling his wife.'

Mirabelle made a sound that confirmed the veracity of this statement. It drew her back to the details. The small changes. The things that were out of place. 'I know.' She ran over it slowly. 'And you're right. He had the opportunity. But it's the motive I can't get a handle to. I mean, even if Billy Randall and Helen Quinn were having an affair . . .'

Vesta took in a sharp breath, as if she hadn't considered this possibility. Mirabelle felt even more weary. It was the easiest thing in the world to jump to conclusions, but you couldn't make people fit into theories just because it was convenient – the method of cracking this case or any other was the opposite way around.

'Maybe you're right – or if Phil Quinn and Vi Randall were at it . . .' the girl started.

Mirabelle shook her head. 'No. That doesn't make sense. If that were the case, Billy Randall would have killed Phil Quinn, surely. Not taken it out on Helen. There's something we don't know yet,' she said. 'More than one thing. We just have to keep digging. At least this is a start.'

'I'll think about it tonight,' Vesta promised. 'I'll reason it through.'

As she hung up, Mirabelle realised that Vesta must have told Charlie about the baby. The girl sounded different. Mirabelle cursed herself for being too slow to have noticed in the moment. There was too much on her mind. Loitering by the telephone box, she considered ringing back, but it seemed somehow intrusive, so instead she walked on to the platform and waited for the train to pull in. A smart woman in a lavender tweed suit marched a Border terrier up and down on a lead. 'Come along now, Barker,' she encouraged the little dog. 'He gets fractious on the train if he isn't tired out,' she explained apologetically, as she passed for the second time. Mirabelle smiled. She felt more than a little fractious herself, as she turned her thoughts to Billy Randall and the possibilities around his strange behaviour.

It was unsettling when death came out of the blue, murder especially. There was no saying how it might take someone, even a man who had seen death before, who had seen action. Even someone with everything to live for, she thought, as she considered Vi Randall, the house filled with flowers and the baby due to arrive over the next few weeks. Had Billy Randall dallied with his wife's best friend? Was the friendship between the Quinns and the Randalls more than it seemed and, if so, how had they managed to hoodwink Mrs Ambrose? Mirabelle had a sudden vision of the net curtain of number fourteen Mill Lane twitching furiously. The street had been constructed in such a way that the houses overlooked each other. On the upside, it made for neighbours who knew each other well, but, on the downside, it was difficult to hide anything and certainly not an affair.

When the train pulled in, Mirabelle settled in a first-class carriage. It felt good to sit down. The journey passed in a flash and, before she knew, it she was standing outside Brighton Railway Station and the light was fading from the sky. The air felt cleaner down here, the breeze off the ocean refreshing after a long day in the city. Behind her a porter blew his whistle, as a train pulled out of the station. It was still early and, suddenly revitalised, Mirabelle decided she wasn't ready to quit for the day. Not by a long chalk. Jack always said that finding out what you needed to know was a matter of asking the right people the right questions. Maybe, she thought, it was more than that. Maybe you had to ask the right people the right questions at a time when they could answer. She had pussyfooted around enough, she thought as she cut off Queens Road in the direction of Old Steine.

Catching the bus northwards, it was only a short journey to Mill Lane. As she approached the Randalls' house, Mirabelle was glad to see that although he might have been out for the last two nights Billy was at home this evening. Vi sat in the fireside chair reading a magazine. At this stage of her pregnancy, she was too large for the chair's dimensions and perched uncomfortably, looking as if either she, or the chair, might topple at any moment. Billy was behind her at the table. He had rolled up his shirtsleeves and was attempting to repair what looked like a clock face. The casement window was open only an inch or two and the sound of music floated towards the pavement. A fat ginger cat sat on the front doormat. With the light on inside, Mirabelle knew it would be difficult to catch Billy's attention. She stalked up the path to the window. Oblivious, Vi turned a page and moved her weight from one hip to another. The back of the chair creaked. Billy, likewise, was concentrating on what he was doing. Mirabelle leaned towards his line of sight and waved smartly, but he didn't notice her – men had such poor peripheral vision. She jumped up and down, but he still didn't look up. Then she considered knocking on the glass, but that was risky. It was Billy she wanted to speak to, not Vi. In desperation, she hissed, but the music was too loud inside the room.

Sighing, she sneaked towards the front door where she knelt down and petted the fat cat before scooping it into her arms. Then she rounded the far side of the house. The Randalls' back door was not locked. Mentally, she berated them – after everything that had happened. Tonight, though, it proved lucky for her. After stroking the cat one last time, she slipped the animal through the doorway and on to the tiled floor of the Randalls' kitchen, clicking the door shut behind it. Then she waited. It was only a matter of seconds before Billy appeared in the kitchen and slung the cat back into the garden. A more slender tabby followed the interloper up the grass like a shot. 'You see him off. Cheek of it,' Billy exclaimed.

Mirabelle stepped into the slice of light the open door cast on to the path.

'I want to talk to you,' she said, keeping her voice low. 'On your own.'

Billy looked up, clearly startled. A call came from inside the house. 'How did he get in?' Vi shouted.

'I don't know. Bleeding animal.'

'We can't talk in front of your wife,' Mirabelle hissed, realising it sounded as if this was an entirely different kind of assignation.

'I'm going to the Michaels',' Billy shouted over his shoulder. His expression relaxed. It was interesting, Mirabelle thought, that he didn't take her to task, accepting that they needed to speak. 'I'll borrow a smaller screwdriver. I'll be back in a jiffy.'

He stepped outside and closed the door. Mirabelle retreated further into the darkness. The sound of cats fighting floated from the top of the garden.

'Well?'

'I know you quit your job. Where were you the other night, Mr Randall? The night you didn't come home.'

'What's it got to do with you?'

'You haven't told your wife.'

Billy let an easy grin cross his face. 'Are you threatening me?' He sounded as if he might laugh.

'I'm trying to find out who killed your wife's best friend.'

Billy Randall pointed to punctuate his words. 'You're just a busybody. That's all you are.'

'Don't you want to find out who killed Helen?'

His eyes flashed with anger. 'Sling your hook, would you? You're not wanted here.'

'I promised Vi I'd figure out who killed Helen Quinn and I'd say that I'm the best chance there is of finding out what happened the night she died. The police have charged Phil and he definitely didn't do it. Was it you, Billy? Is that what it is? Did you kill that poor woman?'

Randall's eyes narrowed. He seemed somehow deflated. 'Is that what you think?'

'Where did you get to the other night? What were you doing up in London?'

'Who says I was in London?'

'I followed you. To Belgravia.'

When he reached out, he did so with surprising swiftness. Wiry and fast, he grabbed Mirabelle and pushed her into the bushes. The twigs and leaves scratched her legs and dug into her back as she lost her balance. Well, that's riled him, she thought.

'It looks like you feel threatened now,' she said smoothly. Panicking never helped.

'Who sent you?' he snarled. 'Who?'

Mirabelle's heart raced. He was stronger than she was, but she tried not to let the fear show in her voice. 'Nobody sent me. I'm acting for a friend of Phil Quinn's. There's nobody on his side but us, you see. Still, perhaps we can get him out of this together. If you just tell me . . .'

'You don't know what you're doing. You're going to get more people killed if you're not careful.'

'Were you gambling in London, Billy? Where did you get the money you brought home for the pram?'

'Gambling? God, you haven't a clue.'

'Tell me then.'

He shoved her hard and backed away. 'You're not getting it from me,' he spat. 'You don't know what will happen if I tell you. You don't want to get involved in any of this, a woman like you.'

'I've been involved in worse.' Mirabelle passed a hand over her jacket. She didn't want to look down, but she was certain her stockings must be a state.

'Big words. Look, I didn't kill Helen and that should be enough.'

'Well, it's not. You know who did it, don't you? What's going on, Billy? Did you see something that night? Is that what it is?'

'One dead woman is one too many. And if you don't stop poking about . . .' A vague looked crossed his face as if he was considering what might happen if Mirabelle continued to ask questions. It didn't make her give up.

'I can help. Don't you think you'll feel better if you share what's on your mind?'

Billy laughed. It was a carefree and unexpected sound. Almost a giggle. 'And then we'll have a cup of tea? Nice, like. I've got Vi to think of and a nipper on the way. I'm not going to tell you anything. If you come here again, I'll hurt you. Properly. Understand? You don't know what you're doing.' He paused for a second before he turned back into the kitchen and slammed the door.

Mirabelle's shoulders dropped. She looked down. Her stockings were torn to shreds. Still, she smiled. She'd kept her head at least. She'd read about it in a training manual. If someone pushes themselves against you, you should try to feel what they have in their pockets. There had been the screwdriver, of course. She'd felt that. But she'd slipped her hand inside and when Billy Randall pulled back she'd managed to keep hold of a little slip of card. Now she turned it between her fingers. In the half-light from the window she could see there was a phone number, printed in black. Belgravia 4192. No name. No address. Still, she popped it into her purse and paused momentarily to remove her laddered stockings. That was a better day's work, she told herself. That was worthwhile, however angry it had made him.

As she slipped off the bus and walked towards the front, Mirabelle noticed with a smile that the door to the Boite was open. It had been some day and she decided she felt like a drink. A wash of pink light from the neon stairway landed in a puddle on the pavement. Her heels clicked as she walked through it. Upstairs, you'd never know whether it was lunchtime or dinner. Like all good nightclubs, the Boite always felt like it was the right time to frequent the bar. One of the Italian waiters was engaged in polishing glasses and, as she entered, he emerged to pull out a bar stool with a flourish.

'What can I get you, madam?'

'Champagne,' Mirabelle said, surprising herself by repeating McGregor's order from the other night.

If the waiter was surprised she was alone, he didn't show it. He efficiently produced a chilled glass, filled it and placed a small plate of peanuts at its base.

'Busy day?'

Mirabelle nodded. She looked around. There was only one other customer in tonight – a man on his own in the corner. He was nursing a whisky and reading a book, which even from this distance she could see was some kind of guide to Brighton with a picture of the Pavilion on the cover. 'Is Mr Gleeson here?' she enquired.

'He's upstairs.' The barman gestured.

'Upstairs?'

'In the office. Would you like me to fetch him?'

Mirabelle shook her head. There was no point in troubling

anybody. Besides, she had her lead. She sipped the champagne. 'Do you have a telephone?' she asked.

The barman reached into a cubbyhole and pulled out a cream Bakelite phone on a long wire. He placed it on the bar with a click. The Boite had everything. Of course it did.

'I thought maybe you wanted to talk to Mr Gleeson,' he said smoothly. 'If you like, there's a button to transfer up to the office.' He indicated it, though his eyes fell downwards, over her décolletage. Mirabelle recognised the feeling that fluttered in her stomach – she'd had the same sensation at the Grand in Eastbourne and in the drawing room at Tongdean Avenue. He reckons I'm for sale, she thought. She finished her drink and motioned for him to refill it. The champagne bottle dripped as he drew it out of the ice.

'Is it all right if I call a friend?'

The waiter replied with a knowing smile. She stared back without meeting his grin and he replaced the champagne in the ice bucket and moved away. Then she picked up the handset and called the operator. 'Belgravia 4192.' It took a few seconds to get connected. The bell rang at the other end and Mirabelle worried, momentarily, that it was too late to call. If the number was a private house it was bad manners to ring after nine. No sooner had she dismissed this thought than she worried about what she might say. It was impossible, after all, to make a plan. She had no idea who or what was at the other end of the line. A vision of Vesta with her notepad flashed across Mirabelle's mind's eye but the Prudential's offices were closed now and she couldn't pretend to be filling in a form.

'Hello,' a man's voice drawled slowly, as if it was a tiresome task to pick up the handset. 'Can I help you?'

'Is that Belgravia 4192?' Mirabelle checked, buying a second or two at least.

'Yes. Can I help you?'

The voice gave away nothing. 'Is the lady of the house at home?' Mirabelle tried, careful not to sound flustered.

'The countess is out of London, I'm afraid.' He said the words as if they were some kind of announcement.

Mirabelle hesitated. The edge of the card had become bent in her purse and, with her free hand, she slipped it through her fingers, tapping it on the bar. It helped her concentrate. 'Ah, I've missed her then. Is she in Brighton by any chance?' The words came out of nowhere – as if in walking round all day she had simply been preparing to put two and two together so that, when she did, it was effortless.

'Yes. Brighton.'

'And she is staying at the Grand? I mean, it's the only hotel.' Mirabelle adopted the haughty tone she'd heard the countess use at the reception desk.

The voice hesitated. Giving out the whereabouts of one's mistress was a serious offence.

'I think I may have noticed her as she checked into her suite yesterday,' Mirabelle continued smoothly. 'I simply wasn't sure. It was at a distance you see and I was meeting friends.'

'May I take a name?' The voice sounded more persistent than when it first came to the phone.

'Oh, I'm an old acquaintance.' Mirabelle let the lie slip seamlessly down the wire.

'Ah.' He thought he had understood something. The man's voice switched again, continuing as if by rote. 'Well, Madam's Tuesdays and Saturdays will continue the same in her absence.'

'Good,' Mirabelle said, sounding confident, as if this was what she had rung to check. 'Tuesday is tomorrow. And everything as usual then?'

'Shall we expect you?'

'Yes. Why not?'

The line clicked dead. Mirabelle regarded the frosted

208

champagne flute in front of her. She lifted the glass to her lips. 'Good heavens,' she mumbled. At least the way ahead was clear. It was a connection she would never have made in the normal run of things. But it opened up a plethora of new possibilities. That this card was in Billy Randall's pocket certainly seemed a mismatch.

The waiter removed the phone. Then he reached for the champagne bottle. 'The gentleman sent you a drink,' he said, raising it as if to demonstrate.

Mirabelle glanced at the man in the corner who had put down his book. He nodded as if he was seeking some kind of agreement. 'No, thank you.' She pushed the glass away and slipped off the bar stool. Really, anyone would think she was fifteen years younger and far more available. Perhaps once this was over she might give Superintendent McGregor a run for his money. Perhaps he deserved that. She popped a few shillings next to the peanuts and stalked back into the chilly evening air.

Chapter 22

The woman who deliberates is lost

The Grand Hotel loomed large in Mirabelle's life in Brighton. The first time she crossed its august threshold she had been engaged on her very first case, but, since then, without becoming a regular haunt, it had certainly developed into a feature. Once she had been barricaded into a suite and had to fight off a homicidal maniac. If Fred hadn't equipped her with a gun, she probably wouldn't have survived. Now, she stalked into the lounge and sat on one of the comfortable seats, near where Vesta had stationed herself that afternoon. When the waiter approached, she ordered a pot of tea and a plate of ham sandwiches.

'On white or brown bread?' the man enquired.

Mirabelle did not respond well to choices of this kind. Over the last year, she noticed that there appeared to be more of them. 'White,' she said, feeling uncertain. In the old days, they'd simply have brought you whatever they had.

'Very good,' the man replied, as if confirming that she had made the correct choice.

Before he turned to leave, Mirabelle leaned forward. 'I wonder if you might help me. There's an old school friend of mine staying at the hotel. She's a titled lady. I hoped to visit but I wonder if I have missed her. It's rather late.'

A waver of expression crossed the man's face like a shadow. 'Ah. I see. The countess has been receiving visitors this afternoon. I believe she is still entertaining. Shall I call up to announce you?'

'I wouldn't want to disturb her if she has visitors.' Mirabelle pointedly checked her watch. Visitors arriving in the afternoon invariably left before dinner. 'Perhaps I'll just pop up after my sandwiches.'

'You have to be announced,' the man said. 'We can't just allow people who aren't guests . . .'

'Oh. Quite,' Mirabelle reassured him.

As he left in the direction of the kitchen, Mirabelle realised how quiet the hotel was this evening. A couple arrived and checked in, flirting with each other as they did so. One or two customers nipped in and out of the bar, but, apart from that, there was hardly anyone around. The waiter returned in due course and she nibbled her sandwiches. Across the deserted hallway, the man behind the reception desk disappeared into a back room. A bellboy walked smartly into the luggage store and emerged with a leather cosmetics case under his arm with which he bounded up the stairs. Mirabelle laid a couple of shillings on the table and got up to follow him. The moment she placed her foot on the first step, an older man appeared ahead of her.

'Madam?' he enquired.

'I'm just going up?'

'To?'

Mirabelle hesitated. To say she was a guest might catch her out. 'Visit a friend?' she hazarded.

'I can call up for you. It is only staff who can go up and down, you see. We like to announce callers at the Grand.'

'I thought I'd be a surprise. It would be rather fun, do you see?'

The man raised a solitary eyebrow. There had been several divorce cases spawned by people who were surprised by their visitors. Some had made the papers. 'I'm sorry,' he said, raising a hand to direct Mirabelle back to the reception desk. 'Why don't you give me your friend's name?'

Mirabelle squirmed. 'Oh it's fine. I don't want to bother anybody. Perhaps you might direct me to the lavatory?'

'Of course.' He gestured across the hall and Mirabelle stalked off, aware his eyes were on her. Behind the mahogany door, she washed her hands and stared at herself in the mirror. She looked tired. Faded even. She ran a sink of cold water and splashed her face. At least she felt refreshed, though, she noticed, the dark shadows under her eyes persisted. She reached into her purse and powdered her nose. Then she walked back across the hallway and waved cheerily to the man on the desk. 'Good night,' she said to the doorman, and turned along the front.

The streetlights were low tonight. That would help, she thought, as she turned smartly at the corner of the building and headed to the rear. The doorman appeared oblivious as she caught a last sight of him, his hands clasped behind his back and his hat pulled low over his eyes. At the back of the Grand, a kitchen porter sat smoking on one of the bins. He blew a long stream of smoke into the night air and watched lasciviously as Mirabelle approached. 'I'm late,' she said, dropping one or two consonants and lengthening her vowels. She hoped it would be enough. 'And I'm new. They showed me where to get the chambermaid uniform but I can't remember. Will you help me? I don't want to get into trouble.'

The man sucked air through his teeth. 'You'll have to smarten up your game if you're going to last at the Grand. What's your name, then?'

'Mary.'

The fellow stubbed out his cigarette and got to his feet. 'The higher-ups won't like it, Mary. But I'll show you just the once.'

The hotel was as quiet behind the scenes as it had been upstairs. The smell of baking bread pervaded the basement floor as preparations started for the next day. A boy passed with a trolley of shoes ready to be polished, each sporting a label with the name and room number of the guest. The kitchen porter showed Mirabelle to a scuffed door. 'The women go in here,' he said. 'Remember now?'

'Oh yes. Thank you.'

As he disappeared round the corner, she slipped inside. To the rear of the changing room there was a locked laundry cage, the shelves and rails crammed with uniforms for waitresses and chambermaids. The air smelled of soap. She fumbled in her handbag for her SOE lock picks and made short work of the mechanism. Inside, she found a pair of flat shoes, more or less the right size, a housekeeping apron and a black shift. Grabbing these, she changed quickly. The shift was roomy, but with the apron tied over the top it wasn't too obvious. In a tiny mirror propped above a solitary shelf, Mirabelle put up her hair in a tidy bun and removed her jewellery, stashing it in her pocket along with the lock picks. She hung up her own clothes and hid her crocodile clutch underneath her skirt. 'Well,' she whispered, checking herself as well as she could in the mirror. 'That will have to do.'

Glad it was quiet, she slipped down the corridor and up the service stairs, which unexpectedly brought her into the main hallway. It seemed bright now in comparison to the poor lighting on the interior stairs. The man on the desk, who had stopped her so politely only a few minutes before, gesticulated frantically for her to return through the swing door. He looked furious. Mirabelle realised she'd never seen a chambermaid at the Grand. They clearly weren't allowed in the public areas of the hotel. She dropped her head and retreated into the basement to start again. This time she navigated the building more successfully. As her heels sank into the thick carpet of the penthouse floor, she found herself hoping that the countess wasn't occupying the suite where she had been detained two years before by the man she had shot using Fred's gun.

She need not have concerned herself. The steady beat of background music quickly confirmed that her mark was installed front and centre in a suite that must have commanded a prime sea view – the best in the hotel and, arguably, in Brighton. She fumbled for the lock picks and made straight for the next unmarked door. After checking over her shoulder, she picked the lock and slipped inside. The cupboard was stacked with linen and boxes of soap. It smelled of honey and vinegar. Mirabelle grabbed a short stack of hand towels and balanced them on her arm as she'd seen maids do somewhere, although she couldn't recall where or when. Then she returned to the corridor, where, ahead of her, two waiters carrying champagne buckets had appeared at the head of the service stair. One of them knocked smartly at the countess's suite. Mirabelle passed, pretending to be on her way up the corridor. The sound of laughter and the syncopated rhythm of a jazz recording emanated from the open door – there was some kind of party going on. Mirabelle halted round the corner and peered back as the waiters disappeared inside. She bit her lip. This operation was more nerve-wracking than she had anticipated. She leaned against the wall, keeping her eyes peeled. Five minutes later, the waiters emerged. One pocketed a shilling. Mirabelle rounded the corner, trying to look as if she was in a hurry.

'It's a bit late for service.' One of them eyed her.

'They sent me because of the party. The bathroom.' Mirabelle rolled her eyes. 'What's it like in there?'

'It's lively all right. I haven't seen you before.'

'I usually work the other shift. What are they up to?'

'You don't want to know.' The waiter winked. 'Hasn't anyone told you?'

Mirabelle shook her head.

'Well, you'll find out soon enough.' He grinned.

Mirabelle knocked, as the men shoved open the swing door

and disappeared back into the belly of the building. Ahead of her, the entrance snapped open and a man in evening dress, smoking a cigar, leaned back as if he was taking in a view or considering a painting. 'Yes?'

'Service, sir? Towels for the bathroom.'

He stood back to let her pass. The suite wasn't as full as the one to which Jinty had taken Mirabelle further down the coast, but it was just as noisy. After what the waiters had said, Mirabelle was relieved to see that nothing particularly nefarious was going on. In high spirits, a group was throwing dice around a low coffee table. Opposite this game, the countess sat alone sipping a recently topped-up glass. She paid Mirabelle absolutely no notice as she passed into the bedroom where several coats were laid on the bed. Mirabelle peered back round the door frame. The man who had let her in whispered something to the countess. It was difficult to lip-read when you didn't know the subject matter being discussed and Mirabelle couldn't make out what he said. However, when he had received the countess's assent, he disappeared through double doors on the other side of the suite. These, Mirabelle knew, led to a private dining room. Charlie had shown her once. Up here, the suites had their own facilities. A system of dumb waiters was equipped to ferry food from the kitchens below and there were limited cooking facilities on site – a gas ring. 'For crêpe Suzette,' Charlie had said with a smile.

Mirabelle couldn't smell food over the swirling haze of cigarette smoke and alcohol but, she thought, perhaps there was a private party through there. Still, the main action, it seemed, was here, and her attention was drawn back to the room as a cheer broke out. A woman at the table threw what must have been a winning pair of dice and flung her arms around the man next to her. Money changed hands and the countess appeared to take more of an interest. There was a flurry of cigarettes being lit and two men retreated to the window to have a private conversation, which appeared fraught. Mirabelle stood back just in time as a woman in a pale-blue satin cocktail gown burst through the bedroom door.

'Oh,' she said, casting her eyes towards the bathroom. 'Is it clean?'

'Yes, madam,' Mirabelle replied. 'I was only going to change the towels.'

The woman pushed past brusquely and it struck Mirabelle that she wasn't normally treated with such disdain when she wasn't attired in a black dress and a white apron. Two more women came through the door, so tipsy they almost fell over the threshold. They made for the dressing table and began to fumble with their clutch purses without acknowledging Mirabelle's presence.

'Really, it's too much!' one declared, as she applied a thick layer of hot pink to her top lip and then blotted it on to her lower one.

The second woman counted a small sheaf of five pound notes. 'I'm so glad the countess came to Brighton. It's just a bit of fun, Katie.'

'Well, she must be making a fortune,' Katie said, looking round frantically, as she stuffed the lipstick back into her purse. 'You,' she snapped at Mirabelle. 'Give me one of those.'

Mirabelle handed her a towel. The woman did not say thank you. Instead, she dabbed her face. 'Do you think she'll be much longer?' the first woman sighed, casting her eyes to the bathroom door. It was a rhetorical question that neither Mirabelle nor the other lady answered. In any case, the door opened a few seconds later and the woman swept back into the fray. From the dressing table, the other lady practically shoved Mirabelle out of the way as she dived in to use the lavatory. Katie didn't notice these bad manners and instead sniffed a bottle of perfume, which must have belonged to the countess. She sprayed some on to her wrist and then checked her hair. Reluctantly, she removed her earrings – a pair of rubies set in gold – then dusting herself down, she left trailing a cloud of violet and amber scent. As Mirabelle peered after her, she noticed a baize-topped card table had been set up in the main room. Next to it, some of the dice-rolling crowd were playing gin rummy. On the sofa, the woman who had just left the bedroom cosied up to the countess, who suddenly became more animated. The earrings changed hands and the woman returned to the tables. Well, well, Mirabelle thought. The countess has set up a casino right here at the Grand.

Gambling was illegal. Brighton was famous for its horse racing and the dog track, which attracted thousands of visitors. But they operated within the law. Mirabelle had attended both several times. It was fun to lay a bet now and then. But this was different. And it didn't make sense – not in terms of her investigation. Billy Randall wouldn't fit in here. These people were far too smart. They wore evening dress and smoked Sobranie cigarettes. And, she noticed, as the bets were laid, the stakes were high. You could buy and sell a lot of prams for the wagers laid on a single hand at these tables. Billy hadn't netted his winnings laying bets here.

The woman emerged from the bathroom and disappeared into the fray. Mirabelle busied herself replacing the towels. Then she slipped unnoticed back through the main room and into the hall where she bundled the dirty laundry into the cupboard. At last, she secreted herself in a doorway further along and waited. It was after eleven o'clock. It struck her as strange that the waiters must know what was going on. All the staff must know and yet no one from the hotel appeared to be concerned that the countess was running an illegal casino on the top floor. But then, the things that went on in hotels were often shady – look at the party at which she'd found herself only a few days before. There was an argument that was more morally reprehensible than a few friends gaming. Feeling slightly stiff after a day of walking, Mirabelle leaned against the door, but gradually she slipped down the frame, succumbing to tiredness. No one went in or came out for what felt like a long time. Surveillance was always tiresome, she thought, as her eyes became heavy. She shifted on the carpet, turning like a child in its sleep as, slowly, she drifted off.

When Mirabelle woke, she felt disconcerted. For a moment, she had no idea where she was. As she stirred, she realised she couldn't feel her left arm and her hips were stuck in an uncomfortable position. She rubbed her shoulder and raised her eyes to the man who was bending over her. He sported a waxed moustache and he smelled of stewed tea. As his voice came into focus, she remembered where she was and what she had been up to.

'A chambermaid asleep? At the Grand? I've never seen the like. Did Moxon take you on, woman?'

Mirabelle scrambled to her feet. 'Sorry,' she mumbled.

Behind the man, two waiters loitered, peering at Mirabelle as if she was some kind of curiosity. One of them hazarded a cheeky wink.

'I won't have it,' the man continued. 'In the old days you'd be dismissed on the spot, young lady. Just because staff are hard to come by doesn't mean that I won't fire you. Just like that.' He snapped his fingers.

'Sorry,' Mirabelle repeated. There didn't appear to be anything else to say.

This did not appease the fellow. 'I can't imagine what you're doing up here. Service to the rooms started half an hour ago but there's nothing on this floor at this time of day. Guests in suites invariably don't rise until later – generally they don't dress till lunchtime. You should be working on the lower floors, especially if you're new.'

There was no natural light in the hall, the windows being dedicated to the rooms. Mirabelle cast her eyes to the carpet, glancing at her watch as she did so. It was shortly after eight o'clock. She ran her tongue over her teeth. 'I'll go down straight away,' she said.

'Sir,' the man hissed emphatically.

'Yes. Sir. Sorry. Sir.'

'Second floor. Go and help Florence.'

She stumbled towards the lift, only remembering at the last moment to continue to the service stairs. Behind the swing door, she peeked back as the man disappeared inside the countess's suite with the waiters. One of them wedged the door open and the sound of glasses clinking cut into the still air. They were clearing the room so it would be ready for use when the countess woke. The Grand looked after its guests – illicit and otherwise. Good hotels, unlike good guest houses, didn't pass judgement. Mirabelle shifted, realising she must have slept through the countess's guests as they left in the middle of the night. God knows what time that had happened.

Turning, she began down the stairs, snatches of the night before appearing in her mind's eye. The smell of the countess's perfume. The little stacks of money changing hands. That woman's ruby earrings. Running through it, she continued to the basement, looking left and right, exiting in the direction of the kitchens. There were more people around this morning – sous chefs and laundry girls. Making sure the coast was clear, she made her exit step by step. She briefly considered checking to see if Charlie was about, but decided there was no point in disturbing him. It was more important to figure out how Billy Randall was connected to this. Was he an enforcer? Did he do her job, or at least, McGuigan & McGuigan's – a kind of upmarket debt collector? She pictured him trying to threaten her in his back garden and realised he was too slight. When

219

tempers were up, life's enforcers didn't just push you into the bushes. So what was Billy Randall up to? By the time she came to her senses, she was outside, and the door had closed behind her. A seagull perched beside a rubbish bin and looked up slowly, its elegant neck pulsing as it choked down something it had eaten off the concrete. It was only then she realised that she was wearing a uniform and her clothes were still inside, hanging in the staff changing room.

Chapter 23

The savage is never quite eradicated

McGregor couldn't help resenting Robinson, who was drinking tea and joking with one of the sergeants on the other side of the main office. At his desk, behind the glass, he tried to concentrate on George Forgie's service record. The file was impressive. Quite besides the amount of missions he'd flown, in 1943 the Flight Lieutenant had been shot down in France and made it home in an impressive nine weeks. Between the lines, McGregor spotted references to heavy drinking and two occasions when Forgie had been absent without official leave. Once he had been found with a married woman in a local hotel and the second time he turned up at the Grand National where it transpired he had pawned a recently acquired medal in order to lay a bet, which he subsequently won. Like many pilots, Forgie had sundry car accidents, one of which, a doctor's report revealed, he should not have survived. He'd been afforded a good deal of leeway – his skills were too valuable to the war effort to take a harsh line.

McGregor sat back. Robinson was reading the newspaper now. The superintendent clenched his teeth. He was about to go out and give the inspector something to do (though not what he should have been doing – clearing Phil Quinn's name) when the figure of the chief constable appeared at his door. The chief hadn't been down here in a long time. Not that the superintendent could remember anyway.

'Alan.' He shook McGregor's hand and took a seat. 'Flight Lieutenant Forgie? How are you getting on?'

'There are unanswered questions, sir.'

'Such as?'

'Why the body was moved and where he killed himself.'

'Do you know why he did it?'

McGregor's hand sought out the file. 'He was a daredevil, sir. High spirits and low spirits, I expect. He's outdone the cat's nine lives – dodged the bullet over several years. It was a matter of time, I expect, before he died one way or another.'

'And it's suicide?'

'Seems that way. A bullet in the gullet and powder on his fingers.'

'I see. Do you think the hotel where he was staying panicked?'

'I doubt it. He'd been missing for thirty-six hours when he killed himself. Forgie was a gambler, sir. If he was in Brighton it's probable he was playing cards for high stakes somewhere. That's my real interest, I suppose.'

The chief rubbed his palms together. He licked his lips. 'My feeling is that it doesn't matter, if you get my drift.'

McGregor paused. 'It doesn't matter, sir?'

The chief's eyes bulged very slightly. 'No. The poor chap killed himself and it's a tragedy – war hero and all that. But it doesn't matter where he did it or what he was up to. In fact, I'm not sure it matters why his body was moved. Not really.'

McGregor nodded slowly. The chief had received a phone call, that much was clear. 'But someone moved the body – I mean, they didn't report it,' he pointed out. 'And if Forgie was gaming—'

'A tragedy, as I said,' the chief cut in. 'But you're going to close the case, McGregor. Mr Forgie's profile requires discretion. He knew what he was doing. He made his choice. We must leave him in peace. Investigating what happened isn't going to do anyone any good.' The chief's forehead was clammy now.

'Right you are, sir,' McGregor said. 'I'll send the file back to Whitehall.'

'Capital.' The old man got up to leave.

McGregor watched as the chief stopped to shake Robinson's hand on his way out of the office. The snake. Keeping his eyes on their exchange, McGregor picked up the phone and dialled the typing pool. 'Betty,' he said, 'I'm sending a file back to London, but I'd like you to copy it first.'

Chapter 24

The greater the difficulty, the greater the glory

Walking towards the office, Mirabelle practically creaked. Her limbs were stiff and, catching sight of herself in a run of polished glass as she passed the first of the shops, she realised how ill-fitting the maid's outfit was and that the dark bags under her eyes were even more pronounced than they had been the night before. She felt like a marionette, as she made her way along the front, wondering if she ought to turn back and reclaim her clothes. But the thought of the manager at the penthouse put her off and, besides, it was busy today on the service floor. It seemed unlikely she would get away without being questioned about what she was doing, especially as it would look as if she was arriving part-way through a shift. No, she decided, it was too much of a risk. People were so rude to maids, almost as if they weren't really people. She found herself thinking of the maid at Tongdean Avenue. She hoped she hadn't been as unpleasant to the old dear as the women had been to her the night before. Her shoulder ached. She must have leaned against the door frame for a good six hours as she slept and she was still exhausted.

She passed a bakery and considered buying breakfast, but realised she had no money – not a penny. Her clutch purse was hidden under her skirt at the hotel. Suddenly, she felt terribly alone. For years after Jack died the feeling hadn't bothered her. If anything it had been a comfort, but now, in only a couple of days, the people she'd come to trust seemed suddenly absent. Would Vesta quit the office and give herself over to motherhood? One way or another, this baby was going to change things. You couldn't bring a pregnant woman or even a young mother on investigations. And as for McGregor. She felt an ache in her stomach, like hunger. She had no idea what might quell it.

Rolling her shoulder now to ease the pain, she turned up East Street and it took her a moment to recognise the super-intendent's figure approaching the office from the opposite direction. He raised a hand breezily as he came down the hill. When he leaned in to kiss her cheek, he smelled clean and his skin felt smooth. He'd slept in a bed the night before. But which bed? Normally, she'd be delighted to run into him, but now Mirabelle couldn't stop thinking about his visits to Tongdean Avenue. She pictured him in the chair in front of Ernie Davidson's desk. Who was Irene? Had the girl been upstairs the day Mirabelle visited? She stiffened as McGregor touched her arm. He was wearing the blue scarf Jinty had described. It was tucked into the collar of his jacket.

'I haven't heard from you in a couple of days. How did you get on finding out about Helen Quinn?' he said cheerily. 'And why are you dressed like that?'

Mirabelle shrugged. She fumbled in her pocket and took out her SOE lock picks. The key to the office was in her handbag back at the Grand – along with everything else. McGregor followed her into the hallway. She wanted to shout at him, but instead she remained silent. The sound of them climbing the stairs echoed. At the top, Mirabelle made short work of the office door and took a mental note to get Vesta to have a lock fitted that would be trickier to crack.

'I've been thinking.' McGregor removed his hat and pulled out a chair. 'You're right of course, if nobody knows about

Helen Quinn's background maybe she kept it secret for a reason.'

Mirabelle shook her head. 'I looked into it. She was Helen Lindley. Her maiden name, I mean. She lived just off Cremorne Gardens, in Chelsea. If she was hiding anything it was probably out of shame – it's a very poor area. A slum really.' Mirabelle pursed her lips. She found she could trust herself to express matters of fact, but she didn't want to hazard an opinion or her anger might tumble out. She hadn't realised how cross she was. How hurt.

Oblivious, McGregor nodded, taking in the information. 'Hmm,' he said. 'It's pretty rough in that part of town. Maybe she left someone behind, or thought she had.'

'That occurred to me too, but she seems to have kept to herself while she lived there, which was wise, I should say. She had no family. She worked in a dress shop.'

'Well, that's progress, isn't it? At least we know where she came from.' His tone grated. She decided not to mention Billy Randall's trip to London or their conversation in the back garden at Mill Lane. 'So, are we back at Hove Cars? Anything come up there?'

'Only what I mentioned before.' Mirabelle found her hand was quivering. She stuck it behind her back. 'Hove Cars ferries prostitutes around the city. You said I shouldn't look into it, but . . .'

'I'll put out some feelers. I've been caught up on another case. A suicide whose body was moved and I don't know why.' McGregor's tone was matter of fact. 'Anyway, leave this to me – I'll follow it up. I don't want you getting caught up in that kind of place, Belle. It's nasty.'

'Of course not.' Her stomach turned.

'It's not for a lady. My lady.' His grin was charming. But, she knew he'd been there. She knew he'd stayed. She felt anger rise, hot in her belly. How dare he?

'It'll be warm today. You won't need that scarf,' she said.

McGregor pulled it off and stuck it in his pocket. 'I suppose it's almost summer, isn't it? I better get back to work.'

She turned to fill the kettle so that he wouldn't kiss her cheek again. She wanted to put as much distance and as many obstacles between them as she could – a sink, a kettle, a million miles. What had she been thinking? It seemed crazy. McGregor didn't notice the change – he hadn't noticed anything.

'See you later,' he said and the door banged airily as he left.

Mirabelle sank into her chair, her hand resting on her stomach. When she looked down a McGuigan & McGuigan card was still in her hand. She wouldn't be in this position if she wasn't such an investigator. Her face crumpled. She shoved it into her pocket as she scrambled for a handkerchief. But she didn't have a handkerchief. It was all still at the hotel.

Making up for several days of being at work at least an hour before McGuigan & McGuigan Debt Recovery opened its doors, Vesta didn't arrive at the office until well after half past nine. Bill Turpin had strolled in on the dot, by which time Mirabelle was muddling through the papers on her desk. As Vesta finally burst through the door, Bill looked up and mumbled his good mornings. For an ex-policeman he was not terribly observant and had not remarked that, having removed the apron, Mirabelle was wearing an ill-fitting black shift – a colour she associated with mourning and therefore rarely sported unless she was due to attend a funeral. Neither had he noted that she was wearing a pair of flat shoes.

Vesta was a different matter. She removed her coat, laid her newspaper on the desk and just stared.

'I need your help,' Mirabelle said.

The girl grinned. 'I'll say.'

Mirabelle held up the apron, which she had secreted behind her chair. 'Long story,' she said.

Bill scraped his seat along the floor and got to his feet. 'I'll leave you ladies to it, shall I?' There was a plethora of subjects which Bill considered 'women's business'. He avoided them assiduously and this had the feel of being one. He lifted his papers and called his dog, Panther, to heel.

'Well?' Vesta demanded after the door had closed behind him.

'My clothes are on the service floor of the Grand Hotel. In a changing room used by female staff. I need to get them back.' This wasn't the main thing on Mirabelle's mind, but it seemed a practical place to start.

Vesta grinned. 'Ah,' she said, 'I assumed you'd swapped clothes with a nun.'

'Chambermaid,' Mirabelle said flatly. 'But not so much swapped, as, well, stole. I left my handbag – keys, money, the lot.'

A wry expression played on Vesta's lips. 'Well,' she said.

'It's not the clothes that are most important.' Mirabelle tried to ignore the fact that Vesta was clearly enjoying this. 'I think I'm on to something. I've made a connection between Billy Randall and the countess.'

'The countess?'

'The Russian woman. Staying at the Grand. The one you picked out in that magazine. She's here, in Brighton.'

Vesta's eyes narrowed. 'Yes. I saw.'

'Billy Randall had her card. Or at least, a card with her telephone number on it. Her number in London. I picked his pocket. She's been running some kind of casino in her hotel suite. I think perhaps she does the same thing in town – twice a week. She must be making a fortune.'

Vesta leaned against her desk. 'I see,' she said, though her expression was quizzical. 'She's been complaining. About the food at the Grand. About everything.'

Mirabelle nodded. 'That sounds like her. I followed Billy to

London. It turns out he was there on Saturday night and on Sunday. That's why he didn't come home. Whatever he was up to he didn't want to tell his wife about it, which is why he came up with the lie about working overtime.'

'Poor Vi,' Vesta mouthed.

'I challenged him, but he wouldn't come clean. He got quite agitated.'

'Was he gambling, do you think?'

'I wondered that. The thing is, he has nothing to gamble with. Not at this level. These games are well beyond the reach of the Randalls. Though I suppose he might be gaming somewhere else. It's not as if they couldn't use a big win.' Both women paused, remembering the worn carpet that Vi Randall had paced when they first questioned her about Helen Quinn's murder. 'Besides,' Mirabelle continued, 'he brought home enough money to buy a pram. It's hardly a good night at the tables.'

'Muscle?' Vesta hazarded doubtfully.

Mirabelle's nose crinkled with dubiety. 'He doesn't seem the type – not really. He tried to threaten me, but I could hardly take him seriously. There's a game in London tonight. At least I think there is. It's Saturdays and Tuesdays. I rang the number on the card.'

Vesta turned over her newspaper thoughtfully. 'And how does this tie in with the murder of Helen Quinn?'

'I have no idea. I accused Billy Randall of killing her and he denied it. He doesn't have any motive that I can figure out, but there's a connection. He definitely knows something.'

Vesta reached for her coat. 'We better get your clothes back,' she said.

It was easy enough to have someone fetch Charlie. Lunch service was nowhere near started. He appeared in the doorway at the rear of the hotel, his kitchen whites luminous as he cracked a 'Hey, baby,' in the direction of his wife.

'Congratulations.' Mirabelle shook his hand.

Vesta blushed. 'Oh for heaven's sake,' she said. 'Look, Charlie, we need help. Mirabelle's left her clothes inside.'

'Inside?'

'In the hotel. She stayed here last night.'

Charlie's face lit up. 'Mirabelle,' he teased. 'Really?'

'Oh stop it! She was on a case.' Vesta defended Mirabelle's honour. 'Can you get us into the women's changing room? The one for the staff?'

Charlie shrugged. 'Both of you? I mean, we don't give guided tours, but I could probably take one of you in if the coast was clear . . .'

Vesta raised her eyebrows. 'Want to toss for it?'

'You go. Charlie might be bringing you into the kitchen for another reason. And, besides, I don't want to bump into the manager I met this morning. I left my clothes to the right-hand side. My handbag is hidden under the skirt.'

Vesta held up her hand. 'Don't worry. I'll find everything. Your stuff is going to stick out – most waitresses don't have your style.'

'Did Vesta tell you the news?' Charlie lingered on the doorstep, as he shooed his wife ahead.

'About the baby? Yes. It's wonderful.'

'No. About the High Court. We ain't got no more racial segregation in the States. Not on buses.'

Mirabelle recalled Vesta toying with the newspaper that morning. She normally brought in the *Picture Post*. She should have realised something had happened, but then she'd been preoccupied. 'Well, that's wonderful,' she said.

'Charlie's cock-a-hoop,' Vesta cut in.

As the door banged behind the young couple, Mirabelle realised they had had a conversation to which she hadn't been privy. Charlie had asked Vesta what she thought about moving to the States. Vesta had always said that the Americans treated the blacks worse than anywhere in Europe, let alone in England. But now, with this decision, Mirabelle wondered if things might be changing. She backed off, loitering out of the way by the rubbish bins. She'd hate to do without Vesta, but then she'd never want to hold her back. That was the trouble, you couldn't replace people. The truth was, you were always alone, or, at least, it seemed she was.

Shuddering at the thought, Mirabelle considered moving into a small square of bright sunlight on the other side of the byway. She was about to do so when a car appeared at the end of the run. It drew up slowly at the door. Mirabelle stepped backwards, skulking round the side of the bin. She didn't want anyone to see her. Then her eyes widened as the man who had been on duty in the countess's suite the night before got out and lit a cigarette. He stepped into the sunny spot Mirabelle had considered. Then he exhaled, checking his watch. He must have been on time, because he had no sooner finished this manoeuvre than the service door opened and Billy Randall stepped on to the tarmac, accompanied by another man Mirabelle had never seen before.

'All right?' the man enquired of the driver.

'Did she give you a bollocking? You're trying her patience, son.'

Billy Randall looked almost tearful. Next to these men, his frame seemed particularly slight.

'Aww. Don't make the baby cry,' the man teased. 'You want to be thankful you're gold dust. Or you'd be gone by now. Long gone.'

Billy looked as if he was about to say something, but then he spotted Mirabelle. He stared right at her. Mirabelle's heart pounded, but Billy didn't give her away. It was confusing. She'd assumed he was on the other side, but then these things could be complicated. She smiled. Then one man pushed him into the back seat of the car and the other man got into the driver's seat. The engine fired and the car backed down the lane. Mirabelle had to make a split second decision, but then what else could she do? Leaving Vesta to pick up her worldly possessions, she ran after the car as it disappeared around the corner. At the front of the hotel, there were two taxicabs. She ducked into one of them.

'Are you from Hove Cars?'

'Yes, love,' the driver turned in his seat.

'I don't have a penny, but I can see to it that you get paid later. My name is Mirabelle Bevan. I'm on the trail of Helen Quinn's killer and I need you to follow that car.' She pointed at the motor, which was receding westwards along the front.

The driver hesitated then switched on the ignition. 'Right,' he said.

'Try to hang back,' Mirabelle instructed. 'Don't let them see you.'

The car turned up First Avenue and the taxi followed discreetly.

'Is the murderer in there?' the driver asked, as he indicated.

'I don't know. But the men in that car know who did it.'

'Mrs Quinn was a nice woman.'

'I know.'

As the car drove north, Mirabelle sat on the edge of her seat, clinging to the leather strap above the window. She was familiar with the area they were passing through. These streets were not far from her flat on the Lawns. As the journey continued, the houses were set back further from the road. They became more spread out and the gardens surrounding them greener. When the car turned into a driveway, the taxi driver pulled up on the street. Mirabelle took in the vista of one of Brighton's most expensive addresses. What were the men doing here? Billy Randall wasn't a tough guy or a high roller. What did he have that brought him to the Grand and then here of all places? When the man said he was gold dust – what did he mean?

'Want me to drive in, miss?'

'No.'

The house had wrought-iron gates. The building was partially obscured by trees, though Mirabelle could make out a turning circle and a couple of rose beds at the top of the drive. She reached for the door handle.

'If you contact Superintendent McGregor at Bartholomew Square, he'll pay you,' she said.

The driver shrugged. 'I can wait if you want.'

Mirabelle considered it. This is what drivers did for the women who lived on Tongdean Avenue. 'No,' she said decisively. 'I'll be fine.'

It took only a moment or two for Mirabelle to disappear through the gate and up the drive. The house was impressive. She guessed it was Victorian – a sprawling brick edifice with a small tower built on to one gable. The car had parked to one side of the front door. Mirabelle kept out of the way, slipping up the right-hand side of the drive and using the planting to shield herself. That was one advantage of wearing black, she mused. It was great camouflage. At the top of the drive, she peered through a window. Inside, a grand room was only partially furnished. Two men on ladders were painting the cornice. Mirabelle continued around the perimeter. There was a dining room and, to the side, some kind of pantry, a laundry, a lavatory and a service entrance. Around the next corner, the extent of the grounds became clear as the grass stretched towards a tennis court and a small cottage hidden by a bank of trees, which, she supposed, must have been built to accommodate a senior member of staff. Turning back to the main house, she noted the rear windows opened on to a large kitchen and, beyond that, a conservatory and some kind of public room – a sitting room, perhaps. Mirabelle made her way towards this when the startling sound of someone knocking on a window halted her in her tracks. On the other side of the glass, a plump, older woman gesticulated towards the back door. Mirabelle froze. The woman disappeared and then the door opened.

'You're meant to come to the side,' she scolded loudly. 'And you're late.' Without waiting for a reply, she stepped back to let Mirabelle enter. There didn't seem a lot of options and, besides, Mirabelle wanted to see inside. 'There's a power of work to do,' the woman continued. 'I'm Cook. What's your name?'

'Mary,' Mirabelle said, as if by rote. It had worked at the Grand, and here too, the cook didn't question it.

'I don't know.' The woman turned back into the kitchen, casting an eye over a pot that was bubbling on the stove. 'The painting isn't even finished in some of the rooms. There's three workmen still full time and her ladyship decides to throw a party. She's sick of the hotel, she said. We're nowhere near ready.'

'A party? Tonight?'

The older woman nodded and rolled her eyes to confirm this ridiculous idea. 'The furniture isn't even all delivered. They got the billiard table in, but there's nowhere near enough chairs. Empty bedrooms. You name it.'

'It's a lovely house,' Mirabelle observed.

Cook looked bemused at this comment. 'It'll take some keeping – these old places. Where did you work before?'

'Belgravia.' Mirabelle found the lie tripping off her tongue.

'Well, it's different in Brighton. It's not the big city. First off, you'll need to make up her ladyship's room. She may want to use it.'

'Her bedroom?'

'She's staying in the hotel just now, poor soul, but at least she can use it to powder her nose.'

Mirabelle found herself unable to pity the countess her three-room penthouse at the Grand.

Cook continued. 'She's bound to need somewhere to retire. Seventy guests. No dinner, mind you. Thank the Lord. Well. Get on with it then. First floor. It's pale blue and gold. You'll find linen in the cupboard at the top of the stairs.'

Chapter 25

*When the gods wish to punish us,
they answer our prayers*

Beyond the kitchen, the house smelled of fresh paint and cigarettes. It was enormous. It reminded Mirabelle of a smaller version of Brighton Pavilion, where she had tracked down a murderer only a few years before. Then the Pavilion had been in disrepair whereas here the countess's house was light and, although not completed, seemed in good order. Crystal chandeliers with cameos set into the frames were hoisted over thick carpets and the rooms were mostly decorated, downstairs, at least. There was hand-painted red wallpaper of a Chinese design in the dining room and then, further along, a games room with the billiards table Cook had mentioned. It might be smaller than the Pavilion, but the place was better appointed. It felt very private – close the door on one of these rooms and you could get up to whatever you wanted.

Mirabelle was considering this when she found herself distracted by the sound of men laughing and, checking over her shoulder, she decided to investigate, setting off past the billiards table. Loitering in the doorway of the room that led off it, she noted half a dozen card tables had been set up and, at one end, a roulette wheel. The room itself, however, was deserted. Then the laughter sounded once more – this time from a room off that. The door was ajar and Mirabelle approached with caution and glanced inside. The anteroom was smaller – only one table had been set up inside. Leaning against the wall, the driver she'd seen at the Grand smoked a cigarette, while round the table Billy Randall was holding court. He looked as if he belonged there. In front of him, three young men were observing carefully as Billy dealt cards.

'You think this is a face card,' he said, turning one over with an elegant flick. 'But it's a two. And this is the three. And here is the four.'

The sound of young men being impressed emanated, as Billy casually worked the pack, naming each card before he turned it over.

'Are you dealing from the bottom, Mr Randall?' one of the boys asked.

Billy laughed. 'Fool's game. You'd spot that.' He continued to turn the cards effortlessly on to the surface in front of him. So this was what he could do for the countess. This was why the Randalls had left London. This was what Vi meant when she said Billy was good with numbers. This was worth a fortune.

Mirabelle shifted in the doorway, as she realised the possibilities. Spotting her movement, the driver looked up. He swung back the door and glared.

'Sir,' she said, bobbing a curtsey. 'I came to see if you might like tea?'

Billy looked alarmed. He stopped dealing.

'Tea?' The driver's tone made it clear that tea would be unnecessary. 'We're busy in here, love.'

'Yes, sir. Cards.'

'Play a little, do you?'

Mirabelle shook her head. 'No, sir.'

'Not even canasta? You must like a flutter now and then. Come on. Take a seat. Let Billy deal for you.'

'Leave her alone, Roberts,' Billy objected, but the man was not to be put off. He took Mirabelle's arm and pulled her into the room. The young men shuffled to make space. 'She's a punter, Billy. A green one. Go on. You show them how it's done. You don't mind, love, do you?'

Mirabelle sat at the table. Billy motioned one of the men to take a place opposite her. 'Five card poker,' he announced. 'Might as well start at the beginning. Now, we want the punters to gain confidence. Nobody plays cards to lose, do they?'

There was a general murmur of assent.

'So let's say they get half a dozen decent hands just playing straight. They might win, they might lose. If they're losing too much you give them a nudge, so they win. We want them to win, see. At first. The stakes are never less than ten guineas here and, on the private tables, higher, so on a table like this, this lady might have won fifty guineas before I'd step in. Some nights, a hundred.'

He started to deal – one hand for Mirabelle, one for the man and one for the house. 'I've given you two sevens and smash, you got three twos. But the house has four tens. Nothing flash, see. Hope is interesting. It makes people do all kinds of things. Now, miss, if you give back three cards, not the sevens, mind.' Mirabelle obliged, sliding the cards across the table. 'Now, I'd deal you a sneaky third seven and an ace. The ace doesn't do nothing, but people like them. They think they're lucky. You've got to give the punters enough to keep them betting. Three sevens is a good hand. This lady thinks she's winning.'

'I can't see how you're doing it,' one of the men complained.

''Course you can't, son,' the driver snarled. 'That's what you're here to learn.'

Mirabelle stared at Billy. She couldn't see how he was doing it either. 'What do I do now?' she asked.

'Well, if you were sensible you get out. Walk away.' Billy looked her directly in the eye. He wasn't talking about the cards. 'But you won't, will you? People like to gamble. So probably you'll up your stake.'

'And I'd lose?'

'Over the course of the night I make sure of that. We set up one or two big winners but the biggest winner of them all is Her Ladyship. The house, I mean.'

'Oi,' the driver objected, as if stating it so baldly was going too far.

Billy didn't reply. 'So, now you're betting on each round and you're confident so you're betting big. There's, say, the full fifty guineas in the pot. And—' he flipped over his cards to reveal his run of four tens '—the house wins.'

A murmur of satisfaction assailed the table. Mirabelle folded. 'How do you do it?' she asked.

'I've always been able to do it. I see the numbers. I have done since I was a kid. But it can be taught.' He pulled out fresh decks and handed them to the men, who eagerly tore open the packs. 'Thank you, miss,' he said, dismissing her. Mirabelle slipped off the seat. Roberts held the door. 'Pays your wages,' he said sagely, almost as if it was a threat. 'Pays all our wages.'

Billy's eyes were still. He seemed resigned.

'Will you be working tonight, love?' Roberts asked, eyeing Mirabelle as she passed into the main gaming room.

'I think so,' she replied. 'Can I get you anything, sir?'

'Not now.'

'Well, I best get on.'

'I'm going to the lav,' Billy announced. 'You lot shuffle. I want to see your pivot cuts. That's the first thing.'

'Pivot cuts,' one of the men complained, as if this was too basic.

'Oi,' said Roberts again.

Mirabelle remembered this was Vi's speciality. Billy had been impressed with her when they first met. It seemed sad now. She walked past the empty tables in the main room and wondered if the roulette wheel was loaded. Of course it was. Out in the hallway, Billy rounded on her.

'What are you doing here?'

'These men killed Helen Quinn, didn't they?'

'Of course they did.'

'They killed her because they wanted you.'

Billy sighed. Then he came clean. He owed her the explanation. 'We thought we'd got away. I had a job. Nothing much, but it was out of this. It was good for a while. But these people . . . when they found me . . . I didn't want to come back, you see. You should get out of here, Miss Bevan.'

'They were trying to scare you, weren't they? To make you work for them. That's the motive.'

'They scared me all right. Look, there's nothing you can do.'

'And they stabbed Helen Quinn in the stomach because Vi is pregnant. It was a warning. But it wasn't aimed at Phil Quinn. That's where we all went wrong. It was for you. God, you must have been terrified.'

Billy didn't answer.

'You need a safe house, Billy. You and Vi. I'll see if I can . . .'

'No. They've made it clear what'll happen.'

'But Vi must be beside herself.'

'Vi hasn't figured it out yet. And I'm not going to tell her till after the baby arrives. Look, you should get out. You're in danger. If they find out why you're here . . .'

'But the police . . .'

Billy snorted. 'Don't you understand? The police won't tackle this. You don't know who she entertains in her place in London – judges and MPs. There's actors too – a bit of glam. Half the room's got a title any night of the week. People of standing. They call it the establishment. They like her and they aren't going to put her away. She's got too much on them. Don't you see?'

'Helen Quinn was murdered . . .' Mirabelle objected.

'Better Helen than Vi. Better Helen than me,' Billy snapped. 'And what about Phil?'

'The police have got nothing on Phil. They'll have to let him go.' Billy dropped his hands by his side as if he had given up. 'Jesus,' he said. 'Don't you get it? People like this, they love it. They want the thrill. They'd screw the house if they could. And, instead, the house screws them. Everyone wants risk since the war. Luxury and risk. It's like a drug. There are drugs here too. They get themselves into it because they want to. And there's so much money that nobody matters, not you, not me and not bloody Helen, that's for sure.'

Mirabelle was about to push him further. But, before she could find the words, the front door swung open at the other end of the hall. There was a pause and then the countess wandered into the vestibule dressed in a long mink coat. She was followed by a man. With the light behind them, it was difficult to make them out. It was not the same in the other direction.

'What are you doing?' The countess's sharp eyes spotted Mirabelle and Billy immediately, out of place.

'I'm giving the girl directions,' Billy said. 'She's new.'

Mirabelle bobbed a curtsey. The countess clearly didn't recognise her, but then why would she?

'Well, get on then.' The woman raised a languid gloved hand and flicked it in the general direction of the interior. 'Haven't you got things to do?'

Billy dropped his head and, with only the merest hesitation, he turned back towards the gaming rooms. Mirabelle watched him. She was about to step on to the stairs when the man behind the countess followed her into the hallway.

'Well, well,' he said.

Mirabelle blushed. In the light, she could see the countess's companion. Ernie Davidson was eyeing her with a look of delight on his face.

'What are you doing here?' The words were out of Mirabelle's mouth before she could stop herself.

'I'm visiting the neighbours, as it were. But you know all about that. I thought I'd come and see the new establishment,' he said, with a shrug. 'Fancy seeing you here.'

'You know this girl?'

Davidson hesitated. He winked. 'She used to work for a friend of mine,' he said. 'She showed promise, as I recall.'

'Brighton. So small.' The countess removed her mink coat and gestured Mirabelle to take it. As she did so, Davidson patted Mirabelle's bottom and handed her his hat. A seam of outrage flashed through her gut and she struggled to control her temper. It felt as if all the evil in Brighton was converging on this grand house and there was nothing she could do.

The countess stalked towards one of the public rooms. 'It's not nearly finished,' she drawled.

Davidson leaned in. 'Our little secret, Belle.' He winked. 'I've got you now.'

'We need discretion, you can see how it is . . .' the countess continued, her voice disappearing as she walked away.

Davidson followed, leaving Mirabelle alone in the cavernous hallway with the mink draped over her arm. Which one of these men murdered Helen Quinn? she wondered. Who had come up with such a cruel, horrible idea? The only decent soul was Billy, she realised. She'd misjudged him. He didn't want to be caught up in this, but there he was, fighting for his life and for his wife and child, and all anyone else seemed to care about was money.

Chapter 26

No one can give you better advice than yourself

Scouting the upper floor, Mirabelle was joined by another maid. The girl was boss-eyed and her auburn hair was tucked untidily under an old-fashioned, white cap. Her uniform fitted her perfectly though and Mirabelle eyed it jealously.

'I didn't know there was going to be two of us,' the girl said proprietorially.

'Well, it's a big house.' Mirabelle ran a palm over her ill-fitting skirt. 'There may be more yet, don't you think? What with the party.'

The girl shrugged and removed a pile of linen from the cupboard, wrinkling her freckled nose. 'You better pull your weight. Mary? Isn't it? I'm Louise. Come on, we'll tackle it together.'

The countess's room smelled of perfume. A large, cut-glass bottle, identical to the one in her suite, sat on the dressing table. Mirabelle wondered if the woman had these in each of her houses – in Belgravia, here and who knew where else? It seemed somehow careless. Even kings and queens used to travel with their personal possessions rather than strewing them around a succession of homes.

Louise pulled the curtains. The room overlooked the back garden. 'You take that side,' she directed, opening a linen sheet and flinging the edge across the mattress. During the war, Mirabelle had been trained by the First Aid Nursing Yeomanry and she knew how to keep the corners tight.

'Do you know what goes on here?' Mirabelle asked.

Louise nodded. 'Why do you think the pay's so good?'

'It's not only gambling.' Mirabelle was hoping for an ally.

'That's not my business. Nor is it yours.' The girl's gaze was stony as she squared off the sheet. 'I'd keep my head down and save up if I were you. Someone told me there's tips. I'll check the lavatory,' she announced and walked off.

Through the window, Mirabelle noticed the countess and Davidson walking down the lawn. The countess had fitted a cigarette into a long, amber holder and Davidson was solicitously lighting it. She waved her hand elegantly as if demonstrating the view, then took off in the direction of the copse of trees and the little cottage. Mirabelle threw a last pillow into place. She contemplated the receding figures and then, keeping an eye out for Louise, she slipped across the hallway and back downstairs. Biding her time at the kitchen door, she waited until the cook nipped into the pantry and then, careful not to be seen, she sneaked into the garden.

Down the lawn, at the copse of trees, in the shade, the cottage door was open, just a slice. The ground felt soft under her feet, as she strained to see. Inside, two rooms led off a tiny hallway. One was set up as a bar with comfortable chairs, beyond which there were French doors on to a small patio. It was empty. Mirabelle slipped round to the rear where she discovered the second room was shuttered. She put her eye to a tiny chink, but she only caught a glimpse. Davidson was standing with his back to her. She could hear his voice but not what he was actually saying. With a shrug, Mirabelle completed her circuit, making for the open front door where she hoped to make out the conversation better. As she rounded the corner, she pulled back just in time. The other man, the one she recognised from the car that morning, was heading towards the cottage. The trees made it easy for her to hide. He pushed the door wider as he entered and Mirabelle moved forward and strained to hear.

Inside, the countess was laughing. It was a throaty sound and quite unaccustomed. Davidson's voice, by contrast, came in snatches.

'And you think there's a demand?' he said.

'Oh yes. I'm certain. People will pay.' The countess's tone was serious. 'We've tried it already. Sit down,' she invited him. 'Sit.'

There was the sound of a chair scraping across a tiled floor. A moment later it seemed Davidson must have got to his feet, because there was the sound of it scraping again.

'No. Sit.' The countess sounded like she was talking to a dog. 'Are you afraid?'

'Any man would be afraid.'

'I'm not. I will sit,' she rebuffed him. 'Are you too scared to sit with me?'

The chair scraped more slowly this time, but it seemed he gave into her. After a short silence there was a mechanical click and Davidson's voice raised again. This time he sounded panicked.

'Jesus,' he said. 'What are you doing?'

'You think you are some big man with your stable of mediocre whores?' The countess's voice was set once more at its usual timbre as she laid into him.

'No!' Davidson sounded as if he was pleading.

'Why did you think I brought you here? A social occasion? Friends between thieves they call it?' She sounded as if she was spitting the words. 'And you want a cut? Some business from me? As if I couldn't find a mediocre whore if I needed one, without the help of a man such as you.'

'Look . . . this is my patch . . . ' Davidson's breathing was shallow. He didn't get any further.

There was the sound of a scuffle, a shout and then a loud bang. Mirabelle jumped. She curled her fists into balls and forced herself to keep listening.

'Oh, really,' the countess's voice drawled. She had gone back to complaining. 'Have you thought what you will do with him this time? Because that other one has been found, you know. I had to make several telephone calls.'

'I'll do what I always do,' said the third voice. 'That's what the Downs are for. That's why we're here.'

'Well, bury him properly this time,' she said, as she got to her feet.

Mirabelle's stomach churned. She pulled back as the countess stalked out of the cottage in the direction of the house. From inside, there was the sound of something heavy being dragged. She watched as the man emerged and followed the countess across the lawn. Then, carefully, Mirabelle edged along the front of the cottage. She stiffened as she caught sight of Davidson's body slumped in the hallway. Tentatively, checking over her shoulder, she sneaked across the threshold and expertly checked for a pulse but there was none. His skin was still warm and clammy from those last moments of terror. She shuddered, pulling back her hand as a smear of blood disappeared into the black material of her blouse. It had happened so quickly. There had been nothing she could do. Glancing behind his body, she could see the room was tiled floor to ceiling like a hospital operating theatre. Along one wall, behind a mahogany table that was set with six chairs, the splatter of blood told its own story. She hovered in the doorway. This was a killing room – a place of execution. Easy to clean.

'You were greedy,' she whispered, 'but you didn't deserve that.'

She found she couldn't bring herself to feel sorry. Not quite. She wondered if Jinty might cry. The girl had shown a marked lack of emotion about Helen Quinn's death, but then she hadn't relied on Mrs Quinn for her living. Davidson's murder might be different. Then, from the direction of the house, the man stepped back on to the grass with another fellow. Mirabelle looked round frantically. There was no way out now without being seen so she slipped across the hallway and crouched behind the bar in the other room. Her breathing became shallow as the men blundered in.

'She's got it in her head, Harry,' the second man said. 'I mean, the other night, the six of them were delighted. One poor bugger copped it, but the rest were as high as kites, mad bastards.'

'Too afraid to kill themselves any other way.'

Mirabelle held her breath.

'Well, who's going to clean up this then?'

'Why do you think I came to get you?'

'I thought you needed a hand with the body.'

'This time I'll be coming with you to make sure you don't just dump him.'

'All right. All right.'

There was the sound of fumbling and Mirabelle realised they were turning out Davidson's pockets. 'Cash,' one said, sounding satisfied. The notes crinkled. 'And I'll take that signet ring and all.'

'You'll get identified with that. That's the lovely thing about cash. No one knows where you got it. Take the ring, but we'll have to dump it. Or melt it down.'

Mirabelle heard footsteps as one of the men came closer. Above her, he leaned over the bar and poured himself a drink. The scent of whisky settled on the air cutting through another, more animal smell of blood and sweat. Mirabelle's heart began to pound again. She could feel it rising in her chest. She closed her eyes. She read somewhere that's what people do, when they don't want to be seen. Illogical. But she found herself doing it. The man sniffed. He put down the whisky. Her heart sank as she realised that if she could smell him then he could smell her. The lavender soap, if any of it lingered on her skin, or maybe the scent of the linen cupboard.

'What's this then?' she heard him say.

She opened her eyes just in time to see his hand reaching out to grab her so she sprang backwards, knocking the bar and jolting his whisky on to the floor. He grabbed her arm and slapped one hand over her mouth as he pulled her upwards. She tried to bite his skin but he was too large for her to get any purchase. Instead, she kicked frantically. All she kept thinking was Vesta doesn't even know where I am. I just walked off. Then the man pinned her against the wall using his knee. He stared, nodding for her to be quiet as he raised a thick finger to his lips.

'Now,' he said, loosening his grasp. 'What are you doing here?'

'I was sent down to clean the bar,' Mirabelle said, her voice shaking. She wanted to be braver, but her body appeared to have taken over.

The man laughed. 'You were just here? Unlucky, like?'

'I didn't see anything. I only heard. Why did she kill him?'

'Oh she didn't kill him, love. I did. On orders. You don't want to know, though, do you?'

Mirabelle shook her head.

'Have you ever seen a dead body?'

It was a lie but she shook her head again. It was what he wanted to hear and what was most likely to get her out of here alive.

'That's what I call bad timing,' he said. 'Who'd have thought it?'

He removed his leg from where it was jamming her into place and Mirabelle slumped.

'Clear that up.' He motioned to the fallen glass. She fell to her knees and picked up the shards, dabbing the whisky with her apron as he made for the door. The other man hoisted

Davidson's body over his shoulder. 'Well, what are we going to do?' he whispered.

Still low to the ground, Mirabelle backed towards the French doors and flicked the catch that locked them. She slipped on to the patio and turned, throwing the glass on to the grass as she began to run. She had no idea what was at the bottom of the garden. There was no time to think that far ahead. She got perhaps twenty yards before they called out and started after her. By then, Mirabelle was into her stride. The lawn tailed off in a patch of mud and three Victorian rollers, covered in moss, were propped against a high, brick wall. She scrambled up one and tried to pull herself over, but she wasn't fast enough. The man caught her leg and hauled her down. Landing with a thump, she felt the cold earth, musty against her body. Her jaw ached where she'd hit it. Then her scalp stung as he pulled her up by her hair.

'Fucking bitch,' he said. 'You just lost your job.'

She was forming the words to reply, because you had to go down fighting – that was her nature – but then, quite suddenly, there was a searing pain and the words turned into a deep gasp that spiralled into blackness.

Chapter 27

What you seek is seeking you

Vesta hadn't only managed to procure Mirabelle's clothes from the staff changing room at the Grand, she had also sneaked out four rock buns and jam (not Hartley's). Now, she parcelled two of the buns in a paper bag for Bill to take home when he called at the office at the end of the day. The remaining two she arranged on a plate. She broke off a craggy outcrop of sugar and raisins and slipped it into her mouth. Ideally, she'd like to brew a pot of tea and have a natter with Mirabelle as they tucked in together, but Mirabelle had disappeared.

Vesta wasn't perturbed when she emerged into the sunlight at the service entrance of the hotel and discovered Mirabelle had gone. She hovered, hopefully, for a moment and then walked to the front of the building and peered in both directions. Mirabelle may have decided to head back to the office, she told herself. Or she might have gone home. She had looked as if she could do with a freshen-up. Vesta had never seen her friend look so faded. In extremis Mirabelle usually sparkled, but this case was taking its toll. Murder was always harrowing, but when the victim was a woman, Mirabelle took it worse and this time the crime had been so violent.

Vesta returned to the service entrance. Sometimes Mirabelle left a note – some kind of clue – but this time there was nothing. She peered around the side of the old bins and stared at the tyre marks on the tarmac, trying to recall if they had been there earlier. Then she shrugged and returned to the office where now, sitting at her desk, she leafed through the papers in front of her. McGuigan & McGuigan's affairs didn't hold her attention for long and she soon turned to the newspaper. Charlie's suggestion was on her mind. The prospect of moving to America was tantalising. It would certainly put paid to Vesta's worries about her mother becoming overbearing when the baby came. But then Vesta felt that she was British and that she belonged here, no matter what people sometimes intimated about the colour of her skin. England was home.

Gradually, the clock ticked towards lunchtime. Her tummy gurgled. She broke off another piece of rock bun and smeared it with jam as she stared accusingly at Mirabelle's empty chair. Perhaps Mirabelle had gone home and fallen asleep. Perhaps something had come up. Perhaps . . . It was no use. Popping the last of the bun into her mouth and licking her jammy fingers, Vesta put on her coat and locked the office door. She turned down the street and headed on to the front. It was almost like summer. The sky was searing blue, streaked with wisps. Some of the souvenir shops had put postcard stands on the pavement. Vesta wondered how large her stomach might get and how quickly it might happen. Would she need new summer clothes and, if so, what might she choose? She considered her favourite red summer frock and wondered if she would be able to alter it.

At the Grand she hovered. The most likely thing was that Mirabelle had gone back to her flat, but still. The doorman eyed her as she loitered on the pavement and Vesta approached him, waving to stop him opening the door.

'Hello,' she said. 'Were you on duty earlier this morning?'

The man's blue eyes sparkled beneath his well-brushed top hat. 'Well, I saw you, if that's what you're asking.'

'I'm looking for a friend. Same height as me. Auburn hair.

She was wearing a black dress. She was with me, but she left on her own. Just before I came round, probably.'

'Darkie too, was she?'

Vesta restrained herself from the sigh that twisted in her throat. 'She's a white lady. Like you.'

The man's lips puckered. 'No,' he said. 'I don't recall anyone in particular, but then a lot of people go by.'

Mirabelle's outfit might have been remarkable to anyone who knew her, but it was commonplace if you didn't – far less noteworthy than her usual clothes. Vesta knew she was the one everyone noticed. 'Thanks.' She walked back on to the pavement and was about to check around the back of the hotel again, when she noticed the taxi rank. This, she thought, was exactly the kind of inquiry for which the police used Hove Cars. Perhaps she ought to follow their lead. There were three cars waiting, two of the drivers smoking and enjoying the sun and one reading a newspaper.

'Excuse me.' Vesta kept her voice breezy. 'I wondered if you'd seen a woman this morning who came from the back of the hotel? She was white, wearing a black dress.'

One of the smokers nodded. 'Oh yes,' he said. 'The chambermaid? Owes me the fare.'

'She got into your taxi?'

'Two shillings and six-worth.'

Vesta scrambled in her handbag and withdrew three shillings, which she thrust into the man's hand. 'Here,' she said.

'She said the police would pay. Some bloke called McGregor,' the driver objected.

'Don't worry. I'll cover it. Where did you take her?'

'Out to the suburbs,' the man said mysteriously.

Vesta opened the car door. 'Take me,' she said, as she scrambled inside. 'Wherever it was.'

The street came as a shock. Vesta had never been out here before. This part of town was poorly served by buses and there were no shops – only a few streets of grand houses set in their own grounds. As she stepped on to the pavement, she was aware that few visitors must arrive unannounced and hardly any of them black.

'Here?' she checked with the driver.

'You want me to wait?'

Vesta considered this. 'Did Mirabelle want you to wait?'

The man shook his head.

'No then. Thanks.'

'Are you sure? She was positive she was on to something to do with that murder. I was thinking perhaps I should go to the police anyway.'

'I'm sure Mirabelle has it in hand. We work with the police. You can go,' she said and turned away.

Walking up the drive was daunting. Vesta hovered between the gates as the car turned along the road. Then she took a deep breath and headed up the drive. There was no point in ringing the doorbell. If Mirabelle was here, she'd have to find out under her own steam. Just as Mirabelle had done a few hours before, Vesta peered tentatively through the windows at the front and then made her way along the side of the house. It was, without doubt, the most palatial house Vesta had ever seen. Like Mirabelle, Vesta thought of the day they had broken into Brighton Pavilion. Now, the building had been opened as a museum, but then it was uncared for – an easy target. Here, the house was undeniably posh and even appeared to be occupied. At the back, linen had been hung out to air and the door to the conservatory lay gaping. Vesta loitered at the corner as a dumpy maid, her hair tucked into a white cap, emerged to check the drying laundry. The girl ran a hand down the damp tea towels and aprons and returned to the house.

Vesta edged towards the conservatory. The view through the glass was shielded by rows of plants, some of them exotic. She wasn't much of a gardener. Mirabelle would know the names – she took more of an interest in that kind of thing. At least the greenery provided some kind of cover. As Vesta stepped inside, the warm air closed around her like a winter coat. A few wicker chairs were grouped around a table. Someone had sat here recently – the ashtray had been used. Vesta checked the stubs – Dunhill – suitably upmarket. A solitary glass sat beside them and there was a whiff of scent on the air, despite the cigarette smoke. That meant expensive perfume.

The conservatory led on to a sitting room, through which she passed into the hall. Ahead of her, the same maid who had checked the sheets trotted efficiently around a corner and headed upstairs. Vesta waited for the girl to disappear. Then she sneaked into the dining room and then, hearing a woman's voice, she turned towards what looked like a study. Boxes of books were stacked beside empty bookshelves, the place in disarray. At the desk, the countess was on the telephone, her voice cutting the air into snippets.

'We'll start later in Brighton. It's so déclassé to game early. Nothing before nine-thirty, perhaps even ten. I mean, people have to have dinner.'

Vesta detected a smug note in the woman's voice. She liked dictating what would happen. Vesta leaned in to hear more.

'The house is adequate. Once I have it running properly I can move in.'

Vesta smiled. There was something ludicrous about considering this beautiful house unready for occupation. She'd passed paintings stacked against the walls and pots of paint piled ready for use, but it was lovely here. She wondered what the countess might make of the tiny house where she and Charlie lived. The front door had needed fixing for weeks and Charlie kept saying he would buy a refrigerator, but, when it came to it, they hardly ever ate at home. This thought reminded Vesta that she had missed lunch and her stomach turned. Then she was brought back to the situation by the click of the telephone being hung up. She took a step backwards, wondering if she would be safer ducking into the dining room, but before she could move she was tapped sharply on the shoulder. An old woman in a white apron gasped as Vesta turned. She let out a cry of dismay and dropped a piece of paper on the floor as she jumped to the wrong conclusion.

'I won't have it,' she said, keeping her eyes on Vesta's face. 'The agency can't expect me to work with darkies. Madam.' The cook swept into the study and laid the paper on the countess's desk. 'I won't do it. I won't have them in my kitchen.'

The countess peered over the cook's shoulder. 'Who sent you?' she enquired languidly.

'The agency, madam,' Vesta found herself saying.

'And how did you get in?'

'The door was open.'

'I won't have a darkie in my kitchen,' the cook repeated.

The countess perused the menu the cook had put on her desk. 'Fine,' she said. 'Serve the little sausages. The English seem to like them.' Her fingers flew elegantly towards the telephone handset. 'Hello,' she said, 'I want to speak to the Silver Service Agency.'

Vesta's palms started to sweat. 'I'll just go,' she said, backing out.

The countess made a gesture as if she was swatting a fly. 'Hello,' she snapped down the phone. 'Hastings Hall. You have sent us a maid. A black one.'

Vesta took another step down the hall. She raised her eyes to the front door as the countess spoke into the handset.

'I don't know how many girls they think we need. What with the other two. It's a kitchen maid I could really do with,' the cook murmured.

The countess replaced the telephone. 'Well,' she said, 'they don't seem to know anything about you. Though we will be getting a housekeeper shortly.'

'There must have been some kind of mix-up. I'm sorry. I'll just let myself out.' Vesta cast her eyes towards the door.

'You can't go out the front,' the cook said. 'Who do you think you are?' She made a gesture to direct Vesta towards the kitchen. It was the kind of movement you might make towards an animal you didn't want to touch and of which you were slightly afraid.

'Yes. Of course,' Vesta breathed gratefully, as she turned down the hall.

The countess appeared in the frame of the study door. 'No,' she said. She stalked on to the carpet. 'I've seen you somewhere before.'

'I doubt that, madam,' the cook said. 'A girl like this.'

The countess's eyes were determined, her gaze steely. 'I never forget a face,' she said.

Vesta thought of that lunchtime in reception at the Grand Hotel. She had got up and followed the countess outside, eavesdropping on her spat about the taxi. The countess's eyes narrowed as if she was honing in on the same incident.

'You were at the hotel.'

'I don't know what you mean.' Vesta felt as if she had been punched in the stomach. Slowly, a feeling of nausea spread across her chest like a stain.

The countess took a step towards her. She reached out and grabbed her arm, the carefully manicured nails like talons, the touch of her skin icy. Vesta pulled back. 'Who sent you?' she said. 'Was it that ridiculous woman from Mayfair? She and her lame little boys are no competition.' A smile spread across her face though she didn't look in the least happy. 'Roberts,' she called loudly. 'Roberts.'

A broad man appeared in the opposite doorway. There

was something blunt about him. 'What do we have here?' he asked.

'A spy,' the countess said. 'I think she is a spy.'

'I've never heard anything so ridiculous. Not me,' Vesta objected.

'She said she was sent by Silver Service, but they have no record of her. She was snooping around the house.'

'Where did you come from, my lovely.' The man adopted a sleazy tone. Vesta restrained herself from saying 'Bermondsey'. 'I was told there was a vacancy,' she said. 'My friend went to the agency and I thought I'd try my luck.'

The man considered this. Then he snatched Vesta's handbag and opened the catch. He rifled through her purse, the pen Charlie had bought her for Christmas, two clean handkerchiefs and a five pound note secreted in the inside pocket. 'Well, well,' he said. 'Rich pickings for a maid.' Then he took out a business card – Vesta always kept a few handy. 'Debt collectors, eh?'

'I'm owed money. I was going to engage them,' Vesta tried.

'Curious,' the man continued, as he drew a McGuigan & McGuigan business card from his pocket. 'I found another of these, earlier today. Another lady who was snooping around.'

The countess looked like a cat about to pounce. The corners of her mouth twitched. 'Find out what is going on, Roberts,' she said.

The room was at the top of the house and to the side. At one time it must have contained servants' quarters. The ceiling cut through it in a sharp coombe. As Roberts pushed Vesta ahead of him, she cracked her head off the low plaster and reeled, losing her footing. Not for the first time. She'd fallen twice as he pushed her up the stairs. As she stumbled over the threshold, there was a shout and she looked up to see Mirabelle reaching towards her from the corner. Her face was badly bruised. Vesta gasped. She'd never seen Mirabelle look so damaged. The black dress was smeared with mud and her hair fell about her face.

'I came to find you.' Vesta managed a smile.

'No.' Mirabelle's eyes filled with tears. Then she drew herself up. 'Let this girl go. She's having a baby. You have to let her go.'

Roberts laughed. It sounded like a rattle being shaken. 'No one's being let go. I want to know who sent you two? What are you doing here?'

'No one sent us.'

He pulled the business cards from his pocket. 'McGuigan & McGuigan? Maybe I should get in touch with them.'

'We are McGuigan & McGuigan, you idiot,' Mirabelle spat.

Roberts replied with a sharp jab to her jaw. She fell backwards on to the floor. 'Don't try my patience,' he snapped. 'Debt collectors? You two?'

Mirabelle put her hand to where he'd hit her. It ached. 'Our client is owed money,' she tried. 'That's what we're doing here.'

'The countess doesn't owe anyone a penny.'

'You don't understand. The guy who owes our client is coming tonight. He's one of the countess's guests. We've had trouble getting hold of him so we went undercover.'

'Who is it?'

'Name of Jenner,' Mirabelle said. 'Him and his wife.'

Roberts cocked his head as if considering this. She had gambled. Jenner, like Whiteside or Thomas, was one of those names that always sounded familiar. Jack had a list he used. 'I'm here to see Mr Cunningham,' or 'Mrs Falconer sent me,' were standard responses that always sounded plausible.

'We're out of our depth. You're right.' Mirabelle tried to shrug, but her shoulder wasn't stiff any more, it was actually painful. 'It was a stupid idea.'

'Who's your client?'

It seemed to be working, at least. 'Mr Cunningham,' she trotted out. 'He runs a game in Norwich. That's why he engaged us. He didn't want to come all the way down here to deal with it. He's small-time. We're small-time. We shouldn't have troubled you.'

Roberts snorted. 'Yeah,' he said. 'You shouldn't. It's a shame, really.'

'Do you think the countess might consider . . .' Mirabelle let the sentence linger.

Roberts stared. 'You'd be a looker, you know,' he said, as if he was noticing her for the first time.

'Well, I've been told I'm not bad when I'm brushed up.' She managed a smile. It didn't sting too much. 'Why don't you ask her? Please? We're sorry. We'd happily disappear if you'd let us.'

Roberts shook his head. 'You made a helluva mistake.'

'We'd both owe you one.'

'We don't need debt collectors here,' he chortled. 'No one reneges, or at least not for long.'

She let the silence sit. It didn't seem more difficult for him to hit a woman than to hit a man, but still, there was something there.

'All right,' he relented. 'Let me see what I can do.'

'Thank you.'

The door closed.

'We haven't got long,' Mirabelle said.

Behind her, tears were streaming down Vesta's face. 'What do you think he'll do?' the girl managed.

'He'll kill us. She's not going to let us out of here. Why should she? She's suspicious. She's right. We have to find a way out. I tried the window, but I couldn't get any purchase.' Mirabelle cast her eyes upwards to the small skylight. It had a heavy, iron frame. The glass was too small to make any difference if they broke it. Vesta got to her feet and pushed her hand upwards, but it didn't move. 'Give me a lift,' Mirabelle said. 'If both of us push together, it's double the weight against it.'

Vesta didn't like to say there was no weight to Mirabelle. She clasped her hands and Mirabelle stepped up, using them as a ladder. She thumped painfully against the window but it didn't move. Back on the ground she tried again. No dice.

'Let me have a go,' Vesta said.

Mirabelle jimmied the girl upwards and Vesta thumped hard against the glass. It jumped. 'There,' she said. 'I'm heavier. Let's try again.'

The second effort did it. Vesta pushed open the window and peered outside. The roof was steep. She hauled herself on to the slates and leaned back to pull up Mirabelle behind her. 'Be careful,' she said. A steep drop of three storeys gaped below. Carefully, Mirabelle closed the window and surveyed the situation. The roof was complicated – a series of flat areas punctuated by sheer slates. She led Vesta up to the top and then across the width of the house where a sturdy iron downpipe dropped twelve feet on to an old extension. 'Come on,' she said, glad of her flat shoes. Vesta was not so well equipped. She slipped off her kitten heels.

'You shouldn't have followed me,' Mirabelle scolded. 'In your condition.'

Vesta hesitated. She agreed, but, if she hadn't, Mirabelle wouldn't be on the roof now. 'It's just as well I did,' she snapped back. 'These people are hateful.'

Mirabelle didn't reply. She lowered herself over the side, her legs dangling before she curled them around the pipe. Then, taking a deep breath, she held on to the gutter as she left the safety of the roof and, clinging to the pipe, began to clamber down. Vesta loitered. 'I can't go over the edge,' she said.

'Don't make me come back up,' Mirabelle replied. 'You've got to.'

Vesta closed her eyes and fell to her knees. Then she realised she needed to see what she was doing. Her hands felt clammy and they were shaking. She wondered if she might be sick. But there was no time. 'Vesta. Come on,' Mirabelle said sternly. Gingerly, following her friend's lead, Vesta took a deep breath as she edged off the roof and dropped into place on the pipe. 'It's easy once you get started,' Mirabelle encouraged her. Vesta began to cry quietly as she shimmied down. At the bottom, Mirabelle gave her a hug. They held hands as they made their way across the slates, still a good fifteen feet off the ground. The garden was deserted. Mirabelle wondered where the men had put Davidson's body. She didn't want to trouble Vesta with the enquiry. 'It's only ten feet if we go over the side and then drop and roll,' she said. A vision of the boy at the cricket ground flashed across her mind. 'Like the SAS.'

Vesta nodded. This seemed easier for Mirabelle. She obviously wasn't afraid of heights.

'Drop and roll,' Mirabelle repeated, as Vesta sat on the edge and slowly let herself hang from the gutter. Then she dropped. The roll was more difficult than expected and her ankle stung. Mirabelle managed better, dropping and rolling like a professional. She got up and dusted herself down. Vesta realised that her friend didn't know how awful she looked. She limped over and smoothed Mirabelle's hair.

'There,' Mirabelle said. 'Thank you.'

Momentarily, Vesta wished she'd asked the taxi driver to wait. He'd offered after all. The women moved to the perimeter of the garden and began to make their way towards the front gate. Mirabelle glanced over her shoulder. Vesta could feel her ankle swelling, but she didn't want to make a fuss. It hurt more with every step. As they made their way along the last stretch of hedge, Mirabelle pulled the girl aside.

'We have to split up once we get out of here, Vesta. It's too dangerous.'

'What do you mean?'

'Someone here killed Helen Quinn. I still intend to find out who it was. And that's not the only murder. If they'd done for us, we wouldn't have been the first people they'd killed today.'

'You can't stay, Mirabelle.' Vesta's voice was peppered with shock.

'I have to,' Mirabelle insisted. 'Billy Randall is in there. If I can find him again . . .'

'It's too dangerous. This is a matter for the police. We need to get McGregor.'

'That's exactly what I want you to do. Tell McGregor about this place – what's going on. Tell him there's been more than one murder here. Go on.'

'What is going on here?'

Mirabelle let an impatient gasp escape her lips. 'It's a casino. There is a big party tonight and the tables are rigged. That's what Billy Randall does – he's a card sharp. A good one.' She decided not to tell Vesta about the cottage in the wood. There was no point – an illegal casino ought to be enough to bring McGregor. She'd mentioned that more than one person had been killed, after all. 'I don't have time to explain, but you have to fetch the superintendent. Promise me.'

'What are you doing to do?'

'I don't know, but I don't want to leave. Oh dear. You're hurt. Look at you.'

A wave of nausea broke over Vesta's body as she realised this was true. 'It's strained,' she said. 'It's not broken. There's a bus stop back on the main road.'

'Can you make it?'

'I think so. But promise you'll be careful.'

'I'm always careful.' Mirabelle cracked a smile. 'You get yourself patched up and fetch some help. I'll see if I can get

Billy Randall out and figure out which one of these men killed Helen. Go on.'

Vesta squeezed Mirabelle's hand before she turned to go, limping the last few yards and disappearing through the gate with a backwards glance. Mirabelle raised her hand cheerily and then leaned against a run of laurel. She stared at the house, wondering if it was Roberts who had stood behind the Quinns' place and waited for everyone to go to sleep. He seemed too large, somehow, to have sneaked in and poisoned the Quinns' gin bottle. Perhaps it was the other fellow. It was almost as if Jack whispered the word to her. Surveillance. Yes, she thought, she'd wait here for a while until she could figure out what to do.

There was no movement in the house for a good five minutes and Mirabelle ran back through everything. Someone was missing, she thought. There was someone she didn't know about. Not yet.

Then, a car turned off the main road and up the drive. She watched as it parked and a lean, green-eyed, familiar figure got out of the driver's seat. 'Now that's interesting,' she whispered under her breath, as Marcus Fox made his way through the front door. Mirabelle felt as if there was a calculating machine in her head, almost as if her brain were knitting. She stared at the facade of the house as if it might help her, but it didn't. Then, suddenly, as she checked her watch, she realised what she needed to do. With a backward glance, she sneaked towards the gate. Peering up and down the street, she made sure Vesta had gone and then she turned in the direction she guessed was opposite to the one the girl had taken to catch the bus into town. It was the long way round, but she'd get where she needed to in the end.

Chapter 28

*Nothing shows a man's character more
than what he laughs at*

Mirabelle stopped at home and slipped the spare key out of its hiding place on the door frame. The flat seemed too quiet. Inside, she discarded the muddy, blood-smeared chambermaid's uniform on the floor of her bedroom, gratefully slipping into a plain but well-tailored blue suit that was clean. She swept her hair into a bun. There seemed no point in applying make-up when her skin was mottled with bruises. Still, she dabbed on witch hazel and contented herself that at least now she was tidy. She picked a navy handbag from the wardrobe and slipped in some cash, two clean handkerchiefs and a spare set of keys she kept in the kitchen cupboard. Forty minutes later, she tripped up the steps of the hospital and turned in the opposite direction to the baby ward, passing a row of tea trolleys abandoned after the four o'clock service. A small pile of leftover Huntley and Palmers tumbled across a green plate.

The ward was quiet. She made straight for Fred's bed, where he was lying flat, heaving for breath. His eyes lighted as Mirabelle appeared.

'Gosh,' she said, 'would you like a pillow?' Fred shook his head. Then his brow furrowed as he took in her appearance. 'I know,' she confirmed. 'Sometimes I wish they'd given me combat training.'

Fred's exhalation rattled with a chortle. On the other side of the bed, a young nurse appeared.

'I'm sorry,' she said. 'It's not visiting time. Are you a relation?'

Fred reached out his hand and, vice-like, curled his fingers round Mirabelle's wrist.

'Please. I need to talk to him,' Mirabelle pleaded.

The girl looked over her shoulder and Mirabelle wondered if every matron terrified her charges in the same way. 'I'd offer you money,' she continued. 'I'm desperate. But you're a nurse.'

The girl looked embarrassed. 'It's what's best for the patients. Routine,' she tried to explain.

Fred's breath betrayed another chortle. 'I'll . . . be . . . gone . . . by . . . tomorrow,' he managed with considerable effort.

The nurse didn't deny it. She hesitated and stepped away. Fred cast his eyes at the chair beside him and Mirabelle sat.

'Where's your wife?'

Fred looked upwards this time. He reached on to the bedside cabinet and, with his hands now quivering, grasped for a pencil and a notepad. *Don't waste my time*, he scribbled.

Mirabelle smiled. 'OK,' she said. 'I've come about Marcus.' Fred's head moved fractionally away from her. 'I'm sorry,' she said. 'But I think he's involved in something bad. Something dangerous.'

Fred closed his eyes. When he opened them again he reached for the notepad. *He was always trouble. The things he saw before I brought him back.*

'Is that why you kept him away from your wife?'

Fred shook his head. Again, the movement was tiny, but it was clear he was making a huge effort. *Bitch*, he scribbled, now unable to keep the letters in a straight line. Mirabelle took his hand. She squeezed it.

'The boy might have killed somebody, Fred. A woman. That murder in Portslade.'

Fred's cough faltered. His eyes were rheumy. He pulled back his hand. It was then she understood. 'You know about it,' she said. 'Oh God.'

'He's . . . my . . . son,' Fred managed. 'Manners of a saint. He loves me. But a black heart.'

He was drawing in breath desperately now, as if he had a vacuum inside. Mirabelle couldn't think what to say. Fred's eyes focused once more. He fumbled with the pencil as she held the pad in place. *Keep away from him.*

'This wasn't his first murder?'

Fred didn't bother to reply. *Does anyone else know?* he scribbled.

'If you're asking will the police prosecute, I don't know. People have died. A local man as well as the woman. I was there when they shot him today. In cold blood.'

A sliver of a smile crossed Fred's face. *Not Marcus?*

'No,' she said. 'That wasn't Marcus.'

He gave a half-shrug and Mirabelle felt her temper rise. 'You're his father, you should have reined him in,' she snapped. 'Your son murdered a woman just to scare her neighbour into doing what he wanted. What kind of man . . .'

Fred's breath rattled again. He looked as if he was remembering something. Mirabelle stopped. During the war, they'd have encouraged this kind of criminal behaviour if it had advanced the Allied cause. She knew what he was thinking. Fred had done worse. And this boy was his son. She sighed. There was no point in berating a dying man – least of all someone she cared about. Fred managed a smile and the picture of Marcus Fox sitting in short trousers on the grey sofa at the Marylebone Hotel all those years ago returned to her mind's eye. She cursed herself for being naive. Not everyone who was rescued from Europe was an angel. She wondered what the boy had experienced before Fred found him. What allowed him to be so personable and yet so deadly. Whatever it was, he had been old enough for it to affect him. Still, anyone who could poison a bottle of gin and stab a drugged woman to death, just as a warning – well, it didn't bear thinking about. *When I die, it's Marcus who'll be here*, Fred managed.

'Has he been like this since the beginning? Since you brought him home?'

Fred tried to breathe. She gave him plenty of time, but he didn't reply. There was no point. He wanted Marcus to get away with what he'd done.

'I'm going to do something about it,' she said at last. 'I can't leave it. I'm sorry.'

Fred looked perturbed. He picked up the pencil. *He'll have you*, he wrote.

'Maybe,' Mirabelle admitted. She shifted in her seat. 'They have a cottage where he's working. It's tiled floor to ceiling. Do you remember, Fred, during the war? The ones who killed themselves – soldiers on their last night of leave. Women desperate for their husbands. Men who just couldn't take it. We used to play it down – the newspapers wouldn't report it. Bad for morale, they said. Well, they've made a game of it. People pay to play – Russian roulette. You know – a single bullet in a chamber and you don't know who'll be the one to die. It was a war hero who died first. A pilot.'

Fred's movement was a mere shrug. There was no point in staying here, she thought. It would only torture him. He grappled the pencil as she rose. *Everyone wants something. That's how I always made money.* She didn't reply, only nodded in the direction of the nurse, who was stripping a bed on the other side of the ward. 'Goodbye,' she said and planted a kiss on Fred's forehead. His skin seemed too thin, but he was still there. His eyes lingered. 'If there's anything you want to say, you better say it now.' She waited. But Fred stayed silent and, after a minute, he closed his eyes.

* * *

It took almost an hour for Vesta to make it back to the office, finding the stairs, surprisingly, easier than walking on the flat. As she burst through the door, she hopped to the cupboard and pulled out the first aid kit. Unused for long periods, the kit contained a few aspirin, a small bottle of iodine, another of witch hazel, a tube of arnica cream, a thick roll of Elastoplast and two rolls of crêpe bandage fixed with safety pins. Vesta sat heavily on her chair and stared momentarily at the kettle, deciding for the first time in her life, it seemed, that it wasn't worth making tea. Her ankle was swollen and bruising was coming up on her dark flesh. She thought she might cry. Mirabelle was so much braver. She always seemed to know what to do. Vesta removed one stocking and was about to address herself to the bandages when the door opened and Bill swept in with Panther at his heel. The dog trotted over and licked Vesta's knee.

'You look like you've been in the wars,' said Bill. 'What happened?'

Vesta sighed. It was a very long story and Bill couldn't help much. He always disapproved of these kinds of cases when what the women had got up to came out later. 'I tried to drop and roll,' she said. 'But I dropped too hard.'

Bill accepted her explanation without question. He picked up the aspirin and fetched a glass of water from the sink.

'Start with that, eh?' he said, dropping to his knees to inspect the injury. 'Go on, wiggle your toes.'

'It's not broken.' Vesta sniffed.

Bill smiled. 'I'd say you're right. But that doesn't mean it's not sore, does it?'

Vesta gulped down the painkillers.

'May I?'

She nodded. Bill prodded the injury with some expertise and Vesta winced. Then he carefully applied a long smear of arnica cream. 'It's a bit late for this but all hands on deck, eh?'

he said, as he picked up one of the bandages. 'It needs support.' He began to wind the crêpe tightly round the swelling. It felt better immediately. 'You'll need a lift home,' he said cheerily, as he pinned the bandage in place. 'You shouldn't walk too far on it. I'll call a cab, shall I?'

Vesta sighed. She'd walked quite far already. 'No,' she said. 'I'll get one myself, thanks.'

'It needs rest.' Bill continued his diagnosis. 'Though, of course, women in your delicate condition actually heal faster.'

Vesta let out a frustrated yelp. 'How come everybody knows?' she said. 'Who told you?'

Bill shrugged. 'My missus and I weren't blessed, of course. But a fella picks things up. Will you be all right? Are you sure?'

'Yeah. I'll be fine.' Vesta resigned herself to the fact that she hadn't kept any kind of secret. 'Turns out the stairs are easy.'

Bill smiled. He drew a sheaf of papers from his inside pocket and laid them on his desk. 'What's this?' he asked, as he found the paper bag she'd left earlier.

'Oh, rock buns,' the girl replied distractedly. 'I thought you'd like to take them home.'

'Very nice.'

He put the buns in his pocket and called Panther to heel. Vesta stood up, trying out her improved situation. She felt tired now the pain was diminishing.

'You sure you'll be all right?' Bill checked.

'I'm fine,' she assured him. 'It won't take long for a cab to get here. I'll call one now.'

As the door closed, Vesta waited to make sure he had gone. Then she picked up the telephone and called the police station.

'I'd like to speak to Superintendent McGregor,' she said. 'My name is Vesta Lewis.'

The WPC tried the line. 'No reply,' she said, 'but I can take a message.'

It always struck Vesta that over the telephone she was treated differently. People couldn't see the colour of her skin and it showed in the tone of their voice. 'It's an emergency,' she insisted.

'Well,' the WPC replied, 'I can put out a call, if you like. But you'll have to hold. It may take a while. It's the end of the day.'

Vesta reached out to plug in the kettle. A solitary rock bun remained on her desk. 'I'll wait,' she said.

The phone clicked intermittently for a long time. Now and then, she could hear the movement of a busy office – a murmur of voices and the clatter of a typewriter. She made a cup of tea and sipped it. After a good three or four minutes, there was a loud click and a man's voice came on the line – an English accent.

'Hello. Detective Inspector Robinson speaking.'

'Good evening, Detective, I'm looking for Superintendent McGregor,' Vesta announced.

Robinson sounded short already. 'McGregor's out,' he snapped. 'Who's calling?'

Vesta hadn't anticipated this. In her mind, if Mirabelle needed help, McGregor would simply be there. 'My name is Vesta Lewis,' she said. 'I work with Mirabelle Bevan.'

The sound of a long, low sigh emanated from the earpiece.

'It's an emergency,' Vesta insisted. 'Mirabelle is in trouble. There's an illegal gambling operation and someone involved in it killed Helen Quinn.'

'Helen Quinn?' Robinson's tone was flat.

'Yes. And another fellow too. It's a private house called Hastings Hall.'

'Two murders?' Robinson's tone became ribald. 'I'm sorry, Miss Lewis. Did you say there had been another murder?'

'Yes.'

'And you witnessed this?'

'Not me. Mirabelle. If I could speak to Superintendent McGregor . . .' Vesta persisted.

'The super had to nip out. He won't be back today. Funeral, see.'

'Oh I am sorry.' Vesta's manners clicked in. 'The thing is, Inspector, Mirabelle is still there. At the scene. At Hastings Hall. And it's dangerous. She needs help.'

'Miss Bevan needs help?'

'Yes.'

'Well, leave it with me, Mrs Lewis. I'll send down the cavalry. Hastings Hall, you say.'

Vesta, full now of painkillers and tea, didn't detect the irony in Robinson's voice. 'Thank you,' she said. 'Would you?'

'Of course.'

Robinson rolled his eyes as he hung up. 'I don't know how McGregor puts up with it,' he remarked to a junior officer. 'Hysterical, bloody women.'

Chapter 29

Evil is easy and has infinite forms

Surveillance was everything. It was dark by the time Mirabelle returned to the rear of Hastings Hall and settled down in a spot with a good view of the public rooms. The house was lit for the evening and now the sun had set so it was easy to see what was going on inside. Tonight, the moon was almost full and Mirabelle was aware it afforded less cover than she might have liked. Still, she was a shadowy figure at best and people tended not to look beyond the light around them. This was how Marcus Fox had staked out the Quinns' house.

At first the vast rooms lay more or less empty. The plump maid padded across the carpet, setting out glasses. There was nothing of any interest to see and, checking her watch and recalling the countess's comments about the party starting late, Mirabelle decided to take another look inside the cottage. Slipping through the copse towards the building, she put her hand to the cold glass of the window and peered inside. The front door was locked, but the French doors had been left open. She took a deep breath and a wave of nausea broke over her as she recalled what had happened there. Her eyes soon got used to the darkness, the light of the moon casting shadows through the trees, dappling the carpet. She slipped past the bar and hovered in the hallway, avoiding stepping where Davidson's body had lain. It was only superstition, but she couldn't help herself. The little house felt haunted. In the tiled room, on the mahogany table, there was a wooden box.

Mirabelle opened it. Inside, she found a revolver and a box of bullets. As she lifted the gun, she realised it was one of the weapons Fred had bequeathed to his son. How could she have been so stupid? On the butt were the three notches that had made her shudder. Now, she shuddered again, flicking open the barrel. It wasn't loaded. Not yet. She'd been planning to throw the weapon into the sea before Marcus took it. Now, she slipped it into her handbag.

Through the window, she caught a glimpse of movement at the main house. Time was marching on. A bank of staff had arrived to man the card tables and the roulette wheel. The casino room seemed wholesome by comparison to what was on offer in the cottage and she slipped back through the patio doors and took up a position behind a chestnut tree where she could see what was going on. It occurred to her that she always found herself on the outside of things. This would be her second night of waiting. She didn't, however, have to wait long. Just before ten, the countess's guests started to arrive. The countess graced the rooms, arrayed in a sky-blue satin evening gown. As she flitted between her customers, she motioned with her amber cigarette holder, upon which she periodically took a draw. Just glancing, Mirabelle thought, you'd think this was a party. A raft of smart-looking waiters served drinks on trays – the dumpy maid had been relegated. Mirabelle wondered if she resented the resulting lack of tips.

Little by little, she found herself drawn towards the light and the movement. Leaving the cover of the tree, she moved closer. Several tables were in play though Billy Randall was nowhere to be seen. But then, she thought, he was bound to be in a private room, dealing for high stakes. She lingered in the shadows, as, bit by bit, the room filled. A cluster of women gathered on a loveseat. One threw her head back and laughed, another opened her handbag and brought out gambling chips, clearly explaining to her friend what they were for.

Mirabelle cast her eyes over the array of well-dressed couples, the best of Brighton out to try their luck. Then there were the men on their own, who headed straight for a particular table, more businesslike in their approach. The countess greeted each of them, fawning over someone occasionally and moving them to another room, where, it might be expected, there was a game that would suit them better. The clock struck eleven. And then half past. Mirabelle wondered what she might do. There was no sign of Marcus Fox or Roberts and nobody was making their way to the death house, which still lay in darkness behind her.

Then, as she peered through Hasting Hall's long windows, she squinted at a party in evening dress that had just arrived. Three men moved towards a table near the fireplace where five-card stud was being dealt. Tommy Fourcade and Dan Gleeson of Hove Cars had brushed up well and, with them, Alan McGregor, who looked somehow different. Mirabelle's brow creased as she tried to figure out what it was. Then it came to her. She'd never seen him look so smart. She had no idea he even owned a dinner suit. But she had learned all kinds of things about the superintendent in the last few days. Still, she was glad he was here.

Nonetheless, the others weren't police officers. It was a puzzle. She shifted, wondering what the men were doing. Gleeson sat down to play cards, laying a generous pile of chips on a single hand, as the countess fussed over him. She brought a new dealer to the table. Gleeson looked as if he was settling in. A waiter served a drink and he lit a cigar. McGregor and Fourcade wandered over to the roulette wheel. Mirabelle strained to see as they laid a solitary bet on red and lost. Fourcade laid another, but McGregor looked around the room and then headed for the door as the wheel spun. Mirabelle didn't hesitate. She sneaked across the lawn, making straight for the back entrance to the house, and gingerly turned the handle. It wasn't locked. As she carefully slipped inside, the smell of pork sausages emanated from the kitchen. She turned in the opposite direction, cursing herself for being in the wrong outfit. It seemed she hadn't worn clothes that fitted for days and now her blue suit was entirely inappropriate – daywear in a sea of evening dress. She peered into the main hallway, but McGregor wasn't there. Grateful there was carpet to cover the sound of her footsteps, she headed for the countess's study and slipped inside just as the front door bell sounded.

'Are we terribly late?' a woman's voice drawled, as a waiter took her coat and showed her to the gaming room.

Mirabelle watched her disappear. Then she checked the surface of the desk, but nothing had been unpacked and the drawers were empty. With a shrug, she sneaked back into the hall, mistiming her entrance so that the waiter with the coat still over his arm almost barrelled into her.

'Madam?'

'I'm lost,' she said. The man didn't appear to notice the lack of a cocktail dress. A lucky break. 'I'm looking for the lavatory.'

He pointed the direction and she set off, aware of his eyes upon her. Round the corner, the door was locked, so she took a moment to collect herself, sitting in a small chair beside the window. It was the spark that caught her attention. It was difficult to see anything outside, despite the moon, but the sudden illumination lit the darkness and, in the flash, she saw figures on the lawn. Two men, smoking. Roberts and McGregor. She edged the chair backwards, aware that she didn't want them to see her, framed in the light of the casement. Carefully, she reached out and slipped the catch. Then she strained to hear what they were saying.

'My friends enjoy a wager, but I'm not so keen. The dogs, perhaps.' McGregor's voice floated towards her.

'It's just a bit of fun, isn't it?' Roberts replied. 'You should go back and have a go. You never know your luck.'

'You do the security then? Much need for that?'

'Not everybody wants to pay up at the end of the night. Though they're a decent crowd mostly. You just have to deal with things quickly.'

Roberts sounded practically benign. Mirabelle found her lip curling in outrage. You'd never believe he'd beaten her, knocked her out, killed Ernie Davidson, when it came to that.

'What's your line of work?' he asked McGregor casually.

'Me? Well, that's why I'm here. I'm a policeman.'

There was the sound of a scuffle and a body dropping. Mirabelle couldn't hold herself back from peering through the glass. She felt relief wash over her, as she realised that, on this occasion, Roberts hadn't dealt with his problem quite quickly enough. McGregor was now pulling the man's body towards the rear wall, where nobody would see it from the windows.

Mirabelle slipped back through the hallway and outside. McGregor stood beside a rose bush with Roberts slumped behind him. He looked up sharply.

'It's me,' she said, holding her hand ahead of her.

'Mirabelle. You have to get out of here,' McGregor objected, as she approached. 'Jesus.' His tone changed as he caught sight of her bruises. 'What happened to you?'

'He got hold of me.' She kept her tone light. 'Didn't Vesta tell you?'

McGregor turned and kicked Roberts in the ribs. 'Bastard,' he spat. 'No, she didn't. Are you all right?'

Mirabelle didn't reply. 'I thought you'd come to rescue me,' she said drily.

'You've never needed rescuing,' he said warmly. She didn't

enlighten him, only nodded as he continued. 'These people killed Helen Quinn, Mirabelle. And worse. Phil killed himself this afternoon. He hung himself in his cell. It's been a terrible day. I think he just lost hope. He left a note. It said he had no reason to go through a trial and there was nothing worthwhile afterwards anyway. I blame bloody Robinson and his cack-handed investigation. Phil didn't stand a chance. I should have stood up to the chief. I should have pushed to be allowed to visit the poor bloke . . . but they kept saying I had to stay away.'

'So you're here to arrest them?'

McGregor eyes fell to the ground. 'Not exactly. I was warned off. The chief got a call from London. I think he's a gambling man, if you see what I mean. I think there might be a few gambling men on the force. First, he stopped me looking into George Forgie's death. Now, I can't bust the house here, but if I can find the fellow who killed Helen, maybe I can salvage one arrest, if we can keep all this out of it and I can get a confession. That's what I came for.'

'But—'

'Don't.' McGregor tried to cut her off.

She ignored him. 'But that's disgraceful. They killed Forgie here, McGregor. Or he killed himself. Down in the woods. There's a house. A private house. It's for Russian roulette,' she said. 'They kidnapped me and Vesta, though we got away. And today they shot Ernie Davidson. You know him, don't you?'

In the half-light McGregor looked rough. The scuffle with Roberts had messed his hair. 'You can't stay here,' he said. 'Leave this to me, Mirabelle. Please. If I can find out exactly who killed Helen Quinn then there's a chance of at least making one charge stick.'

Mirabelle ignored him again. She knew more. 'I know who killed her. Marcus Fox,' she said. 'I've been watching the house and I haven't seen him tonight, but that may be because his father is dying. Roberts appears to be on his own.'

'Fox. Marcus,' McGregor repeated. 'Right. There'll be one or two more monkeys. A place this size. You have to go, Mirabelle. Now. It could easily get nasty.'

'So you're taking matters into your own hands? Just you and Phil's friends.'

'It's what you usually do,' he snapped.

'You asked me to look into this. You came to me.'

McGregor sighed. 'I couldn't bring other officers. Everyone's under specific orders to leave this place alone. But Fourcade and Gleeson are good men and now with Phil dead. . . They just want a go at whoever killed Phil's wife. Killed Phil, if it came to that. And if that's the price I have to pay to get a confession then that's the best I can do. At least I'll clear Phil's name. Look, I have to go inside,' he said. 'They'll come looking for me if I'm much longer. That's what we agreed. And Marcus Fox isn't here, you reckon?'

'His father is in the infirmary. Ward twelve. He's dangerous – the son, I mean. But he's your man. I'm sorry about your friend,' she said softly.

McGregor ignored the opportunity to talk. He stuck to the case. 'Do you have proof it was this man?'

'Nothing concrete. He's the one, though. His father as good as told me.'

McGregor nodded. 'Go,' he said. It was an order, not a suggestion.

As the superintendent disappeared into the house, Mirabelle stared at Roberts. He was still breathing. She kicked him half-heartedly. Then she sat on the grass and removed the gun from her handbag. After considering for a few seconds, she took aim and fired in his direction, wondering what it would feel like to kill somebody so defenceless. As the hammer hit the empty chamber, she realised she couldn't do it – not even

278

in revenge. People like Roberts and Marcus Fox should be dealt with by a judge. But the law was hampered. Toothless. Corrupt. Poor Phil Quinn, he hadn't stood a chance in the face of this tangle of motives, dead bodies and protected interests. Maybe McGregor was right. Maybe he could still salvage an arrest after Fourcade and Gleeson had beaten a confession out of Fox. If Fox cracked, that is.

Through the window, she saw McGregor whisper in Fourcade's ear. Then the men moved to the game of five card stud and picked up Dan Gleeson. Together they made for the door. It seemed wrong that they were leaving the premises when Davidson's killer was right here. When she'd been kidnapped by the same man, and Vesta too. Roberts shifted in the rose bed. She bent over and tied his shoelaces together. Her thoughts were conflicted. Two wrongs might not make a right but she had to do something. Vesta and she might have died and Mirabelle wasn't just going to let that pass.

As the men left by the front door, she made off down the lawn. At the cottage, she slipped across the patio efficiently and threw the gun into the empty fireplace. Then she snatched bottles from the bar, pell-mell, and spilled the contents over the furniture. The smell of alcohol lit the air, as Mirabelle picked up a box of matches. The year before she'd been trapped in a fire and the memory still scared her. Now though, she lit one match and then another, throwing them on to the whisky-soaked chairs. Quickly, as they caught alight, she fled into the garden. As she walked up the grass, the fire took hold in a wall of flame and smoke. Slipping down the side of the property, she saw the back door of the main house open and several waiters run outside. There was the sound of shouted instructions, a sense of panic. Roberts got to his feet and fell over. This was revenge, she thought. It didn't feel entirely good, but it felt better than doing nothing. And then there was another matter on her mind. A rescue.

The private game was on the opposite side of the house in the panel-lined room where Billy had given his masterclass. She made it, round the long way. Billy was still at the table. He was holding the countess's money and only a fool would leave with that. The punters, however, had been distracted by the fire and people had filtered outside. Mirabelle peered through the window and watched Billy counting a pile of five pound notes next to a stack of gambling chips. She knocked sharply on the glass and he looked up.

'Jesus,' he said, slipping the catch on the window. 'What happened to you?'

'Marcus Fox will be out of commission tonight and the cottage in the grounds is on fire. If you want to get away from this, now is a good time.'

'Someone's pinched Marcus?'

'Not yet. They will. He's the one you're really afraid of, isn't he?'

Billy didn't answer and Mirabelle didn't wait. There was no point in having a discussion. She'd told him, that was enough. She stepped away and made her way down the side of the drive.

The street was lined with cars. A huddle of chauffeurs smoked cigarettes, leaning against a smart-looking Bentley. Mirabelle turned so they couldn't see her face. The panic hadn't spread this far yet, all sight of the fire obscured by the main house. However, when it did, she didn't want anyone to be able to furnish a description. She was glad now about the unmemorable navy suit. Behind her, the front door opened and two women, speckled in dress jewellery, rushed out, clutching each other. One hailed a driver and he snapped to attention, almost sprinting towards his car.

As she made her way along the leafy street, Mirabelle listened as the sounds of panic emanating from Hastings Hall receded until there was only the click of her heels on the paving stones in the otherwise silent darkness. It was too late to catch a bus and out here there were no taxis. Goodness knows where the nearest telephone box was. She had been thrown on her own resources and, apart from anything else, she felt angry with McGregor for dismissing her so lightly and leaving her so he could go off with his friends. She'd given him the information he needed and, still, he'd cut her out. But the night wasn't over yet and she wasn't prepared to let them just get on with it. Not by a long shot.

Chapter 30

*Never befriend a man who is
not better than yourself*

People were creatures of habit and men in particular, or, Mirabelle considered, they were creatures of motive at least. Once you understood what was important to them, you knew what they would do. McGregor and his friends had a car so she was at least half an hour behind them. There was no point in going to the infirmary, that much was certain. What she needed was to anticipate their move after that. One step ahead. McGregor couldn't return to the Arundel with Marcus Fox in tow, and he couldn't take the boy in without a confession. Both Gleeson and Fourcade were married men. The safest place to take any kind of action at this time of night was Hove Cars.

The superintendent's face betrayed his distress that she was there, standing on the cobbles when the car drew up. There were four of them in the vehicle, just as she had expected. Behind her, the office was still open. The disabled dispatcher was alone tonight. As the engine cut out, he came to the door.

'Go home, son.' Fourcade nodded as he got out of the driver's seat.

'What about the calls?'

'Go home.' Fourcade glared. 'You ain't seen nothing. And I don't know what you think you're doing here.' He sniffed in Mirabelle's direction.

The dispatcher closed the office and limped down the lane,

peering over his shoulder as he turned the corner. They all waited.

As he disappeared, Mirabelle spoke. 'Good evening, Mr Fourcade,' she said. She kept her voice calm. There was something that happened once a man had done violence and Marcus Fox wouldn't have come easily. McGregor sensed it too. He interposed himself between the two of them.

'You shouldn't be here, Mirabelle,' he said.

'You wouldn't have found him without me. You think if I don't see, I won't know. Is that it?'

'So you reckon we should just let this toerag get away with what he did to Helen? Phil's dead and the police can't do a thing.' Fourcade pushed round McGregor. 'What kind of justice is that? We've lost a friend. A good man.'

Mirabelle peered into the back seat of the car. Gleeson sat next to Marcus, who was in handcuffs. Mirabelle wondered if the boy had been crying. It was difficult to tell in the darkness.

'Did Fred die?'

'Yes. I'm sorry,' McGregor said.

Fourcade snorted. 'Who cares?' he spat. 'Some old man. Who bloody cares? We're going to see to that boy and there's nothing you can do about it.'

'We need a confession, Mirabelle,' McGregor cut in. 'It's the only way.'

Mirabelle nodded. 'I understand,' she said. 'But I'm part of this. I'm going to watch.'

'What?'

'I can't stop you. Three big men. The police aren't going to do anything – you're right. But I can be a witness.'

'Don't you get it?' McGregor was losing his temper.

Mirabelle stayed calm. 'I don't mean to be a witness in court. And I'm not saying the boy doesn't deserve it. But I'm going to be here. That's what I mean.'

Fourcade laughed. 'We're the good guys, Miss Bevan.'

Mirabelle cast a glance at McGregor. 'I wish things were that simple,' she said.

Fourcade opened the car door and took the keys from his pocket. He unlocked the cuffs and hauled Marcus out of the back seat by the scruff of his neck. The boy's eyes burned. It was patent even in the darkness that he wasn't contrite or even grieving. The sheen that came off him was one of pure fury. Gleeson slid across the back seat on to the cobbles. He nodded apologetically at Mirabelle. 'Miss Bevan,' he said.

'Well, this is a fix,' Fourcade snapped at McGregor. 'Can't you do something with her?'

McGregor shrugged. 'You better take him inside,' he said. 'The local bobby will be doing his rounds. We don't want things to get more complicated.'

Gleeson nudged Marcus towards the closed garage doors. Fox leered at Mirabelle as he passed. 'Dad wanted to fuck you. He'd wanted to fuck you for years,' he sneered.

Mirabelle's eyes were still. 'He was proud of you. God knows why.'

'I'd do it again. We always get what we want,' he spat.

Fourcade hit the boy squarely on the jaw and Marcus reeled, falling to one side. He laughed as Gleeson hauled him to his feet and into the garage. Some people just didn't crack, Mirabelle thought. These men didn't seem to know that. But the kind of bloke who laughed when you hit him so hard he fell over was probably going to be a tough nut. Marcus Fox wasn't afraid of anything. Not pain and not death either. Fourcade pulled the door almost shut so that there was a gap – a strip of light reflected on the cobbles.

McGregor turned towards her. 'The world isn't ideal. We can't make everything right. We just have to do our best.'

'This is your best?'

From inside the garage, there was a stifled shriek. Gleeson and Fourcade weren't holding back. McGregor looked over his shoulder. 'And this is for Helen,' they heard one of them spit.

'Doesn't sound much like an interrogation,' Mirabelle pointed out. 'You better make sure there aren't too many marks on him. And really, one of you ought to ask him a question, don't you think?'

McGregor nodded. There was another shriek. 'I don't want you to see it,' he said.

'I know what goes on. I don't think you should be doing this.'

'Phil was my friend, Mirabelle.'

McGregor peered at the garage door. He wanted to get in there. Mirabelle stepped forward and together they opened it. They'd tied Fox up. Gleeson was standing in front of him with a knife in his hand.

'No,' McGregor shouted, as he realised the man's intention, but he was too late. Gleeson stabbed like a piston three or four times. Once in the boy's stomach and then into his heart. Fourcade stepped forward and twisted the boy's neck.

A sharp crack sounded on the chill air.

'This isn't what we agreed.' McGregor launched himself at Fourcade. The big man held him off, but McGregor laid a couple of punches.

'You thought we'd let him walk out of here? After what he did?' Fourcade was furious. 'They don't want charges to stick. No matter what. You know that, McGregor.'

'Sorry,' Gleeson said. 'But there was no other way, Alan.'

'I should arrest you for this,' McGregor spat.

'I'd happily go down. Happily.' Fourcade's eyes were burning.

Mirabelle just stared.

'You think this is my fault.' McGregor turned on her.

'Don't blame me. I said it was a bad idea.'

'The thing is you didn't see service, did you, McGregor?'

Fourcade was getting into his stride. He had a knack for a soft piece of flesh, Mirabelle realised. 'You don't know what it's like to fight alongside a man. To have a comrade in arms. Phil's life was ruined over nothing. He said you'd not seen service, you know. That it made you different from the rest of us.'

'Well.' Gleeson cleaned the knife on a white handkerchief he withdrew from the pocket of his dinner jacket. Ruthie had probably ironed it for him. 'Are you going to take us in? Or are we going to bury the body?'

The men waited. McGregor's eyes were frantic. 'You're going to bury him,' Mirabelle's voice said. 'You have to. Otherwise, everyone has to go down. You too.' she turned to McGregor.

The superintendent's eyes were focused on something in the distance, as if he was running through everything that had happened, trying to understand where it went wrong.

'We *should* all go down,' he said. 'But, even then, they probably wouldn't let it come out.'

Fourcade began to loosen the knot on the rope that was holding Marcus Fox's corpse in place. 'Well then,' he said. 'We've a couple of spades in the cupboard.'

Mirabelle looked away. It was the right thing to do, but that this had come out of a close bond – a friendship – felt twisted.

'I can take you home,' McGregor offered, but she shook her head.

Too many people had died today. Mirabelle wondered which, if any, of them, might be missed. Who really cared about Fred or Ernie Davidson or Marcus? They were all bad men, in their way.

'On the Downs?' she checked.

'Have you done this before?' Fourcade lit a cigarette. 'You want to watch that too, do you?'

She rounded on him. 'It's not a joke. It's not some schoolboy prank. You've murdered someone. He had a father who loved him more than anything in the world.'

'He had a knife. He had a vicious bloody knife,' Fourcade spat back at her. 'And he used it on a defenceless woman. And because he worked for someone with money, someone who had his back, he'd never have paid for it. And worse, he'd have done it again.'

Mirabelle exclaimed in frustration – a sound that came from deep inside. 'You bury him with dignity,' she said. 'You make sure you do.'

It was four o'clock when she finally got home. She sat on the end of the bed and kicked off her heels. She'd never sleep, she realised. Not now. No matter how tired she was. MI6 had done worse. MI5 too. MI9 for that matter, but there was something about this case – the death of Helen Quinn – that Mirabelle realised would stay with her for a long time. She'd never held any operation against Jack, no matter what he'd had to do, but now she had two things she was holding against McGregor. It seemed impossible they could even be friends.

Chapter 31

Every earth is fit for burial

Ignoring the reflection that appeared in the mirror in the hallway, Mirabelle mounted the stairs at McGuigan & McGuigan Debt Recovery later that morning. First in the office, she sat in her chair and tried to figure out if matters looked any different from Brills Lane. When Vesta arrived, it felt like an intrusion.

'Did McGregor get hold of you?' the girl asked cheerily, as she filled the kettle. 'They said he'd been at a funeral.'

'It was fine,' Mirabelle found herself saying. 'Though Phil Quinn died.'

'Oh no.' Vesta peered across her desk, concern lighting her expression.

Mirabelle turned over the newspaper. The headline told the story of a man who had caught a large sea trout from Palace Pier. She pushed it away.

'He died in custody. He killed himself.'

'That's terrible,' Vesta said, as the office door opened. Mirabelle looked up to see Marlene standing, in tears in the frame.

'What is it?' Vesta went to comfort her friend, distracted immediately from the news.

'He was a rat.' Marlene sniffed. 'I can't believe it.'

'A rat?'

'Marcus. I saw him yesterday with one of the Ward Twelve girls. He was—' she struggled to find the word '—canoodling.'

'Oh goodness. Marlene, I'm sorry.'

'I thought he was the one.' The girl slumped into a chair and pulled her handkerchief from her sleeve. 'I can't believe it.'

Mirabelle looked away.

'His father died last night and I thought he might want to talk about it, but he's just disappeared. He's ashamed of himself, I suppose.'

'Well, you could go and find him.'

'I don't even know where he lives. And then I thought, I wonder how many other girls he's got. Flashing around drinks at the Grand like that. I can't believe I fell for it.'

Mirabelle got to her feet. She reached for her jacket. 'I'm just going to pop up the road,' she said.

Outside, she strode up to Bartholomew Square police station and stood regarding the smooth, classical columns. It seemed too clean. Too peaceful. From an office on the first floor, Robinson peered out of the window and then turned away. She walked on, up the hill. What was wrong with the world? At the top, she stared at the lane where Fred had worked and then she turned down, towards the sea, settling on one of the benches on the front. It was too early in the season for the click-click girls, but down on the pebbles a man was shooting Cine film of his daughter – a child of about three years, who was trying to catch the waves as they broke on the shore.

Mirabelle sat down and watched them. When McGregor appeared, she half stiffened and half relaxed. He tipped his hat and took the seat next to her. Mirabelle noticed he had a file rolled up in his pocket. She caught the words 'Forgie' on the side. But all that was useless now.

'Robinson said he saw you in the street, heading in this direction,' McGregor said. 'At least he's useful for something.'

'I don't think I'm ever going to forgive you, Alan.'

'I hope you can.' His voice was low, the tone contrite. He reached out and stroked her hair where it curled around her ear.

'Would you do it differently?' she asked.

McGregor shrugged. 'I don't know. Yes, of course. But . . .'

Mirabelle felt her heart sink. She had lost something now. Yes, it had definitely gone.

'Did you tell Vesta?' he asked.

She shook her head. How could she ruin the faith the girl had in the world? She was pregnant after all. 'Did you tell Irene?' she snapped at him, struggling to keep calm.

'Irene?' McGregor sounded mystified.

'At Tongdean Avenue? I expect the poor girl is in a fix this morning. Ernie Davidson is gone.'

'Yes. I saw the report. Robinson's dealing with it. He has a lead. For once I'm glad he's the one who got the case. If there's anything guaranteed it's that Robinson will get nowhere with it.'

Mirabelle's jaw tightened. 'There really isn't any justice, is there?'

'Not always. No.'

'And if they come for me?'

'I don't think they will, Mirabelle. They're more likely to come for me. I told Roberts I was a policeman. He'll remember that.'

'And you're not going to admit to the girl? Irene?'

'I don't know what you're talking about.'

'At Tongdean Avenue, Alan. The youngest girl in Ernie Davidson's house.'

He looked concerned for a moment. 'You mean Rene?' he said. 'What about her?'

'What about her?' Mirabelle thought she might cry.

McGregor waited. The penny dropped slowly. 'You think I slept with Rene.' He said it as a matter of fact.

'You visited her.'

'Yes. Now and then.'

'Are you saying she's an informant?'

McGregor's gaze was steady. 'I have nothing to be ashamed of, Belle. Not in that regard. And if I don't tell you everywhere I go and everyone I speak to, it's only to protect you. But it seems you won't accept any protection. None at all. I wish you hadn't come last night. You being there didn't change anything that happened, and look at us. I've made you an accessory to murder. It's the last thing I wanted.'

Mirabelle shrugged. When it came down to it, she didn't trust him any more. There was no point in arguing. He kissed her cheek gently, but she didn't turn towards him.

'Damn you,' she said quietly. 'How could I have stayed away?' She was at least as involved as he was and now he was trying to make this terrible mess her fault because she had been present. It wasn't the first time she'd seen someone die. He was treating her like some kind of rookie.

'Fine,' he said. 'If you need me, you know where I am. George Forgie's second cousin is coming from Crewe to positively identify the body. And then I can sign it off.'

He got to his feet and she watched him walk away. As he rounded the corner, she caught a glimpse of his face. His cheeks were wet. Down on the pebbles, the little girl fell over and giggled. Mirabelle stood up. She didn't want to feel powerless like this. She walked along the front and stopped at a telephone box. She hauled open the heavy door, pausing before she lifted the handset. She had to do something. When she'd finally made up her mind, she called the operator and asked for Mayfair 7662. The man who answered did so smartly.

'Hello,' he said.

'You don't know me. I don't have a keyword any more.'

'Madam. You must have the wrong number.'

'I don't think so. Just listen.'

The voice didn't object.

'Hastings Hall in Brighton is owned by a white Russian woman. She calls herself a countess. I don't think she is. This woman has infiltrated the British establishment. She has an address book that takes her to the heart of Whitehall. She runs a gambling operation and I think you'll find she has connections back in Russia. Do you understand me?'

'Who is this?'

'Your people have been compromised.' Mirabelle tried to sound stout-hearted and certain. She held the phone a moment longer.

'Who is this?' the man repeated. 'Give me a name.'

Mirabelle hung up. She leaned against the glass panes, the sea stirring behind her. 'At least they'll have to look at it now,' she whispered. Somewhere there must still be honourable people who cared.

The rest of the day passed in a blur. Marlene went back to work. Vesta chattered. A fish-paste sandwich appeared on Mirabelle's desk at lunchtime and wordlessly she ate it. After work, there was no question of going home. Vesta headed off to pick up fish and chips, kissing Mirabelle on the cheek as if nothing had happened. There was no point telling her.

As the light began to fade from the sky, Mirabelle walked, aimlessly at first, but then she realised she was heading towards Portslade. Mothers hurried their children home, baskets over their arms. Shopkeepers dismantled their displays. With a heavy heart, Mirabelle turned up Mill Lane. The smell of frying peppered the air as pans were heated. The curtain of number fourteen twitched and Mrs Ambrose appeared in her doorway.

'What are you doing back here?'

Mirabelle shrugged. She had nowhere else to go.

'Well, they're gone,' Mrs Ambrose announced. 'I was thinking I should telephone Bartholomew Square and tell that nice inspector. It's fishy, isn't it?'

'Who's gone?'

'The Randalls, of course.' The old woman's voice betrayed her impatience. 'Who else?'

Mirabelle's eyes lit just a little. 'Last night?' she checked.

'This morning. Early doors. I saw them – two suitcases and didn't they look guilty.'

'They just needed a fresh start,' Mirabelle said.

Mrs Ambrose sniffed. 'So you don't think I should tell the inspector?'

'Leave it with me.' Mirabelle felt her step lighter as she turned. The dark windows on the other side of the street seemed suddenly an optimistic sign.

Mrs Ambrose peered short-sightedly across the road. 'Well,' she said. 'Teatime.'

The word sunk in slowly as if it was foreign. Mirabelle wondered if the Boite was open. Perhaps she might have a glass of champagne and some peanuts. She'd achieved something after all – saved two people, at least. And then, she thought, she might sleep. Yes, tonight, with this news, maybe after all, she'd be able.

Acknowledgements

Writing novels is a particular form of communication and with it goes the fun of playing inside other people's heads. However, no writer does it alone. Many thanks go to Jenny Brown, my brilliant agent and to the team at Constable who love Mirabelle Bevan as much as I do. The Society of Authors Trust helped me financially when I was writing this book – I don't know what I would have done without them. Encouragement was received from Marianna Abbots and Sarah Brown in the form of suggestions and the high jinx of using Marianna's name for a Baddy. The joys! To my many patient friends and my ever-patient family, thank you for putting up with me talking about murder over breakfast, lunch and dinner. And to all of those who have contributed in the office at Sheridan Towers – interns, publishing students, clever people passing through – thank you, thank you, thank you.

Questions for readers' groups

1 How difficult is it to believe a wholly innocent person can become embroiled in a crime?
2 Do neighbours no longer care about each other – is Mrs Ambrose right?
3 How different would Vesta and Charlie's lives be today? How far have we come?
4 Should Billy Randall have come clean at the beginning?
5 If you could go back to the 1950s, would you?
6 Would you trust Superintendent McGregor? Under what circumstances could he be a hero?
7 Do you condone vigilantes?
8 Gambling was legalised in the early 1960s. Should prostitution be legalised now?

The quotations and misquotations used to open each chapter are taken from the following sources:

Mystery: a matter that is difficult to understand: definition. True friends stab you in the front: Oscar Wilde. The wise are instructed by reason: Cicero. Everyone has been made for some particular work: Rumi. A cat in gloves catches no mice: traditional. Doubt grows with knowledge: Goethe. Imagination decides everything: Pascal. Music and woman I cannot but give way to, whatever my business is: Samuel Pepys. Undercover: to disguise identity to avoid detection: definition. Mysteries are not necessarily miracles: Goethe. We make war that we may live in peace: Aristotle. An early morning walk is a blessing for the whole day: Henry David Thoreau. There is no instinct like that of the heart: Byron. Love is not a fire to be shut up in a soul: Racine. Clue: guiding information: definition. Vices are only virtues carried to excess: Charles Dickens. All evil comes from a single cause, man's inability to sit still in a room: Pascal. All travel has its advantages: Samuel Johnson. Make the most of your regrets: Henry David Thoreau. No one ever became wicked suddenly: Juvenal. Silence is one of the great arts of conversation: Cicero. Grit: courage, resolve, strength of character: definition. Experience is the name we give our mistakes: Oscar Wilde. The woman that deliberates is lost: Joseph Addison. The savage in many is never quite eradicated: Henry David Thoreau The greater the difficulty, the greater the glory: Cicero. When the gods wish to punish us, they answer our prayers: Oscar Wilde. No one can give you better advice than yourself: Cicero. What you seek is seeking you: Rumi. Nothing shows a man's character more than what he laughs at: Goethe. Evil is easy and has infinite forms: Pascal. Never befriend a man who is not better than yourself: Confucius. Every earth is fit for burial: Christopher Marlowe.